Also by C R Chaston

HEAVEN'S TEARS (Available April 2009)
TAGS (Available October 2009)

For more information on C R Chaston and his books
visit www.janskipublishing.com

HEAVEN'S DOOR

C R CHASTON

JANSKI PUBLISHING

JANSKI PUBLISHING
The publishing division of
Janski Productions Ltd
Office 404, Albany House
324 Regent Street
London
W1B 3HH

ISBN HARDBACK: 978-0-9560396-0-6

Typeset in 13.5 / 16 pt Monotype Garamond by
Hope Services (Abingdon) Ltd, Abingdon, Oxfordshire

Printed and bound in Great Britain by
Biddles Ltd

For

Kim and Daniel

HEAVEN'S DOOR

PROLOGUE

N<small>O SOUND</small>, not even the most piercing of screams, could be heard emanating from the secret crypt below the chapel. Cardinal Biloweiki nodded his approval. His imposing stance gave him the air of a military officer. The practised, no nonsense expression on his face projected a warning to anyone foolish enough to challenge him.

He spoke in a monotone American drawl to the small gathering sitting before him on the hard wooden pews.

'Brothers, our work is God's work. Heretics must repent and accept their punishment. If not, the Anti Christ will triumph and everything we believe in will cease to exist. Bring in the next accused.'

A priest, flanked by two Cistercian monks in traditional white robes, entered the chapel. Cardinal Biloweiki spoke.

'Father, you are accused of giving succour to the Anti Christ by denying the divinity of Jesus in your sermons, in radio interviews and on your website. How do you plead?'

The priest's sunken eyes stared at Cardinal Biloweiki. His face scowled with hatred.

'So you are the new inquisitor…'

Cardinal Biloweiki interrupted.

'Silence! I asked if you plead guilty or not guilty, nothing else.'

'I plead guilty,' said the priest, spitting the words out with explosive force. Cardinal Biloweiki ignored the priest's venom.

'See that he repents his sins before he is judged by God.'

Holding the priest by his arms, the two monks dragged him towards the wooden steps leading down into the crypt. Struggling to free himself, he viciously kicked out, aiming for the monks' shins. His kicks had no effect. The anger inside him turned to rage. His voice snarled and he bared his teeth like a cornered animal facing a pack of hounds moving in for the kill.

The monks tightened their grip. He turned his head towards Cardinal Biloweiki and his eyes, red with fury, drilled into him. Then, like a demented vampire, he sank his teeth deep into one of the arms holding him, forcing the monk to release his grip. Swinging his free arm he aimed for the face of the other monk. Reaching their target, his fingers clawed and dug their way deep into the monk's eye sockets. The monk fell to the floor, holding his face and screaming in agony.

Instead of trying to escape, the priest leapt towards Cardinal Biloweiki. He wrapped his arm around the Cardinal's neck and exerted enough pressure to break it with one twist, should he resist.

Unseen by the priest, another monk quietly slipped from the pews into the shadows of the chapel. The priest spoke.

'Inquisitor, you think you know everything, but you know nothing. I have seen the hidden testaments. I know what prophesies they contain. Early in the third millennium, a musician will challenge all Earth's religions. If he succeeds in his challenge, our Church as we know it will cease to exist. Some of us believe mankind will be best served if he does succeed.'

Cardinal Biloweiki struggled to speak.

'You lie, no one except the Most Holy Father has access to the hidden testaments.'

'You don't believe me? Ask him yourself. The musician is with us now. People are already leaving our Church to follow him and his philosophy. When the time is right the Catho...'

The arm around Biloweiki's neck suddenly released its grip. The priest slid to the floor with the knife still in his back. His body twitched three times before he finally lay still, blood dribbling from his mouth.

'It's a shame he didn't have a chance to confess his sins before meeting God,' said Cardinal Biloweiki, straightening his robes. 'You may pray for his soul in private.' His usual monotone voice gave no indication of any emotion.

Before walking away, Cardinal Biloweiki noticed a ring on the priest's finger. As he suspected, the priest worked for the Vatican. Others will now investigate. *Oh well*, he thought, *I'll be ready for them when they do…and may God have mercy on their souls.*

CHAPTER ONE

Rodeo recognised her instantly. In the second's delay between the full stage lights dimming and the follow spot almost blinding him, he saw her, three rows from the front. Digging down to the deepest recesses of his memory he couldn't say who she was or why he knew her. One thing he did know, he must meet her. His band played.

'Shit!' He missed his entrance. They busked along till he joined them with the opening line. 'Walk with me.' Rodeo's unique voice ranged from a soft and gentle baritone to a screaming, piercing countertenor without any discernable break. Where in row three was she sitting? What was she wearing? 'God, I don't know.' A very apt line. He could only remember her face and her eyes.

'Maybe now or maybe just another day.' He sang the last line of the song unaccompanied. His voice, pure and warm, totally captured the essence of the lyrics.

After a millisecond or two of almost deafening silence, the audience erupted. Screaming, shouting, stamping. Rodeo humbly accepted their applause, their admiration and their love.

'Thank you all. Thank you for your love. I can really feel it. Your love feels so good. You know, maybe you should share it around a little. Give a little more to your families and your neighbours. When I talk of love I'm talking about kindness, warmth, charity, goodwill, even just a regard for someone.'

He paused and turned his face up towards the lighting technician. 'Can I have the follow spot cut please? I want to see everyone in the audience. I want to channel some of the love here in this arena back to you people who could do with a little more of it in your lives. I need to see your faces.'

Suddenly he saw the audience. His eyes made a beeline towards row three. He scanned along the row. Maybe it was row four, or row two? She wasn't there. Christ! She must be somewhere.

Then he saw her. She wasn't clapping or cheering. Instead, tears ran down her cheeks. Behind her eyes sat the unmistakable look of sadness. Who was she? What attracted his attention to her? Where did he know her from? She appeared to be about the same age as most of the audience, at a guess early twenties.

'There's one lady here who I'd like to meet after the show.' The audience let out a barrage of cheers and whistles.

'Only one?' he heard someone shout out. 'Rodeo you're slipping!'

However much he tried to look at her, all he could see was a mass of souls, all searching for that elusive experience called love.

The band played again. Security moved to form a line in front of the stage. Every single member of the audience stood and gyrated with the quickening rhythm. Rodeo briefly forgot about the lady in the third row. He had a job to do. Somehow he had to share himself with all these people. They all wanted and needed a little piece of him.

A few people attempted to avoid the security staff and climb onto the stage. One of them succeeded and, egged on by the audience, she took off her top. Not wearing a bra, she proudly displayed her pierced double D breasts. Rodeo applauded. He avoided the temptation to fondle and kiss them before security hustled her away. Some girls threw their underwear onto the stage. He picked up a few pairs of panties, bras and g-strings and held them up for all to see. Putting them to his nose he took a deep breath then started to rub them seductively around his crutch. After a few seconds he slipped them into his front pocket creating a larger bulge around his penis. The audience went wild. Some of them stripped off, while a few openly engaged in mutual masturbation and oral sex.

Outside the arena, the Reverend Douglas Claymore addressed his congregation.

'Let us close our eyes in prayer,' he continued, clearing his throat. His mic and the effects box on the small portable mixing desk gave his voice an ethereal, God-like quality.

'Dear Lord, please give us, your humble servants, the strength to fight against all that is evil in this world. Fill us with your Holy Spirit so we may follow your laws. Give us the strength to oppose all that is an affront to your name and all Christian people. Help us in our crusade against obscenities and all those who would lead our children astray.' At this point his voice quivered and cracked with emotion. He paused to regain his composure. 'We look forward to the day when you will once again walk on this Earth, when all righteous people who accept you as their Lord and Saviour will enter the Kingdom Of Heaven. We ask this in the name of our Father, Jesus Christ, Our Lord, Amen.' He looked up and paused for a second before speaking.

'Christian brothers and sisters, do you have any idea what is going on in that arena? I'll tell you. The Devil is using sex, music and obscene language to turn young people, some of them your sons and daughters, against Christ. Rodeo is the devil incarnate and I'm going to stop him. Our local politicians could have kept him out of our town and banned him from using the Arena which was paid for out of our taxes.'

His followers shouted in support.

'We're with you Reverend!'

'All the way!'

'Shame on our town for allowing this!'

Reverend Claymore continued. 'God is telling me to march forward and demand that Rodeo leaves this town and never returns.'

He turned towards the Arena and started to walk purposefully towards it. His congregation quickly joined him. He'd only walked about fifty yards when a police car with lights flashing pulled up in front of him, blocking his path. Two officers jumped out. One of them spoke.

'Reverend, this is as far as you go.'

'Who says?' said Reverend Claymore. 'I am a citizen of this town and can go anywhere on the public highway I choose. I haven't committed any offence.'

'No you haven't, but we're charged with maintaining law and order in this town. If you go into the arena it may affect public safety so we can't allow you to go in.'

'Yet you can allow our children to see all that filth on display in there.'

'Reverend, I understand how you feel,' said the officer, trying to defuse the situation. 'But they are not breaking any law.'

'They're breaking God's law!' shouted Reverend Claymore. The police officer remained calm.

'That's your point of view, which you're entitled to. As far as I'm concerned Rodeo is just another entertainer with a bit of a reputation who sometimes goes over the top. An' Reverend,' continued the police officer quietly, 'you know the town is keeping an eye on Rodeo. The Police have people in the Arena. If any law is broken the show will be stopped. We can't be any fairer can we? I suggest you all go home before someone gets hurt.'

Reverend Claymore turned towards his followers. 'Good Christian folk, tonight we have done our duty to God and to our children. We will not break any laws and we will support our police by doing as they have requested. However, we must prepare ourselves for a great battle against the filth and obscenities in our society. Let us all pray.' The two officers politely removed their hats while keeping an eye on everyone.

*　*　*

Laura Sable couldn't be sure what to expect when she booked her ticket at the Arena. How would she feel when she saw him? Would she still hate him? How could she get to meet him? Even if she did get to meet him, what was she going to say to him? Now, sitting in the third row from the front, she felt even less sure. Was it her imagination or did he actually recognise her?

She watched impassively as Rodeo's three backing singers stripped him down to just a thong, using only their mouths to remove his clothes.

'God, this man has no shame,' she said under her breath, as Rodeo simulated oral sex with them. Closing her eyes she tried to blot out the disgusting scenes being played out on stage. A minute later, unable to resist the forbidden fruit on display, she opened them. Suddenly she caught herself admiring his tanned and toned body. *Laura, how could you?* Thoughts entered her mind, disgusting sexual thoughts. Thoughts she wanted desperately to block out. They were certainly not thoughts a nice Catholic girl should have.

The more she tried to block them the stronger they became, until she just closed her eyes and allowed them to flow freely. Mother of Jesus, how can a man do that to me? A man I should hate, a man that stands for everything I have ever been taught is wrong and a sin.

Tears ran down her cheeks. Surely he hadn't meant her when he said there was one lady in the audience he would like to meet? Deep down she knew he recognised her, or rather thought he recognised her. She just knew he wanted to meet her. But how could she meet him now? How could she continue to hate him when all she wanted to do was make love to him? No, not make love to him – she wanted him to fuck her.

I don't want to be a virgin any longer. I don't want to save myself for my wedding night. I want to be fucked by you, by Rodeo. Her thoughts ran wild. *Okay, I know I could leave, just get up and go. Maybe I should go see Father Ignatius?* Then she remembered how she had caught him looking at her thighs and trying to look up her skirt at a confirmation class. Maybe that's not such a good idea after all.

'Is there anyone here about to be married?' Rodeo put the question to the audience. A few positive yells and cheers came back. 'That's great, all the best to you. I hope you'll be very happy. But I say to you all, don't be forced into making promises you can't keep.

Don't marry because you're told it's what God requires. God doesn't require anything from us.'

Laura listened, open mouthed. God doesn't require anything from us? Isn't sex before marriage or outside marriage a sin?

Rodeo continued. 'Not only does God not require anything from us, there's no such thing as sin. There is only love. As The Beatles said, love is all there is. God is love, he doesn't want to punish us, he wants to love us, and he wants us to experience love and to know what love is like. That's why we all go to what we call Heaven. You know, what Heaven is? It's pure love, a beautiful experience, a real love-in, the ultimate love palace. It's the only way we can learn to love each other, all of us, brothers and sisters all over the World. Anyone who tells you any different is lying.' The audience screamed in delight.

'My next song is called What Would Love Do Now? A question we should ask ourselves throughout our lives.'

'Wow,' Laura said out loud. 'Father Ignatius never ever said anything like that.'

Rodeo sat on a bar stall strumming his acoustic guitar. All the lights on the stage dimmed, apart from one follow spot which produced a halo-like glow around him. Laura waited expectantly for a host of angels to appear. As he sang, the lyrics started to flow like a small gurgling stream, but gradually the stream got bigger and turned into a ferocious torrent of emotion about love and mankind.

'There are angels here,' said Laura. 'No man alone could ever produce such God-like lyrics and music.' Now she wanted him even more than ever. In less than an hour she'd changed from a blinkered, revenge-seeking virgin, to a raging nymphet who suddenly began to understand what life and love were really all about.

The applause had barely stopped when a voice from the back of the auditorium rang out.

'Rodeo! How dare you come to our town with your obscene

show and songs and tell our children that there is no sin and that sex outside of marriage is okay with God.'

Rodeo looked up and responded calmly. 'Sir, you know who I am, would you mind telling me who you are please?'

'I'm the Reverend Douglas Claymore.'

'Hi Reverend, we meet again. Let me strike a deal with you. You preach to your congregation about sin and Hell and the wrath of God, and I'll talk and sing with these good people about love and ways of expressing our love for our brothers and sisters. It might take a long time, but I know who'll come out tops in the end.'

Reverend Claymore almost shrieked his reply.

'I will never make a deal with the Devil. You people here, this man is the Devil in disguise.'

With that the arena exploded into laughter while the band played an improvised eight bars of the song.

'You may well laugh,' said Reverend Claymore, 'but let me warn you. God will punish those who reject his word. When Christ returns only those who accept him as their Saviour and reject sin will enter the Kingdom of Heaven.'

'That's bollocks Reverend,' said Rodeo. 'Band, let's rock.' The band played a loud and percussive intro.

Laura had listened with interest to the banter between the Reverend Claymore and Rodeo. A smile broke out on her face when Rodeo said 'bollocks' to him. She had never ever heard anyone speak to a clergyman like that before. But why not? Why *shouldn't* someone challenge what they say? Who says they are always right? Suddenly images of her sister came to the forefront of her mind and her mood changed.

My God, what am I thinking? What am I doing here? This man helped my sister kill herself, now he's seducing me.

'God, please help me, please,' she said under her breath. Closing her eyes she prayed silently for guidance. As she prayed, the loud rock number came to an end and Rodeo spoke to the audience.

'This next song is very special for me. I wrote it after a very lovely person decided she didn't want to carry on with her life here on earth. My Beautiful Laladee.'

Laura opened her eyes. God had answered. Tears streamed down her face at the mention of her sister's name, or rather the name her sister liked to be called by.

Rodeo sang a Negro spiritual-like tribute to Laladee, who Rodeo said now lived in Heaven experiencing the ecstasy of oneness with God. She would never forget the tenderness in his voice as he sang her sister's name.

As a young child Laura couldn't say Melody, her elder sister's real name. It came out as Laladee. Eventually everyone called her Laladee. When Laura was twelve, Laladee confessed to her that she had allowed a boy to touch her breasts and vagina. A few days later Laura argued with her sister and, out of spite, told her parents what Laladee had told her in confidence. There then ensued the biggest row ever. The whole family screamed and shouted, using words Laura had never heard before. She remembered her mother crying and pleading with her father not to cause a scene with the neighbours as he marched up the street to confront the boy and his parents. After that episode Laura and Laladee were never close again. She bitterly regretted what she'd done. She blamed herself that in her hour of need Laladee hadn't felt able to talk to her. If only Laladee had spoken to her things might have worked out differently.

I have to meet him. I have to find out exactly what he did or said to her to make her want to kill herself. She walked to the back of the Arena and introduced herself to one of the security staff.

'Excuse me Sir. I'm Laladee's younger sister.'

'You're who?' he said, with barely disguised annoyance.

'The song he just sang about the girl who killed herself? I'm her sister. I need to speak to Rodeo after the show'

'Yeah, you and a few thousand others. Wait here please.' He walked a few paces away and called his supervisor on his radio. 'This is Alpha Sierra Four Zero Two, over.' He paused and listened.

'I know you're busy but I have a Delta Two Zero. Says she's the sister of a girl Rodeo knew who killed herself, over.' There was another pause. 'Hold on, I'll check with her.' Then, calling over to Laura, he asked 'Are you sitting in row three?'

'Yes I am,' replied Laura.

'That's a positive, out.' He clipped the radio to his belt and said 'Follow me please.' He led her through a maze of corridors until they arrived at a door marked 'security'. He lightly knocked on the door. She heard a gruff voice from the other side of the door.

'Enter.'

The security guard beckoned her to go on in. A large black man, maybe three hundred pounds and almost as wide as he was tall, stood by a solid wooden desk covered in papers. He turned and spoke to her.

'Hi my name's Mathew, I look after Rodeo. So you had a sister who was a friend of Rodeo's and she killed herself? What was her name?' His voice resonated like a perfectly tuned cello.

'Well everyone knew her as Laladee, but Melody was her real name, Melody Sable,' said Laura not quite sure what to make of the big man.

'Do you have any ID?'

'I have my driver's licence.'

'May I see it please?'

'Sure,' she said, opening her clutch bag and rummaging through till she found it. He took it from her and studied it for a few seconds.

'If I agree for you to see him I have to make a photocopy of this,' he said. She began to feel more at ease with him.

'That's fine,' she said. 'No problem.'

He placed her driving licence on a photocopying machine, took a copy and then handed it back to her.

'I heard you were sitting in the third row.' It came across more like a question than a statement.

'Yes I was,' she said.

'You know he noticed you, out of all the thousands of people in the audience. Said he couldn't put a name to you but he wanted to meet you.'

'Mathew – is it okay for me to call you Mathew?' He nodded.

'Can I ask you a big favour? Don't tell Rodeo who I am, please. I'd like to surprise him.' She gave him a big warm smile.

'Okay, you win,' said Mathew. 'With a smile like that you could melt anyone. I won't tell him unless he asks. You see, Rodeo and me go back a long, long way. We trust each other completely and I won't break that trust,' he said, almost emotionally.

'That's fine,' said Laura.

'Do you trust me?' said Mathew.

'I suppose so,' said Laura, a little unsure.

'That's good, because I'm taking you to where he's staying so as you can meet him.'

'Thank you,' she smiled as she said it. Mathew seemed like a nice guy and she was genuinely pleased he would drive her to meet Rodeo.

'Follow me please, Miss Sable,' said Mathew. She followed him out of the building to a large parking lot. To her astonishment, instead of a limousine there stood a chopper in a cordoned off area. Laura paused. The spinning rotary blades and deafening noise frightened her. Mathew beckoned her to carry on.

'It's okay, perfectly safe, I promise,' he shouted, hoping she could hear him above the din of the engines.

Mathew slammed shut the door and secured their safety harnesses. Seconds later, the chopper rose vertically then banked steeply to the right. The pilot turned round to Laura and smiled. Laura's eyes nearly popped out of her head. She hadn't expected Rodeo to be piloting the chopper.

'Mathew, aren't you going to introduce me to our guest?' said Rodeo.

'Sure boss, this is Laura, the mystery lady from row three. I'll let her introduce herself properly when we arrive at Heaven's Door.'

'Heaven's Door?' asked Laura, sounding a little worried.

'Heaven's Door is the name of my ranch where I like to chill out with my friends after a gig,' said Rodeo.

'Why's it called Heaven's Door?'

Rodeo gave her a really cheeky grin. 'You'll find out in precisely thirty-five minutes. Till then just sit back, relax and enjoy the ride.'

CHAPTER TWO

'EVERYONE WELCOME.' Laura read the plaque on the solid wooden door. Rodeo saw her looking.

'Same as is written on Heaven's door.'

'Hey that's beautiful,' she replied. 'So that's why you call this place Heaven's Door.' It never crossed her mind to ask him how he actually knew 'Everyone Welcome' was written on Heaven's door.

Inside she expected to find an opulent palace, but all the furniture looked old, plain and dusty. In fact there wasn't much furniture at all. Just an old worn out sofa, a circular pine table with six chairs that had definitely seen better days and a 1960s jukebox.

'Let's have some music,' said Rodeo. 'I'll stick a few dimes in the jukebox and Mathew, can you rustle up some pizzas or something?'

'Sure boss,' said Mathew.

The jukebox started to play Simon and Garfunkel's 'Bridge Over Troubled Water'. Rodeo beckoned Laura to sit down on the sofa. He sat on one of the chairs around the table and pulled up another to put his feet on.

'Bet I know what you're thinking,' he said. 'How come a superstar chills out in a dump like this?' He didn't wait for an answer. 'Well, to me this is Heaven. All I need is somewhere to rest, recuperate and relax. I don't need luxury to do that. This is a wonderful place to meditate, no distractions. I've written some of my best music here.'

'My Beautiful Laladee,' said Laura with a touch of cynicism. 'Did you write that here?'

Suddenly it all clicked into place for Rodeo. He now knew why he wanted to meet the lady in the third row. 'Laura,' he said.

'You're her sister, aren't you? You're Laladee's younger sister?' Laura took a deep breath and looked directly at him before replying.

'Why did you let her kill herself? Why did you stand by and do nothing? It's like you killed her yourself. You left her alone here while you went off to a gig. You knew what she was going to do. How could you do that? How could you go off and leave her when she was in that state?' Laura's voice began to verge on the hysterical. Rodeo stood up to try and placate her.

'I hate you! I hate you so much, I despise you. I wish you were dead!' She screamed the words at Rodeo. 'Why didn't God take you instead?'

Two years of anger and guilt poured out of her as she beat her fists against Rodeo's chest while sobbing uncontrollably. Rodeo held his arms up in the air and let her beat him until she stopped. Still sobbing, she put her arms around him and pressed her head against his chest. Rodeo bought his arms down and put them around her back. She felt incredible warmth from his hands through her dress. She didn't want to move. They held each other. Rodeo broke the silence.

'My beautiful Laladee,' he sang the last line of the song. As he held her, Laura could only feel love. Love for her sister, love for Rodeo and love for herself. She no longer hated herself for what she had done when she was twelve.

'Pizzas have arrived,' said Mathew entering the room, holding six large plates, three in each hand. 'Want some more music on the jukebox?' he asked, putting the plates down on the table. 'There's anchovy and pepperoni with extra cheese and lots of Pepsi.'

Why did Mathew have to interrupt them? thought Laura. She wanted to carry on holding Rodeo and…

'Here, have a slice of the anchovy pizza, fish is good for your brain,' said Mathew as he put a slice on a plate and handed it to Laura. She shook her head.

'Come on, you have to eat.' She smiled and took it from him.

'That's the spirit,' said Mathew, pleased she was going to taste his creation.

All three of them sat at the table. Rodeo spoke first.

'Mathew, this is your own pizza? You made it?'

'Yes I did and you know why? Because you can never trust those take-out pizzas. The numbskulls that make 'em might do anything; you know, like use the wrong kind o' cheese or even worse, tinned anchovies. You have to use fresh ones.' Laura chipped in.

'Best pizza I ever tasted.' Mathew felt a surge of pride. They all tucked in.

'Is there anyone you need to tell that you're here?' Rodeo asked Laura with his mouth full.

'No it's okay, I told my folks that I was going to a show in town with a girlfriend then crashing out at her place afterwards.'

'Tell me, what's the best feeling you ever had in your life?' Rodeo looked at Laura as he asked the question, the kind of look that said I already know the answer you're going to give.

'Do I have to tell you the truth?' She had the expression on her face that said if I tell you the truth I'll feel a little foolish, embarrassed even.

'That's up to you,' said Rodeo. Laura giggled nervously.

'This is really difficult for me. No I can't.' Her hands covered her eyes and then she opened them up so she could see. It was like looking at Rodeo through a short tunnel. 'Alright, it was when...' She moved her hands away from her face and put them in her lap. She felt strangely calm despite knowing that what she was about to say could change her life forever.

'When you just held me, I felt this incredible warmth from your hands. I've never experienced anything like it before. It said to me "I'll take away your pain, I'll make you feel good".' Mathew interrupted.

'My boss is a healer, that's what he does. In fact, he wants to heal the whole world, make everyone feel good.'

'How are you going to do that?' said Laura. 'You couldn't even heal my sister's pain.' As soon as the words came out of her mouth she regretted them.

'That's a fair question,' said Mathew. 'How are you going to do it boss? That sure is a hell of a task.'

'Well, that's where you're wrong,' said Rodeo. 'It's actually a heavenly task. First I'd like to talk about Laladee. Laura, I want you to know Laladee's a beautiful spirit and her soul knows only love. When she lived here on Earth her young mind and body knew only about sin which is quite natural, because generally that's all we tend to be taught from birth. So when she became pregnant by a man she didn't know and would never see again she experienced a terrible conflict. On the one hand her soul felt happy that in a brief moment of love she'd become one with another soul and together they had created a baby. On the other hand, her mind and body were in turmoil. How could she face her parents and her community? What would her priest say? What would God say? She couldn't face it so she had an abortion. After her abortion, I received her letter. It came with all the fan mail, which I always acknowledge with a signed photo and a message of love. As I read the letter, love poured out of every word, every line. Love for her baby, her parents, for you.'

He looked at Laura in a way that said yes, she did love you. 'It took Mathew here two weeks to find her. Before she came to Heaven's Door she had made a decision. She wanted to be with her baby.'

At this point Rodeo's voice began to quiver. 'When she saw the sign on the door she knew she had made the right decision. You see, she knew what unconditional love was. She knew she would be welcome in Heaven, no matter what she'd done, and she knew her baby, untouched by the notion of sin, would welcome her and want to be with her. Her soul didn't need to experience further pain on Earth because her soul overflowed with love, unconditional love.'

He paused before continuing, looking at Laura. 'We returned home from a book signing and found her unconscious in the bathroom. Doctors pronounced her dead on arrival at the hospital. Even though we took her in the chopper we were too late. That evening I wrote My Beautiful Laladee.' His eyes focused on Laura. She knew he was talking honestly.

'Laura, she died with me. I want you to understand I wasn't just there. Our souls were together. Can you imagine the elation of being surrounded by nothing but unconditional pure love after going through what she'd been through? Well, she could, that's why she chose the path she did.'

Tears streamed down Rodeo's cheeks. Laura looked at the tears. They seemed to become larger and then she saw Laladee with her baby. They were smiling and obviously happy. She smiled back. Then they were gone.

'Was the father of my sister's baby black?' asked Laura.

'Yes,' said Rodeo. 'Why are you looking at me like that?' Then he understood. 'You saw them, didn't you?' Laura nodded.

'Yes I did. She looked so happy, and the baby, he's beautiful. But I don't understand. Your tears, I saw them in your tears.' Rodeo paused for a second before speaking.

'I know you did, but there's nothing strange in that. You see, tears don't come from sadness, loss or despair, they come out of love. If you look into a teardrop all you will see is love, love in its very purest form.' Rodeo looked at her and smiled.

'Boss, the coaches are here,' said Mathew, looking at a message on his cell phone.

'Okay,' said Rodeo, 'let's party.' Mathew picked up what looked like a TV remote control. Suddenly the ceiling appeared to be moving further away. Laura realised the room had become a giant lift.

'This way,' said Rodeo, beckoning Laura to follow him through a door which, ten seconds before, had seemed to be just a plain wall.

Laura struggled to find words to describe it. There were marble pillars and huge fountains, as if they were on some weird film set.

There must have been a couple of hundred people, some dancing to the latest hip hop, some drinking at a long bar draped with flowers and some openly making out on what looked like a virtual beach.

'Laura,' said Rodeo. 'I have to mingle with my guests. If at anytime you want to leave just go to the door. I've left instructions for Mathew to see that you get home safely.' Rodeo left her and joined some partygoers at the bar.

Laura plucked up courage to explore on her own. Everywhere she looked were trees and bushes growing every kind of fruit imaginable. Pineapples, coconuts, kiwi fruit, plums, cherries and some she had never seen before. There were so many. People just picked what they wanted as they passed. Party guests played in huge swimming pools, having fun with giant multicoloured beach balls. What looked like Roman or Greek pillars surrounded one of the pools making it appear as though people were playing in some sort of mythological fantasy.

A field of snow sat between the two pools. She saw semi-naked people playing snowballs. Part of her wanted to join in but the other part said no, it's wrong. What the heck, it's only a game of snowballs! She wasn't going to fuck anyone. As she slipped out of her dress she hoped Rodeo might notice her slim, trim figure and full breasts. A snowball hit her on her back. She turned round and grinned at the culprit.

'I owe you one,' she shouted.

'Come and join us, we're outnumbered,' someone shouted back. Laura didn't really know who she should throw at or run from, but then did it matter? No one seemed to mind. Everyone eventually ended up splattered with snow. Who would have thought playing snowballs semi naked would have given her such a sense of freedom, of living and being alive? She felt a strange sense of disappointment as she put her dress back on. I have to, don't I? After all, nice girls don't just walk around half naked, even somewhere like this, do they?

She continued her exploration on the virtual beach. She found beautiful white sand, palm trees… and sunshine. *Now this is miraculous, how's he do this? How much did it cost?* Reaching up, standing on tip toes, she picked a shiny red apple off a tree, still full of blossom. *An apple tree on the beech? Strange.* She half expected a serpent to appear and try to tempt her. Tempt her to do what? To have fun playing snowballs while half naked? *Well, you're too late, I've done that, or… or to find Rodeo and fuck his brains out? God! What am I thinking?* She knew what she wanted, what she craved. Where is he? She had to find him.

She searched along the beech. A few people made love on the white sand. She looked, Rodeo wasn't one of them. Then she noticed a group of maybe twenty or more sitting on the sand, all holding hands.

'They're attempting to meditate as one,' explained Rodeo as he walked across the beach towards her. 'You know, the only way they can achieve individual satisfaction, or what you may describe as inner peace, is by letting go of their own desires and thinking of the needs of the one, and the only way they can do that is through love. Love for themselves and love of the one. You should try it one day. You'll be amazed at what you can remember.'

'Remember?' said Laura, surprised at his choice of words.

'Yes, you'd learn to remember what life is like in heaven. If we spent more time meditating we'd have less time to fight, and if we meditated as one we'd have fewer people to fight with and more people to love. Think about it – people don't fight in Heaven.' Laura looked at him, open-mouthed, as he walked away.

She watched Rodeo sit down with the group and join hands.

'I'll see you safely home,' said Mathew walking across the beach towards her. 'Follow me please.'

He led her to a stretch limo outside the main door.

'Would you like to sit up front with me so we can talk, or would you prefer privacy in the back?' said Mathew.

'I'll sit with you so we can talk, if it's okay with you that is?'

'Sure it's okay with me, I like company when I'm driving,' said Mathew as he opened the door for her. 'It's a three hour drive. Just let me know when you're tired and want to sleep in the back.' Mathew closed her door and went round to the driver's side.

During the first five miles neither of them spoke.

Mathew broke the silence first. Not because he found it uncomfortable but because he needed to somehow try and put things into perspective for Laura's sake.

'Rodeo's quite a guy. He never graduated. His mother wanted him to go to college but he insisted on looking after her. He wanted to support her so she didn't have to work.'

'What about his father?' said Laura. Mathew carried on looking straight ahead as he spoke.

'His father left when he was born. Told his mother Rodeo's not his son, called her a fucking slut. He's never heard from him since. You see, Rodeo's mother's white and so's his father. But his mother's father, Rodeo's grand-daddy, was black, a fact she never told her husband and Rodeo inherited his grand-daddy's fine afro hair-style and a nice suntan.'

'So how do you fit in?'

'How do I fit in?' asked Mathew. 'I did bad things, real bad. By the time I reached sixteen I had convictions for rape…' He looked into Laura's eyes and saw panic. He felt an inner sadness. 'You have to understand,' he said. 'That was then, before I met Rodeo.'

'So how did he get you to change?' said Laura.

'We were in jail together.'

'You're telling me Rodeo went to jail?'

'He served eighteen months for arson. A court convicted him of setting fire to his local church.'

'Why did he do that?'

'He didn't, someone framed him. You see, one Sunday he went to church and interrupted the preacher during his sermon. Told the preacher he was talking crap and even told the congregation that God didn't want them sitting in a fucking church worshiping him and singing stupid hymns, they'd all be better off having a mass orgy.'

'No, you're kidding me!' Laura was shocked by these revelations.

'It's true, and you know what? The preacher that interrupted Rodeo at last night's concert, he's the very same preacher. Anyhow, in jail I tried to be the big tough guy, but Rodeo turned out to be the tough one. He held the respect of everyone. Not through physical strength or brute force you understand but by... it's difficult to explain, but nothing and no one ever scared him, especially me. We all loved to sit and talk with him and listen to him sing. That's where he first started singing. If it hadn't of been for Rodeo I'd never have come out of there alive. Since then I've been looking out for him, well at least that's what he pays me for. But if truth be known, it's really the other way round. He doesn't need looking after but, if I had to, I'd die for him because I know he'd do the same for me.'

'Wow, that's beautiful,' said Laura, hardly believing what she'd heard.

'Yes it is, it sure is,' answered Mathew. 'Can you enter your address into the GPS gadget for me please?' Laura input her zip code. 'We should be there in a little under three hours,' continued Mathew. 'Why don't you get some sleep in the back?'

Mathew stopped the limo. Laura lay across the long seat in the back covered by a tartan blanket, a popular travel accessory in the 1930s.

'Will I see you again? You and Rodeo I mean,' said Laura.

'Well Laura, that depends on you. I'll give you a card, you can call anytime. On the card there's a number, nothing else. When you call just leave your name and a number we can reach you on.' Mathew smiled a warm friendly smile. 'You try and get a little sleep now,' said Mathew as he closed the rear door.

To Laura it seemed like only a few minutes had passed when the limo drew up outside her home. Mathew opened the door for her.

'You take care of yourself, maybe we'll meet again sometime,' said Mathew.

'Thanks, I hope so.' Laura smiled at him as she climbed out. She didn't notice the black sedan across the street, in which sat three men in sharp suits all wearing the same designer shades, despite the fact that the sun had just risen. As she let herself into her apartment, Mathew pressed a button on the car phone.

'Boss, Laura has company, three spooks. Call me back when you finished partying.'

*   *   *

The door buzzer sounded.

'Hold on, I'm in the bathroom! I'll be right there,' Laura shouted, hoping whoever it was could hear her. She put on her bath robe and opened the door with it still on the chain. Standing outside were three men.

'Laura Sable,' spoke one, showing his badge. 'We're from the FBI. We'd like to talk to you about Rodeo.'

'Rodeo? My God, what's happened? Come in,' she said apprehensively. Laura felt petrified. Something dreadful had happened to him. It didn't cross her mind to ask herself why they would want to contact her if anything bad had happened to him. She assumed it was because she was the last to see him alive, but how would they know that?

'Laura – do you mind if I call you Laura?' The man who asked the question seemed polite enough. He looked kind of handsome – square jaw, fair haired, clean cut. He sat down uninvited and beckoned Laura to do the same. The other two, who looked rather more menacing, stood in the hallway.

'Last night you visited Heaven's Door, Rodeo's private residence. We're investigating claims that Rodeo has had and continues to have sexual relationships with underage girls and boys, which in most States is statutory rape.'

This wasn't what she expected. Images of what happened surged through her mind. Desperately she tried to remember faces, sizes, ages. How old were the guests? Some of them could have been underage, but then again it was difficult to tell. Then she remembered.

'My driving licence, they took a copy of my driving licence, which shows my age. They insisted. I assume they do that with everyone who goes to Heaven's Door.' As she spoke she felt protective towards Rodeo.

'Yes they do. When we interviewed Rodeo that's what he told us and he provided records, but it's all a little too convenient. There's no guarantee that underage girls aren't smuggled in. That's why we need your help. We have to find out exactly what goes on there. I know your sister died at Heaven's Door, please accept my condolences. Okay she wasn't underage, but her death is just another example of why we need to investigate the place and maybe put Rodeo behind bars. I need you to go back to Heaven's Door and provide us with some evidence that will nail Rodeo and protect our children. Will you do that for us?'

* * *

Rodeo phoned back. 'Matt, are you and Laura okay?' He sounded concerned.

'I'm fine Boss,' said Mathew. 'She's with the spooks now. Don't worry they won't hurt her, they just want her to do their dirty work.'

'Matt, come home, I need you here.'

'Okay, I'm on my way Boss.'

CHAPTER THREE

REVEREND DOUGLAS CLAYMORE left the Arena feeling like a giant. He'd fought Satan. The few supporters who'd stayed greeted him with loud whoops and cheers. He raised his hands to silence them before speaking.

'Tonight I faced the Devil in his own backyard. I told him that the time of reckoning will come and he will be judged along with those that support him. Good people, we must continue our struggle against all that is evil. For this reason I'm inviting you all to a meeting in my church tomorrow evening at seven when we'll pray and ask God for his guidance.' The crowd shouted their support.

'God bless you Reverend! We're with you all the way!'

Douglas Claymore spoke again. 'Goodnight and may God bless you all and keep you safe. I'll see you tomorrow night at seven. Spread the word among your families and friends'

Douglas Claymore never missed the Preston Quick Talk Show. He loved the way Preston stuck the knife into his celebrity guests by asking loaded questions with an angelic holier-than-thou smile on his face. The guests, who were by and large atheists, squirmed as Preston twisted the knife with each question.

He turned on the TV. The show had just started. *Good, I haven't missed any,* he thought to himself. Preston sang the show's opening number.

'My wit is untrained in any kind of art.' He was surrounded by five girl dancers. Every single one of them was over six feet tall, making him look substantially smaller than his five feet eight inches.

When the song finished Preston went into his usual overly long introduction of his guests.

'Ladies and Gentlemen, the mark of a showbiz legend is glamour, talent and the ability to entertain.'

Douglas Claymore knew this part of Preston's patter off by heart and moved his lips along with Preston's.

'And tonight we're going to meet a legend. He's a man who's become one of the world's greatest performers. His empire stretches all around the world and his many admirers include politicians, princes and queens,' he paused. 'Yes the pink dollar is very important, please welcome the one and only, the voice and song writing genius of the century… Rodeo.'

'Damn it, damn that man!' Reverend Claymore said to himself, but he wasn't going to miss a second of it. How he wanted to see Rodeo humiliated!

Rodeo sat on a bar stool strumming his guitar, singing a song from his latest album. Reverend Claymore had never heard it before. He wanted to hate it but found himself listening closely to the lyrics. A beautiful ballad about unrequited love.

'How can I ask her to love me when I can't even love me myself?' sang Rodeo. Douglas Claymore's mind began to drift. If only he hadn't been so priggish when Sarah, his long-time fiancé, confessed to him she wasn't a virgin anymore. It only seemed like yesterday; it must be…nearly thirty years. As he thought about her, his eyes became moist. It still hurt so much. He felt the same tightness in his chest that he felt when she had first told him.

'Why did I have to ask her? Why? Sarah, I miss you so much.'

Rodeo joined Preston on his couch. Preston started the interview.

'It's no secret that you hold God and religion in contempt. It's even been said the reason you simulate sex acts in your stage show is to bait the religious right, the Christian Evangelicalists. Why is that?' Rodeo nodded before he answered, buying himself valuable thinking time.

'Well first of all, if I held God in contempt I'd hold myself and the whole of humanity in contempt.'

Preston interrupted. 'Why do you say that?'

Rodeo cleverly reflected the question back to Preston. 'Okay, when you say God, who or what do you see?' Preston thought for a second before answering.

'Well, God is God, the main man, our creator.' Rodeo jumped in.

'You say man – does he have a penis? If he does, how does he use it? Is there a Mrs God? Or is God a virgin?' Preston knew he'd been trumped.

'Okay, what's your point?' he said, a touch annoyed.

'My point is this,' replied Rodeo. 'I am God and I am a creator because I'm a part of God, so are you and everyone else on this planet. We are all one, all creators. Our sum total is God and it's through our physical lives that God experiences the full spectrum of life, what you would describe as good and bad. It's because we are all one, all a part of God that we are all loved. Preston, may I ask you a question?'

'Sure,' said Preston, wondering where this was leading.

'When Adolf Hitler died where did he go?'

Preston paused before answering. 'I believe he went to burn in Hell's fires for all eternity.' Again Rodeo took the lead by asking another question.

'Why do you believe that? I suggest only because that's what you were told from a young age so that's what becomes your reality.'

'Okay, so he just went into nothingness then.'

'Where will you go when your physical life ends?' asked Rodeo. Preston played his answer to the audience.

'I've booked my place in Heaven, you can be sure of that!' 'Well don't be too shocked when you bump into Adolf,' replied Rodeo. 'You know, he's quite an important person up there.' Some of the audience began to jeer and slow handclap. Preston intervened.

'Okay, let him explain please, thank you audience, thank you.'

Rodeo continued. 'God – and that's all of us souls here on Earth – want to progress to the ultimate love-in and all be one together.

But while we live our lives we become bogged down with things like nationalism, racism and religion. They're like a huge barrier to achieving our gigantic love-in. So every now an' then someone up there has to volunteer to be the catalyst which challenges humanity to choose another path. Hitler was that catalyst and the result of what he did is that humanity had a horrific experience that challenged it to move forward with far more love than it had before. Look at Europe now. The European Union, countries that were former enemies, are working together in harmony and using the same currency. Now other countries want to join them. Imagine if the whole world eventually joined as one. Resources would be shared, there wouldn't be any hunger or starvation and there wouldn't be any need for war.'

Douglas Claymore knelt on the rug in front of his TV, closed his eyes and put his hands together as he had been taught as a child.

'Please God, nail this son of bitch.' He turned his attention back to the TV. Preston asked Rodeo another question.

'So what's your take on religion then?' Rodeo took a sharp intake of breath before replying.

'Okay, you asked the question. This is my take on religion. Jesus never told his followers to form a Church or to worship him or sing hymns praising him. He didn't invent Catholics, Anglicans, Baptists or Methodists. All he wanted was for people to live as he did, with love for everyone. He behaved like a role model. He told us that only by living with love for everyone could we move forward to the Kingdom of Heaven, you know, create Heaven on Earth.'

Preston looked directly into Rodeo's eyes before replying.

'When you were eighteen you interrupted a church service. You told the minister he was talking crap and you told the congregation they'd all be better off participating in an orgy rather than singing and praying in a church, except I understand you used more colourful language. Then you went on to burn down the church. It seems to me you have no religion and no conscience, which is why you regularly take part in orgies with your young and vulnerable fans and why you tried to cover up the death of a young woman whom you invited to join your sordid orgies.' The knife started to turn. Reverend Claymore looked up and spoke to God.

'I knew you wouldn't let me down.'

Preston spoke again. 'Before you answer we have to take a break. We'll be right back.'

Reverend Claymore spoke to himself. 'Thank you God, thank you. He can't get out of this one, he'll be finished for good.'

The adverts seemed to take for ever. Eventually Preston welcomed everyone back.

'Before we went to our break I asked Rodeo about orgies at his ranch and the death of a young fan. So Rodeo, how do you explain these orgies that you regularly partake in?' Rodeo looked at Preston and nodded before answering. 'Preston, you grew up as a young man in the nineteen sixties.'

'Yes I did,' replied Preston.

'And you took part in some peace protests.'

'That is correct,' replied Preston again.

'And you also carried a placard that read make love not war?' Preston agreed.

'I did that too.' Rodeo pressed home with his advantage 'So why did you then join the army and fight in Vietnam? Wouldn't it have been better if you had spent your time shagging and taking part in orgies rather than killing in Vietnam?'

Preston, now on the back foot, answered.

'I was drafted, I had no choice. Anyhow, taking part in orgies is wrong.' Rodeo jumped in. 'Who told you that? What's worse, fighting and killing in Vietnam or shagging?'

'Rodeo,' Preston said, trying to regain control of the interview. 'You're missing a key point. My county demanded that I go fight in Vietnam. You get that? My county demanded.'

'So, if your country demanded you go and jump off the top of the Empire State Building you'd go and do it?' said Rodeo. Preston started to become annoyed and agitated.

'Okay what's your point?' he said sharply.

'My point is we always have a choice and nothing we do is right or wrong. If I chose to take part in orgies, which incidentally I don't, it wouldn't necessarily make me bad. Right and wrong and good and evil are a human interpretation. With love or without love is all that matters. With love humanity can move forward, without love nothing changes. Do you mind if I expand on this?'

'No, go ahead, be my guest, only this time remember it's my job to ask the questions.' Rodeo spoke directly into the camera.

'After Nine Eleven America chose to pursue a war on terror. We invaded Afghanistan, then Iraq. We did exactly what Al-Qaeda wanted us to do. We fell right into their hands. But we had a choice.'

'Did we, you really believe that?' said Preston.

'Yes I do,' replied Rodeo. 'Our government could have asked the question, what would love do now? And you could substitute the word love with God because love and God are one of the same. If we had asked that question we might have come up with some different answers.'

'Like what?' said Preston.

'Like the Muslim world and our non-Muslim allies expected us to retaliate with military power. But what if we had retaliated with love?'

'With love?' said Preston. 'How can we do that?'

'It's easy,' said Rodeo. 'We forgive, after all isn't that what Christ told us to do? We sit down in dialogue with people all around the world and invite them to join with us in working to overcome all the world's difficulties. We could spend money on housing, schools and hospitals and we could ensure the whole world has enough food and water, instead of spending money on guns and bombs.'

'And in the meantime Al-Qaeda keeps attacking and killing us,' interrupted Preston.

Rodeo nodded. 'They might well do that, but they are doing that anyway. How many of our soldiers have been killed in Iraq and Afghanistan? How many more of our soldiers and civilians will die

31

in future attacks and how long will it continue? Five years? Ten years? A hundred years? On the other hand, if we adopt the love approach, humanity will be the only winner, divisive religion will eventually cease to exist, the extremist's rants will be ignored and humankind will move forward to a new era of love.'

Douglas Claymore shouted at the TV. 'Preston you had him! You let him go, you could have nailed him.'

Suddenly his phone rang. 'Darn!' he said, answering it. 'This is the Reverend Claymore.' A voice at the other end began to speak.

'Douglas, its Jack. I'm sorry I won't be able to join you at the special service you called for tomorrow, I have to work late. I'll see you on Sunday.'

'Thanks for calling Jack,' said Douglas before slamming the phone down. Jack, his Church Secretary, had dropped out.

The phone rang again. He picked it up. 'Hello this is Reverend Claymore speaking.'

'Reverend, I'm sorry, Donna and I can't make tomorrow evening after all, I know we promised but her mother's been taken sick and we have to look after her.'

'That's okay Bob,' said Douglas lying through his teeth. 'Give my love to Donna and her mother. I'll pray for them. Thanks for letting me know.' He left the phone off the hook. 'Damned liars! You just heard what I heard and you fell for it. I hate you Rodeo. You're a piece of shit and you should rot in hell.' He turned his attention back to the TV.

Rodeo sang 'My Beautiful Laladee'. After the applause he spoke to the audience.

'My Beautiful Laladee is the girl who died at my ranch. She made a choice and she chose love over life.'

The camera focused on Preston. He looked deep in thought and for a second the camera caught him unawares.

'Thank you for that lovely song,' said Preston. 'Come and join me back on the sofa.'

Preston sat down with Rodeo.

'Now's your chance Preston, no more Mr Nice Guy, nail him once and for all,' Douglas urged.

'There are rumours running through all parts of the media that you engage in sex with underage girls.'

'Go Preston, go, go, go! You got him now, he's on the ropes' said Douglas.

'Those rumours are not true,' said Rodeo in response to Preston's question. 'Any person who visits any of my homes has to provide identification; this is for my protection and theirs.'

'He's lying, he's lying,' said Douglas shouting at his TV, his fists clenched in anger. Oh how he wanted Rodeo in front of him so he could beat the truth out of him.

Preston wound up the interview.

'Rodeo, I want to thank you for coming on my show and talking candidly about some of the issues that are close to all our hearts, and some that have been mentioned recently in the media, as well as entertaining us with your beautiful music. Ladies and Gentlemen...Rodeo, a great artist and humanitarian.' Preston went into his closing routine and Rodeo hugged him, a close warm hug. Douglas wasn't impressed.

'Preston you bastard, you're supping with the Devil. You're supping with the fucking Devil.'

CHAPTER FOUR

W HEN MATHEW returned to Heaven's Door, Rodeo appeared in a pensive mood. They embraced, neither wanting to let go. Love flowed between them. For a while no words were spoken, until Rodeo broke the silence.

'You remember my interview with Preston Quick?' Mathew nodded. 'They broadcast it last night.'

'So now you're a target for Christians, Muslims, Al-Qaeda and the US Government. How the hell am I meant to protect you from all of them?' They both looked at each other and laughed.

'I can just picture it now,' continued Rodeo. 'A Government agent takes a pot shot at me, you see just the glint of his high powered rifle in the sunlight and manage to push me out of the way. The bullet strikes you instead and then an Al-Qaeda operative takes a swipe at me with his sword, but you're there again and you disable him with one blow to his skull despite your wound.'

'I can do that Boss.'

'I know you can Mathew, but ours is a higher purpose. I need you alive to manage things.'

'But Boss I'm no good at managing things. I'm just not educated enough.'

'Mathew, you're more talented than any man I know. Anyhow you won't be alone, you'll have Laura Sable and Reverend Claymore.'

'You're kidding me? Reverend Claymore, the Reverend Claymore?'

'Yes, there's only one Reverend Claymore as far as I know.'

'But Boss, he hates you.'

'Hate, Mathew, is only another aspect of love. Consider this: a man and woman marry. He has an affair with her best friend. She feels angry and let down. She hates her husband for what he has done and she hates her best friend. If she didn't love him there would be no emotion – she wouldn't care. What she's really feeling is jealousy, betrayal and a sense of inadequacy. She's pissed off that he needed to go elsewhere to find physical love, but isn't that really a declaration of love for her husband? Our Reverend Claymore loves God. By acting the way he is towards me he feels he's somehow protecting God. We just have to show him more love than he has ever known in his life.'

* * *

Reverend Claymore's body jerked and his eyes opened as the doorbell rang. For a moment he didn't know what day or time it was. His mind was still locked in the dream. Why did they have to interrupt him? He desperately tried to recall the dream. The doorbell rang again. Slowly his brain began to kick into gear.

'Okay I'm just coming.' He made his way to the front door. 'Who is it?'

'Reverend Claymore this is the FBI, we need to talk with you regarding Rodeo.'

'Hold on.' He undid the chain on the door. There were three men in sharp suits and designer shades.

'May we come in?' one of them asked.

'Sure.' He beckoned them in.

Two of the men stood by the door while the third, a fair-haired man, sat down in one of the armchairs and gestured for Reverend Claymore to do the same.

'So what do the FBI want with Rodeo and how do I fit in the picture?'

'We believe he's running a paedophile ring and using his rock superstar status as cover to recruit young girls and boys. We understand you have been leading a campaign against his immorality on stage and were kind of wondering if you may have stumbled across any information that may help us.'

'Well, no I can't say I have. I've heard lots of stories about immoral goings on at parties he attends, but other than that…I'm sorry I can't be of more help.'

'No, thank you Reverend. It's campaigns like yours that often uncover unsavoury truths about people. If you think of anything that might help, however small or seemingly insignificant, please don't hesitate to call us.' He passed Douglas a card.

'Just call the number on the card.'

As they left he breathed a sigh of relief. For a moment he thought someone had complained about his campaign or they found out he had framed Rodeo for the fire at his church. What troubled him more were all the thoughts running riot in his head. Thoughts triggered by last night's altercation with Rodeo at the arena, the talk show broadcast and now…the dream, that cursed reoccurring dream. Anyhow, time was moving on and he had a meeting to go to.

*   *   *

Reverend Claymore looked at his watch for the third time in less than a minute. Nearly seven fifteen. He'd called the meeting for seven and no one had turned up.

'Maybe there's been an accident on the highway,' he said to himself. As he looked at his watch for a fourth time two people entered the church. They sat down and prayed silently for a couple of minutes. He didn't recognise them as regular members of his congregation.

'Welcome to our Church,' began the Reverend, 'and thank you for coming to this very important meeting. I'm Reverend Claymore. I don't believe I've had the pleasure of making your acquaintances before.'

'We come from a neighbouring county.'

'Yeah, we heard you called a meeting this evening and thought we'd come along and support you.'

'Ah, you must be from St Mary's. I visit there occasionally. I thought you looked vaguely familiar. Time's moving on so shall we make a start? Let's hope some more join us later. Let's join together in prayer. Our father who art in Heaven, hallowed be thy name, thy Kingdom come thy will be done on Earth as it is in Heaven. Give us this day our daily bread and forgive us our trespasses as we forgive those who trespass against us. Lead us not into temptation and deliver us from evil and for thine is the Kingdom the power and glory for ever and ever Amen.'

'Thank you Reverend,' spoke one of the strangers. 'You know, you have a mighty stirring voice. I'm not surprised God called you into his ministry.'

'Why, thank you. Yes I believe God did call me, but I haven't made the impact I thought I would when I was a young man. I thought I was destined for great things. Now, I call a meeting to lead a crusade against a man who I've just been told by the FBI is running a paedophile ring and no one bothers to turn up, except you good people of course.'

'We support you all the way, Reverend,' spoke the second stranger.

'That's right, last night on TV he said we should surrender to the terrorists and that we shouldn't have invaded Iraq or Afghanistan…'

Reverend Claymore interrupted the man.

'No he didn't say that exactly, he said we should fight them with love.'

'Is that right Reverend? Ain't that what Jesus said, love thy enemies an' turn the other cheek?'

'Yes he did.'

'Reverend, may I ask you a question?'

'By all means.'

'Is Rodeo your enemy?'

'I believe he is in league with the Devil, so I suppose that makes him my enemy.'

'So that means you have to love him then?'

'Wait a minute, I…'

'You said that's what Jesus told us to do.'

'Well, yes, I suppose…okay, I'll say a prayer for him but we still need for him to repent.' He cleared his throat. 'Dear Lord, if giving my love to Rodeo will help him see the error of his ways, then let this be your and my will and may our love be never ending. Amen.'

'Reverend?'

'Yes.'

'I have a confession to make. I've never been Baptised, neither has my friend.'

'That's not a problem, I'd be honoured. Do you know, after praying for Rodeo and sending him my love I feel…'

'Loved?'

'Yes, loved. For the first time since, do you know I can't remember since when, I feel loved.'

'That's because you are loved, Reverend,' replied the stranger. We love you and one day the whole world will love you.'

'I know God works in mysterious ways, but I don't think even God could work that one.'

'Why not? If he can create the whole World and the Universe, why can't he do that?'

'Well, if you put it like that, I suppose anything is possible.'

Just then the church door opened.

'Sorry we're a little late Reverend but the notice on your gate said the meeting was being held at the Community Centre down town an' when we got there they told us they knew nothing about it.'

'Ah, that notice must have been left by our ladies' group. Sometimes they hold their meetings there,' replied Douglas. 'I'm sorry about that, but you're just in time, I'm just about to baptise my two friends from St Mary's. This is going to be a wonderful meeting.'

Eventually sixteen people filed in and sat down.

'Let us pray,' said Douglas to the audience. 'Dear Lord, thank you for sending my two friends from St Mary's to be with us at this meeting tonight. They reminded me that Our Lord and Saviour Jesus Christ said we should love our enemies, so I prayed for Rodeo and sent him my love. I now ask you all to do the same. We ask you that by sending our love he will repent and follow the example shown to us by your son Jesus Christ. Amen.'

Everyone responded with 'Amen'. Reverend Claymore continued.

'The Lord is here. His Spirit is with us. Jesus Christ came that we might have life and have it in all its fullness. In St John we read that Jesus said to Nicodemus by night: No one can enter the kingdom of God without being born of water and the Spirit. Nicodemus asked how it was possible for anyone to be born again in this way. God loves us before we love him. Though we cannot understand such love, he invites us in baptism to accept it with the openness and trust of a child. In the waters of baptism, God sets us as a seal upon his heart, for his love in Christ is stronger than death. We are given Christ's journey from death to resurrection to be the pattern of our lives, in union with him. Jesus himself was baptized by John in the Jordan. His baptism found fulfilment in the Cross, where he gave himself for the life of the World. We have been buried with Christ by baptism into death, so that, just as he was raised from the dead by the glory of the Father, so we too might walk in newness of life.'

He paused and looked at the two men before him.

'Brother, what is your name?' he asked one of the strangers.

'Mathew Lopez.'

'Mathew Lopez, you have come for baptism, in response to the call of Christ and the leading of the Holy Spirit. Let us hear that you confess your faith in Christ.

Do you confess your faith in one God, Father, Son and Holy Spirit, taking the Father to be your Father, the Son to be your Saviour and Lord, the Spirit to be your helper and guide?'

Mathew smiled, showing his mouthful of gold teeth.

'I do, I sure do,' replied Matthew.

'Kneel please.' Mathew knelt. 'Mathew, I baptise you in the name of Jesus Christ our Lord. Amen.' As he said the words he poured a jug of water over Mathew's head.

'Brother, what is your name?' he asked, looking at the second man.

'Rodeo.'

The jug crashed from Reverend Claymore's hand and he collapsed to the floor. The people in the congregation gasped in amazement.

'Call an ambulance,' someone shouted out.

Rodeo knelt down and rested the Reverend's head in his lap.

'There's no need.' Everyone gathered round. He kissed Reverend Claymore on the forehead. 'You gave your love to me, now I give you my love for all eternity.' Rodeo kissed him.

The Reverend's eyes opened and he looked around.

'Am I in Heaven?'

'Well Reverend, as good as. You're surrounded with love which is a very similar experience. Would you like a glass of water?'

'Do you have something a little stronger?'

'When you have another baptism to perform? Reverend, I'm surprised at you.'

Reverend Claymore's hands didn't stop shaking as he baptised Rodeo. He wasn't sure if it was shock or excitement.

'Rodeo, I baptise you in the name of Jesus Christ our Lord. Amen.' At that point the congregation broke out in spontaneous applause. Everyone shook each other's hand and embraced.

'Reverend, you performed a miracle today.'

'You're God's main man.'

'I don't know how you did it Reverend, but you deserve a sainthood or something.'

He felt overwhelmed, but why had God bought Rodeo to him, to his Church, to be baptised? While these thoughts raced through his mind, a dazzling bright white light enveloped him like a warm blanket. The feeling was like nothing he had ever experienced before. He wanted to wallow in the light forever. After a few seconds it evaporated, leaving him feeling pleasantly exhilarated by the experience. Everyone present witnessed the white light envelop the reverend.

As Rodeo sat down, Mathew beckoned everyone to do the

same. Reverend Claymore sat between Rodeo and Mathew. He waited until everyone was seated before he stood up.

'Brothers and sisters, you have all just witnessed me experiencing the full love of God. Believe me it's like nothing, nothing you have ever experienced before. I've used the phrase "God is love" many times without really knowing what that means. I thought I knew but in reality I knew nothing. Now I really do know. Through Rodeo and his friend Mathew I have experienced God's love. It didn't come to me because I'm a Reverend or because I'm righteous. There weren't any preconditions. I didn't have to pledge my life to Christ, confess my sins or ask for forgiveness. God's love came to me because I allowed it to, because I accepted it and because I asked for it and because God's love is all there is. I call on Rodeo to lead us in prayer.'

Rodeo had never been called on to lead a group in prayer before. He looked at his audience before he spoke, communicating with them on an almost telepathic level.

'Think of prayer as a communication between many souls. Mankind can achieve great things when prayers are used as a mass channelling of love. Our brother Jesus Christ and God our father do not require praise. They do not require that we pray to them or sing hymns espousing their glory. All they ask is their will be done on Earth as it is in Heaven. In Heaven there is only love. Can you imagine what Earth would be like if there was only love? Why is there so much hate and anger on Earth? It's because there is so little love.'

Reverend Claymore stood to speak. What he wanted to say he found really difficult, especially in front of some of his congregation. He looked around nervously, trying to summon up the courage.

'I have a confession to make.' He turned toward Rodeo. 'Because of me, you went to prison.' Rodeo looked at him and smiled and then looked across to where Mathew was sitting.

'Reverend we have all, everyone of us here, committed what you would call sins. But that doesn't mean that God will judge us. If we do something that's without love we only harm ourselves, we deny our soul what it wants, which is oneness with God. What you did Reverend, you did for love. You see, you were trying to help me by having me punished and by doing that you actually saved Mathew's life.'

'I did?' Reverend Claymore looked shocked but happy, as if a weight had suddenly been lifted from his shoulders.

'Yes you did. You see, if I wasn't in prison with Mathew, he'd have ended up dead.'

'But I didn't know that. I didn't know. I wanted you hurt, I wanted you punished for your blasphemy and tonight, tonight I dreamt of leading a huge movement against you and against immorality. Now…now?' He looked towards the roof of the church. 'God, why have you done this to me? Why?' His voice reached a piercing crescendo on the last word. Rodeo's voice stayed stoically calm.

'I want you to fight immorality, the immorality of a world devoid of love. Leave what you're doing here, join Mathew and me. Set your soul free and join us on stage in our forthcoming World Tour. Listen to your soul, look at what's happening in our world. You've felt God's embrace. Everyone on this planet can experience what you have, they just need some help and now you're perfectly placed to give them that help.

* * *

Laura Sable hadn't slept since arriving home. Laying in bed, all she could think about was Rodeo. His touch felt like nothing she had ever experienced before. She wanted him to hold her again. Closing her eyes she tried to imagine what it would be like to feel him inside her.

'Fuck the FBI, what do they know? He wouldn't mess with underage girls or boys…would he?'

Her mind fought against answering her own questions because she knew Rodeo didn't share traditional values. The more she fought against them the more worried she became.

'I have to ask him if it's true, I have to. God, please don't let it be true, please.' For the rest of the day her mind lay in turmoil. Tears continually ran down her cheeks. Then she remembered what Rodeo had told her. Tears don't come from sadness, loss or despair, they come out of love. She picked up the phone and read the number off the card.

'This is Laura, please call me, please.' She realised there sounded more than a touch of longing in her voice. She didn't want to let go of the phone. How long would it be before he returned her call?

*   *   *

Reverend Claymore never felt happier or more loved. Even though he felt a little sick after the flight in the chopper it didn't dampen his spirits. He didn't quite know what to expect as he entered Heaven's Door. The sign on the door caught his attention and he gave a wry smile.

'Welcome to my house, Reverend,' spoke Rodeo. 'Please make yourself at home. Anything you want just ask.'

'This…is your home?' Reverend Claymore asked incredulously.

'Sure, I'm a simple man with simple tastes. Okay, there is another part of the house which is a little wacky, where I entertain guests at parties, but this is where I live.'

'Oh yes, the parties.'

'Douglas – may I call you Douglas?'

'Yes by all means, please do. I might as well drop the Reverend title, after all they've probably already decided to defrock me.'

'But when we left the church they all loved you.'

'Yes, but they weren't the church elders. You don't know what the church elders are like.'

'Believe me I do, I do.' Rodeo put his arm around him. Douglas winced just a tiny fraction, but it was enough for Rodeo to notice. He deliberately hugged him even closer. 'You know, you don't have to attend any of the parties while you're here, but I would like you to. I would love for you to experience the oneness and the freedom of love but, most of all, I want you to learn to love yourself. If a

man can't love himself how can he bring himself to love others?'
Douglas turned to him and gave a worried grin.

'Look, if I'm going to help make the world a better place through love I think I had better attend, don't you?'

'Absolutely Douglas, absolutely.' Rodeo smiled. He liked Douglas, he really did. Mathew chipped in.

'Boss, Laura called, she left a message. She wants to speak with you.'

'Mathew, call her back, tell her you'll come and pick her up.'

'Okay Boss, I'll catch you later.'

CHAPTER FIVE

EDITH LLITJOS, a slight, gorky French girl, first attended confirmation classes at the age of twelve. She amazed Father Jacques, her parish priest, with her understanding of the scriptures. By the age of thirteen she no longer looked slight or gorky. She had developed curves and learned how to make the most of them to attract much older boys. To her parents' relief, Edith's interest in older boys didn't appear to be sexual. She loved the idea of romance and being swept off her feet by a knight in shinning armour. She made a pledge to save herself for her wedding day, whenever that day may be.

One week before her fourteenth birthday, Edith agreed to go on a picnic with Jerome Picat, the handsome seventeen-year-old son of wealthy neighbours. All her friends teased her about making sure he wore a condom. She just laughed it off.

'Jerome's not like that,' she said. 'He's gentle and respects me. If he's lucky I might let him kiss me, and if he's very lucky I may even open my mouth a little and allow him to use his tongue.'

She wheeled her bike out of the garage.

'Edith!' called her mother. She knew what was coming and turned to face her mother.

'Edith, Jerome is a nice boy from a good family, but he is much older than you. Boys of that age can easily become carried away. You know what I am saying?'

'Yes I know.'

'Okay, just be careful, don't give him any excuse.'

'Don't worry, I won't.'

'Good girl.'

Edith raised her eyebrows in exasperation of her mother.

The sky looked a shade of blue that artists describe as owing more to Technicolor than Mother Nature. No light or shade, just one continual swathe of the same rich blue. The maize in the fields was a pastel green colour.

'Where are you taking me?' asked Edith, pedalling alongside Jerome.

'I know the perfect place for a picnic.'

'What makes it so perfect?'

'Trees for shade, a stream to paddle in and...'

Suddenly Edith's front wheel hit a rut in the unmade road. It forced her handle bars and wheel to turn at a ninety degree angle. Her bike stopped as if hit by a brick wall. Edith flew over the handle bars. She landed on the hard-baked mud. Jerome heard the sickening sound of a breaking bone.

'Edith, don't move!' he shouted as he raced towards her. She grimaced with pain.

'I think my arm's broken.' Jerome looked. Her right arm above the elbow appeared twisted and had swollen to double its normal size.

'Are you hurting anywhere else?

'Not really, I think it's just my arm.' Jerome tried to call an ambulance on his cell phone.

'Damn it, there's no signal, there's no fucking signal. Can you walk?'

'I can't move, it's too painful.' Tears began to stream down her face.

'Hold on, I'll go and find a phone or raise some help. You stay here, I'll be as quick as I can.'

Jerome cycled off down the lane in the direction from which they came. About a mile down the lane he saw an old Renault van heading towards him. He dismounted and stood in the middle of the lane with both arms raised above his head. The van stopped about six feet from him and the driver wound down his window, asking what the problem was.

Jerome quickly explained what had happened. The driver nodded and beckoned Jerome to jump in beside him. They drove towards the scene of the accident in silence. The van pulled up just a few feet from Edith. Jerome jumped out, followed by the driver. Edith suddenly screamed. Jerome turned his head just as a small wooden club smashed into the back of his skull. Immediately he fell to the ground, his body still and lifeless. Edith screamed again. Her brain told her to run but her legs felt like jelly. She couldn't move.

'Shut up, you fucking little bitch!' The driver spat the words at her as he grabbed her hair and pulled her towards the rear doors of the van. 'Get in. If you scream any more I'll kill you.'

She focussed on the pain from her arm while he raped her. She welcomed the pain, letting it envelope her and shut out everything else. Eventually she felt no more pain, only a desperate emptiness.

*   *   *

Doctors induced a coma to allow her body time to recover from the trauma. A week later, still heavily sedated, she woke. Evelyn and Henri Llitjos sat at her bedside with Father Jacques waiting for her to regain consciousness. Her eyes opened and she tried to speak but the words wouldn't form.

'It's alright darling, don't speak. Just know that Papa and I are here with Father Jacques.' Tears formed in Evelyn's eyes as she spoke to her daughter.

Edith tried to speak again. 'J...Jer...' They knew what she wanted to say. Father Jacques spoke.

'I'm afraid Jerome didn't make it. I'm so sorry. We are told he died instantly.' Edith turned her head to one side and closed her eyes.

Three months later, Father Jacques sat down with Edith and told her that the man who had raped her and murdered Jerome had been caught. He'd confessed to everything and his confession had been backed up by forensic and DNA evidence.

'But why did he do it? Why did God allow it to happen?' Her voice, calm and measured, belied her young years.

'I wish I knew, I wish I knew how someone could conceive of such evil, let alone carry it out. All I know is God has given us all free will. Some people do good and some bad and some a little of both. But why that is, I don't know.' He hesitated before continuing. 'Edith, there are people who feel that the man who did what he did to you and Jerome doesn't deserve to live.'

'You mean they think he should be executed?'

'Yes, but the laws in France will not allow that to happen. As a man of God it's difficult for me to ask you this, but I have examined my conscience and prayed for guidance. Would you support a campaign to change the law to allow the execution of child rapists and child murderers?' He didn't wait for her to answer. 'It would mean people would learn of your identity but by going public you could help protect children throughout France.' She closed her eyes and put her hands together as if praying.

* * *

'Once again I thank you. Monsieur, Madame Llitjos, Edith. This is a very great sacrifice you have agreed to make. I'm sure the people of France will appreciate your heroic contribution to our fight against those who commit evil sexual crimes. The days and months ahead will be very difficult and painful for everyone, but remember, whatever happens, no matter what you hear, you may take comfort from the fact that you will be helping to make France a safer place for our children to live in and…'

Father Jacques interrupted. 'One day Edith, you will sit at the right hand of God with our Blessed Virgin Mary.' The reporter continued.

'Publishing your story will create an unstoppable wave of emotion around France, maybe even demonstrations and strikes. No government will be able to resist our newspaper's call for the execution of child rapists and child murderers.

* * *

The Cardinals and Bishops listened intently to Cardinal Biloweiki. As usual, he showed no emotion when speaking.

'Eighteen months have passed since Barnabus became Pope. The plan for his World sojourn is now complete. First he will visit India.' A surprised whisper of discontent rippled around the richly decorated hall.

'India has a population of over one billion people, which includes thirty million Catholics.' He looked over his bifocals at the gathered assembly. They quickly quietened like admonished school boys. 'He will then continue on to his native Philippines and from there to Africa where he'll visit Nigeria and the Democratic Republic of Congo. South and Central America haven't been finalised yet, however it is expected he will visit Brazil, Bolivia and Mexico in that order. After a well-earned three week rest he will visit the United States, Ireland, France and Spain. You will all receive the precise details within the next three to four weeks.' His tone and body language gave no invitation to the ensemble of Cardinals and Bishops to ask questions and none were asked.

Barnabus would meet and give blessings to over ten million of his flock and reach many more by radio and television. By his reckoning less than a tenth of that number would see 'that' musician live and, if Cardinal Biloweiki was right, television companies and radio stations would agree not to screen any Rodeo concerts or interviews in return for exclusive interviews and audiences with himself.

Jesus mixed with the people, with sinners, the poor, the blind and crippled, and he would do the same. He would be the voice of God, a voice that people respected and loved. Yes, he would tell them of God's love, but he would also remind them that they must repent their sins and follow the example given by Christ or face the wrath of God and be denied entry to the Kingdom of Heaven. In Africa, Bishop Aphalardi's strict teachings had started to be accepted. He would echo those teachings.

During the past year, Barnabus revisited the Aramaic language. He hadn't studied it since his university days. As an academic, his natural curiosity needed satisfying. He wanted to enhance his understanding of the Hidden Testaments. He discovered that the word given to him as meaning 'musician' had been translated from Syriac, an eastern and early Christian version of Aramaic. It worried Barnabus that the same word in Hebrew translated as 'of David'. Could there be any connection? No, surely not. King David was a musician, that was the only connection. He put it out of his mind.

*   *   *

'Edith,' called her mother. 'Come quickly, Father Jacques is here and he has some wonderful news for you.'

Edith came rushing down the stairs. Father Jacques, already sitting down, beckoned her to do the same. She looked at him expectantly. Father Jacques bubbled with excitement.

'Come on Father Jacques tell me or you will explode,' joked Edith.

'You are to have a private audience with Pope Barnabus when he visits France next June. He has asked especially to meet you.' He said it all in one breath. 'Are you happy?'

'Yes I am...but what will I say to him? I just know I'll be like a dumb mute.'

'No you won't, you'll be your charming and intelligent self.' He paused for a second and looked more serious. 'There is something else I have to tell you. It's likely that The National Assembly will pass the new laws when they reconvene next month and it is proposed that the new law be retrospective. You know what that means?' She closed her eyes and nodded.

*   *   *

In order for the new law to be passed by the National Assembly allowing the execution of child rapists and murderers, the proponents had to agree on a form of execution other than the guillotine or hanging, which the Government considered equally barbaric. In the end they proposed lethal injection. Even though the new law had massive public support, the government felt lethal injection to be less contentious. Almost like putting down a sick or wounded animal.

When Philippe Luquet, Edith's attacker, learned of his fate he asked for permission to write to her to apologise for his crimes. The court granted permission provided it went through her parish priest and not directly to her.

On the eve of his execution he refused the company of a priest; instead he asked if he could listen to Rodeo's music. He sat on the only chair in his cell and tried to make himself comfortable. He couldn't understand the English words to the songs but something in Rodeo's voice reassured him he had nothing to fear. The next morning he went into the sparse execution chamber feeling calm and almost relieved that the trials and pain of this life would soon be over. He kept hearing a line from one of the songs in his head: 'what would love do now?' He didn't know what it meant but it somehow comforted him.

The guards strapped him to the moulded plastic execution table in a standing position. He felt the sensation of a warm blanket being wrapped around him, keeping him safe. His mind thought about what he would do next time if he had the chance to live his life again. I'd be like Rodeo singing about love. Yes that is what I would be. He felt the first needle jab go into his wrist.

*   *   *

Father Jacques received the letter the day after the execution.

'I am sorry for what I did to you and your friend. I wish he wasn't dead. I wish I was never born and it would not happen and you would be alright. You are a good girl. I hope God looks after you always. I should die for what I did and God must punish me'.

The words, written in large uneven scrawl, hit Father Jacques like a rock. At the trial the defence revealed Philippe had hardly ever attended school because his parents, who physically abused him, had forced him to work on their small farm until he ran away from home at the age of fourteen. He had always been a loner and had never had a girlfriend. Another piece of paper accompanied the letter. Father Jacques unfolded it. He looked at the crayon drawing. His eyes glassed over. The picture showed a big bright yellow sun in the top right hand corner and a blue sky. Three matchstick type characters, a man, woman and child, all held hands and looked happy. Written on it were the words '*what I dreamed for as a child. I kept this picture in my shoe*'.

'You see...' Father Jacques tried to explain the picture to Edith.

'Father Jacques, I'm not a child anymore. I understand. Jerome and me, we both had what he always wanted, what he never had or would ever have, a loving family. Do you think God will ever forgive him?'

'You always ask such difficult questions. I believe God is our Father. All fathers become angry but eventually they come round, even our Bishop does, so why not God eh? Edith, can you forgive him?'

'I already have. I couldn't live with my heart full of hate for the rest of my life.'

CHAPTER SIX

WITH THE party in full swing, Laura and Douglas sat on the edge of the pool, their backs leaning against the pillars, dangling their legs in the water. She'd decided to go topless. Douglas felt a little concerned about his flabby physique and chose to wear a baggy cotton shirt with Bermuda shorts. Looking at her, he admired her gorgeous body. Why had he let all those years slip by without having a woman to love, to physically love? He felt a stiffness between his legs. His brain told him, this shouldn't be happening, it's wrong and what's she going to see in a staid, slightly greying man more than twenty years her senior?

Laura felt a sense of freedom. When she returned to Heaven's Door with Mathew she resolved to go with the flow. Mathew had reassured her that no girls or boys younger than eighteen were ever invited and even then there were stringent checks on their ages.

She looked at Douglas and sensed his struggle with his conscience. His greying hair aside he looked…she couldn't quite make up her mind. Yes, he looked more like a film star just reaching his prime than a Baptist minister. With a little exercise to tone his body he'd be really quite fit…and if rumours about the size of a man's hands were true…

'Have you seen the beach yet?' said Laura.

'No, not yet.'

'Come on, let's go and build some sandcastles.' They walked through the snow field. Despite there being no snowball fight going on, Laura picked up some snow and threw it at him. It hit him full in the face and covered his glasses. He wiped the snow off.

'Right young lady, you asked for it.' He threw a quick salvo of balls at her. She screamed and ran. He soon caught up with her. She turned and fired another snowball that splattered his cotton shirt. He hadn't had so much fun for…he couldn't remember when. He noticed her long stiff nipples. *It must be the snow*, he thought.

When they arrived at the beach the sun had gone down. Light from the moon glistened on the water which gently lapped at the sand. A few couples walked along the beach holding hands. Laura sat under a palm and invited Douglas to sit next to her. He glanced at her firm breasts. He desperately wanted to kiss her nipples. *I'm a clergyman for God's sake. I'm supposed to uphold moral values. Who's moral values are they? Where had they come from?* Laura interrupted his thoughts.

'Have you ever made love?' Laura suddenly asked. He hesitated before he answered. He shook his head. Laura smiled.

'Me neither.'

She rested her head on his shoulder. Douglas wanted to put his arm around her. What if she didn't want him to? He didn't have to answer the question. She took his left hand and placed it on her breast. It felt smooth, firm and wonderful. His fingers caressed her nipple. She leant over and kissed him. Douglas pulled away and went to speak. She put her fingers on his lips to stop him and pulled him down to her side. Their lovemaking became frenetic, each of them giving and taking pleasure, both revelling in their new found freedom.

The next morning saw Rodeo cooking breakfast. Mathew, Douglas and Laura all sat around the old kitchen table. Rodeo spoke as he turned an egg.

'Today is a special day because today I'm going to try an' spread a little more happiness around the world. I've decided to give an impromptu concert in the park.' Mathew screwed his face up and put his mug of coffee down.

'Boss, I thought we agreed no more impromptu concerts. You promised.' Rodeo gave him a cheeky grin.

'How can I keep you safe? How can I be expected to provide a competent level of security?' Rodeo shrugged his shoulders.

'Last night I wrote a new song. Sorry I left the party early but I had to get this song down.' Mathew gave him a quizzical look

'I knew it, you want to try this song out on a live audience.' Rodeo grinned.

The park wasn't particularly busy. A few people walking their dogs, a family playing a game of soft ball, a couple of cyclists and some kids trying out their roller blades. Mathew breathed a sigh of relief. Maybe this wouldn't be so bad after all.

Laura and Douglas laid out the car blanket on the grass while Rodeo took his acoustic guitar out of its case. They all sat on the blanket except Mathew, who preferred to stand some distance away to observe. He liked to be able to spot any trouble before it arrived.

Word spread pretty quickly. Rodeo's playing his guitar in the park! Within twenty minutes a crowd of at least fifty watched Rodeo sing and play. They listened and politely applauded. Some of them asked for autographs. Rodeo told them he would sign for everyone before he went if they formed an orderly queue.

Mathew became anxious. The crowd had grown to over a hundred. Ten minutes ago it was only fifty. Rodeo performed his new song. The crowd seemed to appreciate it just as much as all his others, maybe even more. Then Mathew spotted trouble. He saw two uniformed police officers making their way across the park towards them. He tried to catch Rodeo's attention but Rodeo was too involved in his song to notice. Then to Mathew's relief the two officers stopped some distance away and just watched. At the end of the song an elderly gentleman walking with the aid of a stick pushed his way to the front of the still growing crowd.

'Rodeo, my wife has cancer. She's in a lot of pain. But you know, when you were on TV the other day she suddenly felt a lot better for a couple of days. Is there any chance you could stop by and see her? We only live just the other side of the park. It would really make her day.' Rodeo smiled at the man and addressed the crowd.

'I want everyone to stand up and hold hands. Rodeo took the elderly gentleman's hand and Laura held his other hand. I want everyone to wish this man's wife well. Let's all send her our love.' Rodeo started to sing his new song. Soon everyone was holding hands and joining in the chorus. He pointed to Mathew.

'You give that man over there your address and we'll be round later.'

For the next hour Rodeo signed autographs, even the two police officers asked him to sign for their kids, not for themselves of course. Gradually, to Mathew's relief, the crowd dispersed.

'What was that address he gave you?' Rodeo asked Mathew, who pulled a crumpled piece of paper out of his jacket pocket and handed it to him.

'We'll walk across the park. You meet us outside with the car in about a half hour.'

'Okay Boss, but you take care. A lot of people know you're around here now.'

As they walked across the park, Rodeo took a sidewise glance at Douglas and Laura.

'How did the party go last night?'

Laura looked at Douglas before answering. 'I had a wonderful time.'

'Yes and so did I' added Douglas.

Rodeo looked at them with mock concern. 'Well I hope you didn't do anything that you regret today.' Douglas smiled.

'Rodeo, my only regret is that I didn't do it years ago.' Rodeo felt a certain smugness in turning the Reverend Douglas Claymore from a middle-aged Bible thumping conservative clergyman to a champion of swinging and free love in less than three days. Well, maybe champion of swinging and free love was an exaggeration, but his transformation was remarkable all the same.

They approached the elderly gentleman's house, a modern two bedroom condominium. Seeing them walk up the short drive, he opened the door ready.

'Come on in, come on in,' he said excitedly. He showed them through to the living room. A lady wearing a pink bath robe was sitting in a raised armchair supported by three or four pillows. 'I told you they'd come! I told you but you wouldn't believe me, would you.'

'Jacob Goldberg, you've been so full of bullshit all your life that I never know whether to believe you or not,' replied his wife.

Rodeo smiled. He liked this couple.

'Mrs Goldberg, Jacob your husband tells me you felt better when I was on TV a few days ago.'

'Yes I did. Even felt like a bit of passion from Jacob, first time in years. Silly old fool though, he couldn't rise to the occasion.' Jacob looked miffed.

'If you'd have been thirty years younger I'd have been fine,' he said. Rodeo interceded. 'Mrs Goldberg, I'd like to introduce you to Douglas and Laura, both friends of mine. Douglas is going to lay hands on you and make you feel better.' She gave Douglas a disapproving look.

'I'd feel a lot better if *you* put your hands on me.' Rodeo smiled. Douglas looked at Rodeo as if to say 'can I do this?' Rodeo nodded affirmatively.

Mathew, meanwhile, had pulled up behind a blue Mercedes parked outside the house. He looked at his watch. *Shouldn't be too long now*, he thought. Another blue Mercedes pulled up behind him and pushed his car, sandwiching it between the two. He jumped out to remonstrate.

'Hey, what are you playing at?' He felt the barrel of a gun being pushed into the small of his back.

'If you know what's good for you you'll get back in your car,' said a voice. Another man opened the car door and pushed Mathew onto the front seat. The man with the gun sat in the rear.

'What's all this about?' said Mathew, trying to buy valuable thinking time.

'Shut it! Just sit there and do nothing until I tell you.'

* * *

Douglas put his hands on Mrs Goldberg's head. She looked at Rodeo.

'I can't feel a thing.'

'That's normal, Mrs Goldberg. With hands-on healing all you feel is a warm sensation.'

'No, I mean I can't feel a thing, my pain is gone, all gone. I feel fine.' Douglas held his hands up and looked at them in disbelief. In all his years in the church he'd never ever healed anyone.

Mrs Goldberg beamed. 'Douglas, I'm going to give you a big kiss and when I've finished with you I'm going to give my Rodeo an even bigger kiss and then Jacob you can take me upstairs.' Rodeo wondered how Jacob would cope with Mrs Goldberg's new demands. He smiled to himself.

As they walked out the door, Rodeo looked up the short drive to the car.

'Laura, Douglas go back into the house,' he ordered. 'Don't argue, go now, go.' They didn't argue.

Something's wrong. Mathew always stood by the car when waiting for Rodeo. He could see Mathew sitting in the driver's seat looking directly ahead.

'Shit!'

Rodeo carried on walking towards the car. A man moved alongside him.

'Rodeo, get in the car.' He opened the rear door of the front blue Mercedes and pushed Rodeo in.

Mathew felt helpless. What was this shit? The man in the rear seat told him to follow behind the blue Mercedes. Mathew followed. He whispered to Rodeo under his breath.

'Hold on there my friend. These punks are beginning to annoy me.'

He flicked a switch on the dashboard. Immediately the rear doors locked and a glass panel sprung up, separating the rear passenger compartment from the front. The man in the rear raised his gun to the glass panel.

'I wouldn't do that my friend,' said Mathew. The man just grinned as he pulled the trigger. The bullet hit the glass panel, ricocheted and hit the gunman in his right shoulder.

'Now what did I tell you? Why didn't you listen to your uncle Mathew, eh? You better pray that we sort this mess out before you bleed to death.'

Mathew managed to let traffic in between him and the lead car.

'Hopefully they'll think we just got separated in the traffic.' He switched on the tracking device. 'Good, it's working. Rodeo's managed to activate it. Now where are we going? East, highway two eleven, that takes us to the Central Industrial Estate.'

The blue Mercedes pulled into a dilapidated garage adjoining an abandoned factory unit. The garage doors shut behind them. A tall bald man with heavy gold jewellery hanging from his neck opened the car door and beckoned Rodeo to get out. He ushered him towards a small chubby man smoking a large Cuban cigar. Two other men in sharp suites stood nearby.

'Rodeo, I'll cut straight to the quick,' spoke the man. 'You're pissing off some good friends of mine with your negative comments about Christianity and Catholicism in particular. You gotta start to learn some respect. Now, just to help your education, your buddy Mathew Lopez is probably meeting his maker as we speak. Look, I'm a fair man. You can continue performing but you better start to show some respect to the Church. Just to remind you, I'm going to cut off something about three inches long. No, not your dick, I'll only cut that off if you carry on pissing off me and my friends.'

Rodeo remained calm. Mathew's too good. No way is he about to meet his maker, but he's taking his time. The tall, bald-headed man took hold of Rodeo's arm. Rodeo visibly stiffened as one of the other men picked up a large pair of bolt cutters. Suddenly Rodeo heard the sound of sirens and a chopper overhead.

'Come out with you hands up, you're surrounded.' The four men appeared surprised.

'What do we do?'

'Shut the fuck up.'

Suddenly Mathew's car smashed through the garage doors and did a handbrake turn. The four men jumped clear. Rodeo dived into the front seat as Mathew opened the nearside door. He slammed the door closed. A double salvo of bullets hit the car. They had no effect on the two inch steel plate or bullet proof windows. Mathew drove straight back out through the wrecked garage doors.

'Hey Boss, the surround sound worked a treat.'

Rodeo turned round and saw the man in the back, laying across the rear seat obviously in some amount of pain.

'He did it to himself, I never touched him, honest.'

'Mathew, take him to the hospital before he dies.'

'Okay Boss.'

Rodeo gave the hospital a hundred thousand dollars to cover any costs. The wounded man couldn't believe it.

'Rodeo, I don't know of another man on Earth who would do what you're doing. I owe you, one day I'll repay my debt. I promise. Here, take my marker.'

He handed Rodeo a folded piece of paper.

In return, Rodeo gave him a card with just a phone number on it.

'Call me if you need to. Just leave a message and someone will call you back.' Mathew gave him a look that said don't mess with me again as he turned and walked away with Rodeo.

Back at Heaven's Door, Laura quizzed Rodeo and Mathew about what had happened.

'So you're telling me you took him to the Hospital and paid a hundred thousand dollars for his treatment?' She looked almost angry. Rodeo took her hand.

'Laura, what would love do now, remember?'

'But he was going to kill Mathew and they were going to cut one of your fingers off.' Mathew interrupted.

'He couldn't have killed me. He was an amateur. If you ask me they were all amateurs. Boss, what were they playing at?'

'I don't know, maybe they only wanted to frighten us,' answered Rodeo. Then, turning to Laura he asked, 'You're a Catholic, aren't you?'

'Well kind of lapsed,' she replied.

'Do you have any contacts?'

'Only father Ignatius, if he's still alive. He used to be my parish priest.'

'Well that's a start. Pay him a visit, find out anything you can.'

'May I go with you, to keep you company?' said Douglas. Laura walked around the table to Douglas and put her arms around his neck.

'Sure, I'd like that.' She kissed him on the cheek.

'That settles it then, you both leave in the morning,' said Rodeo. 'Mathew, we have a meeting with Old Iron Knickers.'

'But Boss, do we have to?'

'Afraid so, we have a World tour to plan for and Old Iron Knickers ensures everything runs like clockwork.'

That night, Douglas didn't sleep. All he could think of was Laura. How could he tell her his feelings without making a fool of himself? Was it purely a physical act, a sexual release, or had she really taken a shine to him?

Laura knocked on Rodeo's door. He opened it slightly.

'What's wrong?' he said through the crack.

'I can't sleep, I'm scared.'

'You better come in. Sit down.' He motioned for her to sit on the bed. He made no attempt to cover his naked body.

'Can I get you a drink? A glass of water or orange juice?'

'No, I'm okay thanks. Rodeo, do you find me attractive?'

'Yes I do, very attractive. You have a beautiful body and a beautiful soul.'

'I want you to make love to me.' She stood and released the straps to her negligee. 'I've wanted you since the first time you held me when I was trying to beat seven tons of shit out of you.' Her negligee fell to the floor.

'Laura look at me,' replied Rodeo. 'I love you, possibly more than you can ever know.' She looked into his eyes. She saw sadness, genuine sadness.

'But if we spend the night together Douglas will know, and I love Douglas too, not in the physical sense. Put yourself in my shoes and ask the question what would love do now? What would your answer be?'

Picking up her negligee, without bothering to put it back on, she stormed out of the room, banging the door shut behind her.

Rodeo stood dumbfounded. 'Shit!'

Douglas had at last dozed off. When Laura climbed in beside him he didn't stir. She lifted the quilt. He awoke to the most amazing sensation he had ever experienced. Laura made sure Rodeo would hear them. Rodeo smiled to himself.

CHAPTER SEVEN

O LD IRON KNICKERS appeared to be on top form. Mathew always felt intimidated by her. Rodeo, on the other hand, used to ply her with compliments till she giggled and blushed like a love-struck schoolgirl. When they entered her office she gave Mathew a scowling look.

'You still around? Anyone would think you two were joined at the hip.'

Mable Hillthorpe, a spinster in her mid forties, dressed like someone twenty years older. Rodeo guessed she wanted to hide her enormous breasts. He always teased Mathew that she fancied him and all he needed to get into her knickers was a tin opener. Mathew shuddered at the thought.

'Well, you certainly screwed things up this time.' Rodeo and Mathew looked at each other blankly and then back at Mable.

'Don't tell me you don't know?'

'Know what?' they answered in unison.

'Don't you ever read any of my emails?' They both looked at each other again.

'Your World tour. We agreed you would visit India, Japan, the Philippines, Brazil, Mexico, the USA, Great Britain, Ireland and France, right?'

'Yes, that's what we agreed.' Rodeo didn't know where she was coming from.

'It's going to be a disaster. Every TV network in every country except Japan has declined to film any of your concerts and there are no planned radio or TV interviews, nothing. We're even having trouble booking suitable venues.' Mathew sensed an opportunity to score a home run.

'Mable, you must be losing your touch.'

'Losing my touch?' She screamed the words. Rodeo stepped in.

'I'm sure there's a logical explanation.' Mable looked daggers at Mathew.

'Well, the only one I can think of is that you two must have upset a whole lot of people all around the world.' She was quite close to tears at this point. Rodeo decided to use a little flattery.

'What excuses did they give? After all, I'm sure you used all your wonderful feminine charms like you usually do. Normally you have them eating out of your hands.' Mathew nearly threw up. She brightened up almost immediately.

'Well, they said they couldn't fit us into their schedules.'

'All of them said that?' She nodded. Rodeo smelt a rat.

'Mable, will you do something for me?' He didn't wait for an answer. 'I want you to contact all the big land owners that own land on the outskirts of the cities we planned to perform in. Offer them mega bucks to allow us to use their land for a concert. They must arrange all the necessary permissions and licences. When they're confirmed I want you to place full page adverts in all their major newspapers. All net profits from these concerts are to go to local charities. Local accountants will verify the figures.'

*   *   *

Douglas sat in the passenger seat while Laura drove. She hadn't spoken a word since they left Heaven's Door two hours ago. Douglas tried to pluck up courage to say something. Laura beat him to it.

'I went to Rodeo's room last night. I asked him to make love to me but he wouldn't, said he had too much love for you.' Douglas felt shocked, not because Laura had gone to Rodeo, but more that Rodeo cared so much for him.

'So why did you come to me?'

'Because I needed love and a little piece of me wanted Rodeo to hear what he'd missed.'

Douglas took over the driving and Laura rested her head on his shoulder. *This is another world*, he thought. He looked back to the world, he'd left. A world full of fire and brimstone but not much else. Now he'd experienced love he strangely felt closer to God.

'Take a right here.' Laura's directing bought him back to the present. We must be getting near, he thought.

Saint Michael's looked like a relatively modern church. It had beautiful stained glass windows depicting the Last Supper and the Virgin Mary. The steeple, probably sixty feet tall, had a bell tower at the top of it. The grounds looked well cared for with gorgeous rose beds, clematis and manicured lawns. A stone path led from the church gate towards a hedge and a modern, well kept detached house.

'That's where he lives.' Laura pointed to the house behind the hedge. 'Well, here goes.' She started to unbutton her jeans.

'What are you doing.'

'It's okay, I know what Father Ignatius likes. Don't ask me how, don't even go there. But if we are going to find out what's going on I need to use all my charms. Here, give me a hand to pull these boots off, they're a little tight.' Then she took off her high-necked top to reveal a white blouse.

'There, how do I look?' Douglas looked at her short, pleated tartan skirt and white socks.

'You look like…a schoolgirl.'

'Great, because that's exactly what he likes.' Douglas watched her walk down the path swinging her hips. He admired her long legs and shapely butt. His thoughts went back to last night.

Laura rang the door bell. An elderly lady answered and immediately gave Laura a disapproving look.

'What do you want?' she said almost accusingly in a strong Irish accent.

'I'd like to see Father Ignatius please.'

'He's busy preparing his sermon for Sunday. He won't see you now. If it's confession you're after, that's weekdays between five and seven.'

'Mrs Keegan, who have we at the door?' A white-haired elderly man appeared. Laura recognised him as Father Ignatius.

'Father, it's me, Laura Sable.' He paused for a second, his mind trying to think back.

'Ah yes, Laura, Laura Sable. You've grown a little since I last saw you. Come on in my dear, come on in. Mrs Keegan, please be a dear and put the kettle on. Laura, come into my study.'

She looked at the two upholstered leather chairs on either side of a coffee table. *Exactly how I remember*, she thought. *Oh, and the biscuit tin on the table.* They sat down. Laura knew exactly what the tin contained. He hadn't changed one bit.

'I'd offer you a lollipop, but I suppose you're a little old for them now.'

'It's you I blame for my two fillings, all those sugary lollipops you used to give me.' Father Ignatius smiled.

'Well my dear, life would be so dull if we couldn't be tempted by the odd lollipop, wouldn't it? So, to what do I owe this pleasure?'

Laura crossed her legs allowing her skirt to ride up her thighs, an action that did not go unnoticed by Father Ignatius.

'I'm a journalist, freelance. I've decided to write an article on Rodeo, you know, the rock star. I believe he was complicit in my sister's death and maybe my writing about him will help me come to terms with losing her. Some of his views on life, God and religion are quite controversial and I wonder what the Catholic Church's take on him is?'

He shifted in his chair and looked a little uncomfortable. 'Well, that's an interesting question. Will you be quoting me?'

'That's up to you, if you'd prefer I could just say a source inside the Catholic Church.' Laura felt concerned about his reticence. She toyed with the top button on her blouse.

'I think a source inside the Church would be better. It's quite a coincidence that you should call today and ask me about Rodeo. Only a few days ago I was having a conversation with a Cardinal. He's a confidant of our Most Holy Father you know. We spoke about Rodeo…no, I shouldn't be telling you this…no I cannot.' Laura undid her top button.

'What shouldn't you be telling me, Father?' His eyes focused on the cleavage now partly revealed.

'He told me Rodeo was a danger to the whole of Christianity as well as other religions and our World order. He believes he's the Devil himself and must be destroyed. Even Barnabus Our Most Holy Father has given his full backing to this.'

'But why? Why does the Catholic Church believe he is such a threat? Why do they believe he is the Devil?'

'That I cannot tell you, my lips are sealed.' She toyed with another button.

'Father, do you mind if I take you up on the offer of a lollipop? My mouth is a little dry.'

'The tea will be here shortly but help yourself, you know where they are.'

She leant over towards the tin. Father Ignatius took the opportunity to steal another glance at her cleavage. Mrs Keegan bought in a tray with the tea and what looked like homemade scones.

'Thank you Mrs Keegan, just leave them on the table.' She put them down and gave Laura a filthy look.

'If you want any more just call me.' With that she turned and left.

'Now, where were we?' He looked at Laura who licked her lollipop, making great play with her tongue.

'Shall I be mother?' Not waiting for an answer, he poured the tea from the pot. He put two teaspoonfuls of sugar into his cup. As he stirred he spoke.

'The New Testament is made up from twenty-seven separate books, but in Rome at the Vatican there are another eleven. What they contain I don't know. Only Our Most Holy Father is allowed to see them. But what I can tell you is that one of these eleven books tells us that early in the third millennium, after the birth of our Lord, a musician will challenge the established world religions for the hearts and minds of all the people on our planet. If he were to succeed it would mean the end of the Roman Catholic Church, Christianity and all the World's religions.' He stopped stirring. Laura frowned. Shit, this is getting deep.

'So you think Rodeo could be this musician?'

'We don't know for sure you understand, but we cannot take any chances. We have to stop him. He is already building a large following.'

'How are you going to go about stopping him?'

'That I cannot tell you.' Laura undid another button on her blouse. Father Ignatius could see the lacy cups of her bra. She uncrossed her legs.

'Well, I…' Her legs parted a little to allow him to see the tops of her stockings. 'We have asked contacts in the FBI to investigate him for anything that could link him to paedophilia. If any link could be proven it would almost certainly destroy him. We have also arranged for some not very nice friends of ours to frighten him.'

'What if all that fails?'

'No, no more. I cannot tell you any more.' Laura opened her legs and put her hand down the front of her white lacy panties.

'Mother of Jesus, why do you do this to me?' Father Ignatius cried out, now in a very agitated state.

'Because, let's face it Father, you're a dirty old man and always have been. If you want me to give you a treat you had better tell me.'

'Alright, Our Holy Father is going to be touring the World at the same time as Rodeo, the people will see who is the voice of God and who is the Devil.'

'Thank you Father. Interview terminated.'

'But what about my treat?'

'You've already had more than you deserve. Don't bother to get up, just carry on playing with yourself. I'll see myself out. Goodbye.'

As she got in the car she said to Douglas, 'Drive, just drive.'

Tears welled up behind her eyes. Douglas looked at her but thought better of asking her what happened. That can wait till later, if she wanted to tell him.

The curtains twitched as they pulled away. Father Ignatius felt satisfied she was gone and breathed a sigh of relief.

'She's a very pretty girl, father.' He turned in surprise as Cardinal Biloweiki addressed him.

'How did you get in?'

'Oh, Mrs Keegan let me in the back way. Lucky she did or I'd have missed your treachery.'

'But I didn't tell her anything.'

'Don't lie to me, I heard every word you said. You betrayed my confidence and my friendship and for that you must pay the ultimate price. Mrs Keegan please.'

Cardinal Biloweiki stood back as she raised a gun and pointed it at Father Ignatius at point blank range. He didn't have time to react. A bullet hit his forehead causing his skull to disintegrate. She looked at the Cardinal, he nodded. Calmly she made the sign of the cross then raised the gun to her temple and pulled the trigger.

*　*　*

Rodeo and Mathew were deep in discussion when Laura and Douglas arrived back at Heaven's Door. Mathew tried to persuade Rodeo to pull out of the world tour.

'Boss, it's too dangerous. It's obvious that someone is working against us, someone with a lot of power and influence.'

'Mathew's right,' joined in Laura. 'You want to know what I found out?' She didn't wait for an answer. She told them exactly what Father Ignatius had said. When she finished they all sat in silence. Rodeo broke the silence first.

'I'm just a musician, a fucking musician who sings and entertains people, that's what I do.' His voice sounded angry. Mathew had never heard him sound like this before. 'Okay, I talk about love and God but why does that give them the fucking right to try and stop me reaching my audiences? How the fuck does Barnabus think I'm going to destroy Christianity and Catholicism and every other fucking religion? They're so far up their own fucking arseholes – Barnabus!'

He looked up as he shouted, as if Barnabus was up in the sky looking down on him. 'Fuck you Barnabus! We're going on tour. Can you hear me Barnabus? We're going on fucking tour. We're gonna rock, fucking rock. All I want to do is bring a little more love into the world, and into people's lives. That's all I want to do. I challenge you Barnabus. You do your fucking tour and I'll do mine. Let's see who can bring the most love into the world, let's see what you can fucking do with your fucking blessings and prayers. Me? I'm going to spread a little love around the world with my music and if you don't like it you'll know where to send your henchmen to fucking find me.'

Douglas silently watched as Rodeo ranted against Barnabus, strongly rejecting the prophecy of the hidden testament. Then it hit him. Rodeo really doesn't know who he is, what he's capable of. In his eyes he's just a rock musician with ideas about love and how love is the only way humanity can progress. That's how he sees things. That's how things are for him. My God, what a man, what a man.

CHAPTER EIGHT

THE CONCERT at Fenway Park had sold out. Five thousand fans bought tickets. Rehearsals went well and Rodeo's voice sounded in fantastic shape. Douglas had come a long way since he saw Rodeo at the Arena, but even so he still felt a little uncomfortable about some of the show's more outrageous sexual acts. Somehow he'd taken on the role of front man. He had to introduce Rodeo after the warm-up act. Rodeo, to his credit, had given him a free hand.

'Whatever you do Douglas is okay by me.'

Douglas had never introduced anyone on stage before let alone in front of five thousand people. What did he have to say and do? Laura worked with Mathew, organising security which included vetting people who applied to go to the party after the concert. Only people who'd been fan club members for at least two years were considered and even then they had to bring at least two forms of photo ID to the party.

After the kidnapping, Mathew seriously stepped up security. Now, another car always followed them with at least two unarmed security staff, plus another two stationed full time at Heaven's Door. Mathew had hand-picked them. They had experience, impeccable references and could stop an army if necessary, but Rodeo insisted they didn't carry guns. He did allow tasers though.

The night before the concert Mathew found a message on the phone.

'I want to talk to Rodeo. I'm the guy he dropped off at the hospital. My name is Alfredo Benando, he has my marker, I owe him. Call me back tonight on this cell phone number.'

Mathew decided to call him without telling Rodeo. Rodeo

mentally prepared for concerts by relaxing and meditating. He wouldn't want him disturbing him for something like this.

Mathew dialled the number. It rang for an eternity before someone answered it.

'This is Mathew Lopez, I believe you wanted to speak with my employer. I'm afraid he's busy right now so you'll have to speak with me.'

A voice answered. 'Mr Lopez. I'm sorry for what I tried to do to you. I don't know who you and Rodeo upset but three of my associates have been wasted an' they already made one attempt on me, you ...'

'Who's they?' interrupted Mathew.

'I don't know, but I'm assuming it's the same people who employed us.'

'And who might that be?' said Mathew.

'Mr Lopez, I don't know, it was arranged through a priest who didn't give his name. Look, I'm a dead man, but I would like for you and Rodeo to take care of my daughter Carlotta.'

'Why? Can't she take care of herself?'

'Mr Lopez, she's ten years old and as long as I'm alive she's in danger.'

Mathew thought for a second. For some reason, which he didn't really understand, Mathew decided to take him at his word.

'Can you both stay safe until tomorrow night's concert at Fenway Park?'

'As safe as we can hope to be under these circumstances.'

'Okay, when you arrive at the concert just speak to anyone on security, tell them you have a registered package for Mr Lopez. They'll be briefed on what to do.'

'Mr Lopez I want to thank you. We'll see you there tomorrow.'

Mathew slowly put the phone down. How the hell were they going to look after a ten-year-old girl? But worse than that, he had a nasty feeling in the pit of his stomach. This ain't gonna be no picnic in the park.

Alfredo looked at Carlotta, gently squeezing her small hand while she looked trustingly at him. Her big, sparkly brown eyes reminded him of her mother. He smiled a wry smile. All his life he'd tried to do the right thing but where had it got him? Into this shit, that's where. If only he'd worked in some steady drudge of a job he wouldn't be in this mess up to his fucking neck. What could he to say to her? She put her arms round his neck and started to cry.

'It's alright baby, it's alright. Look we're going to be okay, I promise. I want you to go and stay with Rodeo and Mr Lopez. They're nice men and will take good care of you.' She looked worryingly at her father. He wiped the tears from her cheeks.

'But Daddy, where are you going to go? I don't want you to leave me.'

'I know baby, I know, but some bad men want to find me. I have to go and stay with your uncle Giorgio until things have quietened down a little.' As they hugged he felt fresh tears on his cheek.

'Daddy, have I ever told you that you're the best daddy in the world and that I love you?' Tears welled up in his eyes.

'Have I ever told you that you're the best daughter in the world and that I love you too?'

*　*　*

The sound check took place right on schedule. One thing bothered Rodeo. Satellite TV pulled the plug at the last minute, citing a strike by their outside broadcast staff. He smelt a rat. First of all he'd been kidnapped by mobsters, then Laura found out the Vatican wanted to threaten his world tour and now this. It had to be Barnabus. Did he really think that he, Rodeo, could be the musician mentioned in the hidden testaments? He smiled to himself. The only thing that will destroy religions is their lack of love. If it ever did happen, it would be by their own hands, certainly not his.

Douglas hid in the home team's dressing room to finalise his introduction. He didn't want to sound like he'd just stepped out of the pulpit, yet on the other hand he didn't want to sound like some middle-aged man trying to appeal to the predominantly young audience by using modern language that he clearly wasn't comfortable with.

Then it hit him. Preston! How would Preston Quick introduce him? What would the master of manic introductions say? His mind started to flow with ideas. Ten minutes later he'd completed the introduction. Now he just had to practise it, or should he? Maybe it would sound better off the cuff? No, what if nerves took over? If he practised he'd stand a better chance getting through it. Practising definitely seemed the safest thing to do. He had two hours before the start of the concert.

Mathew knocked on Rodeo's door. Rodeo didn't like being disturbed before the start of a concert but this was important.

Mathew told him about the arrangements with Alfredo Benando, the man they dropped off at the hospital. Rodeo's face showed real pain when he heard the fate of the men who had threatened him.

'You did the right thing. Is there anyway we can help her daddy?'

'I don't know, we could try but we might be putting ourselves and your audience in danger. These people, whoever they are, obviously don't fuck about.'

'I know, do your best though…and Mathew, thanks for telling me.'

*　*　*

'Keep still darling, nearly done.' It broke Alfredo Benando's heart to have to cut his daughter's beautiful long hair so short, but it would be safer for them both if she looked like a boy. 'There that's not so bad.' He stood back and admired his handiwork. Carlotta looked in the mirror. 'Don't worry my little angel. When all this is over it will soon grow back again. She gave him an impish smile.

'I don't mind Daddy, lots of models have short hair.' He didn't deserve a daughter like her.

'Now, you leave me alone in here, its time for me to change.'

'Okay Daddy.'

'Go watch TV in the other room.' He felt really strange, almost feminine-like, as he shaved his legs and put on the women's clothing. Thank God he wasn't a big man. With a little padding in the right places he could just get away with it. That would have to do. He found putting on the make-up really difficult. He looked in the mirror. *You're not so bad as a dame*, he thought to himself. *I've seen worse.*

He'd gone for the affluent, conservative look. Three quarter length skirt with a single pleat, a high necked top, light cotton jacket and sensible shoes. He chose the brunette wig specifically not to draw attention to himself. Carlotta burst into the room. She stared at him in disbelief.

'Daddy, is that you Daddy?'

'Yes it's me, but from now on you call me Mama, understand?'

'Yes Daddy, I mean Mama. Daddy, sorry I mean Mama, your make up's wrong. Can I?'

'Sure go ahead, help your Mama with her make up.' A little later, they were ready to leave. Alfredo Benando let out a sigh of relief when he closed the car door. So far so good.

'Mama.'

'That a girl.'

'Boy, Mama. I'm a boy.'

'You're right...son, just testing you.'

'Yeah right.' She raised her eyebrows at him. As he moved up through the gears he kept checking the rear view mirror, just in case someone was following them. They'd only gone two blocks.

'Holy shit!' An enormous explosion followed by plumes of black smoke and flames, a hundred feet high, came from the apartment they had just left.

'Don't look back darling, please don't look back.' Carlotta didn't look back, but felt her stomach knot up. She knew something bad had happened.

* * *

Douglas paced up and down backstage, mentally rehearsing his introduction. Mathew looked at his watch and checked the signal on his radio pack.

Alfredo parked in the main stadium parking lot. His daughter's life depended on him. He couldn't fuck this up. Adrenalin began to kick in. He looked around before opening the car doors.

'Keep close to me. If I shout "run" at any time, just run. No matter what happens to me just keep running, you understand?' She nodded. He felt reassured by the comforting coldness of the revolver inside his light cotton jacket.

They had an eight hundred yard walk to the main stadium from the parking lot. Did they know he was here?

'Programmes, souvenir programmes for tonight's show. Would you like a souvenir programme for your son?' As he handed over the ten dollars, the seller didn't raise an eyelid. *Another test passed*, he thought.

* * *

Laura kissed Douglas and wished him good luck. She looked across to Mathew. On the surface he looked pretty cool, but he gave away his true state of mind by constantly looking at his watch. She'd agreed to be the one to take care of Carlotta. Not just because she was female – well, yes, that was part of it, but also because Carlotta would probably be more comfortable with her, and Douglas wasn't used to children. Rodeo, he'll be on stage and Mathew well, he's likely to be otherwise engaged in security issues. She sidled up to Mathew.

'Do you think they're safe?'

'I don't know. A news report said a gas main exploded in an apartment on the city's west side about an hour ago but no one was hurt.'

'Too much of a coincidence?'

'Yeah, too much. Maybe they left just in time to come here.'

'So you think they would have been followed?'

'I *know* they would have been followed. People don't go to that much trouble and then let their prey just walk away, especially these people, whoever they are.'

'We have to find them.' Laura felt scared, not for herself, but for the little girl.

'No. If we go looking for them it becomes obvious to the bad guys that something is up and that we're in on it. We wait until they make themselves known. I think somehow, for the moment anyway, they've managed to give them the slip.'

'I hope you're right.'

So do I, so do I, thought Mathew.

Alfredo crouched down to speak to Carlotta.

'This is where I have to leave you. See that security guard over there?' She turned and nodded.

'Give me two minutes and then go over and say to him "I'm the registered package for Mr Lopez". You got that?'

'Yes Mama.'

'That a g…boy.' As he turned and walked away his eyes filled with tears. Would he ever see her again? Carlotta watched him walk away. She wanted to cry out "Daddy" but somehow she managed to control her emotions.

'Dear God, please keep my Daddy safe,' she said out loud. 'Please, I'll do anything you want, I promise.' She started to count

'One hundred eighteen, one hundred nineteen, one hundred twenty.' She stopped counting under her breath and slowly walked across to the security guard.

'Excuse me Sir, I'm the registered package for Mr Lopez.' Unfazed, the guard spoke into his radio,

'This is Alpha Sierra Six Five Seven at zone two four, copy. I have the package.'

Mathew jumped as his radio came to life.

'Laura, follow me.'

They made their way to zone two four. He knew they'd monitor the radios and each of the security zones as well as watch the chopper. They spotted the guard with Carlotta.

'Laura go, get her. I'll decoy with the chopper.' She approached Carlotta and the guard.

'Bobby, where have you been?' said Laura to the child. 'You're always getting lost. Now come here.' Carlotta walked towards her and clenched Laura's outstretched hand tightly. 'Now don't wander off again. Let's go watch the concert.' Quickly they made their way to the turnstiles and what Laura hoped would be safety.

Douglas paced up and down backstage. Nerves kicked in.

'However you introduce me,' Rodeo had told him, 'whatever you say will be cool. Just speak from your heart with love.' Even so, he still felt worried about making a complete fool of himself and ruining the evening for Rodeo. He thought back to the last concert he attended. Paul's conversion on the road to Damascus was the closest he could come to explaining his change of heart and allegiance.

'Five minute call.' No warm up act tonight, just two hours of entertainment from Rodeo. Douglas breathed deeply. His mind raced. Copy Preston Quick. Be bold and brash, he told himself. As he paced up and down the band started. Douglas listened for his queue. The stage manager spoke.

'Go Douglas, go, you're on, you're on.' Douglas strode out onto the stage. He felt blinded by the lights and the music sounded deafening. Surely they can't hear me over that? Then the adrenalin took over. He waved his arms in the air to the beat of the music and put his mouth near the mic on the stand.

'If you can hear me and you love Rodeo wave your arms in the air.' The whole stadium erupted in an enormous cheer and waved their arms, mirroring Douglas. Could he really have such an impact on thousands of people?

'If you believe Rodeo is the greatest entertainer on the planet give…' Before he finished an almighty cheer went round the Arena. As it subsided he continued.

'Not only is he the greatest entertainer, I don't know a man on Earth with more love in his heart.' Another enormous cheer went up.

'Listen to what he says tonight, it might just change your life like it has mine. This is his last concert before he embarks on his World tour, so let's give him a huge Boston send off. Lets give him all our love to take with him and let's rock!'

The band struck up into an energised orgasmic sound of lead guitar with a strong bass beat. Fireworks exploded at the front of the stage, creating a blaze of sparkling colour as the chopper descended into the stadium. Rodeo made his way from the chopper to the stage, almost hidden by smoke from the fireworks. As he did so, Laura and Carlotta did the reverse. They went from under the stage to the chopper, hopefully unseen.

The whole changeover only took thirty seconds. Mathew turned round to Laura and Carlotta, grinning like a Cheshire cat with two tails.

'Douglas had the audience eating out of his hand. I had the fold back patched into my radio.'

CHAPTER NINE

SEVEN DAYS after the concert at Fenway Park, Alfredo Benando phoned and left a message for Carlotta. He promised he'd try and do the same every seven days.

Mathew struggled to make sense of what had happened. Who had murdered Alfredo's three associates and tried to kill Alfredo and Carlotta? The Catholic Church?

We know from Father Ignatius that they're behind the accusations of paedophilia at Heavens Door, he thought to himself. Douglas and Laura both had visits from the FBI, or persons claiming to be from the FBI. What reason would the Catholic Church have to murder four men and a little girl? It didn't add up. *They must know something else, something so sensitive to someone we don't yet know, that it sealed their death warrants.*

'I bought you a cup of tea.' Mathew looked up, his concentration broken.

'Thank you.' Douglas sat down opposite him and spoke.

'You look mighty engrossed. Penny for your thoughts?'

'I'm just trying to make sense of what's going on. None of this adds up. The Catholic Church don't go around killing people.'

'I thought maybe you should see this.' Douglas passed him a broadsheet newspaper. Mathew looked at the headline, then read the article and opening paragraph out loud.

'Support Slipping For Champion Of The Christian Right. Senator Michael Heaney who is seeking to win the Republican Presidential Nomination has seen his support in the Southern and Mid-Western States drop dramatically. Recent polls suggest his support amongst the Christian right has fallen to an all time low. Senator Heaney denies this is the case, citing Christian rallies in

Ohio, Kentucky and Tennessee which recently gave him their full support in his nomination bid.' Mathew looked at Douglas quizzically.

'I don't understand. What are you getting at?'

'There's more, read on, read on.'

'Recent figures show attendances at Churches throughout the South and Mid-West have fallen dramatically, by as much as five million during the past two years. In a recent phone interview of one thousand former church goers, eighty-one percent cited Rodeo and his message of love as the main reason they no longer attended church. When questioned about the results of the phone interviews, Senator Heaney dismissed the results as nonsense and said "Rodeo is nothing more than a sinner who will one day have to answer to God".'

'So what do you think?'

'I think we are going to pay a visit to the person who wrote this and try to find out a little more.'

'We can't.'

'What do you mean we can't? Why can't we?'

'Because he's dead. This paper is two weeks old. They found his body floating in his swimming pool yesterday, a suspected heart attack.'

'How do you know that?' Mathew was surprised by Douglas' self-assuredness.

'I phoned the paper earlier today for some contact details and they told me.'

'Shit, so what do we do then?'

'How about I pay Senator Heaney a visit? I went to theological college with him, we weren't exactly buddies but I knew him well enough.'

'You do realise he may know you're working with Rodeo?'

'Sure, but I figure if I follow Rodeo's lead and show him as much love as possible I'll be ok.'

'You figure?'

'Well, that and having you as the Calvary close behind me.' Mathew smiled.

'You reckon eh? Okay, it's a deal, but lets keep it to ourselves. We don't need to worry Laura or the boss.'

'Sure, I'm cool.'

Mathew looked at Douglas with amazement at his choice of words. He'd changed, he really had changed.

On the drive to see Senator Heaney at his offices in Little Rock, Douglas spoke to Mathew about his days at Matheson College and his recollections of Michael Heaney.

'As I recall he was always full of himself, liked to be the centre of attention all the time. Boasted that one day he would be president of the United States because it's God's will.'

'How did he know that? Does he have his own direct line?' asked Mathew.

'In a way, we all did. It was how we justified everything we did, that way we didn't have to take responsibility for anything. But we were all lying. We kidded ourselves and others so much that in the end we really began to believe it was true, you know, that God had spoken to us.'

'Did Michael Heaney ever give you any idea that he was capable of using violence to achieve his goal?'

'No, not that I can recall – except maybe once…' Douglas hesitated.

'Go on tell me, let me be the judge.'

'Well, one day he was very quiet, you know, not his normal self. I asked him if everything was okay. He told me to mind my own business. Then rumours began to spread that his sister had become engaged to a black guy, a Baptist minister as it happens. A while later the college asked us to pray for Michael Heaney and his sister. A hit and run driver killed her just a week before the wedding. I know, I shouldn't have, but when the college told us, just for a moment, I wondered whether Heaney had killed her? I soon banished such unchristian thoughts from my mind, until today that is.'

'So you're telling me you think he might have killed his sister because she was marrying a black man and that wouldn't have fitted in with his plans to become President?'

'Yup, that's about the sum of it.'

Mathew felt a chill go down his spine. If Douglas' suspicions were right, Michael Heaney would obviously go to any lengths to achieve his ambition of becoming president.

They arrived on the outskirts of Little Rock and pulled into a Key Mart parking lot.

'Time to call Senator Heaney and make an appointment,' said Douglas. Despite the car's air conditioning, Douglas sweated profusely as he made the call.

A young female answered in the manner typical of corporate America.

'Hello, this is Senator Heaney's office, how may I help you?'

Douglas put on his warm, friendly voice.

'Hi, my name is Douglas Claymore. Michael and I were pals at college. In fact we roomed together for a while. I appreciate he's very busy, but I'd like to meet up with him, talk about old times and wish him all the best in his quest for the presidential nomination. Maybe I can even help him.'

'Please hold the line, Mr Claymore.'

Douglas waited and wondered if the piped music would carry on for all eternity if no one reconnected the other end.

'Mr Claymore,' her voice cut in almost unexpectedly. 'Mr Heaney will see you in his office tomorrow for half an hour at two thirty. Please be prompt.'

'Don't worry I will, I will…and thank you.' He put the phone down. 'Result, I got a result.' Mathew looked at him knowingly. Douglas had really gotten into his new life.

'So what do we do now?' said Douglas, as if he couldn't wait until tomorrow afternoon.

'Now we find a motel for the night and then we surf the net for anything and everything about Michael Heaney.'

Douglas looked at the plush downtown office block. Michael Heaney had taken over the whole of the top floor, including a luxury penthouse apartment. Every visitor went through an airport-style security check. Douglas felt relaxed as he entered the elevator. Why not? He had nothing to hide and was quite looking forward to crossing swords…was that the right term? Maybe not, but whatever happened he wasn't going to be intimidated by Heaney.

As he stepped out of the elevator a young and pretty blonde woman dressed in an expensive business suite greeted him.

'Mr Claymore, this way please. Michael will be with you in five minutes.' She led him into a plush office. Pictures of past US presidents and bible texts covered probably eighty percent of the available wall space. One in particular caught his eye. *Revelations 2.26, And he that overcometh and keepeth my works unto the end, to him will I give power over other nations.* Douglas winced.

'Michael, he's clean, no weapons. The scans and x-rays show he's not bugged and he hasn't swallowed anything nasty.'

'Okay, but make sure you monitor all frequencies. How do I look?' It was a rhetorical question. 'You know I always like to look my intimidating best.' He grinned and winked as he left the room.

'Douglas how are you?' He didn't wait for an answer. 'It's been a long time.' Douglas went to rise from his chair. 'No don't bother to get up, this is informal.'

They shook hands with Douglas still sitting down. Heaney poured two glasses of sparkling spring water from a bottle on the table and passed one to Douglas.

'So tell me, are you still studying that God forsaken forgotten language? Syriac, is it? And what happened to that long-term girlfriend of yours? Sarah, I think it was. Do you know, when I heard you two had split I was stunned. Some nasty malicious gossips said it was because you're a closet homosexual but I put them straight. No way I said, no way. I think it's because she had an affair with someone and confessed. Still, that was a long time ago. Bet it still hurts though.'

Douglas looked him straight in the eye. Heaney knew how to hit the spots that hurt.

'I've moved on since then.'

'So I hear. Now you're screwing around with a Rock Star and all his hangers on. Douglas, what's happened to you? You were always a rock, a pillar of Christian values.'

Douglas focused his response.

'I found love.'

'You what? You found love?'

'Yes, I found love, the purest love a person could ever hope to be surrounded by. I hated Rodeo with a passion at first.'

'So I heard. I was really proud of you, leading those rallies and demonstrating against him. So what changed?'

'He showed me love, a love totally missing from my life, a love that can only come from God.'

'Whoa, whoa, Douglas, that's a pretty strong statement.'

'Michael, this man is going to change our world forever. Look, even the Catholic Church are trying to stop him because they believe he's a Musician who's mentioned in some hidden testaments. They believe he's going to consign Christianity and other religions to the history books and replace them with a philosophy of love.' He watched Heaney's face for any tell tale signs that he knew what was going on. There were none.

'The only way Rodeo will change the World forever is by unknowingly helping me to become President of the United States of America. So Douglas, if I can't persuade you to leave him and come and work for me, promise me you'll help keep him safe because, at the moment, I need him live and well.'

'I will, don't you worry, I will.'

'Before you go, I have to ask your forgiveness for something I did a long time ago.'

'My forgiveness? You want my forgiveness?' said Douglas, looking surprised.

'Yes. I already asked God for forgiveness and he forgave me, but he asked me to seek forgiveness from you as well. You see, I was too weak to resist your Sarah when she came on to me. I must admit she was great, trouble is I've felt a little guilty ever since.' Douglas felt a surge of emotions he'd kept suppressed for years. His chest felt tight. His voice took on a new high pitch.

'You're lying, you're lying. She wouldn't have, not with you.'

'Oh it wasn't just me. I popped her cherry, but by the end of the night I think everyone in our wing had fucked her.'

Douglas charged at Heaney. Suddenly he felt a terrifying force hit him, like running into an electrified wall. He screamed in pain as fifty thousand volts surged through his body. His whole body became rigid then crumpled to the floor. Apart from a few involuntary jerks he lay still. Heaney barked orders to his staff.

'Take him outside and revive him. Make sure he's okay before he leaves here. I don't know what the world's coming to. He joins a fucking rock musician who preaches free love, then tries to attack me when I ask his forgiveness for partaking in a free love session nearly thirty years ago.'

Mathew waited anxiously for Douglas to emerge from the building. He spotted him staggering down the steps.

'My God, what's happened to him?' he said out loud. 'What's Heaney done to him? He looks like some kind of zombie.'

Back at the Motel, Douglas lay on the bed crying and trying to explain what had happened. Mathew sat next to him.

'Let it all out man. Let it all come out.' He listened to Douglas struggle to find words to describe what had happened. Only when Douglas finished did he intervene.

'The way I look at it is she was raped. How you describe her tells me there's no way she would have willingly gone with Heaney or anyone else. You have to believe that she loved you. Come on, you're in need of some loving care from Rodeo. He'll know what to do about Heaney and he'll make you feel better. Are you okay to travel?' Douglas nodded affirmatively.

Mathew drove on, while Douglas slept in the back. The whole journey passed in silence which gave Mathew the opportunity to do some much needed thinking. A few things bugged him. Why did Heaney want Rodeo kept safe, at least for the time being? What were his motives?

'Okay the facts are...Heaney needs the Christian right to support him if he has any chance of winning the Republican Presidential nomination. The Christian right hates Rodeo and his ideas on sex, homosexuality, abortion, religion etcetera. I got it. What if Heaney were to blame Rodeo and his liberal values for America's problems and then accuse his political opponents of supporting him? Then Rodeo was found guilty of some terrible crime which went totally against his teachings?' He figuratively pinched himself. Mathew, you're talking shit.

When they arrived at Heaven's Door, Rodeo, Laura and Carlotta were outside to greet them. Rodeo knew that things hadn't gone well. He could see the hurt on Douglas's face and Mathew looked unusually subdued.

'Matty.' Rodeo hardly ever called him that, at least not since their prison days. Mathew gave him a wry smile.

'Boss, I know, maybe we shouldn't have gone but we found out some important information.'

'Okay, that's good, but we were all worried about you.' Rodeo hugged him.

Douglas felt the pain and hurt well up inside him. Rodeo could see him trying to suppress his emotions.

'It's okay, we love you, you're not on your own. Feel my love, feel Laura's and Mathew's and our little Carlotta's.'

They all hugged as a big group and they all shared Douglas' tears. Later that evening, Rodeo and Mathew sat talking on the porch. Douglas turned in at seven and slept soundly. Laura and Carlotta walked around the grounds.

'You know what I'm thinking?' said Mathew pensively. 'I'm thinking what a mighty beautiful sunset. If I ever doubt God's love I just look at that. Every time I see it my heart beats a little faster with a new found joy and wonder. Does Michael Heaney see that? Does he feel the joy and wonder?' Rodeo took a sip from his glass of root beer.

'No, he can't. Only people with love in their hearts can see and feel what you do. He sees people who try to live life with love, as weak. He sees them as people he can manipulate and control. But actually it's the other way round – we're the ones with the power because we can change things and create new beginnings. People without love are powerless, all they get is more of the same. You see, whatever Heaney does he's powerless over love. The paradox is that he's doing what he's doing for power, not love. Mankind will learn from it though and eventually move forward with even more love. Love is always the winner.'

Carlotta crept round behind Rodeo and put her hands over his eyes.

'Who is it?' she said. Rodeo smiled.

'I think it's Cinderella.'

'No it's me stupid.' She giggled.

'Come on honey, time for bed,' said Laura.

'Do I have to?'

'Yes you have to.'

'But why?'

'Because.'

'Because what?' This had become a nightly routine.

'Because if you don't the Honey Monster will get you.'

Carlotta squealed and ran. Mathew and Rodeo both pretended to try and catch her then fell down as if worn out and out of breath.

'You wore us out.'

'You can never catch me, I'm too fast for you!'

'Okay you win tonight but we'll catch you next time.'

'No you won't because I'm too fast. Night Rodeo, night Mathew.' She gave them both a kiss on the cheek.

'Laura will you read me a story?'

'Okay but just a short one.'

'Peter Pan, I love Peter Pan.'

'Okay, first you have to beat me to your room.'

They both ran into the house and up the stairs. Carlotta just managed to win, as she always did.

* * *

At his offices in Little Rock, Michael Heaney shouted at his embarrassed security team.

'How much do I pay you? You're not worth a wank, any of you. Our contacts in the FBI even went to the trouble of telling us where Alfredo Benando is and that Rodeo is protecting his daughter, yet you still can't fucking find him. You're shit. In fact you're worse than shit, you're all fucking shit shafters. Look! What don't you fucking understand? We need Alfredo if we're going to persuade his daughter to do what we want.'

'Excuse me Sir'

'Excuse you? Why should I excuse you? I suppose you're going to tell me you know where he is?'

'Not exactly Sir.'

'What do you mean, not exactly? Either you know where he fucking is or you don't.'

Keanan Horris did not look like a typical member of the security team. He weighed no more than ninety-five pounds and looked about sixteen years old, complete with spotty face.

'Well, we could make a virtual copy of him.'

'A virtual copy? What's a fucking virtual copy gonna do for us?'

'A computerised image that's pre-programmed to look and sound like whoever we want it to. I can put the image on any computer in the world and he'll look, move and talk exactly like the real Alfredo.'

Heaney stopped in his tracks and pointed at Keanan.

'This man's a genius. How much do I pay you? Don't answer, cause whatever it is it just doubled – no trebled, no fuck it, quadrupled.'

'Thank you Sir.'

'I want my virtual copy of Mr Alfredo Benando completed in three days, you work day and night if you have to. The rest of you leave off trying to capture Mr Benando – I don't need him any more, just kill him. Now let's pray to God and ask for his help in defeating the fucking Muslims.'

*   *   *

Carlotta lay awake. The hot and humid weather didn't help. She kept hearing her daddy's voice. However hard she listened she couldn't quite make out what he said.

'Daddy, where are you? Daddy I can hear you, why can't I see you?' Then she picked out the word computer. It sounded like 'I'm on the computer'. She leapt out of bed and lifted up the lid of her laptop. Her eyes lit up.

'Daddy, Daddy!'

Keanan Horris managed to reproduce exact virtual replicas of Alfredo Benando's voice and facial features from recorded phone recordings and surveillance cameras. Sirrus, his new Trojan programme, allowed him to connect to a PC and control it remotely even if it had no internet connection. A computer parasite he had developed used the world wide GPS signal as a host, allowing him to locate and connect to any computer anywhere in the world. The parasite bypassed fire walls and allowed him to control computers without leaving a trace.

Michael Heaney beamed when Keanan showed him how it worked.

'This is mind-blowing stuff. It means I can access and control any computer in the world undiscovered. My opponents won't stand a chance.'

Heaney had only one problem. Keanan would have to go. He

couldn't afford for this to leak out or for anyone else to have the technology.

'You've done well Keanan, really well. You deserve a holiday.'

'Thank you Sir.'

'Where would you like to go? You can go anywhere in the world.'

Later that day, Heaney spoke to a friend on a public phone. 'I need a favour, yes I'll pay, usual rules apply. There's a kid, name's Keanan Horris. I want him detained for a while, maybe a drugs charge, but if I need him, say in the next year or so, I have to be able to get the charges dropped. Is that clear? Oh and by the way, no bail. I just want him out of circulation for a while, maybe even for life.'

Keanan's technology allowed Heaney to speak with Carlotta as if they were communicating by webcam.

'Daddy, how did you get on my computer?' Her voice sounded really excited.

'Carlotta, I love you so much. I'm safe at the moment. I need you to do something for me but you must never tell anyone, not even the people you're with. My life depends on it, do you understand?'

'Yes Daddy, I won't tell anyone. It's our secret.'

'Good girl, I'll speak to you again in a few days, my darling.'

'Good night Daddy. I'm so pleased I can see you.'

'Me too my precious, now you go back to sleep and I'll see you again in a few days.' The screen went blank as Heaney cut the link.

'Yes! Wow! White House here I come.'

*   *   *

Cardinal Biloweiki's concerns grew. He hadn't heard anything about the fate of the four men employed to put the frighteners on Rodeo. 'Should I make enquiries?' he asked himself. 'No, I'll wait two more days.'

On the second morning, after mass, a small package arrived. It contained a cassette tape. He went into his study and put the tape in a small portable player and sat and listened.

Three hysterical, terrified men begged for their lives. *God knows what fate awaited them*, thought Cardinal Biloweiki.

'May God have mercy on their souls.' Then a voice on the tape addressed him.

'Cardinal Biloweiki, as you probably gathered the men are now dead, their bodies untraceable. Unfortunately one of the men escaped, but not for long. Don't worry, by the time you listen to this tape there will be nothing left on this planet to show that any of the four men ever existed.'

A chill ran down his spine. He pressed the button on the cassette player to remove the tape. The cassette player burst into flames, burning the tips of his fingers and destroying the tape. *Very clever*, he thought, *very clever*.

CHAPTER 10

THE START of the Papal world tour coincided with the release of Rodeo's new album, 'Heaven's Door'. Barnabus and his advisors weren't slow in picking up on this. Three weeks before the release of the album, T-shirts and badges emblazoned with pictures of Barnabus and the slogan Only Christ Can Forgive and Open Heaven's Door were on sale in all the countries Barnabus planned to visit. The Roman Catholic Church enjoyed a great revival. Congregations and their offerings nearly doubled from the previous month, delighting Priests and Bishops worldwide.

India became a huge success for Barnabus. Wherever he went, huge crowds of Catholics and non Catholics greeted him. A crowd estimated to be around a half a million lined the streets, all hoping to catch a glimpse of him when he visited a children's home run by nuns in Goa. He won many plaudits when he praised India for being the largest secular democracy in the world with religious freedom for all and for refusing to be drawn on the issue of India's ban on Dalits being allowed to convert to Christianity.

Images of him were beamed around the world, creating a huge media frenzy guaranteeing the success of his world tour. *Rodeo will not be able to compete*, thought Barnabus. *Why, when my tour is so successful, should I even think about a mere rock singer?*

His heart told him he had nothing to worry about but his intellect said otherwise. He remembered the offending verses he'd translated from Syriac...

'(1) A musician (He of David) sings of love till all people listen, their thirst and hunger satisfied.(2) He (of David) is the curse of all Holy people. (3) The Church of Peter (Fall) into the abyss.(4) Followers of the prophet move into the ascendancy.'

Barnabus felt nauseous. His heart beat faster, his stomach churned and a pain surged through his temples across his forehead. Why should these thoughts re-enter his head today of all days, his last in India? His mind screamed with frustration as he struggled to keep the symptoms under control. He kept asking himself whether Rodeo was the Musician and, if he was, how could he stop people listening to him?

The more he tried to erase thoughts of Rodeo from his mind the stronger they became. What if the Catholic Church's clumsy attempt to silence him ever became public? The consequences would be unimaginable. Questions will be asked like who sanctioned it and why? No mention could be made of the hidden Testaments, we couldn't use them as an excuse because in theological terms they are only rumour and speculation.

Barnabus tortured himself with thoughts of Rodeo. Eventually he decided the Church must stop him. He'd become a nuisance to Christian authorities all over the world. Church attendances for all denominations had nosed dived during the last four years. Islam appeared to be growing. Frighteningly for Barnabus, the sharp drop in Church attendance correlated perfectly with Rodeo's rise in popularity. But as much as he prayed, he had no answers. For Barnabus, God was strangely silent.

* * *

Rehearsals for the forthcoming world tour went well. The band, the backing singers and the roadies couldn't wait to get on the road. Rodeo felt encouraged by reports that every venue had sold out. If Pope Barnabus and his advisors tried to sabotage his tour they hadn't succeeded. Old Iron Knickers really had come up trumps with the alternative venues. The only thing she hadn't managed to negotiate were TV appearances but, with all the venues already sold out, that wasn't too much of a problem, although it would affect album sales.

Rodeo had no idea how the Indians would receive him. Album sales compared to other countries on the tour were relatively small, but Old Iron Knickers insisted India was the world's fastest growing market for recorded music and he needed to be a part of it. He'd booked to play four dates in two cities, Hyderabad and Bangalore. The venues, both temporary and built to seat ten thousand, met all his requirements. All the performances were sell-outs, so Rodeo made a decision to place giant screens outside the venues for the benefit of people who couldn't buy tickets.

Rodeo had a concern. By and large the people of India were naturally conservative with strong family values. Would they accept the explicit sexual content of the shows? Douglas tried to persuade him to tone things down but Rodeo's instinct was to keep everything the same, although he didn't want to be the cause of any riots or anything similar. Laura hit on an idea.

'How about writing to both the City Councils explaining your quandary? Tell them that you don't want to cause offence to anyone. Let them decide, maybe make it an open letter to the people of both cities.'

'Okay, I'll write to the people of both cities care of their councils.'

Douglas breathed a sigh of relief. He'd had visions of the venues being flattened by rioters and them having to flee for their lives. Laura squeezed Douglas' hand.

The feedback from the road crew who arrived three days ahead of Rodeo and his entourage sounded really positive. They reported that the Indians couldn't do enough for them and were thrilled that Rodeo had included their cities on the first leg of his world tour. They also felt honoured that Rodeo had consulted them about the content of the shows, but most of all they were intrigued about his take on life and religion and how his shows reflected his beliefs. As it turned out, the councils and people of both cities agreed the shows should be in their original format, but all advertising had to make clear that the show contained explicit simulated sexual acts because they were a part of the life beliefs of Rodeo.

Rodeo strolled around the hotel's lush Mughal gardens in the warm spring sun. He didn't know the names of the flowers or plants, so he decided to give them names of his choice. One highly scented yellow orchid-like flower he called Laladee. Another plant with small pink buds clustered around large lime green leaves he called Maya after the Hindu Goddess of illusion because, although the flowers are very beautiful, they also trapped and ate any fly that dared to land on them.

He sat on a small square of grass almost hidden between some Laladee, Mayas and Cremes, a name given to them by Rodeo because of their sweet toffee-like scent. He closed his eyes to meditate on what he had seen and heard in India so far.

'Master.' He heard a faint whisper coming from immediately behind him. 'Master, I am not allowed to be here but I have to speak with you.'

Without turning around, Rodeo replied. 'Okay speak, I'm listening.'

'Master, many people here are interested in your ideas about God and love. You say you are God, a part of the whole and we are all the same, that is what we believe. Also you say we are eternal beings, that we live forever, that is also what we believe, and Ramanuja's Bhakti yoga is faith in a loving God which you also say is true. Master, there is talk in the city and villages that you are a manifestation of God. People believe, that when they see you, they are seeing God and they have given you a name, Kalma-deva, which means God of love. Master, there will be many devotees attending your concert tonight all hoping to hear and see you. Thank you for listening to me Master. If it pleases you, I would like to be of service to you. My name is Achanda but I like to be called Davey, you know like Davey Jones in the Monkees.'

Rodeo smiled. 'Well Achanda, I mean Davey, you had better show yourself so I know what my new guide in India looks like.'

'Master, I'm here.' A small-framed teenager tumbled out of the bushes. He grinned at Rodeo showing all his immaculately straight white teeth. He wore a cheap blue cotton t-shirt and mud stained white shorts with open plastic sandals.

'Thank you master. Would it be too much if I asked for twenty-five rupees a day to be your guide in India?'

'Twenty-five rupees a day? Let me see, I reckon that works out at about fifty cents a day. Okay I agree, but if you do a good job for me you have to promise that you'll accept a little bonus, is that a deal?'

'Yes Master, that's a deal.'

'Okay, now high five me to seal it.' Davey flung his hand in the air to meet Rodeo's.

'Have you ever flown in a chopper?'

'No Master'

'Well tonight that's your first duty. You fly with me to the venue and show the chopper pilot where to go. But first, let me get you one of our official Heaven's Door tour t-shirts.'

*   *   *

The first two shows in Hyderabad were at a site near to Durgam Cheravu Lake. The temporary venue consisted of hundreds of wooden benches around three sides of the stage and another five thousand tiered seats behind the benches. A fifteen foot canvas barrier surrounded the whole venue. Local entrepreneurs had been busy for weeks sowing cushions to sell to the audience.

Others produced a variety of souvenirs ranging from carved statues commemorating the event to brightly coloured paper decorations of all types.

The chopper approached the lake. Mathew and Rodeo looked at each other open mouthed. They saw hundreds of thousands, maybe even millions, of people making their way to the temporary arena by foot. It seemed as if the whole city had turned out to the event.

'Look Master, I told you. Everyone wants to see and hear Kalma-deva.'

The chopper landed on a patch of ground ringed by security staff, just fifty metres from the arena. Mathew, Rodeo and Davey made a dash to a small door in the arena's canvas barrier.

'Where's Douglas?' Rodeo looked around for him. Douglas suddenly appeared, holding his practice script. 'I don't want to worry you or anything, but tonight we have an audience of maybe millions. As we flew over here it looked like the whole city has turned out.'

'Gee thanks, no more pressure then,' said Douglas.

'Douglas I know you'll be just fine,' Rodeo reassured him.

'Fifteen minute call, fifteen minutes everyone.'

Rodeo called everyone backstage around him.

'Everyone, lets kick off this tour with a fantastic show. Energy, lets keep up the energy tonight and use the energy to show them our love. Lets go.'

The band struck up prior to Douglas's entrance to polite applause. Douglas literally ran onto the stage. He wasn't sure if that's what Rodeo meant about energy, but at least he was trying.

'People of Hyderabad, everyone involved in this tour wants to thank you all for your wonderful friendship and your love. We love Hyderabad and all its people.' The audience responded with a mixture of cheering and polite applause.

'Rodeo believes that mankind can only progress and create Heaven on Earth through love. Everything you see and hear in tonight's show is about love. So, without further delay, please welcome the greatest rock legend on the planet – Rodeo.'

The band revved up the tempo and the volume. The audience chanted 'Kalma-deva, Kalma-deva' but, as Rodeo rose onto the stage through a trap door, the audience stopped. They sat in almost total silence.

For a second it almost threw Rodeo, but he quickly realised they didn't want to miss a thing he did or said.

When he launched into his first number he felt their love radiating toward him. A few of the audience stood and danced but were quickly told to sit down.

'You are blocking our view of Kalma-deva,' said one.

Overhead a chopper, its engines drowned out by the concert,

filmed the events and beamed them live to satellites. News editors around the globe couldn't believe over two million people had camped outside the temporary arena trying to catch a glimpse of Rodeo on the large screens. They prepared headlines like 'Cowboy and Indians in love Match' and 'Cowboy Draws On More Indians Than The Pope'.

Rodeo reached the point in the show when he invited a female member of the audience onto the stage. He'd noticed an incredibly beautiful Indian girl sitting in the front row. She looked about nineteen or twenty, had pert breasts, sensuous eyes and was dressed in a traditional sari. She'd flirted with him through the whole show, using her eyes, her lips and her hands. He bought her onto the stage. Something told Rodeo to be careful. She looked almost too perfect, like a trained seductress, but he couldn't resist her.

He finished the song and out of sight of the audience briefly kissed her on the lips. For a second he felt her tongue probe into his mouth. Security led her backstage. During the band solo he told Mathew, 'Invite her back to the hotel.'

As soon as he spoke, the same uncomfortable feeling returned. Something wasn't right, but again he couldn't resist her.

The show overran by an hour. The audience kept demanding more by chanting 'Ka1ma-deva, Ka1ma-deva'.

Rodeo felt exhausted. He'd been on stage for almost three hours. Only the adrenalin of the occasion kept him going. He acknowledged his band, all individually, and then finished with a beautiful lullaby accompanied by a sitar instead of a guitar. The sound of the sitar fused with Rodeo's voice and sounded like music made in Heaven, the title of the song.

CHAPTER 11

IN HIS hotel suite, Rodeo stood facing the mystery girl. He held both her hands and smiled as he spoke.

'Tell me about yourself, I don't even know your name.'

'My name is Kamna, which means desire. I desire you and hope you also desire me. But now you are tired after your show. So sleep and when you are refreshed I will be here for you.'

He lay on the top of the bed wearing just his pants. Almost straight away he drifted into a deep peaceful sleep. Kamna lay next to him and made circles on his back with her little finger. He didn't respond.

Her mind drifted back to her time in America, almost three months ago, in Little Rock. She applied to work for a computer software company owned by an Indian. When she walked into his office for an interview she recognised the signs immediately. He was definitely interested in her, at least sexually anyway. He soon made it very clear she could have a very successful career working for him providing she did anything he asked of her. It didn't take her long to agree. Why not? She wanted money and power. At last she'd met a man prepared and able to give her both. Sex was something she'd used from a young age to get what she wanted and if it gave her pleasure at the same time then so much the better.

Rodeo stirred. His sleep became lighter, his breathing wasn't so deep and he started to fidget. Kamna had seen these signs many times before. She moved from the bed. When he awoke she would be ready. Her eyes almost devoured him when he woke and sat up.

'There is an Indian legend,' began Kamna. 'A husband forfeited his beautiful wife in a gambling duel. The lecherous victors, intent on humiliating her husband as much as they could, pulled her sari and tried to unravel the material, but they couldn't reach the end so virtue triumphed. I want to share my virtue with you so I had better remove it myself. There are six yards of material. If you like I could unravel it very, very slowly for you, a few inches at a time.'

'The floor's all yours,' said Rodeo. He sat back, resting his head on his hands.

Even without music her movement was ballet-like in its complexity. In traditional Indian dance style she used her whole face to add more layers of meaning to what her body already said. Rodeo wondered how removing six yards of cloth could be so erotic. *There's no doubt, she's a professional*, he thought.

In the far reaches of his mind the thought of her being professional set alarm bells ringing, but he wasn't going to pass up this opportunity, not in a million years. Gradually the cloth fell loosely on to the floor until he saw all her naked body.

She moved across to Rodeo and started to kiss his bare upper body. Her tongue flicked at his nipples while her hands deftly removed his pants. His penis, already erect, sprang free. Her mouth engulfed it all and her tongue added to the sensations she had created. She knew he wouldn't be able to last too long so, not wanting to waste any of his precious love juice, she manoeuvred herself so his penis just slid into her. Her muscles clenched him to her. Rhythmically she led him to climax. This time she had to forgo her own orgasm. She needed every last drop of his valuable liquid pearls. She felt the torrent of fluid enter her as he arched towards her.

Laying in his arms she said, 'It's alright if you want to go back to sleep. I know you are exhausted. I won't be offended, I promise.'

Within two or three minutes he rolled over and slept like a baby. Calmly she walked into the bathroom to dress. Before wrapping the material around her, not wanting to waste any of her precious cargo, she pulled on a pair of incontinent pants usually worn by elderly ladies.

Quietly she unlocked the sliding glass doors leading onto the balcony. As the doors slid open a security light lit up the balcony. She climbed onto the balcony wall. She leapt, easily managing to catch the branch of a neem tree. Her weight pulled it down the fourteen feet to the ground.

A voice whispered from the bushes to her right.

'Kamna, over here, quickly.'

She moved to the bushes where the voice came from. Neither of them saw Davey crouching down in bushes only six feet away. He looked on in amazement. What was his sister doing coming from Rodeo's room and jumping off the balcony? He hadn't seen his sister for three years and desperately wanted to say something, but the man she was meeting looked dangerous.

'Do you have the cargo?'

'Yes, it's safe.'

'Good, we don't have much time. Let's go.'

He led her to where he'd cut a hole in the security fence. A paramedic ambulance waited for them.

'Quick, get in. The team are waiting for you. They are all prepared, good luck.' The ambulance sped away.

Davey looked on bemused. What cargo? What had she stolen? Why did she go off in an ambulance? Was she hurt? Of course she wasn't, an ambulance would not be stopped. Kamna knew things like that. What should he do? He didn't want his sister to go to prison but she shouldn't have stolen from Ka1ma-deva. Maybe if he told him what he saw and Kamna gave back whatever it was she took, Ka1ma-deva would not tell the police.

Kamna was four years older than Davey. Their mother died giving birth to Davey and their father died fighting for the Indian Army in Kashmir. Their maternal grandmother looked after them and taught them English until she passed away five years ago.

When she died, Kamna took control and looked after Davey. Three months had passed. Davey was playing with friends while

Kamna cooked their dinner. She heard a knock at the door. A large gentleman dressed in a western suit stood there.

'My dear, may I come in? I have some important business to discuss with you.'

'But I don't know you.'

'No, you're right, but I knew your grandmother. We had a business arrangement.'

'What kind of business arrangement?'

'Well, how can I put it? I loaned her money which she used to pay back every month with interest. She was always a good payer. Unfortunately she still owed twenty-five thousand rupees plus some interest when she died and I have come to reclaim my money. I have all the paperwork here. See, it is perfectly legal.'

'But twenty-five thousand rupees? That's all we have to live on. Me and my brother will starve.'

'I'm sure you'll manage. You're a pretty girl, you'll think of something. Where do you keep the money?'

'No you can't have it, I won't let you.'

'Would you rather me call the police? When I show them the legally binding documents they'll give me the money anyway and they'll put you and your brother in a home. Do you want that?'

'No!'

'Look I'm a reasonable man. Your grandmother was a good customer, so you give me twenty thousand rupees and I'll write off the rest. How does that sound?
I can't be any fairer than that can I?'

'Well, alright, thank you.'

Kamna took a small chest from a covered hole in the floor and counted out twenty thousand rupees.

'Thank you, you'll get by, but if you are ever short of money there's always plenty of work for a pretty girl like you. Here's my card. If you're interested come and see me.' She took it and looked at it before placing it in the cash chest.

Kamna lay on the operating table in Hyderabad's Memorial

Hospital with her legs strapped in the air, while a surgeon recovered as much of Rodeo's fresh sperm as he could. She smiled to herself. Her first hundred thousand dollar job and it was so easy and enjoyable. An orderly came in and took away the tubes containing the sperm. She looked at him. *Good, job done*, she thought. The only disappointment was that she would never have a repeat performance with Rodeo. Still, never mind, she could always dream of him when she pleasured herself.

She saw the surgeon preparing a hypodermic syringe.

'What's that for? I'm fine, I don't need anything.'

'Yes you do,' replied the surgeon. 'You see, my boss says I'm to keep you quiet…for good.' He moved towards her exposed bottom with the loaded syringe.

'Oh no you don't!'

Using all her upper body strength she swung herself over the straps and in one movement grabbed the surgeon's arm and pushed it towards his body. His face looked startled and surprised. The needle pierced his skin. He didn't even have time to stop her as she pushed down on the syringe, driving the deadly contents into his abdomen. His convulsing body collapsed, shaking on the floor.

∗   ∗   ∗

'But I must see Ka1ma-deva, it is most important, you don't understand. I must see him.'

Rodeo heard Davey shouting at the security staff outside his suite. He looked around for Kamna but saw that she had gone. He couldn't blame her. He was a washout last night, no good to anyone. He shouted as he pulled his pants on.

'Okay Davey, give me a minute and I'll see you.' He opened the door. Davey fell to his knees.

'Master, something terrible has happened and I must take some of the blame because she is my sister.'

'Whoa, slow down little fella, you're losing me. Your sister? Who's your sister?'

'Kamna…Kamna is my sister.'

'Kamna is your sister?'

Yes Master, I saw her leave your suite last night and she has stolen something from you. Please do not send her to prison, Kalma-deva I beg you.'

'Okay Davey, it's okay, no one's going to prison. Kamna was with me last night with my permission. We made love, but I didn't know she was your sister. I'm sure she hasn't stolen anything, she just left.'

'But Master, why did she jump from the balcony and meet a bad man in the grounds who asked her if she had the cargo?'

Rodeo frowned and bent down to be on the same level as Davey.

'This man she met, was he an American?'

'Yes Master. He spoke like they do in the movies, like you do.'

'So how come you were in the grounds at night when I've booked you a room in the hotel?'

'Master, until the American man cut through the fence I was sleeping.'

'Sleeping?'

'Yes Master, since my sister left me to go to America I cannot sleep in a bed. I like the stars above me, they protect me.'

'Wait a minute, your telling me your sister went to live in America?'

'Yes Master, three years ago.'

'Okay Davey, I'll catch you later after breakfast. First I need to talk to Mathew.'

'I don't like this,' Mathew ranted later that morning. 'I don't like it one little bit. This smells – no, it more than smells, it stinks. What the fuck's going on?'

He directed a worried look at Rodeo. 'Boss, I think we should seriously consider cancelling tomorrow's show until we find out what all this is about.'

Rodeo sat back in his chair.

'Don't you think that's a tad extreme? After all, no one's been hurt and no threats have been made.'

'I don't know, maybe you're right, but I want to find out what's going on an' who's behind it.'

CHAPTER 12

DAVEY SAT on the immaculately manicured lawn of the Raja Hotel in Bangalore, starring blankly ahead. Ever since his sister left he'd been withdrawn. Rodeo watched him from a distance then made his way over to him.

'Davey, you're looking like you have the weight of the whole world on your shoulders. What's wrong? Do you miss your sister?'

'Master, I do not believe you are Ka1ma-deva.'

'I never said I was.' Rodeo sat down beside him. 'Look Davey, I'm just a guy from America. I write songs, I sing and entertain and I tell people what I believe about God, religion and love. Some people like what I say because it makes sense to them. They feel it would make the world a better place if we all took it on board, so they put me on a pedestal. Others feel threatened by what I say so they want to stop me.'

'Master, why do they want to stop you when you talk of love?'

'Because it doesn't fit in with their view of the world, or what they've been taught to believe is right and wrong. Somehow they feel their power will be eroded…'

'What does eroded mean?'

'Taken away. They feel their power will be taken away, but what they don't understand is that without love there is no power. Without love there's nothing, absolutely nothing, because God is only love and we are all part of God.'

'Master, what is love?'

'Wow, that's quite a question! You know, back in the Sates there's a daily newspaper cartoon called *Love Is*. I don't suppose you've seen it?'

'Yes I have!' His eyes lit up. 'I like to read American papers, they're funny.'

'Well the guy who used to draw them and write the captions got it absolutely right. Love is about everything we say and everything we do. You see, everything we say and do can be with or without love.'

Davey tilted his head to one side. 'Do you love my sister? I know she has earned money sleeping with men, but they did not love her. They just used her for their own pleasure.'

'Now I know why you've a face like that stubborn camel I rode yesterday. You think I'm just like the other men that slept with your sister, right? Okay, I slept with her. As I said, I'm just a guy.'

'No, Master, you are not just a guy. You are Ka1ma-deva.'

'Well, how do you work that one out?'

'You told me yourself. Love is being a guide to Ka1ma-deva. Being a guide to just a guy is not the same.' Rodeo took a breath to speak but no words came out as he tried follow Davey's logic.

'Hey Davey, how you doing?' Rodeo looked up and saw Laura walking across the lawn towards them.

'Hi, come and join us,' called out Rodeo. He had to shout so that he could be heard over the noise of the lawnmower. Laura had that concerned look on her face.

'I need to talk to you…alone.'

'Davey, do you want to go and see if Mathew needs any help with our preparation for Japan?'

'I do not know anything about Japan.'

'Don't worry, with your street cred you could guide us anywhere.'

'Does that mean I'm going to Japan with you?'

'Yeah sure, providing we can get you a passport and you want to hang out with us.'

'Master, I'm going to tell Mathew.'

'Good you do that, he'll be thrilled I'm sure.'

Rodeo grinned to himself. Laura looked at him sternly.

'Is that a good idea, telling him he can come to Japan with us?'

'Why not? He's got no one here. I've kind'a adopted him. Besides, the travelling will help his education.'

'Okay you win. Look, I'm worried about Carlotta. Her dad hasn't phoned for over a month now. She puts on a brave face and says he's going to come for her soon, but I'm worried she's hurting real bad. What if he's dead?'

'You're right, we have to take her mind off things…let's have a party…'

'Hold on, I've been to your parties…'

'No, not that kind'a party. Have you seen some of the small villages around here? Let's hold a party for the villagers. Get Carlotta involved in organising it, in fact ask her to plan it with you.'

'You mean that?'

'Sure, don't worry about the cost, but don't put it down against the tour expenses. It comes out of my pocket, agreed?'

'Agreed.'

Laura skipped back across the lawn to the hotel, eager to tell Carlotta about the party. Carlotta played on her laptop.

'You spend a lot of time playing with that thing.'

'I know, I'm sorry but it's too hot to play outside.'

'You're right, but you know what you can use that computer for? You can use it to plan our party.'

'A party?'

'Rodeo suggested we hold a party for the local villages and he asked for you to plan it.'

'He did? Really?'

'Really. Are you up for it?'

'Can we start now?'

'Sure, why not.'

'Great, I can tell my Daddy.' Suddenly she realised what she'd said. 'I mean when he phones I can tell him.'

'Of course you can, he'll be so proud of you.' Laura turned away, hoping Carlotta hadn't seen the tear in the corner of her eye.

They planned the party for the day before Rodeo's last performance in Bangalore. Local musicians, caterers and street entertainers were all employed to help make it a success. They chose the village of Hebbagodi on the southern outskirts of Bangalore. Carlotta chose it because, out of a population of just over sixteen thousand, twelve percent were under six years old. She thought they would really enjoy a party.

Laura, Carlotta and Davey went to see the village council. They thought it a wonderful idea: Hebbagodi had never had a village party before.

'It will certainly enhance the importance of our village and it will make all the other villages very jealous. Rodeo must be mad spending all this money on us.'

Davey chimed in. 'No, he is not mad, he is Ka1ma-deva.'

Rodeo and everyone involved in the tour spent the night before the party in the village as guests of the council. In the morning, just as the sun rose, Davey woke Rodeo.

'Master, Master...'

'What is it? What's the time? You know us rock musicians don't normally rise too early.'

'Master, come and look.'

Davey pointed out the window. Crowds of people of all ages packed the streets. Some swept, others hung flowers and decorations.

'Master, this is going to be a great day.' Rodeo nodded and fell back onto his bed.

'Wake me up in a couple of hours.'

CNN Reported later that day: 'India has never seen a party like it before, in fact the world has never witnessed anything quite like it either. Millions of people who heard about the party in the small village of Hebbagodi, south of Bangalore, decided to gatecrash it. They've come from hundreds of surrounding villages. When asked why they have come to the party in Hebbagodi they all answer the same. They haven't come for the free entertainment or free food, they've come to see Ka1ma-deva. They believe Ka1ma-deva or Love God, though most of us know him as Rodeo, is the incarnation of God himself. The crowds are so vast we can't get near him. This is Scott McKenzie for CNN news in Hebbagodi near Bangalore India.'

Rodeo didn't disappoint the crowds. For sixteen hours he played his guitar, spoke and laughed and joked with the crowd as they filed past him in an orderly manner. No one could stop, they had to keep moving. Hundreds of thousands were able to see him and some even touched him. Many claimed they were healed by touching him or even just seeing him. Rodeo made no such claims.

Mathew stood by his side the whole time, ready to spring into action, but even he admitted the crowd were so good humoured and the atmosphere so loving, that it would be highly unlikely he'd need to step in.

*   *   *

Pope Barnabus arrived in the Philippines, his home country, the following day. When people told him about the party in India he asked for the news to be played to him on the television. He wanted to see it for himself. For five minutes he sat watching, totally expressionless. Barnabus did not easily become excited. As he watched he refused to think of the verses in the hidden Testaments. Instead he asked for one of his accompanying cardinals to play chess with him.

Michael Heaney worked late at his offices in Little Rock. He watched the news unfold.

'This is great,' he told his staff. 'This man, who is an affront to Christians the world over, is now being acclaimed by fucking statue worshippers as a God. Let's stir up a little mischief. Call our contacts in the press, make sure they ruffle a few feathers of some of Rodeo's more liberal supporters like Senator Davis. Ask him what he feels about Rodeo claiming to be some sort of Indian God and what his Christian voters may think about that, and make sure you quote him directly. I want these fucking libs nailed.'

CHAPTER 13

THE FLIGHT to Japan gave Mathew some time to think. Why would the men who met Kamna in the hotel grounds describe the stolen goods as 'cargo?' What is cargo? It's a load that's carried in something. Kamna wasn't carrying a bag or anything; the hotel CCTV pictures confirmed that. So if the cargo wasn't in a bag or parcel…it must be on her…or inside her? Drugs? No. What was she carrying? He smiled to himself. Apart from Rodeo's sperm… Rodeo would never change.'

His face suddenly became serious. That's it. My God, someone wanted Rodeo's sperm! Who on earth would want Rodeo's sperm? But, more worryingly, why? There could only be three reasons that he could think of. Reason one, Kamna wanted to become pregnant and cause a scandal for Rodeo. No, everyone knew of Rodeo's reputation. I'm surprised it hasn't happened before now. Reason two, she wanted to have Rodeo's child and then blackmail him. A possibility. Reason three, she or someone else wants to use Rodeo's sperm to make a baby. Someone wants Rodeo's baby and they paid Kamna to collect the sperm.

Yes that's it! He stood up and walked down the aisle to where Rodeo sat reading.

'Boss can I have a word?'

'Sure, take a seat. What's wrong?'

'Why do you always think something's wrong?'

'Mathew, I've known you a long time, I can always tell.'

'Well, you're kind'a right. Something is wrong.'

'Don't tell me, there's a bomb on board.' He said it with a sense of mischief that annoyed Mathew.

'No Boss, I think I worked out what happened. Someone

wanted your baby so they paid Kamna to collect your sperm. The cargo is the sperm.'

'Are you really serious?'

'Yeah,' said Mathew, pleased with himself for working it out.

'I suppose you're right, that is a possibility,' said Rodeo with a grin on his face.

'But Boss,' said Mathew, irritated by Rodeo's lack of concern. 'Aren't you worried?'

'Why worry about a new life being born?' Mathew thought for a minute before speaking.

'I suppose you're right. I'd be an Uncle.'

Rodeo rested his hand on Mathew's shoulder and gently squeezed. It was something Rodeo used to do to calm Mathew down when they were in jail together.

'Mathew, you'd make a wonderful uncle.

Mathew went back to his seat, talking to himself. 'Okay, you got lucky this time but I'm not going to let you out of my sight. You ain't going to be able to fart without me knowing.' He walked down the aisle to where Davey was sitting.

'Hey Davey, do you know where your sister stayed when she went to America?' asked Mathew, anxious to learn where any paternity suits might come from.

'Yes I do,' said Davey innocently. 'She stayed in a very small village called Little Rock. She sent to me a postcard.'

Mathew looked across to where Douglas sat. Douglas had overheard what Davey said. The expression on Douglas's face said everything...Heaney!

Japan proved to be an inspired choice for the second leg of the tour. The Japanese people took Rodeo to their hearts after he appeared on a Sunday morning talk show, during which the host asked about his recent tour of India. The host, a jovial man named Aldo, politely suggested that it had all been a big PR exercise. Rodeo simply smiled.

'You know,' he said, 'my PR team consists of one fantastic lady called Mable Hillthorpe, who has never ever left the USA and certainly never set foot in India. I'm sure Mable would be flattered by what you're saying, but it's simply not true. I'm just a jobbing musician who's driven to perform in front of audiences, and if I can make a little difference in people's lives by sharing my beliefs about God, religion and love then that's great.'

Aldo nodded politely. 'Rodeo, I'm sure the Japanese people would be interested to hear you views on Shinto, the most prevalent religion in Japan.

'Ok, I'm no expert on Shinto, but my understanding is that there are no absolutes. There's no absolute right and wrong. Nobody is perfect and people are thought to be fundamentally good, which is pretty much what I believe. But you know, I just take it a little further because, although there is no absolute right or wrong, there is with or without love. Without love, it leaves our souls and the world empty, nothing happens, nothing changes. It's like we're in perpetual limbo, all separate, person against person, family against family, neighbour against neighbour and country against country. But if we do something or experience something with love, then that can have an effect, you know, like dancing a conga.'

He saw the blank look on Aldo's face. 'Let me explain. The conga's a dance where one or two start off the dancing linked together and eventually more and more people link on to the chain, doing the same dance but in their own way. Everyone taking part is linked together, having fun and enjoying themselves and experiencing the oneness. Those that don't take part do not experience the fun, the enjoyment or the oneness, so consequently they are unable to relate to those experiences and introduce them into other parts of their lives. So, as I said, they don't move forward. All they get is more of the same.'

'Thank you Rodeo, a very interesting insight. I must say that personally I find your music full of interesting insights. Now you're going to perform one of the songs from your Heaven's Door album for us. Ladies and gentlemen, Rodeo sings River People.'

The studio audience applauded enthusiastically as Rodeo walked across the studio, picked up his McPherson guitar and sat on a very high chrome bar stool. The studio lights dimmed till just a spot with a slight blue tint focused on him.

'River people...' As he launched into the song he had the strangest feeling that, for some reason, this would be the last time he'd perform it.

Within two days you couldn't buy a Rodeo CD in Japan. Every supermarket, record store and gas station had totally sold out. The only way to get hold of one was to order via the internet. The planned four concerts became mega media events. Crowds feted Rodeo everywhere he went. They even awarded him Japan's second most prestigious honour, The Order of the Rising Sun with Paulownia Blossoms, Grand Cordon.

The current Japanese Emperor's reign is called Heisei, which means the achievement of complete peace on earth and in the heavens. Because of the all encompassing influence of the Emperor on Japanese life, the adoption of this name for the reign influenced Japan's policy. It fascinated Rodeo to read that students of Christian prophecy also believed Heisei could be interpreted as referring to the long period of peace and prosperity predicted in Christian theology, a period which must precede great changes prior to the return of Jesus Christ.

He read and tried to digest as much information as he could about Japan prior to actually receiving the award, even though it wasn't due to take place until six months after the completion of his world tour. As he read, he couldn't help but wonder what Jesus Christ would encounter should his soul ever return to Earth.

CHAPTER 13

LIFE COULD have been better for Alfredo Benando. Since he left Carlotta with Rodeo at the Redsox Ball Park he'd survived two more attempts on his life. Both attempts happened soon after he'd left a message for Carlotta on Rodeo's answer phone. He suspected someone intercepted and traced the calls. So far he'd been able to keep one step ahead of them, but for how much longer? The odds weren't in his favour.

The last attempt happened in Herradura, Mexico. After visiting a grocery store he climbed into his four by four Jeep. A passing motor cyclist suddenly crashed for no reason. Instinctively, Alfredo ducked down behind the Jeep. A bullet struck the windscreen, shattering it into a million tiny fragments. Immediately he guessed what happened. A sniper had him in his sights. The motor cyclist took the bullet meant for him.

Keeping low, he opened the near side front door and crawled in. Without sitting up he turned the key in the ignition, put the vehicle into drive and, with his left hand, pushed down on the accelerator while holding the steering wheel with his right. He prayed there was nothing coming. It wasn't until he'd gone over a hundred yards that he sat up and took proper control of the vehicle.

'Shit! That was too close.'

Mexico obviously wasn't safe, but would anywhere be safe? A thought came into his head.

'You're crazy, Alfredo,' he said to himself. You must be to have stupid thoughts like that. The more he missed Carlotta the more the thoughts crept into his mind.

'Where's the next leg of Rodeo's tour?'

* * *

Every night Carlotta opened her laptop, hoping her daddy would come to her. Heaney deliberately kept her waiting for days on end so that, when he did come through, she held onto his every word. Soon his patience would be rewarded, he thought.

Heaney's campaign to win the Republican presidential nomination started well. Reporters caught his main rival, Senator Alun Davis, off guard when they asked him his opinion on Rodeo's elevation to a Hindu God in India.

'Mr Davis, your support for Rodeo is well known, but how do you condone his behaviour in India?'

'How do I condone his behaviour in India? Look he's done nothing wrong. Rodeo is a great ambassador for our country and you can quote me on that.'

'Many Christians are offended by him accepting adulation as a Hindu God.'

'If Christians are offended then that's their problem, not mine.'

'May I quote you on that also?'

In contrast, Michael Heaney, when asked about Rodeo's behaviour in India, sounded eloquent in his responses.

'I believe his behaviour is reprehensible. Many good people have left the Christian Church over the last few years because of the philosophy espoused by Rodeo. But I ask you to think about this. He's scathing about worshiping God in God's House and about praying and singing hymns, but, by accepting praise and adulation himself, as a Hindu God, he's going against everything he's ever said. In my book that makes him a hypocrite or even worse. He's just milking his popularity in India to sell more music albums.'

*   *   *

Keanan Horris had never been in trouble before, not even a parking ticket. So when armed police raided his hotel room in Rio De Janeiro, paid for courtesy of Michael Heaney, he couldn't believe it. For Keanan it was like a scene out of a movie. He wasn't scared, more awe struck. This had to be savoured and enjoyed. At last excitement! Goodbye nerdy life.

Keanan, a committed Christian, had long respected Michael Heaney as a clergyman turned politician who supported Christian values. A year ago he wrote to Heaney asking if he had any job vacancies. Three months went by without a reply so he tagged Heaney's website. A week later, Heaney employed him as his IT Security Specialist.

'May I dress please?' Keanan had just showered and only wore the luxury bath robe supplied by the hotel.

'No you may not. Keep your hands raised above your head and lay face down on the bed.' The Brazilian policeman spoke pretty good English.

Keanan did as he was told. A policemen cuffed his hands behind his back. Two police came out of the washroom with what looked like four blocks of white soap in sealed plastic bags.

'We have the evidence.'

'Señor, it looks like a long sentence for you.' The policeman said it with the biggest smile Keanan had ever seen. He closed his eyes. He'd thought the raid must be a mistake, a joke even…but now?

Keanan needed to be resourceful. For him, logic dictated that there must be a way to out. He'd been set up by Heaney. This much he figured out already, but why? Logic told him that Heaney wanted him to keep quiet about Sirrus, or that he wanted to sell the idea. If that's the case, why hadn't he just had him killed and been done with it? While working for him he'd seen and heard things he maybe shouldn't have. Things that made him believe Heaney would kill if he had to. Maybe he couldn't take the risk. This way he ended up in a cage in some Godforsaken foreign jail and Heaney had Sirrus without any risk.

All these thoughts went through his head for hours.

'I got it! That's it, I can't fight my way out but I can bluff my way.' He shouted across to a guard who was sitting at a large desk in the middle of the cell block. 'Señor, I need to talk to you. Do you speak English?'

'I speak a little, what is it you want?'

'When can I see an attorney?'

'Ah you want to see advogado? Amanha you see advogado, amanha.'

'Amanha? You mean tomorrow right?'

'Si señor, tomorrow.'

'May I make a phone call please?'

'You phone amanha when you see advogado, sim?'

With all sorts of thoughts rushing around in his head, Keanan tried to settle down for the night. One thing was for sure, revenge would be sweet.

The next morning at about nine a guard took Keanan to a small room that contained a desk and four chairs. The guard beckoned him to sit on the chair in front of the desk. Keanan noticed the desk had seen better days and found himself counting the worm holes. After counting the first fifty his mind snapped back to reality. He looked up as two men and a woman entered the room. The two men sat behind the desk and the woman moved a chair and sat next to him. One of the men spoke. Keanan noticed he had cruel eyes.

I wouldn't want to cross you, he thought to himself.

'You are charged with possessing one point three kilos of cocaine with intent to supply. Do you understand the charge?'

Keanan looked directly at him. 'I've been framed.'

The man looked angry. 'I asked you, do you understand the charge?'

'Yes sir.'

'I need some time with my client, alone,' spoke the woman.

The other man spoke this time. 'You have thirty minutes.'

Both the men left the room. When the door shut behind them the woman introduced herself to Keanan.

'I'm Maria Von Hind. I've been asked to represent you.'

Keanan looked at her. 'Are you German? You don't look it.'

'And what may I ask is a German supposed to look like?' She

didn't give him chance to respond. 'My husband was German. But let's move on, we have only a short time. The charge is very serious, you could be jailed for life, maybe serve ten years.'

'But I was framed.'

'Unfortunately, eighty two percent of people on serious drugs charges use that excuse.'

'You don't believe me?'

'I didn't say I don't believe you, but it's not a satisfactory defence.' Keanan looked at her earnestly. She was maybe forty but kind of pretty, with short jet black hair. He took a deep breath before speaking.

'If I can make a phone call I think I can make this easier for everyone.'

'I doubt it, but you can try. Here, use my cell phone.' She opened her handbag and passed it to him. He noticed it was the most up-to-date model available with TV, radio, email and GPS.

Luckily he knew the number off by heart. His heart began to beat faster as he dialled the number. Heaney had to be there, he just had to. An automated voice answered.

'*Hi, you have reached the offices of Senator Michael Heaney. For details of his public meetings please press one. For press enquiries please press two. For all other enquiries please hold.*' He heard three ring tones before a voice answered.

'Hello, how may I help you?' Keanan recognised the voice.

'Debs it's me, Keanan.'

'I thought you were on vacation.'

'I am, but I desperately need to speak to Michael.'

'He's in a meeting, you know he doesn't like to be interrupted when...'

'I don't care, just do it,' interrupted Keanan. 'Please.' The line fell silent for ten seconds but it seemed like an eternity before a voice came through.

'Keanan, what's the problem?' It was Heaney. 'You're meant to be on vacation.'

Keanan put on his best grovelling voice. 'I'm so sorry, Sir, I've let you down.'

'What do you mean, let me down?'

'I'm in trouble, big trouble.'

'What kind of trouble?'

'I've been arrested and charged with possession with intent to supply.'

'Are we talking drugs?'

'Yes Sir.'

'That's serious.'

'Yes Sir, but there's something else. It's to do with Sirrus.'

'Did you say Sirrus?'

'Yes Sir. Timescales to complete the project were tight but I figured I'd be back from holiday in time.'

'In time for what?'

'Well, when the military defined GPS there was always a theoretical threat of a parasite. So they built in a mechanism to combat the possibility. To foil the mechanism I incorporated a cloaking device, it's really ten cloaking devices, each one lasting an hour...'

'So you're telling me we only have ten hours. What happens when they give out?'

'We get found out... but I can design and build other cloaking devices, that could last maybe a year, or longer.'

Maria listened intently.

'Fuck you Keanan. Why didn't you tell me before you went off on vacation?'

'I thought I had plenty of time. I didn't know I'd end up in jail on a drugs charge. They found drugs in the washroom. The previous occupants must have left them there.'

Maria spoke. 'Give me the phone.' It sounded more like an order than a request. He passed it to her.

'Señor, this is Maria Von Hind. I am Keanan's attorney. He is in a very serious situation. Listen to me carefully. Can you afford to pay one hundred thousand American Dollars? If you can, I think I can arrange for his release. The money must be paid today. It's the only way, think of it as a kind of bail. I will text you the bank account details for you to transfer the money.'

She listened intently for about a minute. Keanan strained to try to hear what Heaney said. She switched the phone off.

'You're a very lucky young man. He has agreed to pay the money. When the money is in the account you will be free to go.'

He felt a surge of relief. Maybe he should take up poker?

Meanwhile, Michael Heaney was in no mood to play games. 'If that spotty little fucker has put one over on me I swear I'll kill him.'

He picked up the phone. 'Gill, it's Heaney. You worked with the spotty little fucker on Sirrus. Tell me, is there a cloaking device that expires after ten hours?'

Gill thought for a second. 'Hmmn…there is a cloaking device, whether or not it expires I don't know. But it does change every hour and each one is programmed individually, so it's highly likely.'

'Could you design and build another?'

'No, it would take me years. If I'm honest the technology is a little beyond me.'

'Thanks Gill, that's all I wanted to know.' He made another call.

'Reagan, it's Heaney. I need a favour. One of my staff got himself into a spot of bother in Rio. Can one of your operatives there deliver him safely back to me? He's currently being held at the main police HQ. He's due to be released later today.' He listened, hoping for a positive response. 'Okay thanks, I owe you.'

To Keanan the next few hours seemed endless. Still, it gave him time to plan what to do next. A guard let Maria into his cell, then locked the door behind her.

'Good news. The money is transferred and you will soon be free to go. Tell me, I couldn't help overhearing you talking about GPS, parasites and cloaking devices. Are you in trouble?'

'You could say that.'

'This Michael Heaney, he is an American Senator, yes?'

'Yes.'

'He is sending a man to meet you to take you back to Little Rock safely. We have been asked to hold you until he arrives.' He looked at her with a hung dog expression.

'Can't I go out the back door?'

'I think if you don't go back to Little Rock he will hunt you down and kill you.'

Keanan desperately wanted to tell her about how he'd bluffed Heaney, and his plans were to go anywhere but Little Rock. Could he trust her? What if she's part of it? Maybe he should take his chances with the guy accompanying him back to little Rock. His mind worked overtime on how and where he could lose him. It would have to be at the airport.

A guard unlocked the cell door. He beckoned them to follow him. They walked along a corridor to a small office. A black man, at least six foot seven, three hundred pounds and, by the look on his face, mean, stood by the desk.

He looked at Keanan but didn't speak. Instead he spoke to Maria in Portuguese.

'Portanto isto é a pequena merda quem nos esteve dando toda a preocupação.' She smiled and replied.

'Sim olham-no ele é bastante brilhante e não quer ir a Pouca Rocha.'

The big man gestured to Keanan to follow him.

Keanan was thinking fast. Galeão-Antonio Carlos Jobim airport is located thirteen miles north of Rio and takes about thirty minutes by taxi, depending on the traffic. That gives me enough time to attach some kind of metal object to the big man. It could work. It had to work.

Keanan sat in the rear of the taxi with the big man in the front. The doors centrally looked. The big man turned round and addressed him.

'If you leave my side I will kill you.' He didn't explain or wait for a response, but just turned to face the front.

What can I use? There must be something metal that can do the job. His eyes looked around the back of the cab for something suitable. He needed to be careful not to move too much, in case he attracted the attention of the big man.

On the floor he spotted a large paperclip. *Perfect*, he thought. Leaning towards the window he used his feet, which were out of view of the big man, to try and lift the paper clip off the floor so he could grab it with his right hand. Twenty minutes of the journey passed and he still didn't have the clip. He felt sure the big man was watching him through the wing mirror.

Come on Keanan, he thought to himself. *Focus, you can do it.*

Seconds later he had the clip. That's the easy part. How the fuck am I going to attach it to him?

Keanan observed the big guy knew how to dress well. His tailored suit looked expensive. Maybe he has a certain vainness about him? Well, it's worth a try.

The taxi drew up at terminal one. The driver unlocked the doors then opened the trunk. He passed the two sports bags to the big man who in turn passed some bank notes to the driver. Keanan decided not to move until told. The big man opened the rear door. Keanan climbed out.

The air felt humid after the air conditioning in the cab. The big man spoke.

'Remember, stay by my side.'

For Keanan it was now or never. 'Excuse me Sir, do you know your collar's not straight?'

'Not straight?' He fiddled with it for a second. 'Is that better?'

Keanan shook his head. 'Not really, let me.'

The big man bent down a little to allow Keanan to fix it.

'That's better, nice and straight now.' Keanan breathed a sigh of relief. He'd fixed the paper clip safely under his collar.

'You carry the bags and walk in front of me, understand?' The big man barked his order to Keanan, making him think this guy had either been in the military or the police.

'Yes Sir.' He made his response deliberately meek. Everything he did now had to lull the big man into a false sense of security.

'Walk towards the check-in desks.'

Keanan did as the big man said.

The big man checked in the two sports bags and exchanged a few polite words in Portuguese with the pretty ground hostess. Keanan assumed it was the normal 'have you packed the bags yourself' nonsense. She passed over two boarding passes.

They walked away. The big man stopped and passed one of the boarding passes to Keanan.

'Remember, stay with me or you're dead.'

They made their way to the security check-in. Keanan panicked. Would the paper clip work? What if it didn't? He sweated. I must be in front of the big man.

'Please God, let me go first. The plan won't work if I don't go first.' To his amazement God answered his frenetic praying.

'You go first and remember I'm watching you all the time.'

Keanan walked through. No beep, no sound. He kept walking, gradually quickening his pace. Then he heard an unmistakable beep. Someone activated the detector. He glanced back and saw the big man being searched.

'Please God, make him go through the detector again.' Keanan mouthed the words as he fought to decide whether to go left or right. For some reason he decided on left.

The big man felt ready to explode, he'd now set off the metal detector three times. Each time they searched him they found nothing. It suddenly dawned on him.

'That little shit arse of a fucker.' He felt under his jacket collar and pulled out the large paper clip. He handed it to one of the security guys.

'Here, is this what you're after? Somehow it must have stuck there.' Security let him through.

'Now, where's the that spotty little fucker gone? When I catch yer you'll wish you'd died in that jail.'

Keanan knew he only had a limited amount of time before the big man found him. He'd always believed that in situations like this attack became the best form of defence, but fuck that idea. This guy must be three or four times his weight. Surprise, along with his belt and a plastic bag he'd blagged from one of the airport shops, would be his weapons.

He made his way to the men's washroom located off a twenty metre passage way at the end of the main departure building. Sitting in one of the cubicles he removed his belt and trousers. A pipe ran along the back wall of the cubicle about six or seven feet from the floor. *Perfect.* Standing on the toilet seat he tied one of the trouser legs around the pipe and attached the other leg to his looped belt.

'I reckon I have about forty seconds before things start to get a little uncomfortable.' He knew things could go drastically wrong. He put the thoughts out of his mind and pulled the bag over his head, then placed the looped belt around the bag and his neck. He stood on the toilet seat listening. He heard someone come into the gents.

'Here goes,' he whispered through his teeth. He carefully stepped off the toilet seat while holding onto the belt around his neck. He felt the belt take his weight and then let his arms fall to his side. The big man kicked the cubicle door open. Keanan hung absolutely motionless. The big man recoiled.

'Shit! Mr Heaney won't like this. You're lucky kid, that's a whole lot better than what I had planned for you.'

Keanan waited for the big man to leave the washroom. When he heard no more sound he reached up, grabbed the belt and swung his legs onto the toilet seat.

'Ten seconds to spare. Once again, brains beat brawn,' he said to himself. He knew he wasn't out of the woods yet. He still needed to figure out how he could leave the departure terminal and where he should go.

CHAPTER 14

POPE BARNABUS touched down at Manila's Ninoy Aquino Airport. A crowd estimated at more than a million greeted him, all eager to catch a glimpse of their own local hero.

Cardinal John Sabormo remained an extremely popular local figure. Many Filipinos placed bets at long odds on him becoming Pope and made small fortunes when the Vatican announced his Papacy. The devout Roman Catholic population celebrated and partied for three days.

Barnabus chose to wear a traditional Filipino coconut fibre shirt rather than his usual robes. The crowd loved it.

'This is my country and they are my people,' he beamed. 'Together we will rejoice with God.'

Barnabus had been there for the best part of a week but the frenzy surrounding him was still the same as the first day he arrived.

Antipolo is the national shrine of the Philippines. The statue of Our Lady is carved of wood and stands on a shrine of solid silver. One hundred thousand pilgrims attend the annual ceremony in which a crown of precious jewels is placed with great solemnity upon the Virgin's head. Barnabus chose this shrine and ceremony to be his last official engagement in the Philippines.

A colourful procession preceded the ceremony. Barnabus had taken part in this procession and ceremony many times before. He remembered as a boy looking forward to it more than any other day. The build up and excitement started weeks before the event. A part of him felt sad this would be the last time he'd witness it and be a part of it.

He remembered a day, maybe fifty years ago or more. A woman, really old and ugly, he didn't know her name, called to him as he walked along with the procession.

'John, come here. I have some news for you.'

What news could you have for me? he thought. He walked towards her, slowly, not knowing who she was or what she wanted.

'John, you are to be blessed. One day you will sit here at Antipolo as head of the Church of Rome.'

'John, where are you going?' called his friend. 'Come on, you'll be left behind.'

John turned to his friend . When he looked back the old woman was gone. There was no one there. To this day he had never told a soul about what happened. That day, God called on him to serve him.

His focus returned to the procession.

'John.'

Barnabus went white. His spine tingled. It's her, the same old woman. It couldn't be, it's impossible.

'John you are in danger. You must leave Antipolo now. Go, do not stop, please I beg you.'

Then she disappeared. He turned to his aid.

'Did you see the old woman? Did you hear what she said?'

'I'm sorry your Holiness, I don't understand. Did I see or hear who?'

They were his aids last words. Five minutes later a burst of automatic fire hit him. Bullets struck his abdomen and head, spreading blood and body parts over the papal party.

Barnabus slumped forward in his chair. The chair toppled over onto the sandy floor. Blood poured from wounds in the upper part of his body. People screamed and ran for their lives. Before the Papal bodyguards had time to react the man who discharged the weapon turned it on himself. He opened his mouth and pulled the trigger. Only a bloody stump remained.

CCN news described the Pontiff's condition as very critical. The next twenty-four hours would decide whether he lived or died.

Rodeo immediately decided to cancel the planned concerts out of respect and give everyone their money back. He would join an all night vigil outside the hospital where staff battled to save Barnabus.

Rodeo, Mathew, Laura, Douglas, Davey and Carlotta joined a crowd of over a hundred and fifty thousand, all silently praying for their Pope, their own John Sabormo.

Rodeo whispered to Mathew.

'Could we organise some food and maybe some temporary washrooms for these people? I have a feeling we're all going to be here for quite a while.' Mathew nodded. 'Don't worry about the cost, I'll cover it.'

Then he turned to Douglas.

'Do you think it would be appropriate for me to play something on my guitar?'

'Why not? Might help us channel all this love that's around here.'

Strumming his guitar, Rodeo sang a song Douglas was very familiar with.

Ave Maria
Gratia plena
Maria, gratia plena
Maria, gratia plena
Ave, ave dominus
Dominus tecum
Benedicta tu in mulieribus
Et benedictus
Et benedictus fructus ventris
Ventris tuae, Jesus.
Ave Maria
Ave Maria
Mater Dei
Ora pro nobis peccatoribus
Ora pro nobis

Ora, ora pro nobis peccatoribus
Nunc et in hora mortis
Et in hora mortis nostrae
Et in hora mortis nostrae
Et in hora mortis nostrae
Ave Maria

The huge crowd became hushed. They whispered amongst themselves.

'It's Rodeo, he's singing for our Holy Father!'

Word began to spread around the crowd. People joined in with him. When he'd sung the two verses Rodeo stopped singing but just kept on playing. Soon almost everyone in the crowd joined in. Afterwards, people in the crowd described it as the most moving experience of their lives.

In the hospital, even though connected to a life support machine, Barnabus could see and hear the crowd that gathered outside. While floating above them, he felt the sensation of a soft blanket wrapped around him. The blanket took away all the pain, leaving only a feeling of love for everyone and everything around him.

A part of him wanted to end his days in his homeland but a distant voice told him, 'This is not your destiny. God has other plans.'

News bulletins around the world showed footage of Rodeo leading the singing. Senator Alun Davis grabbed his chance with both hands.

'First of all,' he told reporters, 'I, like many of my countrymen, are praying for the Pope's full recovery. My heart goes out to the people of the Philippines and I'd like to add that Rodeo is a true humanitarian. He cancels all his concerts in the Philippines out of respect for a man with whom he fundamentally disagrees about theological matters and then sits in solidarity with people who are praying for the recovery of His Holiness The Pope. We should be proud that he is an American. He is a man with love in his heart for all people no matter what faith or colour, and as Americans we should all follow his example.'

For forty-eight hours no one knew whether Barnabus would live or die. The crowd around the hospital waited patiently for each hourly bulletin, hoping beyond hope to hear the news they all prayed for. Then the announcement came. A Hospital representative stood on the steps by the main entrance. The crowd hushed.

'Doctors have switched off the life support machine that kept Pope Barnabus alive...'

The crowd groaned.

'...because Barnabus can now breath on his own and doctors say is out of danger.'

Rather than wildly celebrate, the majority of the crowd knelt and prayed. Some wept tears of joy or, as Rodeo called them, tears of love.

CHAPTER 15

IF I'M RIGHT, thought Keanan, *most fire alarm systems go straight into evacuation mode if two or more sensors detect smoke or heat or the glass is broken, and if the buttons are pressed at two or more fire call points. Now, let's test it out.*

For the last hour he'd sat in the cubicle puzzling over what to do. From the big man's point of view he was dead. Even so, he didn't particularly relish the idea of bumping into him again and then having to persuade him he's a ghost.

'That could be a little tricky, even for someone with my talents.'

Causing the terminal to be evacuated definitely appeared to be the best option. He could just merge with the crowds.

Tentatively he opened the cubicle door and made his way out of the washroom and along the passage way. So far so good. He spotted one fire call point on a wall beside a retail outlet selling expensive handbags.

'Now, I need one more not too far way,' he said to himself. He began to walk to the…

'Holy shit!' Ten feet ahead stood the big man. Luckily he hadn't seen him. Too busy talking on his cell phone. Keanan turned and almost ran to the sanctity of the washroom.

'Time for a change of plan.'

He deliberately left the cubicle door open so whoever came in could see him hanging. It worked. Someone looked in and within ninety seconds two police officers entered and let him down. Luckily for Keanan they did. This time he didn't quite get it right, another few seconds and he'd have died. One of the policemen felt for his pulse. He couldn't find it.

'Esta Inoperante.'

They didn't even bother with the kiss of life. One of them put his jacket over him. When the ambulance men arrived they covered him with a white sheet and carried him away on a stretcher. The big man looked on impassively when they walked past him.

It wasn't till he was lying on a slab in the morgue that Keanan came round. Gradually his consciousness returned.

'Where am I? I must either be in a very quiet hospital or a morgue.' Slowly he pulled off the white sheet.

At first he couldn't see a thing. Gradually his eyes became accustomed to the dark. He could just about make out other bodies on slabs. He thought perhaps it was the hospital morgue. He didn't feel too bad considering he'd nearly died. What worried him the most was the fact that no one had bothered to check if he was actually dead. He could have been buried alive or filled with embalming fluid or something equally horrific. Weren't they supposed to do tests to find out if he was brain dead? Oh well, maybe they did.

He looked around. He could see one door that looked as if it led into offices and another that looked like it opened to the outside. *Maybe that's where they bring the bodies in and take them out*, he thought. He slipped open a couple of bolts then tried the handle. To his surprise it opened. *It's not like anyone in here's going anywhere*, he thought, *at least not under their own steam*.

Quietly he opened the door that led out to a deserted alleyway. He looked around. Closing the door behind him he walked along the alley till he came to a main road. A thought suddenly occurred. He felt in his pocket. No wallet, passport, money…nothing.

CHAPTER 16

CARDINAL BILOWEIKI felt uncomfortable speaking to the camera at the press conference three days later.

'The attempted assassination of Pope Barnabus was carried out by a Muslim from the Filipino Island of Mindanao. This is fact. Police positively identified the body. Despite this I appeal to Filipino Catholics not to take revenge on the Muslim minority in Mindanao.' He paused before continuing in his usual no nonsense style.

'I do, though, admonish Muslims worldwide for their penchant to use violence to achieve their ends and I warn you, Christendom will not stand idly by while Islam uses the sword to expand its influence.' The news room erupted.

'Cardinal Biloweiki, those are pretty strong words. Will you expand on them?'

'Cardinal, that almost amounts to a declaration of war...'

'I have no further comment to make.'

'What do you mean by those comments?'

'Gentlemen, ladies, the interview is ended.' With that he strode out of the studio. The media throng swarmed around him as he made his way down the steps to a waiting car. Photographers fought with each other to take shots.

Three days later, Cardinal Biloweiki attended a meeting of the Confederation of American Christian Churches in Washington. The COACC lobby for the interests of Christians throughout the United States. They had invited Senator Heaney to address the delegates.

His speech contained no surprises. After leading prayers asking for the speedy recovery of Pope Barnabus, he outlined what he saw as three key areas of change for American Government Policy. First, the need for an amendment to the US Constitution to allow blasphemy laws already on the statute book to be enforced. Secondly, the US should only give financial aid to Christian countries and, thirdly, local urban development grants should be managed by Christian organisations.

In reality, Heaney didn't give a toss about the three issues. The meeting only acted as a smoke screen for Cardinal Biloweiki and Heaney to meet legitimately without arousing anyone's suspicion, COACC being their only link.

The room at the Catholic study centre was clean, soundproof and monitored by Heaney's staff for any illicit transmissions. The Cardinal and Heaney sat opposite one another around a large oval table made of solid mahogany. There were no papers, no records, just the two of them. Heaney spoke first.

'His Holiness, is he likely to survive?' Cardinal Biloweiki looked uncomfortable.

'Yes, he will survive. Fortunately, however, his time in office will probably be considerably curtailed taking into account the severity of his wounds.' Heaney nodded.

'I liked your press conference. The way you asked for no revenge attacks and then said that Christians would not stand idly by…I'm sure I heard the whole western world say about bloody time.'

The Cardinal nodded, then his lips hardly moved as he spoke.

'I have read the hidden testaments.' He paused and looked over his bifocals at Heaney. 'Unfortunately, Barnabus doesn't take them seriously enough. He will not acknowledge the terrible consequences, but then how could he, coming from a simple farming community?'

Heaney spoke. 'At least now he's out of the way and for a while we can make hay, so to speak.' He leaned slightly forward. 'Let's get one thing straight. Rodeo is to be left alone until I'm ready. Fuck the plan Barnabus had. Let Rodeo's tour be a success, the bigger and more popular he becomes the harder he falls and the bigger the fall out. Now that's what I call a win-win situation. I get to the Whitehouse, you get the papacy. As an added bonus you also get rid of Rodeo in a way that will guarantee his name will forever be linked with evil.' Heaney saw the briefest sign of a smile on the Cardinal's face.

'Are the plans in place?' asked the Cardinal.

Heaney sat back a little and put his hands together. 'We have a small technical problem that we're looking to fix, but whatever happens, one way or another the plan goes ahead. By the way, did you receive my audio tape?' The Cardinal nodded.

'How come you asked me to waste the mobsters who tried to put the frighteners on Rodeo?'

The Cardinal removed his glasses and rubbed his eyes before answering.

'They weren't mobsters, they were actually Papal bodyguards working for Barnabus. Unfortunately for them they stumbled on something they shouldn't have.'

'Really? What was that?'

'If I told you I would have to kill you too.'

'I see.' Heaney decided not to press any further.

'Well, I think that concludes our meeting today,' said the Cardinal.

Heaney nodded, wondering what the enforcers had stumbled upon. Before the Cardinal left the room he turned to Heaney.

'Dare I ask, have you found Benando yet?' Heaney felt an element of criticism in his tone.

'No, he's proving to be somewhat elusive.'

'Then may I suggest you try Rio. Rodeo is currently touring there. Benando and his daughter are very close, he won't be able to stay away from her for too long. Let me know when he's no longer a problem.' With that he turned and left the room.

* * *

Two days had passed since Keanan had walked out of the morgue. Having no money, passport or identification, he quickly realised he fell under the category of non person. Sleeping rough hadn't posed too many problems. The warm dry weather made it easy and he quite liked sleeping under the stars, but being a realist he knew he needed food and somewhere to shelter. For that he needed money. Or did he?

While studying at college he'd earned his living working in a diner. The work wasn't hard and he got to keep all the tips. He decided to look around for a suitable establishment. Two hours later he found it.

The American Diner, only four blocks from the morgue. The owner, a guy named Harry, appeared likeable enough.

'Kid, I can't pay you, business isn't so good, but I have a room you can sleep in and I'll feed you. We share the tips fifty-fifty and if the police come for you I know nothing, you understand? You never worked here.' Keanan agreed.

Now, as Baloo put it, he had the bare necessities of life, even though he was supposedly dead.

* * *

Tonight, Rodeo was due to perform his first concert in Rio. Harry agreed that Keanan could have the night off. Maybe he could blag his way in and warn Rodeo about Heaney?

Keanan sat in the back room drinking a coffee. Harry called him.

'Kenny,' we got a customer. Go take his order while I mop the floor.'

Keanan walked out the back room and stopped dead in his tacks. He turned to Harry and whispered.

'I can't do it.'

'What do you mean, you can't do it?'

'I can't take his order.'

'What? Do you know who that is? That's Titus, he like kinda rules Rio. Nothing happens here without his say so.' He noticed Keanan shaking like a jelly. 'Okay, I'll serve him. You stay here out the way.'

When the big man had gone, Harry sat down with Keanan in the back room.

'So why were you shaking kid? How come you know Titus?'

Keanan wasn't sure how much to tell him. Harry seemed like a nice guy. If he couldn't trust him who could he trust? When he'd finished, Harry looked pleased.

'You let me know when all this is over, and I'll tell everyone how you put one over on Titus. Maybe then people around here will laugh at him and not be so frightened of him.' Harry paused as if he had just thought of an idea. 'You want a ticket to see Rodeo tonight? I'll get you one. I know a tout who owes me. You know what, you're the first person I know who's crossed Titus and lived to tell the tale!'

The concert at Estádio do Maracanã, known to the locals as Maraca, sold out months ago. Over a hundred thousand tickets sold in less than twenty-four hours. After the cancellation of the Filipino tour Rodeo couldn't wait to go back on stage again. Performing had become part of his life force, as much as breathing.

Donning his new baseball cap and large shades, Keanan made his way towards Maraca with Harry by his side. It just so happened Harry's contact had two tickets. Exactly what he'd do at the concert Keanan wasn't sure. He had some vague idea about meeting Rodeo and telling him about Heaney.

What precisely is Heaney doing? He couldn't figure it out. All he knew was that Heaney used Sirrus to put a virtual man on a computer that Rodeo or one of his team used.

'Kenny, you're pretty quiet,' said Harry. 'What's up?'

'Nothing. I'm just thinking, if I meet Rodeo what do I say to him?'

'You worry about that when you meet him. First let's enjoy the show.' Digging Keanan in the ribs he grinned. 'I heard his backing singers are something special, if you catch my drift.'

Keanan noticed Harry had said 'when', not 'if' he meets him.

When Mathew received a message via the Maraca box office

that Harry from Three Rivers would be at tonight's concert he couldn't wait to tell Rodeo. Harry had always said he'd live in Rio if and when they released him.

'Well, knock me down with a feather!' Mathew said, as he put the phone down. What a reunion they were going to have tonight… He wouldn't tell Rodeo until afterwards. Yeah, let it be a big surprise.

His mind drifted back to when he first met Harry. He was sobbing his heart out. It turned out his baby grandson had died and he wanted to comfort his daughter. The prison authorities refused to give him leave on compassionate grounds. Rodeo spoke to him alone. He wasn't party to what was said, but Harry had picked himself up again and, by the looks of it, fulfilled his dream.

Keanan sat next to Harry ten rows from the front. Neither of them had ever been to a concert before. As the music started, Harry nudged Keanan.

'He's something special Kenny, something special. Not just his singing but his whole persona. I always knew he'd make good. I always knew it.'

Keanan looked at him quizzically. 'You knew him then?'

'Yeah ten years ago…watch the show.'

The concert turned out to be one of the best Mathew could remember and the atmosphere was just electric.

Right from the start the audience were determined to have a good time and, when Rodeo introduced a samba beat into his act, a cheer went up, bigger than at any concert Mathew could remember.

Mathew decided to meet Harry personally and take him back stage. Five minutes before the end of the show he walked down the aisles to row J, dodging everyone dancing the samba and even joining in a little.

There he is…my God he doesn't look a day older.

'Harry…Harry…excuse me, will you give the guy in the red shirt a nudge for me please?' he said to a lady, who had seen him trying to gain Harry's attention. Harry turned round.

'Mathew, I don't believe it! Mathew my boy.' Harry pushed his way towards the aisle and hugged Mathew like the long lost friend which he was.

'Mathew, I want you to meet someone, my grandson Kenny. Hey Kenny, come and meet Mathew.'

'That's wonderful, you have a grandson.' Mathew and Keanan shook hands.

Mathew felt a little confused. Harry's first grandson died twelve years ago while Harry was in prison. Kenny looked at least, at a guess, nineteen.

'Harry, you and Kenny are invited back stage. I know Rodeo will be absolutely delighted.'

When Rodeo came off stage Mathew pulled him to one side.

'There's someone here I think you'll want to meet.'

'Not the girl in the front row, the one with the…'

'No not the girl with the tits to die for…better than that. Turn around slowly.' Rodeo did as Mathew asked. Suddenly his eyes lit up.

'Harry, I don't believe it! Harry, you made it to Rio.' As they hugged, both men's eyes filled with tears. When they parted Harry spoke first.

'When they released me I worked my way to Rio and now I have myself a little business, legit, a diner, but that's not all. Meet my grandson Kenny. Kenny, meet my old pal Rodeo, the finest man you'll ever meet. Rodeo looked a little embarrassed as he held out his hand to Keanan.

'Hi Kenny, how you doing? Your granddad an' me are old pals. Ten years ago they locked us up together along with Mathew here. We've a lot of catching up to do. How about you both come back to our hotel and we'll celebrate our reunion?'

Back at the hotel, the manager had set aside the whole of the English pub for Rodeo and his party. Mathew made sure there wouldn't be any interruptions.

'Kenny, do you like champagne?' Keanan nodded, never having tasted champagne before.

'Harry, what about you?'

'I'll always try something new.'

'Let's celebrate properly. Bartender, how about a couple of dozen bottles of your finest champagne.'

'Right away, Señor.'

'Who's hungry?' He didn't wait for an answer. 'Bartender, can you rustle up a selection of food? Let's see…for about fifty of us?'

'Señor Rodeo, consider it done.'

Rodeo turned his attention to Harry and Keanan.

'Come and sit down over here.' They both sat down on the soft leather chairs with Rodeo and Mathew. The bartender brought over a bottle of champagne in an ice bucket and proceeded to pour.

'Before I forget,' said Harry, 'Kenny here has something important to tell you. But before he does, I have to make a confession. Kenny's not my grandson, I kind'a adopted him.' Rodeo nodded.

'If you say he's your grandson and you treat him as such, that's fine by me. Kenny, what is it you want to tell us?'

He started right at the beginning, when Heaney first employed him. Rodeo and Mathew kept exchanging glances as Keanan told his story. It wasn't until he'd finished describing Sirrus that Mathew interrupted him.

'So you produced a virtual copy of Alfredo Benando? Then Heaney used Sirrus to communicate with Carlotta so he could persuade her to do what he wanted, her thinking it's her daddy?'

'That's about it Sir.'

'Holy shit,' said Mathew. The four of them sat in silence for a few seconds.

'Harry, can you keep Kenny safe here in Rio?' asked Rodeo.

'I guess so, but our big problem is Titus. He comes in the diner pretty often.'

Mathew had his thinking face on. 'Kenny, do you have access to Sirrus?'

'Yeah, I programmed it. Only myself and Gill who worked with me on the project have access, and of course Mr Heaney.'

'Can either of them tell if you've accessed it?'

'Only if they look at the logs, but I could easily bypass them.'

'Right, you need to send an email to Heaney supposedly from Titus…' A waiter came to pour some champagne.

'We'll discuss this somewhere a little more private tomorrow,' said Mathew. Rodeo raised his glass.

'Kenny, thank you. We all owe you a great debt, but promise me you'll take care of your granddad, he's a special guy. Here's to Kenny and Harry.'

CHAPTER 17

WHEN MICHAEL HEANEY received the encrypted email from Titus he couldn't believe what he was reading. Has this guy got a death wish or what?

'Dear Michael, Before the unfortunate departure from this world of your friend Keanan, he told me all about Sirrus, even wrote some things down in an attempt to buy me off. I'm sure you wouldn't want the authorities snooping round. A one off payment of two million dollars will ensure complete security for Sirrus.'

Transfer the funds into Banco Boavista 23-33-44 6688790. Yours truly, Titus

Heaney left the building and drove towards Hot Springs Village. About five miles out from the village he pulled over and took an unregistered pay as you go cell phone out of the glove compartment. He dialled a number.

'Hello, isto é Maria Von Hind.'

'Maria, this is Michael. Mr T has let us down big time. He sent me an email, I can't go into details but I need to terminate his contract...permanently. Of course I'll pay the usual compensation.'

'Okay Michael, consider it done. Adeus.'

He took the SIM card out of the phone, snapped it in half and tossed the pieces into a bush. A mile along the highway he threw the phone into one of the lakes.

Maria thought to herself. *This is a job I'll do my self. It seems such a shame to waste such a talented lover. Why shouldn't I enjoy myself one more time? At least he'll die happy.*

He suspected nothing, after all he and Maria went back a long way. Okay, she was just using him, but what the hell. She's a pretty good screw even though she's getting on a little and, as he'd said before, many a good tune's been played on an old fiddle.

Titus lay naked on the king-size bed enjoying a post coital cigarette. Maria came out of the bathroom. He spoke without looking at her.

'Maria, you taste better with age. I swear your pussy's sweeter than a teenage virgin's.'

'That is a compliment coming from you, Titus, 'cause I have a good idea how many teenage virgins you've fucked.'

Something wasn't right. Maria had been going over the phone call from Heaney in her mind. Then she had it.

'Titus, have you ever used a computer?'

'Aw don't embarrass me, you know I can't even read or write.'

'So, have you ever sent an email to anyone?'

'I don't even know how to turn one of them things on.'

'Titus, you like my sweet pussy. You want another taste?' He moved to open her legs. 'First I need to use the bathroom.'

She locked the door, turned on the shower, then dialled a number on her cell phone. It rang for about thirty seconds.

'Hello.'

'Our client didn't send that email. The fuckwit can't even read or write, let alone turn on a computer.'

'He could have paid someone else to do it. I can't take the chance. Terminate his contract permanently and when you've done that call me. I may require your services on another matter.'

Maria Von Hind liked to tell herself she didn't have a heart. Money, or was it power? Nothing else mattered. Ever since leaving the slums of Brasilia she'd lived by that rule. Now, for the first time, it looked like her heart would rule her head.

She unlocked the door and looked across to the bed. Titus had gone, he'd dressed and gone.

'What the fuck you playing at Titus, you fuckwit? You'll get us both killed.'

* * *

Alfredo checked Rodeo's web site to see where the Tour headed next.

'Rio De Janeiro, here I come,' he said to himself. His excitement about seeing Carlotta again visibly showed. His whole body language changed, even the way he walked.

He pondered on the best way to travel. Flying and airports are way too dangerous, too many people and prying eyes. My only option to arrive there safely is to go by ship. Maybe a freighter?

He worked his passage aboard the freighter Perla Del Mar. The ship, far from being a pearl, smelt more like a rancid oyster and looked similar to how he imagined a Soviet labour camp once looked. Conditions were tough, dirty and basic.

She was due to dock in Rio on the eve of Rodeo's last concert at Maraca. Being at sea gave him plenty of time to mull over who it was that had killed his three colleagues and attempted to kill him.

Before he could answer who, he had to figure out why. The Vatican enforcer's role generally consisted of endless reports on individual priests and bishops, which occasionally resulted in having to use heavy-handed tactics against an individual deemed a threat to the Church of Rome, either by their teachings or actions. The enforcers acted against many priests with paedophile tendencies. Unfortunately, many more had gone undetected by the church until too late. Acting against a celebrity like Rodeo the way they did set an unusual precedent. Nothing made sense. He was missing something.

Supposing, he assumed, the decision to act against Rodeo came from the Vatican through Cardinal Biloweiki, the Pope's representative in the United States? Supposing… Then he heard a news flash on the radio. He listened to the unfolding news of the attempted assassination of Pope Barnabus in his native Philippines purportedly by a Muslim separatist. As he listened he became angry. What were they doing? Where the fuck was his security?

Instinctively he knew his predicament was somehow linked. When the conclave had elected Barnabus there were many rumblings of discontent from the conservative wing of the Church, even rumours of an impending split.

All of a sudden the answers he'd searched for stared him full in the face. The four of them all formed part of the Pope's personal bodyguard when he performed public duties away from the Vatican, like in the Philippines.

Without them Barnabus became more vulnerable, as had been proved. If the elite bodyguards are all dead, they couldn't protect him. So now he knew why. That only left the question, who?

After the ship's purser paid him off and returned his revolver, he decided to take a cab downtown.

'Americano, from the cruise ship?' the cab driver asked happily.

'Yeah you could say that. Tell me, is Rodeo still in town?'

'Si señor, nenhuns bilhetes vendeu toda.'

'No tickets eh? Where's he staying?'

'Nenhum compreenda señor.'

'Rodeo... que hotel?'

'Ahh Hotel Sofitel. You go señor?'

'Satisfaça sim.'

The Hotel Sofitel looked pretty impressive to Alfredo as he sat opposite, on the famous Ipanema beach. Carlotta, his daughter, his pride and joy, played somewhere inside.

'I have to see her,' he said. 'It might be my last opportunity.' Whoever tried to kill him would probably be watching and waiting, knowing he'd want to see his daughter. 'Maybe I'll try my luck at the hotel casino tonight, at least it'll get me in there,' he said to himself. 'In the meantime I have to eat.' He hailed a cab on the promenade.

'Do you know any American diners, you know that serve good wholesome American food?'

'American Diner? Si señor. I take you.'

He walked in and sat down, one of only five customers.

'Kenny,' said Harry, 'can you take that order please?' Keanan walked towards Alfredo who was sitting with his back to him.

'What can I get you Sir?' he asked without looking up from his pad.

'Do you serve southern fried chicken and beans, just like my mother used to make?'

'Sure,' said Keanan. 'Best southern fried this side of Texas.'

He looked up and smiled at Alfredo. Keanan recognised him instantly. Holy mother in hell! He beat a hasty retreat to the kitchen. He pulled Harry to one side.

'Harry, the guy I just served – it's him.'

'Who's him?'

'The guy I made a virtual copy of, you know, to use with Sirrus.' Harry put a hand on Keenan's shoulder.

'Okay, he might look like him but there must be hundreds of guys around the world who look like him.'

'No Harry, it's him, one hundred percent. Even his voice is identical.'

'Okay let's feed him up. I'll call Mathew an' find out what to do.'

Keanan put the southern chicken and beans on the table. 'Enjoy your meal.'

As he turned away Titus walked in. They both just stopped and stared at each other. They stood only four paces apart but Keanan felt rooted to the spot. Titus spoke first.

'You ain't no fucking ghost. No one, no one makes a fool out of me. The Boss thinks you're dead so you might as well be. I've had it with you, adeus you spotty little fucker.' He pulled out a gun that looked big enough to kill an elephant. Keanan closed his eyes, accepting his fate. A single gunshot reverberated around the diner like a thunderbolt.

Keanan felt nothing. He opened his eyes, expecting to find himself in Heaven or the other place. To his amazement Titus lay on the floor, still holding his gun. He had a single bullet wound in his forehead. Blood seeped from the wound like tomato ketchup dipping from a beef burger. Harry beckoned Alfredo into the back room.

'Quickly, so no one can see you from the street,' he said.

Keanan followed them. The other diners, not wanting to be witnesses to the death of Titus, hurriedly left.

'Thank you for saving my Grandson,' said Harry as he held his hand out to Alfredo. 'But why did you do it? Are you a policeman?' Alfredo briefly smiled.

'No, I'm not a policeman, at least not in the sense you mean. Only a policeman for God.'

'For God eh?' said Harry 'Well, he should be mighty proud of you today.'

'I hope so,' said Alfredo, remembering the sixth commandment. 'I have to get to the Sofitel Hotel. What's the best way from here?'

'A cab's too dangerous under the circumstances,' said Harry, thinking out loud. Keanan jumped in.

'Harry, the Sofitel Hotel. That's where Rodeo's staying.'

'Are you referring to Rodeo, the rock star?' said Alfredo.

'Sure, he's a friend of ours,' said Harry. Alfredo could hardly believe his ears.

'I'm a friend of Rodeo too,' he said excitedly. 'He's looking after my daughter.'

Harry interrupted. 'That must be little Carlotta.'

'You know her?' said Alfredo in surprise.

'Sure, we met her just the other night,' said Harry.

'How is she?' said Alfredo desperate for news.

'Oh she's fine,' said Harry 'except she's missing you.' He turned to Keanan.

'Kenny, I'll deal with things here. You take him to Rodeo, use the bus, I'll phone ahead and let him know to expect you.'

'No,' said Alfredo, 'it's too dangerous to phone.'

'Okay, as you wish,' said Harry.

CHAPTER 18

MATHEW WAS finishing checking the final security arrangements for the following night's concert when the phone rang.

'Mathew Lopez,' he said as he picked up the receiver.

'Mr Lopez, this is hotel reception. We have two people here who wish to talk to you. They say it is extremely urgent. Only one would give his name, he said tell Mr Lopez it's Kenny.'

'What does Kenny look like?' said Mathew. 'He looks about sixteen, skinny and his face is spotty.'

'Okay,' said Mathew, 'that's Kenny. Keep them there and I'll be right down to meet them.' He put the receiver down. 'Shit,' he said to himself, 'what's gone wrong now?'

He walked out of the elevator into the lobby. Mathew saw Alfredo with Keanan.

'What the fuck are you doing here?' he said to Alfredo. 'Quick, into the elevator before someone sees you. You should know better.'

* * *

Maria Von Hind knew the places Titus liked to hang out. When Titus walked into the American Diner she watched from a car parked across the street. She was about to join him in the diner when a shot rang out. She stayed where she was. A few people left but not Titus. Then she saw Keanan with Alfredo Benando.

'Meu Deus é Benando com o fucker pequeno manchado,' she said to herself. 'Você é suposto estar inoperante.' Leaving her car she followed them on foot.

Carlotta couldn't believe it when she saw Mathew leaving the elevator with her father and Kenny.

'Daddy! Daddy!' She rushed towards him. He picked her up in

his arms and held her. Tears filled Alfredo's eyes. Mathew watched and wondered what it was like to have a mother or father, or a child. He could only really imagine.

While Carlotta and Alfredo became reacquainted, Keanan told Mathew what happened at the diner. Mathew looked at him in disbelief.

'You say he shot Titus with one shot and hit him right between the eyes?'

'Yes sir,' said Keanan. Mathew thought for a moment.

'He ain't no small time heavy. I'm going to find out who he really is and who he's working for.'

'Carlotta, sweetie,' said Mathew, putting on his best pretty please voice. 'I need to speak to your daddy for a few minutes in private.'

'That's okay,' she said. 'I know you want to talk about grown up stuff. I'll wait outside. Don't be too long.'

'There's a girl,' said Mathew.

'What the fuck's going on?' said Mathew to Alfredo. 'You ain't been straight with me or Rodeo.'

'Okay, but you're not gong to like what you hear,' said Alfredo.

'Let me be the judge of what I like and don't like,' said Mathew.

'Okay. My name is Alfredo Benando and I work as a Vatican enforcer. Most of my time is spent bringing errant priests back into line, if you follow my drift. Putting the frighteners on Rodeo was a little unusual.'

'Who gave you the order to do that?' said Mathew.

'Our orders always come with the blessing of our Holy Father, but in reality they usually come from a senior cardinal. In this case it was Cardinal Biloweiki.'

'Who the fuck is he?' said Mathew.

'Not so quick,' said Alfredo calmly. 'I also have another role.'

'Yeah and what's that,' answered Mathew. 'Chief executioner?'

'No, I'm one of the Pope's body guards,' said Alfredo, 'along with three of my associates who are now dead.' Mathew looked at him as if all of this were unreal.

Alfredo continued. 'Officially we don't exist. We all have our own private lives, jobs, homes and families. Only some senior cardinals are aware of us and our role as enforcers, but even they don't know our identities, only how to contact us, and no one except the Holy Father himself is aware of our dual role as Papal bodyguards. One thing I can guarantee, if we had been there, in the Philippines, he wouldn't now be lying in hospital seriously injured.'

Mathew interjected. 'So what you're saying is someone wanted you four out of the way?'

'Yes, exactly,' said Alfredo. 'But even worse, it means the attempted assassination was almost certainly an inside job.'

'This is heavy shit,' said Mathew. 'What do you know about a man called Michael Heaney?'

'Do you mean Senator Heaney, the champion of the right wing Christians?' said Alfredo.

'You got it in one,' replied Mathew. 'I'll let Keanan here tell you about him, he used to work for him.'

Keanan told Alfredo about how he produced a virtual replica of him for Heaney and how, with Sirrus, Heaney could infiltrate any computer in the world using GPS. Alfredo sat in stunned silence for about a minute while he collected his thoughts.

'I have to speak to Carlotta,' said Alfredo.

Mathew nodded and called the little girl back in.

'Carlotta,' said Alfredo, 'when I was away did you see me or speak to me on a computer?'

'Yes of course, don't you remember? You told me not to tell anyone, not even Laura or Rodeo. You said your life depended on it.' Alfredo let out a big sigh before he answered.

'It wasn't me on the computer, sweetie. It was someone pretending to be me.'

'But Daddy,' she said, almost in tears, 'it was you.' Alfredo beckoned he to sit on his lap.

'I know it looked and sounded like me, but it wasn't. Look, it's alright, you're not in trouble, you weren't to know it wasn't me.'

Alfredo gave her a squeeze. 'Did he ask you to do anything for him?' said Alfredo as he wiped her eyes with a tissue.

'No Daddy, he didn't ask me to do anything.'

'Must have been because I bluffed him about the ten hours. He couldn't take the chance,' said Keanan.

Mathew looked very concerned. 'I don't like it. I don't like it one little bit. How do I know he's not watching us right now on some computer around here? Keanan, you said he'd eventually find out that the ten hours was a bluff. Is there any way you can immobilise Sirrus? You know, stick a spanner in the works or something?'

'Sure I can do that,' said Keanan, 'but then he'll know I'm not dead.'

'Are you prepared to take that risk?' asked Mathew. 'Titus is dead, you can stay with Harry at the diner till all this blows over. Rodeo will make sure you have enough money.'

'You guys and Harry, especially Harry, you're like my family. I don't need money to stick a spanner in the works. It'll be kind of cool, Heaney knowing I'm not dead and that I put one over on him,' said Keanan, relishing the thought.

Alfredo sat listening to Mathew and Keanan then made a suggestion.

'Look, I'm not a technical man, but instead of putting a spanner in the works could we not switch it round and use it on Heaney to find out what's going on and who's involved?'

'Is it possible?' said Mathew to Keanan.

'Sure it's possible. Might take a while, but I can do it and he won't know I'm doing it.'

Alfredo leant forward. 'I'm sorry to spoil your two finger salute to Mr Heaney, but I think this way will be more valuable.' Mathew nodded in agreement.

* * *

Maria Von Hind made herself inconspicuous in the hotel lobby. Keanan left the hotel alone with one thought on his mind: settling the score with Heaney.

She followed him out as he made his way towards the bus terminal. On the bus Keanan imagined the pained and anguished look on Heaney's face when he realised Sirrus had been used against him.

Maria Von Hind stayed on the bus as Keanan alighted near to the diner. How am I going to kill o fucker pequeno manchado? Something painful, something Titus would have enjoyed.

CHAPTER 19

THE PEOPLE of Rio took Rodeo to their hearts. Somehow they managed to acquire an old open-top Route Master bus that had once been driven round the streets of London. Instead of being red they'd painted it yellow and blue, the colours of the Brazilian soccer team.

Rodeo stood on the top deck with his band and backing singers waving at the crowds, all trying to catch a glimpse of Rodeo. Mathew stood at his side.

'Boss,' he said, trying to gain Rodeo's attention. 'Boss, we'll be arriving at Maraca in about five minutes and we need to be ready to make a dash.'

'Okay I'll be ready.' He looked at Mathew. 'You worry too much.'

'Maybe I do,' said Mathew thoughtfully, 'maybe I do, but I have a bad feeling about tonight. I just want to make sure we're there on time and everyone's safe.'

Laura sat with Douglas in his dressing room massaging his shoulders, trying to relax him.

'Why do I put myself through this?' he said. 'I must be crazy. I hope that bus gets them back here on time. The engine didn't sound too healthy to me. How can I keep a hundred thousand fans entertained…?'

'Don't forget the millions watching on TV…' said Laura, impishly.

'Who's watching on TV?' said Douglas, suddenly beginning to panic.

'Didn't I tell you? Now the Papal tour's cancelled, broadcasters all over the world are taking a feed from tonight's show.' He looked at her pleadingly.

'Tell me you're joking, please. I can take a joke.'

'Sorry, it's true,' said Laura with a hint of tease in her voice. 'Just tune into all that loving energy coming from the audience and, oh… don't forget mine.' She kissed him on the lips as she said it. A knock on the door interrupted them.

'Ten minute call, ten minute call.'

* * *

'Harry, come and sit down. Show's about to start.'

'Okay I'm coming, I'm making us some popcorn.' A couple of minutes later Harry walked into the living room above the diner with two huge bags of popcorn.

'Turn it up a little, I can't hear it properly,' said Harry.

'That's because it hasn't started yet,' replied Keanan.

Just as Keanan spoke the band struck up and Douglas ran onto the stage.

'Hey, there's the Reverend,' said Harry. 'I like him, he's a good guy, a real man of God.'

Douglas brought the mic up to his face to speak.

'Noite boa Rio De Janeiro, good evening Rio. Obrigado convidando nos a sua cidade maravilhosa. We love you all and tonight is all about love and music. Let's show the world how to love and how to rock.'

Just then the TV and all the lights in the diner and upstairs apartment went off.

'Fuck it,' said Harry. 'What a time to have a power cut.'

'Maybe it's just a blown fuse,' said Keanan.

'I'll go and check,' said Harry. 'I know where to look. Now, where's the fucking torch?'

'Stay where you are,' said a female voice. Keanan recognised the voice but couldn't place it.

'Old man,' she said, 'you can go but the spotty little fucker stays here.'

Adjusting his eyes to the dark, Harry could just make out a figure to his right, about eight feet away. Turning towards the door he made out he was leaving.

Before she had a chance to react, in one quick movement he swiveled round and charged head down towards her, catching her in the diaphragm with his head.

'Kenny get out! Go!' he shouted.

Keanan hesitated before running out the door and down the stairs into the diner. Knowing the diner door was locked and bolted, he threw himself at it, half expecting to bounce off. The glass smashed and he ended up sprawled across the pavement.

Picking himself up he heard a plaintive scream of pain from Harry, as Maria Von Hind twisted her twelve-inch blade into his abdomen. With tears streaming down his face, he ran in the direction of Maraca.

Keeping to the shadows and alleyways he made the darkness his friend. He ran towards what he hoped would be safety. Suddenly he remembered where he'd heard the female voice – his lawyer, Maria Von Hind. He shuddered to think he nearly told her everything.

Maria Von Hind placed a pan of oil on the stove, lit the gas underneath, then turned on the other three gas taps. Five minutes after she left, a massive explosion burnt the diner to the ground.

Keanan turned to look as he heard the blast. Flames shot skyward, nearly a hundred feet into the air. He knew she'd look for him and probably wasn't far away. How far is Maraca? He wasn't sure. Then he heard the sound of the music carrying through the thin night air, sounding pure and almost holy. Only the sounds of police and fire sirens racing towards the diner interrupted the music from Maraca.

With renewed confidence he picked up his pace and headed towards the music. At one point he must have been only ten feet from Maria Von Hind. She didn't see him hiding in the shadows as she drove past.

Was it her? Keanan didn't know, but he felt a cold shiver run down his spine as the car turned the corner in front of him. He saw the same car four more times on his way to Maraca.

'It must be her. It can't be far now,' he said to himself.

A street lamp at the end of the alley silhouetted Maria Von Hind perfectly. It was her. He stopped, paralysed by fear.

'The old man is dead.' She spat the words at him. 'It's your fault. It should have been you. But at least you won't have to feel guilty about it for very long, because I'm going to put you out of your misery. First I'm going to shoot you. While you're still alive and writhing in agony I'm going to cut off your two-inch dick, você fucker enfrentado manchado pathetic.'

While she spoke, Keanan thought he heard Harry's voice. 'Pick up the brick that's by your feet and throw it at her with all your might.'

Raising her gun, she took aim and pulled the trigger just as Keanan bent down. Picking up the brick he threw it at her, all in one movement. The bullet missed. Caught off guard, the brick struck her on the head with a tremendous force that even shocked Keanan. She fell to the ground as if struck by a poleaxe. Picking up the gun, he held it to her head.

'You fucking bitch, you murdered the only person that has ever shown me any love.' With his finger on the trigger he wanted vengeance for Harry. As tears streamed down his face he heard Harry speak.

'Leave her be, Kenny. Killing her won't bring me back, leave her be.'

He pressed the muzzle of the silencer into her temple till it made an indent. Her eyes opened and blankly stared at him. In panic he dropped the gun and ran, not stopping until he arrived at Maraca.

When he arrived at the stadium all the entrances were shut. He sat and waited for the show to end. Eventually the large exit gates opened. Keanan made his way inside. Unchallenged, he walked up the stairs to the top of one of the stands.

Rodeo talked to the audience, who nearly all held lighted candles.

'This next song is one I wrote only yesterday after I bumped into an old friend of mine, here in Rio. We met in jail over ten years ago. His name is Harry and he inspired me to write this song. Thanks Harry if you're listening.'

The stage lights dimmed around him leaving him standing under a single spot. The rhythm section started to play. After four bars Rodeo joined in with his guitar and vocals. Keanan felt a lump in his throat as he listened intently to the lyrics.

> *Harry Day was a young man with an old soul*
> *Who was sentenced to life without hope.*
> *The only crime Harry Day ever committed*
> *Was a real strong aversion to soap.*
>
> *Harry Day was a drifter in Kentucky*
> *Who one day was in the wrong shady place*
> *The only witness to the shooting at the drugstore*
> *She remembered the wrong fucking face*
> (Chorus)
> *Harry Day was the angel of sing sing*
> *Took the rookies under his wings*
> *Explained that life behind the bars of Thee Rivers*
> *Would prepare us for far better things*
>
> *Harry Day heard me sing in the shower*
> *Told me God had given me a gift*
> *Helped me plan a concert in the library*
> *His wings sure gave me a lift*

'Everyone please join me with the chorus,' said Rodeo.
> (Chorus)
> *Harry Day was the angel of sing sing*
> *Took the rookies under his wings*
> *Explained that life behind the bars of Three Rivers*
> *Would prepare us for far better things*

Harry Day lost a grandson to Heaven
Taken before Harry was set free
Just a baby still walking in diapers
All Harry wanted was to bounce him on his knee
(Chorus)
Harry Day was the angel of sing sing
Took the rookies under his wings
Explained that life behind the bars of Three Rivers
Would prepare us for far better things

Harry Day now lives a life of freedom
And still helps young rookies find their wings
I never knew a man with more love to offer
Except the man we like to call the King of Kings

(Chorus)
Harry Day was the angel of sing sing
Took the rookies under his wings
Explained that life behind the bars of Three Rivers
Would prepare us for far better things
Harry Day was the angel of sing sing
Took the rookies under his wings
Explained that life behind the bars of Three Rivers
Would prepare us for far better things

Keanan screamed at him from the top of the stand. 'Rodeo, he's dead, Harry's dead, Harry's fucking dead.'

There was no way he was going to be heard above the applause. He ran down the steps of the stand. Where he was going he didn't know, he didn't care, he had to see Rodeo.

'Não assim rapidamente,' said the security guard, as Keanan nearly bowled him over. 'Onde você pensa de você está indo?'

'I have to see Ro...' he paused for a second, realising it would be a waste of time to say he wanted to see Rodeo.

'I have to see Mathew Lopez. Please, I must see him.'

'Você quer ver Senior Lopez, O que é seu nome?' said the guard.

'My name,' said Keanan, feeling a little frustrated. 'My name is Keanan, Keanan.' He emphasised his name the second time. 'You got that?'

The guard spoke into his radio. 'Hello controle. Eu tenho um homem aqui quem queira ver o Senior Lopez, ele digo que seu nome é Keanan.'

At least he got my name right, thought Keanan. After about two minutes there was a garbled reply on the guard's radio.

'Si senior,' said the guard into his radio. He turned to Keanan.

'Siga-me por favor.'

Keanan did as he was asked.

* * *

Harry's ashes were laid to rest in a small picturesque cemetery north of Rio. Sixty two people, many of them Harry's customers, stood at the graveside to pay their respects. Rodeo stood with his arm around Keanan while Douglas addressed the mourners.

'Brothers and sisters, we are all gathered here today to pay our respects to a man we all loved. Harry Day was an example to us all. Even in prison he became a beacon of hope to many who were incarcerated there. Some he taught to read and write, while he encouraged others to find and use their talents to create a better life for themselves. For many of them it was probably the first time in their lives that they had experienced any kind of love. Then, after nearly thirty years, he was free and living his dream here in Rio. You know, Harry didn't believe in religion or God or Jesus Christ. He believed in the power of love and he believed that it could transcend death itself. That's why he gave up his life for his grandson. There is no greater sacrifice a man can make.'

The words of the eulogy were going round in Keanan's head as the Boeing 747 with Rodeo's entourage on board flew to Paris. Davey sat next to him in the window seat. He hoped to see the Eiffel Tower, but at the moment he could only see ocean.

Every now and then he spotted a ship and a surge of excitement flowed through his body. He felt comforted to know the plane wasn't the only human vessel on the planet. He turned to Keanan.

'Why did God make the oceans so big?'

Keanan, his concentration broken, frowned.

'How the fuck should I know?'

As he spoke, Laura walked past. She stopped in her tracks.

'Hey Davey, go and sit up front in the cockpit with the captain, he'll teach you how to fly the plane.'

'Thank you Laura, thank you.'

She sat down next to Keanan.

'It hurts doesn't it?' she said, with her hand on his shoulder. 'It's not easy coming to terms with how much we love someone who's no longer with us. Young Davey's on his own – no parents and desperate for news of his sister. He needs all the love he can get. We all do, and you know what? Love is something we can all create and give freely. It costs nothing and the supply is endless. When we create it we feel great and so does everyone around us. Harry knew that, that's what made him so special. Despite spending so much of his life in prison, he left the earth a rich man with the one thing you can take with you, love. I've been thinking, all of us, you, me, Douglas, Mathew and Alfredo, we all wanted in varying degrees to hurt Rodeo. But he never defended himself, all he's ever done is shown us love. Isn't that a …'

'What about Heaney?' interrupted Keanan. 'How the fuck can I love him? I have to stand up to him, I have to assassinate him or something.'

'Then you're the same as him.' Without warning she wrapped her arms around him, pulling him to her. She kissed him on the lips, a long passionate kiss. Her tongue explored every cavity of his mouth. He felt her breasts pushing against his chest through her thin white cotton blouse.

'What feels best,' Laura asked, as the clinch broke, 'physical loving or your hate for Heaney?' Keanan looked at her as if she was mad.

'There's no contest. But when all's said and done, Heaney is still around and he's going to hurt a lot of people.'

'May I join you?' said Rodeo. Keanan moved to the window seat, allowing Laura to move along one and Rodeo to sit in the aisle seat.

'I don't want to panic you, but Davey's flying the plane,' said Rodeo with a mock worried expression. Then he addressed Keanan.

'Laura's right. Sometimes we become so focused on revenge and getting even or stopping someone, that we lose sight of love and loving. But love is the most powerful positive there is, so if we follow that path it's impossible to lose. If you go off on a personal vendetta against Heaney you lose, no matter what the outcome. But if we stick together, sure in what we do, true to our beliefs in love, we might just create a little piece of Heaven on Earth. What do you say?'

Keanan turned away and looked out the window. Under his breath he mouthed the words, 'I hope you're right.'

CHAPTER 20

CASTEL GANDOLFO, the Papal summer residence, overlooked Lake Albano. Barnabus loved the view. He particularly enjoyed the unspoilt ancient woodland on the lake's southern shore. Somehow it reminded him of his native Philippines. Only twelve days had passed since the assassination attempt. God spared him, of that he was sure, but for what purpose? He didn't know. His aid handed him a card from a well-wisher. Over two hundred thousand cards arrived from all over the world. He'd asked his aids to pick out a few for him to read.

On the front of the card was a hand-drawn picture of the Virgin Mary, the message inside written in French. He translated as he read aloud.

'My dear Holy Father, since I heard the terrible news on the television I have prayed for you everyday, but I have a confession to make. Part of my reason for praying is selfish. You see, I was due to have a private audience with you in Paris when you visited France.

Nearly two years ago a man attacked me and also killed my friend. I believe Our Lady looked after me and nursed me back to life. If she would do that for me she will certainly do the same for you. It would have been the very best day of my life to meet you.

Signed your faithful servant Edith Llitjos, age fifteen and three quarters.'

Barnabus smiled as he closed the card. God has spoken to me, he thought. I will go to France and continue my tour. If I die during the tour so what? At least I will die doing God's will.

* * *

Rodeo had originally planned for the Paris concerts to take place in front of an eighty thousand crowd at the Stade De France. The

Papal visit put paid to that. Rodeo had to be content with a stage built on private land on the outskirts of the city. They had permission for a maximum of fifty thousand people. Because of this, tickets were in short supply and, with the added problem of no TV coverage, they sold at more than a thousand Euros each on Ebay.

Edith Llitjos was determined to see him. She had all his albums and listened to his music constantly on her MP3 player. There were two problems. Firstly, Monsieur and Madame Llitjos would not entertain the idea and, secondly, the concert was billed for over-eighteens only. Then she heard that Pope Barnabus was coming to France after all. God had surely answered her prayers.

She phoned Father Jacques. 'Le père Jaques ceci est Edith. Vous avez entendu les nouvelles. Notre père saint vient en France après tout, n'est pas ceci merveilleux? Pouvons nous aller à Paris le voir? She didn't stop for breath.

Father Jacques could not resist her enthusiasm to see the Holy Father. 'Pas aussi rapidement jeune dame,' he said. 'Oui, si vos parents conviennent je vous porterai à Paris.'

'Hooray! Father Jacques is taking me to Paris.'

Now she could formulate a plan to see Rodeo in concert.

CHAPTER 21

'OLD IRON KNICKERS really came up trumps when she chose this place,' said Rodeo as their car drew up in front of the Chateau. Mathew nodded as if in agreement, but had a worried look on his face.

Château De Montvillargenne, situated twenty-two miles north of Paris in serene countryside, looked perfect. To Rodeo it looked like a fairytale castle, but for Mathew it shouted security nightmare. He'd managed to set up a security cordon around the perimeter with the help of the local gendarmerie. Inside the grounds were twenty-four hour patrols with guard dogs. All ground floor doors and windows were specially fitted with alarms, while security guards watched the stairs and lifts leading to the rooms and suites occupied by Rodeo's entourage.

'I just hope I can keep everyone safe here,' said Mathew.

'You worry too much,' said Rodeo, while he opened the car's trunk to allow the porters to take his luggage. 'What's going to happen in a beautiful place like this?'

'Don't tempt fate boss,' said Mathew, then he saw the look on Rodeo's face. 'Alright, I know what you are going to say, but I love you and I care about you.'

'I know you do,' said Rodeo. 'If only the whole world were like you and I, eh Mathew?'

'One day boss, one day.'

Later that evening Rodeo enjoyed a stroll, taking in the scents of the roses from the neat beds that flowered all around the chateau. The eternal optical illusion made the sun look very close and very big as it set. It all seemed very calm and quite serene.

For the sniper hidden in undergrowth nearly a mile away, unseen and unheard, it silhouetted Rodeo perfectly. Unfortunately for the sniper, Rodeo wasn't the target. The sniper would have to wait a little longer for his target to appear.

Rodeo's thoughts were interrupted by Alfredo running toward him. The sniper smiled to himself as he spotted his target through the powerful Russian telescopic lens.

'Have you heard the news? It's a miracle!' Alfredo could barely contain his excitement and didn't wait for an answer. 'Barnabus is going to continue with his tour. He is due to arrive in Paris tomorrow.' Then he suddenly realised that maybe Rodeo wouldn't be so enthused by the news. 'Of course I understand if you...'

Rodeo interrupted. 'No, that's great news, it really is. I'm happy for Barnabus, I'm really happy. My concern is for you and Carlotta. I know you're going to want to go and protect him because that's your job, and whoever wanted him dead hasn't gone away. I'm right, aren't I?' Alfredo nodded.

'I have to go now, Rodeo. Thanks for all you've done for Carlotta and me.'

'She's staying here with us, right?' said Rodeo, not sure what Alfredo had planned.

'Well no,' said Alfredo, worried at what Rodeo's reaction would be. 'You see,' he said cagily, 'everyman and his dog, including Heaney, knows she's here and they probably figured out I'm here too. This place is beautiful but it's not secure. She'll be safer somewhere else.'

'I guess you're right,' said Rodeo reluctantly. 'We'll miss you both, you know that. Have you spoken to Mathew?' Rodeo hoped that if anyone could find a good reason for them not to go, Mathew could.

'No, I hate saying goodbyes. I was hoping you'd tell everyone,' said Alfredo.

'And save you the trouble,' said Rodeo. He could have kicked himself for making that comment, but he genuinely felt disappointed and afraid for both of them. 'I'm sorry, I didn't mean to sound...'

'It's all right. You're right, I should say goodbye to everyone and thank them.'

He turned with Rodeo towards the Chateau.

'Perfect,' the sniper said to himself as he pulled the trigger. Alfredo didn't feel a thing as the minute micro chip entered his bottom, leaving just a tiny red mark as evidence of the invasive object.

*   *   *

Carlotta sulked all the way to the convent of the Sisters of Charity in Saint-Omer. She didn't want to go. Alfredo tried his best to explain the situation to her.

'You know the men that want to do bad things to me?' She didn't answer, so he continued. 'They tried to kill our Holy Father Pope Barnabus. I have never told you before, but it is my job to protect him.'

Concerned they might be followed, he pulled into a farm lane, coming to a sudden stop behind a hedge. Nothing passed. He breathed a sigh of relief and turned to Carlotta.

'They know we are with Rodeo. It's too dangerous to stay there. If we did there's every chance they would try to use you to get to me. This way you are hidden from them, you are safe and I can try to protect Barnabus.' He saw her bottom lip quiver and tears form in her eyes. Nobody ever told him being a father would be this tough. It felt like his whole heart was being wrenched from his body.

The convent wasn't at all like Carlotta expected. The sisters weren't all old and wrinkly. It didn't smell musty and the atmosphere around the convent seemed to be quite happy and jolly. Maybe it wouldn't be so bad after all. Alfredo spoke to her before he left.

'You know my work is dangerous. If anything happens to me I have made arrangements for you to be adopted by Rodeo. Do as the sisters tell you and as soon as Barnabus is safe I will come for you.'

They hugged each other closely before Alfredo broke away. He didn't turn around as he walked down the corridor to the rear entrance because he didn't want her to see the tears streaming down his face.

* * *

Edith Llitjos sat in the audience at the temporary concert arena. Her friend, Henri, sat next to her. The band took their positions on stage. She could barely contain her excitement. *This is definitely the best day ever*, she thought.

Henri looked at her and smiled. If it wasn't for his sister, who she bore an uncanny resemblance to, letting her use her driving license as ID and Henri agreeing to accompany her, she wouldn't have been able to make it. As far as Father Jacques was concerned, she was safely tucked up in bed back at their hotel while he attended a reception for Barnabus.

Lots of her girlfriends fancied Henri. His Gaelic good looks turned many young girls' heads. He could have almost any girl he wanted, so why didn't he have a girlfriend? Then the penny dropped.

The audience, encouraged by Douglas, clapped in time with the band. A huge crane lowered Rodeo onto the stage while the set erupted in a huge explosion of colourful fireworks spelling out the word 'amour'.

Edith found the whole spectacle mesmerising. Everything looked and sounded so much better than she ever expected. She adored the music, Rodeo's voice, the atmosphere. The spirituality of the occasion, which was something she hadn't expected, lifted the whole event to a new level. The way Rodeo fused explicit sex with his theme of love was so beautiful.

She thought about his words as he chatted with the audience.

'All we need to do is choose love, every time, and you know we have that choice. It's up to us; it's always our choice, our responsibility. It makes no difference what someone else has done to us or what we've been through, or what we want from a situation. If you choose love, you and the whole world will always be a winner. They'll be no losers and we'll be creating a better place for our children.'

Her mind drifted. What if Philippe Luquet had chosen love? He wouldn't have attacked her. If his parents had shown him love…if she had chosen love and not revenge… She thought of Philippe's simplistic picture of sunshine, blue sky and a loving family. Love is simple, so why do we have to make it so complicated?

Rodeo launched into a song called 'Love 'n Life'. Edith knew it well, but upon hearing it live the words took on a new meaning. A tear rolled down her cheek. Henri asked her if she was alright. She nodded enthusiastically.

After the concert, Rodeo felt unusually tired.

'Mathew, I'm going to turn in for the night. Apologise to our guests for me.'

'Sure boss,' said Mathew. 'I won't be far behind you, must be all the traveling.'

'Give me the keys Mat, I'll drive myself,' said Rodeo.

'Is that wise boss? Let me send a couple of the security guys with you.'

'Mat, I'll be fine. I just need some time on my own and driving relaxes me, gives me time to think.'

*   *   *

Shutters ensured no moonlight entered through the two large windows. Carlotta woke, sensing someone in the room with her. Her eyes strained to see through the darkness. All the usual shadowy suspects hid around the room. The ogre's face on the curtain, the wild horse by the dressing table the… Then she saw a figure standing at the foot of her bed.

'Sister Maria, is that you?' The figure did not respond.

Fear took over. She wanted to jump out of bed and run to the door, but she couldn't move. Instead, she pulled the duvet over herself and closed her eyes. Then she curled up into a little ball and instinctively put her thumb into her mouth for comfort, like she used to do as a baby.

Suddenly, as the figure pulled the duvet off the bed, she overcame her fear. Jumping off the bed, she made a dash for the door. Desperately she tried to open it but the handle wouldn't turn. She turned round to face her attacker. Before she could scream, a hand clamped over her mouth and dragged her back to the bed. Desperately she tried to bite the hand but there was too much pressure. As she choked, the attacker gagged her with a piece of cloth. She wanted to be sick and found it hard to breathe.

She shook with fear as the attacker tied her hands behind her back. Then her legs were pulled apart and her feet tied to the bed posts. Lying on the bed, helpless, she closed her eyes as she felt an object invade her most private part. She tried to shout out, 'I don't like it, please stop, it really hurts...' But no words could come out.

She started to count the angels which suddenly became visible. One, two three, four, five... As she reached three hundred and forty-five, the attacker held a pillow over her head. Life slowly left her little violated body. She felt strangely calm as the warm, dazzling white light from the angels engulfed her.

* * *

'Time to get up Carlotta,' said Sister Teresa playfully, opening the shutters. The sunshine poured into the room through the grey framed windows.

'Carlotta, come on, it's a beautiful day and breakfast is ready. Carlotta, stop playing games. I'll tickle you then you'll wake.'

She pulled back the duvet that covered her. Expecting the little girl to scream at the threat of being tickled, she was totally unprepared for the sight that greeted her.

'Mon Dieu, mère de Jésus m'aident.' She vomited as she ran from the room.

The Police set up a two-kilometer cordon around the convent. They allowed no one in or out. Media crews set up camp outside the cordon. They asked two questions. Who was the girl and why was she staying at the convent?

When police interviewed Sister Louisa, the convent's mother superior, she told them everything she knew.

'Her name is Carlotta Benando, she is ten years old, just a baby, an American. Her father, Alfredo, was in some sort of trouble and asked if we would provide a safe haven for her here. In that I failed, may God forgive me. I believe he feared someone might try to use her to get to him.'

Inspector Partis raised his eyebrows.

'Did he give any clues as to who this might be?'

'No, none,' she said, 'and I didn't ask.' Then she added, 'But I believe he is working for our Holy Father while he is here in France.'

'And why, may I ask, do you believe that?' he asked coldly.

'He wore a ring. I have seen one like it once before. It belonged to a man I knew who worked at the Vatican, that's all.'

'Hmm, I see. Who else knew she was here?'

'No one, we were all sworn to secrecy and her father told no one else,' she said.

Inspector Partis paused before he spoke again. 'There are no obvious signs of forced entry. How do you suppose the murderer entered the convent?'

'That's easy. Through the front door.'

'The front door?' he looked startled as he said it.

'Why of course,' she said. 'Whoever did this switched off our alarm and let themselves in. I have checked the alarm's security record. The murderer entered the security code at three fifty five and again at eight minutes past four. You see, provided the correct number is input within fifteen seconds of unlocking and opening the door the alarm will not sound. They must have had a key, what do you call them, a skeletal key?'

'And where do you suppose he obtained this skeletal key and the code to switch off the alarm?'

'I have no idea,' she said exasperated. 'Surely that's your job to find out?'

'Oh I will, make no mistake about that, I will. How do we contact Alfredo Benando?'

'I have no way of making contact, he said it was too dangerous. He would collect her when his business was finished and no longer any danger.'

The press briefing took place in a hastily erected small marquee. Inspector Partis made a short statement.

'At approximately seven o'clock this morning, a girl who I believe to be about ten years old was found dead in her bed at the Sisters of Charity convent in Saint Omer. She had been subjected to a brutal sexual assault. I am currently trying to trace her relatives and formally identify her before releasing her name. I will take a few questions.'

'Yes please.' He pointed to John Stowe from the BBC.

'The talk in the town is that she is an American girl. Can you confirm that and are there any local suspects, known paedophiles who live in the area?'

'Until we have formally identified her I cannot say what nationality she is and no, there are no local suspects.'

'Bernice Lefeure, Le Figaro. Are police advising people in the area to secure their homes and be on their guard?'

'Without wanting to panic people, yes, I would ask people to be extra vigilant. We are dealing with a very dangerous man.'

'Jacquie Valais, Radio France, what was the cause of death?'

'Until we have carried out a post mortem I cannot say.'

'Why was she was staying at the convent?'

'Please, no more questions. Further briefings will keep you informed of any new developments, thank you.'

CHAPTER 22

'Monsieur,' the taxi driver looked in his rear view mirror as he spoke. 'The bastard who murdered the little girl last night deserves the guillotine. Lethal injection will be too good for him.' Alfredo looked at his watch. He wasn't really listening. His thoughts were on Barnabus and how to keep him safe.

The traffic moved slowly. He desperately wanted to arrive at the press conference on time. Whoever wanted Barnabus dead could strike at any moment, and what better place than a press conference for maximum publicity?

'Excuse me, what little girl?' asked Alfredo, breaking away from his deep thoughts.

'It's been on the radio all morning. A little girl was raped and murdered at a convent in Saint Omer last night.'

As he heard the words he knew his worst nightmare had come true. He wanted to scream and hit out at someone, anyone, it didn't matter who. The whole of mankind was to blame. Where was God? Why hadn't he saved her?

He buried his head in his hands. His whole body felt numb. His breathing laboured to the extent that the taxi driver believed he was having a heart attack.

'Monsieur, what is wrong?' said the taxi driver as he peered through his mirror. 'Would you like me to stop?'

'No, take me to Saint Omer, quickly.'

'Oui Monsieur, did you know the girl?'

'She is my daughter.' As he said the words he began to sob.

'Mon Dieu, peut Dieu être avec vous,' said the driver under his breath.

Ten kilometres from Saint Omer the taxi pulled up at a police road block. The taxi driver wound his window down. Six police, all armed with MP5 sub machine guns, approached. Alfredo couldn't quite make out the conversation between his driver and the policeman, who looked like the senior officer. Then the driver turned round and spoke to him.

'For us, this is the end of the road. You have to go with them. I believe they will arrest you.'

'For what?' said Alfredo dispassionately, his spirit already broken.

'On suspicion of murdering your daughter, of course,' said the taxi driver as if it were obvious.

Alfredo sat in the rear of the unmarked police car squashed between two police officers, with his hands cuffed behind his back. The worst ignominy was the blanket over his head. How could they believe a father would do such a thing to his child?

The car pulled up in the parking lot of the police station in Saint Omer. Police officers quickly led Alfredo through a side door into the small grim cell block. One of the police guards removed the blanket and took off the hand cuffs.

'Sit down please.' A man in plain clothes gestured for him to sit on a chair in front of a large oak desk. 'My name is Chief Inspector Partis. I'm leading the investigation into last night's rape and murder of a ten year old girl at the Sisters of Charity convent here in Saint Omer. My officers tell me you told the Paris taxi driver that you are the girl's father. Is that correct? Before you answer I have to remind you of your rights. You do not have to say anything without your lawyer being present and under our revised law you are presumed innocent until found guilty, but I must tell you I don't believe in that shit. As far as I'm concerned you're guilty until I say you're innocent. Do you understand?' Alfredo nodded.

'That shouldn't take too long. You see, whatever low life did this left his DNA, if you understand what I mean.'

Alfredo stared at him with piercing eyes.

'I don't need a lawyer, ask your questions. For God's sake she was my daughter. She was all I had that mattered in this world.

Now she's gone I might just as well be dead. I want to see her, I have to say goodbye to her. Afterwards I will answer all your questions because I want to find out who killed her as much as you do, probably more, and when I find out my revenge will be terrible.'

Carlotta looked peaceful. The morticians had done a good job. Her skin had its usual soft smooth sheen. A pure white silk gown covered her body and her hair was brushed. Alfredo gently took hold of her hand.

'I let you down, I'm so sorry my angel. I thought you would be safer at the convent. I expect your momma's with you now. I'll bet she's mad with me but she'll be pleased to be with you again. She'll take good care of you. Ask her to show you round and introduce you to your grandpa and grandma who you never knew. I'm sure grandpa will play some games with you. He was always pretty good at dominos but watch out 'cause he cheats at cards. Don't tell him I said that though, he might come and haunt me.'

Then it hit him. He would never again experience her smile, her infectious laughter or her hugs. As he kissed her on the forehead his tears fell on her face.

The drive from the mortuary to the police station passed in silence. Alfredo puzzled on who murdered Carlotta in such a brutal way and why. No one knew she was there. He had taken great pains to keep her whereabouts a secret. Maybe a drifter forced his way into the convent with the idea of raping a nun and by accident came across Carlotta? But why did Inspector Partis suspect him? It could only be because there was no forced entry. Whoever it was knew how to gain access. So who killed her and why? The people who wanted him dead, Michael Heaney and some people within the Catholic Church, already tried to get to Carlotta through her computer. Surely they would have kidnapped her and threatened to kill her unless he gave himself up to them, not just raped and killed her? Something else is going on, but what, he could only speculate.

The interview took place in a small room with no natural light.

Nicotine stains going back decades covered the plain white walls. The furniture consisted of three chairs in a row with two chairs facing them.

Chief Inspector Partis sat on the middle chair. On his right sat another policeman in uniform and on his left a conservatively dressed, mature lady with grey hair cut in a short page boy style.

'Please sit down,' said the Chief Inspector. He beckoned Alfredo to sit on one of the two chairs facing them.

'On my right is Inspector Lorenze and on my left Madame Pasquale, she will be taking notes. Please state your full name, occupation and permanent address,' said Chief Inspector Partis as he drew on a Gauloise cigarette.

'My name is Alfredo Benando. I work for the Vatican and I am a citizen of the United states of America and I have no fixed address.'

When Alfredo mentioned he worked for the Vatican the two policemen gave each other puzzled glances.

'Will you confirm you refused the offer of legal representation for this interview?'

'Yes, that is correct.'

'And do you also confirm the body in the mortuary is that of your daughter, Carlotta Angelina Benando?'

'Yes, it is her.'

Chief Inspector Partis sat back in his chair and took another drag from his cigarette before continuing.

'So what exactly do you do for the Vatican?' Alfredo thought for a second before answering.

'Okay, if you want to know, I'm a papal bodyguard.' The two policemen looked at each other before Chief Inspector Partis continued.

'So what went wrong in the Philippines?'

'I'd been compromised and three of my colleagues were viciously murdered.'

'Murder seems to follow you around.'

'It's an occupational hazard, but why bring a little girl into it?' said Alfredo, his voice cracking with emotion.

A loud knock on the door interrupted the proceedings.

'Entrée,' barked Partis, annoyed at the interruption.

'Inspecteur En Chef, nous avons uneallumette pour l'échantillon d'ADN,' said a young gangly officer.

'Interview is terminated. It seems we have a DNA match.'

'Who is it?' said Alfredo.

'You will find out soon enough.'

'Am I free to go then?'

Chief Inspector Partis said just one word.

'Non.'

CHAPTER 23

'BOSS, ARE YOU ready for the gig tonight? You look terrible. Look, we don't know if it was Carlotta. Do you want me to cancel? I'll tell them you're sick or something.'

'Mat, will you stop fussing round me like some kind o' mother hen. I'm okay, I'll do the gig.'

Very rarely did Rodeo ever raise his voice at Mathew. He saw the expression on Mathew's face and felt the hurt that his friend felt.

'I'm sorry, I shouldn't have shouted. Come here.' They hugged each other.

'You know boss, it's a shame other people don't make up as quick as us.' Rodeo opened his mouth to speak, but instead decided just to accept Mathew's love.

On the way to the gig everyone on the coach felt subdued. Laura and Douglas both feared the worst. Carlotta had become like a daughter to them.

When Alfredo took her away it left a big hole in their lives. Laura loved having her around. She helped with things like arranging the flowers in the dressing rooms and bringing round bottles of water or teas and coffees for everyone, and before every concert she drew Douglas a card wishing him good luck.

'Every time I received a good luck card from Carlotta I felt so good that a child could care so much about me. How could I ever let her down? So I just went out on stage with that attitude.'

Laura smiled momentarily. 'She made me laugh every time she directed you to where you had to sit on the coach so your card would be in the pouch in front of you.'

Douglas put his hand in the pouch in front of him, disappointed there wouldn't be anything there. He smiled.

'Laura thank you.' He pulled out a white envelope.

'Don't thank me,' said Laura, 'I didn't put it there.'

'Well we'd better see who did,' said Douglas.

Slowly he opened the envelope and took out a card. He looked at the drawing on the front and opened the card.

'Well I'll be damned.' He read the words.

'*Dear Douglas, Laura, Rodeo, Mathew, Davey, Keanan and everyone else I've sent this card...*' he stopped reading.

'Hear, listen up everyone.' He paused until he had everyone's attention. 'There's a card for us all from Carlotta. How she got it on the coach I don't know but I'll read it out.

'*Dear Douglas, Laura, Rodeo, Mathew, Davey, Keanan and everyone else. I've sent this card to wish you all good luck for tonight's gig. I want to thank you all for being so kind to me and my Daddy, all my love Carlotta.* On the front she's drawn a picture of us all.'

A sense of relief passed around the coach that Carlotta wasn't the girl in the news after all.

Douglas, buoyed by the certainty that Carlotta was okay, put his whole heart and soul into his warm up and introduction. Rodeo even asked him if he wanted to lead a prayer and two minutes of private thoughts for the dead girl and her family. He declined, feeling Rodeo would do a far better job, but he felt proud that Rodeo had asked him.

From a security perspective everything ran smoothly. Not too many people tried to rush the stage, no demonstrations outside, no security alerts. Mathew even allowed himself the rare luxury of watching from the wings.

It all changed when Mathew spotted a police chopper hovering low above the makeshift stadium. Then another chopper appeared. He strained his eyes to try to make out the markings.

'What are those markings?' he asked one of the crew.

'Looks like the police.'

'I can see that,' said Mathew. 'I mean the other one.'

'Oh the other one...looks like CNN News,' he said.

'What the fuck do they want?' said Mathew, still staring at the choppers. As he spoke, his radio crackled into life.

'This is Delta Charlie Tango three four we have a Papa X-ray situation. Request Mr Lopez attends at the main entrance, over.'

Mathew responded, 'Copy Delta Charlie Tango three four Mr Lopez acknowledges, give me five out.'

He approached the main entrance and stopped in his tracks.

'Holy shit!' As he looked he estimated perhaps a thousand riot police on the coaches. TV cameras were rolled. A group of maybe ten or twelve uniformed police stood with his security guard and an indiscriminate number of plain-clothes officers milled about.

Mathew approached one of the uniformed police officers.

'I'm Mathew Lopez, head of security for this event. How can I help you?'

A plain-clothes officer stepped forward and put his hand out to shake hands. Mathew accepted.

'Mr Lopez, my name is Chief Inspector Partis. I'm leading the investigation into the rape and murder of a ten-year-old girl in Saint Omer.'

Mathew's heart started to pound. His head felt like it was going to explode. Did they suspect him because of what he'd done all those years ago?

'Mr Lopez, I understand you're not only Head Of Security for this event but you are also a close friend of Rodeo?'

'Yes I am, but what has that got to do with the attack on a ten-year-old girl?'

'Everything. You see, I have come to arrest Rodeo for her rape and murder. How would you say it in English? I have incontrovertible evidence that places him at the scene of the crime.'

'You are joking! This has got to be some kind of sick joke,' said Mathew.

'I never joke about such things,' said the Chief Inspector tersely.

'So that's why you bought the Calvary with you,' said Mathew.

'Yes, I believe it is prudent to take such precautions for everyone's safety.'

'What about the press?' asked Mathew. 'Is it prudent that they come along for the ride?'

'They were not invited,' said Partis. 'It is very difficult to keep these things quiet, especially when large movements of riot police are involved.'

'So you are going to wait till after the concert before you arrest him?' said Mathew.

'Non, he might escape. I intend to arrest him on stage now.'

'Now! You can't do that.'

'Who says I can't? Mr Lopez, you can either make things easy or difficult, the end result will be the same.'

'Okay, but if you or your goons lay one finger on him you'll answer to me personally. Follow me please.'

Mathew took Chief Inspector Partis and two other plain-clothes officers round to the back of the stage while the riot police filtered around the aisles and rear of the stadium.

On stage, Rodeo addressed his audience.

'Everyone, this morning we heard sad news. A young girl was brutally raped and murdered in a small town called Saint Omer. While I sing this next song, I'd like everyone to light their candles or shine their torches and join as one so we can send our love to her spirit, to her family and friends and anyone affected by tragedies around the world.'

As he sang, he noticed police in riot gear filtering around the stadium. Something was wrong, very wrong. He carried on singing. The audience appeared not to have noticed the police. They held their candles and softly sang along with him. It was probably the most satisfying moment he had ever experienced since he first started performing. The love emanating from the audience was physical. He could see it, feel it, hear it, smell it.

As Rodeo played the last chord on his guitar, Chief Inspector Partis and his two colleagues walked on to the stage.

'Rodeo, I am arresting you on suspicion of the rape and murder of Carlotta Angelina Benando in the Covent of The Sisters of Charity in Saint Omer. You do not have to say anything and you have the right to request a lawyer.'

Rodeo's mic picked up every word. The other plain-clothes officers handcuffed his hands behind his back. Mathew appealed for calm as they led Rodeo away.

'Everyone, please stay calm and leave the stadium in an orderly fashion. There has been some sort of mistake. My name is Mathew Lopez, I work for Rodeo. I'm in charge of his security and he's my best friend. I know he's innocent. He would never harm anyone, let alone a ten-year-old girl.'

The closely marshaled crowd, taken aback by the events of the last few minutes, left quickly. Some openly cried, some tore up their programmes. Most left in a state of shock. They just couldn't believe what had happened and left in silence.

The stadium soon emptied. Mathew bought the whole entourage together. They sat on the stage in stunned silence until Mathew stood to speak.

'All of us are in shock. Our beautiful Carlotta has been taken from us and Rodeo has been accused. Douglas, my friend, my brother, would you say a prayer or blessing for Carlotta please.'

Douglas rose and stood before them.

'Dear God, who is in each one of us and in Heaven. We remember Carlotta, a beautiful child, full of life and fun who had love for everyone and everything around her. Take her into your care and let her soul and spirit experience the oneness of love with you in Heaven. Help us all to remember all her good qualities that we may learn from her and use them in our daily lives. Life is eternal and love is eternal. Carlotta knew that, her soul knew that. She knew, humanity can move forward only through love. She gave her life for us. Let's not let her down, we must not lose sight of what we want to achieve. We must not turn our backs on our love for humanity and our love for Rodeo.'

'Douglas is right,' said Mathew. 'If Rodeo had turned his back on me when I was in prison with him and threatening to do nasty things to him I wouldn't be here now. I'd be dead. Douglas, if Rodeo hadn't shown you the love he did, where would you be now? All of us, he loved us, he never wanted anything in return. His love is unconditional, just like ours should be for him. I don't know what evidence they got, but I'm damned sure going to find out. If you love Rodeo and Carlotta, stay with us. Things are going to get tough and our love is the only thing we have to help us get through it.'

'Kalma-deva is innocent,' shouted Davey. 'I know because God has told me.'

'Good boy Davey', said Mathew.

'How did God tell you?' someone asked.

'Today I saw a "love is" cartoon. It said love is always seeing the best in the person you love.'

'What wisdom from the mouth of a child,' said Mathew.

*   *   *

Sitting in the blacked-out police van, Rodeo had no idea where he was being taken. He tried to collect his thoughts. Beautiful Carlotta is dead, that is the tragedy of the situation. His predicament is unimportant. All the people who loved her will be devastated. The world had lost a beautiful soul, for a time at least. Why had they arrested him? What evidence did they have? He had no answer. The van continued its journey. His eyes became heavy, the motion of the van making him sleepy.

A sudden jolt woke him. The van stopped. A police officer unlocked the door with the engine still running.

Outside, floodlights lit the grim-looking courtyard. The walls of the buildings, made of grey stone, looked forbidding and unwelcoming. Two police officers ushered him out of the van.

'Where am I?' he queried.

'La Santé,' replied one of the police officers, 'the French equivalent of Hell. Welcome!'

CHAPTER 24

'Wow, how do you like that? One minute he's singing a song in memory of a ten-year-old girl who's been brutally raped and murdered, the next minute he's arrested for doing it, live on TV. Wonderful things these satellites. Now the whole world can see what kind of a fucking hypocrite Rodeo really is.'

Michael Heaney felt in a buoyant mood as he watched the events being played out.

'I'll give it three minutes before that phone rings.' It rang as he spoke.

'There you are, what did I tell you? Let's make the maximum publicity out of this. Selina, you take the call. I'm not here. I've gone to church to light a candle for the dead girl. I'll meet the press in an hour.'

All the major networks covered the interview.

'Senator Heaney, I understand you delayed this interview so you could go to the church and light a candle for the little girl who was murdered?'

'Yes, because as a Christian I believe my priority should be to pray for the little girl.'

'The French police arrested Rodeo in the middle of one of his concerts in Paris just two hours ago, live on TV. Do you have any comment you wish to make about the arrest?'

'Yes I do. Rodeo was rumoured to have sexual relations with young underage girls at his ranch. Why weren't these rumours properly investigated? If they had maybe he'd be behind bars before now and this young girl would still be alive.'

'So you believe he is guilty then?'

'In France as in the United States, a man is presumed innocent until proven guilty. However, to arrest him in the middle of a concert live on TV they must have some very compelling evidence.'

'May I ask you, what the yellow ribbon in the shape of a cross that you're wearing on your lapel represents?'

'Sure, it's a sign to welcome back people to Christ and the church. People who lapsed or maybe people who left to follow the philosophy espoused by the child rapist and murderer Rodeo. Let me just say to those folks, there is a warm welcome waiting for you, whatever church you attend. All denominations have taken up with the ribbons and will welcome you with open arms.'

'Thank you Senator Heaney, I'm sure we'll be following the trial very closely when it starts in Paris.'

*   *   *

The two policemen led Rodeo into a plush office. Oil paintings depicting scenes from the Old Testament hung on the walls. A well-groomed, middle-aged man with silver hair sat behind a Louis XIV desk complete with quill pens.

'Reposez-vous satisfont vers le bas,' said the middle-aged man without looking up. Rodeo didn't move. The man looked up at him through the top of his bifocals. 'Sit down please.'

Rodeo sat on a wooden chair facing the desk with the two policemen flanking him.

'Rodeo, my name is Monsieur Henri Malblanc. I am the Investigating Magistrate. You are under arrest for the rape and murder of Carlotta Angelina Benando. Because of the seriousness of the charge, you will be held at La Santé jail until my investigation is complete. Do you understand?'

Rodeo nodded. 'Yes Sir.'

Monsieur Malblanc continued. 'You are of course entitled to legal representation. If you do not appoint your own attorney I will appoint one for you. For your own safety, I have asked the Governor to place you in solitary confinement. You understand the nature of the charge, and the fact you are a foreign national makes you a target for some people here. We will meet again tomorrow when I commence my investigation.' He looked down at some papers as the two policemen led Rodeo away.

The cell measured twelve feet by twelve. It contained a small table and chair, a sink with hot and cold water, a portable toilet, a two foot six wide single bed with a thin rubber mattress, one sheet, two blankets and one thin pillow.

'Oh well,' said Rodeo to himself, 'I've experienced worse.'

                    *   *   *

Mathew phoned for a cab to take him to the American Embassy.

'Let me go with you,' said Douglas.

'Thanks for the offer,' replied Mathew. 'I'd rather you stay with everyone else and see they get back to the Chateau safely.'

'Okay,' said Douglas. 'If you think that's best, but when you get back let me know the state of play. Don't worry about waking me. I won't sleep.'

                    *   *   *

The receptionist at the embassy's main desk asked Mathew to take a seat while she found someone who could see him. Thirty minutes passed before a young woman dressed in an expensive business suit approached him.

'Mr Lopez, follow me please.' Mathew felt a distinct chill in the air as he followed her into one of the elevators. She pressed the button for the fourth floor. Despite Mathew's attempt to gain her attention there was no eye contact between them. When the doors opened, she left the elevator like a thoroughbred racehorse out of the traps. He followed her around a maze of corridors. Eventually she came to a door marked 'Interview Room Five'. Using a swipe card she opened the door.

'Help yourself to water, tea or coffee. Someone will be here to see you in a couple of minutes.' She left, closing the door behind her.

Mathew poured himself a cup of water from the dispenser and sat down. A few seconds later a tall man, maybe six foot seven or eight, entered the room.

'Mr Lopez, my name is Larry Hall. I'm what's euphemistically referred to as an Embassy Official. How may I help you?' He didn't offer to shake Mathew's hand.

'Mr Hall, this evening my friend and employer Rodeo was publicly arrested for a heinous crime that he did not commit. As an American citizen, I'm asking for your help.'

'Well Mr Lopez, what help exactly are you looking for?' said Mr Hall. Mathew looked at him with angry eyes

'I want to know where he's been taken to, when I can see him and an assurance he's being treated properly. I also want the best English-speaking lawyer in France to represent him. And one more thing – I want to know what evidence they have that gives them the right to arrest him in the middle of a concert then drag him off to some God forsaken French jail.'

'Mr Lopez, let me tell you a few home truths. Firstly, we will not intervene in the French judicial process and secondly, at this moment in time, Rodeo is an embarrassment to the US Government.'

'So you're refusing to help a US citizen?' asked Mathew, incredulously.

'No I didn't say that, all I'm inferring is don't expect us to push the boat out for him. I'll be able to tell you which jail he's in and I'll put you in touch with the best English-speaking lawyer, just give me a couple of hours. Oh, and one more thing, we will send someone from the embassy to check on his welfare. Other than that, you're on your own. You better leave your contact details at the reception desk on your way out.'

* * *

Half-forgotten sounds echoed through the jail. *All jails are the same*, thought Rodeo, *no matter where they are*. He listened to a prisoner sobbing. His mind went back to Harry. When Harry found out his grandson was dying, he was inconsolable. Did it make any difference to the prison authorities? Like fuck it did. They wouldn't let him go to the boy's funeral or spend time with his daughter because he wouldn't admit to a crime he didn't commit.

No, the sole aim of prison is revenge and what fucking good does revenge do? Nothing, except provide egocentric comfort for people who label themselves victims. His eyes felt heavy as he stretched out on the thin mattress. Once again, sleep provided a pleasant escape.

*   *   *

Mathew's cell phone rang, making him jump. *God! I'm becoming twitchy*, he thought.

'This is Mathew Lopez.'

'Mr Lopez, it's Larry Hall from the embassy. Rodeo is at La Santé Jail in Paris. The lawyer, Philippe Revel, will meet you there in the morning at eight. Don't worry, he's good. I understand he's never lost a case…yet.'

Mathew yawned as he disconnected the call. Events were beginning to catch up on him; he needed to grab some sleep.

Philippe Revel often defended high profile clients, though none of them ever faced charges that carried the death penalty. This case could be tricky. As he understood it, the prosecutors were relying solely on the fact that the autopsy discovered sperm in the victim's vagina and DNA tests later identified a perfect match with Rodeo, but why hadn't they found anything else? He would have expected forensics to find hair or pubic hair, skin or clothing fibres, which would have put the case beyond reasonable doubt.

He doodled with his pencil as he struggled to make sense of his thoughts. After ten minutes, he'd worn the lead down so much it wouldn't write anymore.

He could already hear the prosecution's case.

'Rodeo knew the girl and because of his pedophilic tendencies, which were already under investigation in the States, he became besotted by her. After the concert, he sneaked out of Château De Montvillargenne without anyone seeing him and made his way to the Sisters of Charity Convent in Saint Omer. He knew she was there because a few days earlier he had followed her and her father. At the same time, he identified the skylight as a way to gain entry but then turned off the convent's alarm from the inside to confuse the police. Carlotta didn't scream for help because she knew and trusted him and it was because she knew him he killed her.'

So perfect which, in Philippe's eyes, is what made it so flawed. All he had to do was identify the flaws.

The door to the office opened. Mathew held out his hand across the desk to Philippe and introduced himself.

'Hi, my name's Mathew Lopez. I'm a friend of Rodeo's and I look after his security.' Philippe stood to shake his hand.

'Mr Lopez, please sit down. My name is Philippe Revel. Before I agree to represent Rodeo, I need to ask you some questions. Firstly, do you believe he is innocent?'

'Mr Revel, I don't just believe he's innocent, I *know* he's innocent.'

'And how do you know?'

'I just know.' Philippe raised his eyebrows in frustration. Mathew attempted to explain.

'Mr Revel, Rodeo won't even allow me or any of his security to carry a gun, all we have are tasers. He says protecting our lives isn't a good enough reason to take the life of someone else.'

Philippe paused thoughtfully before answering.

'I see. Ok, I'll take the case, but there's no guarantee we'll win.'

'So tell me Mr Revel, what evidence do they have that allows them to arrest him on stage in the middle of a concert?'

'They found his sperm inside the vagina of the deceased. DNA matches Rodeo's exactly.'

Mathew sat thoughtfully for a few seconds. His mind went back to the Raja Hotel in Bangalore. Suddenly it all clicked.

'Mr Revel, I think I know where that sperm they found came from. Rodeo met a beautiful Indian girl, slept with her and in the morning she'd gone. No goodbyes, nothing. Her kid brother Davey, who'd kind of tagged along with us, told us he saw her leave and meet an American guy in the grounds who asked if she had the cargo.'

Philippe leant back in his chair. 'I see, does Rodeo have any enemies?'

'No, he loves everyone, but some people don't run with his ideas. A while back before we started on the tour we were warned off criticising Christianity by some Papal heavies, one of them was Alfredo Benando, Carlotta's father. Turns out he's a bodyguard of Pope Barnabus and for some reason they want him out of the way. That's why he secretly took her to the convent so they wouldn't get to him through her.'

'Hold on, you say he took her there in secret?'

'Yes, none of us knew where she was.'

'Not even Rodeo?'

'No sir, not even Rodeo.'

'Thank you Mr Lopez, I'll be in touch again very soon.'

CHAPTER 24

D ESPITE HIS frailty, Barnabus continued with all the promised private audiences including Edith Llitjos, the twenty-second of the day. He smiled warmly when she entered the Upper Chapel at Saint Chapelle. Edith looked at the beautiful stained glass windows on all four sides as she tried to remember everything Father Jacques had told her. Make sure your white shawl properly covers your shoulders, kneel down on one knee and take his right hand and kiss his ring

'My child,' he said, holding out his hand as she walked towards him. 'Come a little closer so I can see you and hear you a little better.'

She walked forward another six steps then, kneeling on one knee, took his hand and kissed his ring. She looked up at him.

'Most Holy Father, why was Jesus crucified when he hadn't done anything wrong?'

'What a question from one so young,' said Barnabus, wondering where this was leading. 'Come and sit on this chair, it will be easier to talk.' As she sat down he continued. 'Jesus was a Jew. The Jewish religious leaders at the time felt threatened by his radical unorthodox ideas. So they accused him of blasphemy. Backed by the rabble crowd whom they'd aroused, they called for his execution. He died for our sins, he died that through his love for us we would have everlasting life.'

'That's what I thought,' said Edith in a very matter of fact way. 'Do you know a man, a rock star called Rodeo?'

'Yes I know of him,' said Barnabus guardedly. 'He has been arrested for the rape and murder of a young girl.'

'It's a lie!' said Edith. 'I know he has done nothing wrong. He would never ever do anything like that. He is too full of love, his music, his life, he touches too many people. Most Holy Father, I saw him on stage. The man who attacked me, his eyes held nothing, you understand nothing. But in Rodeo's eyes he holds only love. He didn't do such a thing, I just know, and now because of me they will kill him. It will be like Jesus all over again.'

By this time tears were streaming down her cheeks. Barnabus took her hands and held them between his.

'Edith, you are a brave girl. God in Heaven knows you went through a terrible ordeal. Afterwards you and other people did what you believed was right. Rodeo will be tried and if he is innocent he will be freed.' Edith pulled her hands away.

'But Jesus was innocent and he wasn't freed.' Barnabus looked at her incredulously.

'Edith, he is a rock musician who has filled your head with stories of romance and love.'

'No,' she screamed, 'he's not. He's from God, I know he is.'

'How do you know?' asked Barnabus, trying to remain calm.

'Because I had a dream and God told me.'

'Edith,' said Barnabus a little impatiently, 'I will not listen to this.'

'Why!' said Edith. 'Do you think you are the only person God speaks to? God spoke to Daniel and Joseph so why wouldn't he speak to me? I believe what Rodeo says, that we are all a part of God and because we are a part of God he loves us. God is love and when we follow the path of love our souls rejoice and become one with God. Most Holy Father, you must listen to me please. Through my love for you and for Rodeo my mind has opened. God has told me that when you, Most Holy Father, meet with Rodeo you will know love and you will have no need for the Holy Scriptures.'

Barnabus felt nauseous as the pain surged through his temples and across his forehead. His mind ran through the verse.

A musician (He of David) sings of love till all
people listen, their thirst and hunger satisfied.
He (of David) is the curse of all Holy people.
The Church of Peter (Fall) into the abyss.
Followers of the prophet move into the ascendancy

'Edith, you will tell no one what we discussed, you understand? May God's love be with you forever.'

The large double doors to the chapel opened and a priest ushered Edith out.

'I will see no one else today,' said Barnabus to his aid.

CHAPTER 25

C ARLOTTA'S LITTLE white coffin looked pointedly small in the large black limousine. The funeral cortège moved at walking pace behind the impeccably dressed funeral director, who walked stolidly along the main street towards Saint Omer's impressive sixteenth century cathedral.

Most of the town turned out to pay their respects to the little girl, who was murdered while they slept. TV crews from around the world filmed the sombre procession. The townsfolk laid flowers all along the route through the narrow streets.

Alfredo sat in the lead limousine flanked by two plain-clothes police officers. Looking straight ahead, he looked dazed, almost as if he couldn't comprehend the goings on. Nevertheless, his mind, active and agile, planned revenge, terrible revenge on those he knew to be responsible.

The cortège stopped in front of the Cathedral. Local dignitaries and clergy filed in behind Alfredo and his two minders.

A figure dressed in priests' robes stood high up in the eves on a balcony, which was used to film services at Christmas and Easter. What looked like a camera to the casual observer pointed down at the congregation. Using glasses that magnified the image ten thousand times, he loaded a micron of TRXc3 into the rifle's breach. Made from a very concentrated form of human growth hormones, TRXc3 simulates the effects of a heart attack and is totally untraceable. He only had to hit the target.

The figure looked through the telescopic viewfinder on the disguised rifle. Alfredo and the congregation knelt. He pulled the trigger. Alfredo felt nothing as the micron of TRXc3 entered his body through his temple. Calmly, the figure hid the rifle under his robe and made his way down the three hundred odd steps of the stone spiral staircase. He had plenty of time. The TRXc3 would take exactly sixteen minutes and fifteen seconds to work its magic. He knew this from experience.

The mourners knelt in prayer, Alfredo did not move. His hands covered his face. The pain in his chest reached twelve out of ten on a scale of ten. The two police minders looked at him sympathetically. He fell on the floor clutching his chest and fighting for breath. His face turned blue. The life in his body began to ebb away. He tried to speak. His lips moved but there was no breath to form the words. His eyes glazed over.

One of his minders shouted, 'Nous avons besoin d'un docteur, est la un docteur.'

A woman pushed her way along the aisle. Kneeling down beside him she felt for his pulse. Feeling nothing, she began to give the kiss of life, alternating with pressure pushes to his chest. Four breaths into his lungs, then three pushes.

After five minutes an ambulance approached the cathedral with its siren sounding. The crew ran down the aisle.

'Il est trop tard, il est mort,' she said turning to the crew as they readied their equipment.

CHAPTER 26

KAMNA LOOKED at the TV in disbelief. Rodeo charged with the rape and murder of a ten year old girl? Everything fell into place. Now it all made sense. She now knew why the doctor tried to silence her and why people were asking questions and looking for her, forcing her to keep moving to stay one step ahead.

'I am going to Paris and I will tell the world that someone is framing him.'

At Goa airport she checked in on a flight to Heathrow. Everything went fine, the journey to the airport, check in, security. The fun would start in London or Paris.

She planned to catch a connecting flight from Heathrow to Paris Orly then make her way directly to the Indian Embassy located on Rue de Paradis. Surely they will help and protect her?

* * *

So far so good, she thought while waiting by the luggage reclaim at Paris Orly. Then she sensed eyes watching her.

Her one bag, a white sports holdall, appeared on the belt in front of her. Quickly slinging it over her shoulder, she made her way to passport control and customs.

The passport control officer just gave her a cursory glance as he quickly examined her visa. The customs officers gave admiring looks as she strolled through, but the watching eyes stayed with her. No matter how quickly or slowly she walked towards the arrival terminal, they followed her.

'Boss, she's going for a cab and she's on her own.' Mathew paused for a second before answering.

'Have Ryan tail her. Find out where she's going. Tell him that on no account is he to lose her. You understand?'

'Affirmative boss,' said the man before switching off his cell phone.

Kamna jumped into the first available cab on the taxi rank.

'The Indian Embassy on Rue de Paradis please.'

The driver grunted something unintelligible and pulled away. She relaxed into the comfortable leather seat. Soft rain fell as the taxi made its way into the centre of Paris. Another hour and it will be dark. Darkness helped her feel safer. She could more easily disappear and hide.

'Madame.' The taxi driver woke her from her thoughts. 'Madame, the black sedan behind us, I believe it is following us. Is that possible?'

'Yes,' said Kamna. 'It is very possible.'

'Would you like that I try to lose them?' he asked.

'Yes, please do whatever you have to,' said Kamna trying to smile and remain calm.

Five minutes later Kamna turned round to look. Despite jumping numerous red lights and performing a handbrake turn on Avenue d'Italie, the black sedan managed to stay close behind.

'Can't you do something that will lose them?' said Kamna.

'Oui madam, please hold tight.'

The taxi entered Boulevard Raspall and picked up speed. The black sedan followed suit. Within twelve seconds they reached speeds of one hundred and fifty kilometers an hour.

The driver of the black sedan talked to himself the whole time.

'You ain't gonna lose me you mother fucker. You have to do better than that. Call that a hand brake turn back there? My ten-year-old son could do better.

I'll show you what a hand-brake turn is. I'm like superglue, you and me are stuck together like Bonnie an' Clyde. So why not just admit it? Anyhow, why you's running away from me, I'm the good guy? So that makes you the bad guy. Don't worry honey, I'm gonna save you.'

'Hold tight,' said the taxi driver to Kamna as he pushed his brake pedal to the floor. The force propelled her forward until the seat belt cut in and threw her back leaving her slightly winded. The black sedan swerved to avoid a fatal rear end collision, hit the curb and ended up on top of the crash barriers, straddled across the central reservation. The driver called Mathew on his cell phone.

'Boss he got away, he got lucky but he ain't no cab driver. He's a pro.'

'Shit,' said Mathew as he hung up.

In the cab, Kamna felt amazingly calm after her ordeal. The driver's cell phone rang. He didn't answer it. Holding it over his shoulder, he instructed Kamna.

'Take it, it's for you.'

'But you didn't answer it. How do you know it's for me?'

His tone changed.

'Take it.' He spat the words at her.

Kamna warily put the phone to her ear.

'Hello,' she said. A woman's voice spoke.

'You escaped once, we will not allow you to escape again. You will follow my instructions exactly. If you do not, your brother Davey will be killed.

In the seat pocket in front of you there is a laptop. Take it out and start it up. Then open the media player which is on the desk top.'

Kamna followed the instructions. As the media player opened the movie appeared. Kamna gasped. Pictures from a webcam showed Davey splashing around in the shallow end of what looked like a hotel pool.

Kamna put the phone to her ear. The woman spoke.

'As you can see he is all alone. Drowning is such a painful death, not at all quick. However, it does not have to be like that. You will leave the cab and walk one block to Rue Vaneau. Enter the apartment building immediately on your right and take the elevator to the top floor. You will see a door to the roof that is unlocked. When on the roof, you will jump. Of course if you do not carry out my instructions, we will kill you and your brother. This way at least your brother will live.'

The phone went dead. On the laptop Davey splashed about trying to swim. The sun shone through the pool windows lighting up one end of the pool which gave the water a beautiful reflective quality, not unlike the glistening material of one of her saris.

'My dear, beautiful brother, I love you. I will not let you die because of me.'

The cab driver watched her as she slowly made her way to the corner of Rue Vaneau. She looked up at the apartment block. *It must be at least thirty storeys high*, she thought, as she entered the building. The elevator was directly in front of her with the doors open.

She pressed the top button in the elevator, number twenty six. The doors closed A putrid smell of urine momentarily distracted her thoughts as the elevator made its way to the top. All too soon the doors opened.

As soon as she stepped out on to the landing. The doors closed and the elevator descended.

She looked around for a door leading to the roof. At the end of the corridor a sign read 'Aucune entrée, personnes autorisées seulement'. To the right of the sign she saw a white door with a bolt and padlock.

When she looked more closely the padlock wasn't snapped shut. She removed the padlock, undid the bolt and opened the door. Outside it was now pitch black.

She walked onto the roof. The strong breeze took her breath away. The bright lights of the Parisian skyline lit up the night around her. Slowly she walked towards the edge. Only a railing, no more than a metre high, stood between her and oblivion.

She focused her mind on the pictures of Davey happily splashing around in the pool. Taking a deep breath she prepared herself.

In the street below the taxi driver impatiently looked at his watch. *Why is she taking so long?* he thought to himself. *Do I have to finish the job myself?* Again he looked at his watch. Then it came.

He screwed up his face as he heard the expected bloodcurdling scream followed by the sickening thud. Climbing back into his taxi he made the sign of the cross.

Preparing herself, Kamna closed her eyes and imagined herself bathed in golden sunlight, her body totally engulfed in healing rays, absorbing energy and love. Her mind returned to Davey, splashing around in the pool, with the sunlight pouring in. Then it hit her. The sun had already gone down. Those pictures on the webcam couldn't possibly have been live. They were bluffing.

Frantically she looked around the roof until she saw an old dustbin crammed full of rubbish. She dragged it to the edge. No way could she lift it over the railing, but it might just fit underneath.

'Shit!' The bin had wedged under the railing. 'No you don't,' she shouted at the bin.

She kicked it, nothing happened. Then she kicked it again and again and again.

Nearly there, she thought, as the bin moved a little.

One last kick sent it flying off the roof top. Kamna let out the most bloodcurdling scream imaginable, letting it tail off to nothing. The thud as the bin hit the ground sent shivers through her.

Using the staircase she made her way out of the apartment block.

'No more taxis,' she said under her breath.

In the darkness she felt at home. All cities were similar.

'I will survive and so will Davey.'

$*$ $*$ $*$

Mathew frantically paced the floor.

'We've lost her. Our one chance to defend Rodeo is gone. She's probably dead. Where's Davey? I want him by my side twenty-four seven. They might just try to get to her by threatening him.'

CHAPTER 27

GOD HAD revealed some of his plan through Edith. Of that, Barnabus felt sure. Barnabus knew he must meet Rodeo. However, if anyone found out, the consequences would be…he dare not even think about it.

His health continued to concern his doctors. How much longer did he have? Months, weeks, days, maybe only hours. How could it be arranged? Who could he trust? He prayed for guidance. For five solid hours he sought answers in prayer. Exhausted, he fell into a deep sleep.

The planet Earth looked beautiful as Barnabus hovered above. A blue haze covered the sunlit surface. He could clearly see the continents of Europe, Africa and part of Asia. He looked down in awe and heard what he took to be a heavenly choir. Then he realised the choir consisted of only one voice singing all the parts. A voice that ranged from a rich baritone to a piercing countertenor. He listened to the words.

'I know that language,' he said. 'Syriac, the language is Syriac.'

The singing stopped. A man wearing t-shirt, jeans and trainers hovered beside him.

'Lovely view,' said the man.'

'Yes it is,' said Barnabus curiously. He paused before speaking again. 'May I ask who you are?'

'Don't you know?' said the man, a touch mockingly.

'No, I can't say I do,' said Barnabus, slightly embarrassed.

'I'm Rodeo.'

'But you were singing in Syriac,' said Barnabus.

'Wrong,' said Rodeo, almost triumphantly. 'You *heard* it in Syriac.

People interpret what they see and hear in many ways, whatever suits them. Much like the scriptures really.'

'So Rodeo, you are an expert in the scriptures eh?'

'No, I don't give a fuck about the scriptures,' said Rodeo.

'So what do you give a fuck about?' replied Barnabus.

'Let's see. You and every Catholic, every Muslim, every atheist, Hindu, in fact everyone, every soul, that's who I give a fuck about.'

'Why?' said Barnabus, not to challenge but because he genuinely didn't understand.

'Love,' said Rodeo, 'only love, because everything else is unreal, just an illusion. Look down at our planet. If you took all love away what would you be left with?'

Barnabus felt a shiver run down his spine at the thought of a world devoid of love. Rodeo continued.

'On the other hand, if love were multiplied just ten fold what would our lives on Earth be like? You know, love is really all we have and it's enough to feed our souls for all eternity.'

Rodeo held out his arms to Barnabus, who sensed the presence of God as they hugged. For the first time in his life he experienced God's unconditional love. With love like that Barnabus knew there could be no Hell or Purgatory. How else had religion misled people and, more importantly, why?

Suddenly the 'why' hit him full in the face. He wanted to switch it off or shut it down, do anything but face up to it. Pacing up and down in his cell-like chamber he confessed all to a higher authority. He knew what he had to do, the question was did he have the courage?

Tomorrow at the Stade De France, the venue for his last public appearance in France, he would...yes that was it, Syriac. No one, apart from a few scholars, could speak or understand Syriac. But first, he had six hours during which he wasn't to be interrupted.

As the day's first sunlight shone through the small gaps in the shutters, Barnabus heard a knock on the door.

'Come in,' he said. 'Cardinal Biloweiki, what a surprise. I wasn't expecting you.'

'No I don't suppose you were,' Replied the Cardinal in a matter of fact way.

The Cardinal looked at Barnabus suspiciously. Sensing the Cardinal's distrust, Barnabus tried to align his fears.

'Just putting the finishing touches to my sermon for today.'

'You shouldn't have bothered,' said the Cardinal. 'Here, I have prepared it for you. Nothing controversial, just your usual pet subjects.'

He placed a folder on the desk. Before Barnabus could react, the Cardinal grabbed the papers Barnabus had been working on.

'I'll take these,' said the Cardinal. 'Maybe I can work them into your next sermon for you, whenever that may be.'

'I doubt it,' said Barnabus under his breath.

The Cardinal turned and left. Barnabus drew a sigh of relief. The Syriac written on the papers taken by Cardinal Biloweiki was meaningless nonsense, but it would keep the Cardinal busy for a while. A wry smile appeared on his face as he thought about it. Now, how to get these other papers to Edith Llitjos?

CHAPTER 28

MARIA VON HIND felt annoyed. Sitting in the café smoking a Gauloise she fumed at not being allowed to personally kill Kamna, and why had she not heard anything? No ambulances or police sirens and no chatter. Word would have filtered through. The druggies, pimps and prostitutes in the café would have talked about a jumper on their patch and come to all sorts of conclusions. Maybe she was pushed by her pimp? More likely the police after she failed to pay them.

As she took a drag on her cigarette her eyes widened in amazement when Kamna suddenly walked in and ordered a coffee. *Yes, no mistake, it's her*, she thought. *She hasn't changed since I approached her to sleep with Rodeo and collect his sperm.*

Without hesitation she picked up her glass and walked across to Kamna. Smashing the glass on the table she pushed the jagged edged into Kamna's face, twisting it as it went in. Blood poured from the wound.

'You fucking bitch!' screamed Maria. I'm going to cut your face and cunt up so much you'll never screw around again.' She pulled a stiletto blade from the inside of her boot.

For the people in the café this was first class entertainment. Purely a personal dispute, the rights or wrongs didn't concern them, it was none of their business. It just added another colour to their lives.

Kamna appeared to freeze. Maria smiled, but years on the streets of India had prepared Kamna for this moment. As Maria raised the stiletto to strike the fatal blow, Kamna's perfectly placed kick caught her on the side of her head, causing her to momentarily to lose consciousness.

Maria fell to the floor. Kamna grabbed the stiletto and sat astride Maria. She waited for her to open her eyes. She wanted her to be conscious, to feel the pain. Her eyes opened and Kamna plunged the blade into Maria's head, slicing off her left ear in one movement. Covered in blood, Kamna dropped the knife and calmly left the café. No one followed.

CHAPTER 29

THE STADIUM stood as one and applauded. Barnabus slowly made his entrance toward the temporary pulpit erected specially for the occasion.

He felt humbled and buoyed by their genuine love, but knew that one false move on his part and the plug would be pulled on the TV coverage. Also, if anything happened to him the Vatican would refuse a post mortem. He could be murdered and no one would be any the wiser. Standing as close to the microphones as possible so as not to have to strain to be heard, he cleared his throat. The crowd fell silent.

'God bless you all. Jesus Christ our hope and chief shepherd, guides his Church to the fullness of truth and life, until the day of his glorious return, when all promises will be realised and the hopes of humanity fulfilled. The Church and humanity are walking together towards a future marked by the legacy of the past century with its array of lights and shadows. We are in a new moment of human history in which many question the destiny of humanity and wonder what is in store for the future. The world is engaged in the dynamism of progress and a growing interdependence in economic matters, culture and communications. Still, there are local conflicts, increasing hunger, sickness and poverty. The Church and our love of God are the two constants in our lives. All Christians...' He looked at what followed on the page given to him by Cardinal Biloweiki.

I cannot say this, he thought to himself. To buy time, he recited the Lord's Prayer. As he hoped, the congregation joined him. At the end of the prayer he took a deep breath before speaking.

'In the beginning was the Word, and the Word was with God, and the Word was God. He was with God in the beginning. Through him all things were made; without him nothing was made that has been made. In him was life, and that life was the light of men. The light shines in the darkness, but the darkness has not understood it. There came a man who was sent from God; his name was John. He came as a witness to testify concerning that light, so that through him all men might believe. He himself was not the light; he came only as a witness to the light.' He paused and looked around. 'The true light that gives light to every man is here on Earth with us now. His name…'

Suddenly he felt a little dizzy, he repeated himself. 'His name is…'

He struggled to get the words out…he couldn't swallow, the dizziness increased, his head span. He fell to the floor.

As he fell he felt the sensation of a healing blanket wrapping around him. He didn't hit the floor, the blanket caught him, comforted and warmed him. All his aches and pains went. He felt young again.

When he entered the light he remembered the unrequited sexual pangs of his first love. God! he had a lot of catching up to do.

* * *

Edith Llitjos excitedly opened the small packet. What is it? Who has sent it? She opened the envelope and took out lots of folded pages held together with a wax seal. They all had strange hand writing on them. She spotted a small note attached to the last page.

'My Dear Edith, please tell no one about this, not your parents, not even father Jacques. You must take these papers to the Reverend Douglas Claymore, you will find him near Paris at Château De Montvillargenne. He is a close friend of Rodeo. He will know what to do. May God bless you and keep you safe. Your friend, Pope Barnabus. Amen.'

She gasped. He must have sent it just before he died.

'Mama, you know there is an open air Mass for our Most Holy Father tomorrow in Paris? May I go please? I want to.'

Evelyn Llitjos smiled. 'I know how much you loved our Holy Father. Yes, you may go, but only if Father Jacques can take you.'

'Mama, I already asked him but he is busy,' she lied. 'Henri said he'd take me.'

'Alright, providing you are home before it is dark.' She gave her mum a big hug and kiss.

Early next morning Henri dropped her off at the station.

'If your mother ever finds out I'm not going with you she'll kill me.'

'Then we had better make sure she doesn't find out,' said Edith. 'Providing you don't let her see you today she will never know, will she?' She blew him a kiss. He smiled, knowing she was right. She would always be able to wrap him round her little finger.

* * *

The taxi approached the castle gatehouse. Edith sat in the back, tightly holding her rucksack. She breathed a sigh of relief when the taxi came to a standstill. She paid the driver and walked towards what looked like an office. A uniformed security guard came out to meet her.

'Hi there, how can I help you miss?' For a second she was thrown by the broad American English.

'I have to see the Reverend Douglas Claymore. It is très important.'

'Is he expecting you?'

'Non.'

'Okay, who should I say wants to meet him?'

'My name is Edith Llitjos,' she said in her very best English.

'And what should I say is it concerning?'

'Il est très prive, is private you understand?'

The security guard nodded and went back into the office. Through the window Edith could see him speaking on the phone. He put the phone down and the two enormous wrought iron gates opened, sliding silently apart. The security guard came out of the office.

'Just head down the path towards the main building and someone will come out to meet you. Have a nice day.'

'Hey Douglas, do you know a fifteen-year-old French girl called Edith Llitjos?' asked Mathew.

Douglas thought for a second.

'No I can't say I do. Should I?'

'Well, she's here to see you. She's walking towards us now. I just had a call from security. She gave your name, said she had something very important for you. Go and meet her, you can bring her in here. I'll order some coffee and doughnuts.'

Douglas held out his hand.

'Hi, you must be Edith. I'm very pleased to meet you. I'm Douglas Claymore.' His smile relaxed her. She shook his hand.

'Edith, come with me, I have some very good coffee and doughnuts. You like American doughnuts?'

Edith liked him. He wasn't what she expected. He seemed kind, très gentile.

'Hi Edith, I'm Mathew,' he said, standing up to shake her hand. 'And this is Laura.'

'Hello Edith,' said Laura.'

They sat in the drawing room around a solid walnut Louis XIV table.

'I'll pour,' said Mathew. 'Would you like coffee or soda pop?'

'Coffee please,' said Edith. As Mathew poured the coffee, Edith reached into her rucksack and took out the Papal papers.

'Monsieur Claymore, these are for you from the Most Holy Father Pope Barnabus.'

She passed them across the table to Douglas.

'Boy, you have friends in high places,' said Mathew, smiling broadly.

'This looks like the Papal seal,' said Douglas quietly, examining it. 'It's not written in English, it's in Syriac. Yes, Barnabus was one of the world's leading experts in the now almost forgotten ancient language.'

'So why should he send these papers to you?' said Laura.

'I studied ancient languages at college and published some papers on Syriac – decades ago, you understand.'

'Can you translate these?' said Mathew.

'I'll do my best,' said Douglas his face screwed up in concentration.

'Edith, how come Barnabus sent these papers to you to give to Douglas?' asked Mathew.

Tears formed in Edith's eyes. Laura saw them and thought back to what Rodeo had said about tears coming out of love.

'Douglas, you carry on translating,' said Laura. 'Mathew, I'm sure you have things to do. Edith and I will have a girly chat. Is that ok Edith?' Edith nodded. 'We'll meet back here in a couple of hours.'

Douglas opened his laptop. Two hours eh? Well, he could make a start at least. One hour and fifty two minutes later, Douglas sat back in his chair and silently read back what he'd translated.

'Douglas, you look like you're on another planet,' said Mathew as he sat down.

'Take a look,' said Douglas.' He slid his scribbled notes across the polished table towards Mathew.

Mathew picked them up and began reading.

'My God,' said Mathew. 'This is heavy shit.'

Laura and Edith entered the room.

'Hi guys,' said Laura. 'Edith explained how she had a private audience with Barnabus where she asked him to intervene on Rodeo's behalf. The next thing she knew, these papers arrived in the post.'

'Come and sit down,' said Mathew. 'Edith, this is very important. Does anyone know you have these papers? Have you shown them to anyone?'

'No, no one,' said Edith adamantly.

'That's good, because Douglas translated just the first two pages and they are dynamite. I'm afraid it means all of us here, and that includes you as well Edith, we're all in extreme danger. Some people would kill to destroy this document. It could be a death warrant for anyone who knows of its existence, like all of us.'

Everyone looked at each other in silent disbelief. Douglas broke the silence.

'Look I still have a long way to go with this translation. Leave it with me, nothing's going to happen for a while.'

'What about Edith?' said Laura.

'See she gets home safely,' Mathew replied. 'Edith, you must never tell anyone you received a package from Barnabus or that you came here. Your life and ours are at risk. We must keep it a secret until the time is right.'

'Mais pourquoi, what do the papers say?'

'It's better you don't know. Do you have a cell phone?' asked Mathew. She nodded. 'In an emergency call me.' He handed her a card. 'Give your number to Laura in case we need to call you.'

Douglas returned to translating the remaining four pages. Two hours hour later, Mathew interrupted him.

'I bought you a coffee.'

'Thanks,' said Douglas. 'Put it down over there, I don't want to spill it on the papers.'

'So what else has Barnabus told us?' said Mathew.

'Well, these two pages are extracts from a hidden Testament that's been kept secret by the Vatican for centuries. But these are different. They're not Syriac, I'm certain of that.'

'Here, let me look,' said Mathew. 'These aren't letters,' he said triumphantly. 'These are pictures or, more precisely, pieces of pictures. All we need to do is put them together and complete the jigsaw.'

'How do you know that?' said Douglas.

'Well, you know me, I never was much of a scholar. I always think in pictures rather than words, so to me this makes perfect sense. Let me put them together for you' Mathew drew on a blank piece of paper. Five minutes later he'd produced a picture that needed no explanation but was chilling in its message.

'Holy shit,' said Douglas, as the two of them stared at the drawing. 'So where do we go from here?' he asked finally.

'You know,' said Mathew, 'Rodeo always says ask yourself what would love do now?'

'So what would love do now?' said Douglas.

'Now that is a good question,' said Mathew, 'and I have no idea. But talking of love, is Laura back yet?'

'I don't know, I haven't seen her.'

'Shit,' said Mathew, 'I'll check it out.' As he spoke a member of his security entered the room without knocking.

'Boss, we have a code nine. Two bus loads of gendarmes are heading this way.' His radio crackled into life.

'Alpha two five this is control. The gendarmes appear to be heavily armed. They're surrounding the chateau. I repeat they are surrounding the chateau.'

'Here, give me that.' Mathew grabbed the radio. 'Control, this is Mathew. What visuals do you have, over?'

'Boss, there's three guys, no, two guys and a woman. One guy and the woman are in uniform and the other guy's wearing a dark suit. They're walking down the main drive towards us.'

'Okay, I'm on my way, out.'

CHAPTER 30

EDITH SCREAMED. A white Volkswagen van rammed Laura's small blue Citroen pushing it into the rear of another white Volkswagen van. The airbags inflated. With their seat belts fastened, they couldn't move. They were sandwiched.

Frantically fearing a robbery or kidnap attempt, Laura struggled to release her seat belt. A Gendarme appeared and unlocked the doors and freed them.

That was quick, thought Laura, relieved that the police were on the spot. More Gendarmes appeared. They helped Edith into the police incident vehicle. The doors shut behind them and the vehicle sped off.

Laura felt sick. What had she done? Where were they being taken? Tears formed in Edith's eyes. Her whole body shook.

'Edith what's wrong? You're shaking,' said Laura.

'My parents, they will find out I did not go with Henri to the service for Barnabus.'

'No they won't,' said Laura, reassuringly. 'I will see they don't, I promise.'

Edith looked at Laura, nodded and gave a little reluctant smile.

'I wish you were my sister,' said Edith. 'I often prayed for a sister but God never answered.'

'Maybe he has,' said Laura as she held Edith close to her. 'Maybe he has.'

The Gendarme's van pulled up in a rural road by an old church. Looking through the murky window, Laura made out an unkempt graveyard with old tombs and headstones where the writing had worn away to almost nothing. The van doors opened and a Gendarme ushered them out.

'Where are we? Why have you bought us here?' said Laura in her most assertive voice.

A priest approached them. 'Come with me please,' he said.

'Where are you taking us?' repeated Laura, standing her ground.

'Come, it is for your own safety. We don't want anyone to see you standing out here, quickly.'

Laura and Edith followed the priest through a side door of the church then down some stone steps into a small room that, Laura assumed, was used by the church choir to change into their cassocks.

The priest pulled on one of the coat hooks. Silently a wooden wall panel opened.

'Come,' said the priest.

'Wow,' said Laura, 'this is like something out of James Bond.'

Laura and Edith found themselves in a room, probably a burial crypt, under the church. The floor consisted of large granite slabs. A large rug depicting Jesus riding triumphantly into Jerusalem on a donkey with olive branches strewn in front of him covered most of it. The whitewashed walls were covered in portraits of religious figures. An old leather three piece suite and a rosewood coffee table stood in the centre of the room, looking totally out of place.

'You look surprised,' said a figure dressed in the red and white robes of a cardinal. 'Come and sit down and I'll explain why you were brought here.' His voice sounded calm, gentle and reassuring. Laura and Edith both sat down next to each other on the long leather sofa.

'Can I get you anything, a coffee perhaps?' Edith shook her head negatively.

'No thank you,' said Laura.

'First of all, I must introduce myself. My name is Father Lejon, or Cardinal Lejon. I am from what you would call the liberal wing of the Roman Catholic Church. I believe we are all God's children and that makes Jesus our brother. If he is a deity then we are all deities. Yes, I believe God sent him. He is an old soul, you know, and he set an example for us to follow. You know his main message was one of love. I made reference to old soul. That was deliberate, because we are all eternal beings, we all live forever. Did you know that the Catholic Church originally believed in reincarnation? We dropped it from our beliefs because, if people knew they lived many lives, we wouldn't have any control over them. How could we preach about fire and brimstone and going to hell for all eternity? Anyway, someone born a Catholic in this life might be a Jew or Muslim in another. What I'm trying to say is…I believe Rodeo is a reincarnation of Christ. It is the second coming.'

Laura and Edith looked at one another then at Cardinal Lejon.

'Before Barnabus was murdered…' He saw the look of disbelief on Edith's and Laura's faces. 'Yes, he was murdered, but the world will never know. There will be no postmortem. He wrote a document in an ancient language, Syriac, and then posted it to you, Edith, for you to take to Reverend Douglas Claymore. He is one of the few people in the world who could translate it and he is also a disciple of Rodeo's.'

'Hey, wait a minute,' said Laura. 'Did you say a disciple?'

'Yes, and you are too, and Edith.' Edith smiled. A disciple of Rodeo. A reincarnation of Christ. *That's cool.*

Cardinal Lejon continued. 'The man who posted it for Barnabus worked for me. Before being killed he managed to tell us…'

'Killed?' interrupted Laura.

'Yes,' said Cardinal Lejon. 'He was seen going out to post the package for Barnabus but managed to give them the slip. They tortured him to find out who it was addressed to, then they killed him. I believe he held out long enough for us to bring you here and make sure you're safe.' A shiver went down Laura's spine at the thought of what they might have done to him. 'You see, anyone who even knows of the existence of the package from Barnabus is probably at risk. Now we must leave here. This is only a temporary refuge. They will be here soon, I have no doubt.'

'We have to tell Douglas and Mathew and the others that they're in danger,' said Laura.

'Hopefully and with God's help we have that under control,' answered Cardinal Lejon.

CHAPTER 31

'GENTLEMEN, my name is Mathew Lopez. Can I help you?' Mathew stood in the doorway, his whole bulk acting as a formidable barrier.

'We require to enter,' said the man in the dark suit. Mathew eyed them suspiciously.

'Is that an order or request?'

The man in the dark suit stared at Mathew before responding. 'We can either make this easy or difficult, it's your choice. I have thirty men, fully armed with sub machine guns.'

'Why didn't you say so before?' said Mathew sarcastically. 'You'd better come in, but please wipe your feet 'cause I can smell shit somewhere.'

They sat down in one of the large drawing rooms.

'Monsieur Lopez, the world and Christianity are in great danger so we have come to protect them,' said the man.

'From what or from who exactly?' asked Mathew, sounding a little irritated.

'From you and your friends. You see, I believe you have something that we want. A package with strange writing.'

'You think you can just walk in here and take it?'

'Who's to stop us? Your so-called security are by now neutralised. Don't worry, they are just shot with drugged darts, they will be fine in a few hours, apart from maybe a little headache. We also want Kamna's brother.'

'So you don't have Kamna then? Good girl!' said Mathew.

The man barked an order to one of his cohorts.

'Accompany Mr Lopez and make sure he brings the offending package and the Reverend Claymore as well.'

The cohort drew a pistol from inside his tunic. 'Mr Lopez, after you please.' Mathew led the way.

'Douglas, our friends want the package. As you see, we don't have a lot of choice.' Douglas looked up from the translation. 'They also want you.'

Douglas just nodded. He picked up all the papers and placed them inside the envelope with the papal seal and handed them to the cohort.

The dark-suited man smiled as Mathew and Douglas entered the room.

'Give me the package.' Taking a cigarette lighter from his pocket, he flicked the top and put the flame to the corner. In seconds the package turned to ash.

'Now Mr Lopez and Mr Claymore, I'd like you to kneel and pray for your souls because you are both about to meet your maker.'

The male cohort pointed his gun at them. Mathew struggled to think what to do. Was it meant to end like this?

'You won't get away with this you know,' said Mathew.

'Oh, but we will. We'll leave a note to say you were all part of Rodeo's paedophile ring and the citizens of France took it upon themselves to see justice done for little Carlotta. Now fucking kneel, both of you,' he screamed at them.

As they knelt he pulled a gun from a breast holster. Douglas closed his eyes, waiting for the inevitable. Mathew turned and looked directly at the man with the gun. It distracted the man for a split second. Mathew lunged at him with his whole massive body. Two shots rang out. One passed straight through the forehead of the dark-suited man, the other through the temple of his male cohort.

Douglas expected…he wasn't quite sure, but felt happily surprised he could open his eyes after the two shots were fired.

The female cohort had shot them both. She spoke. They both recognised the voice, but it wasn't a female voice.

'Quickly, get Davey and Keanan, we have to get out of here.'

'Alfredo, is it you?' said Douglas in amazement.

'But you're dead!' said Mathew as he picked himself up from the floor.

'Do I look dead?' replied Alfredo. 'Thanks to TRXc3 and its antidote we fooled everyone. Now let's get Davey and Keanan and get the hell out of here.'

'The chopper,' said Mathew.

'How do we get to it?' said Alfredo.

'It's across the grounds,' said Douglas.

'We'll never make it.'

'Wrong,' said Mathew, 'it's at the airbase being refueled.' He looked at his watch. 'But it's due back in about ten minutes. If only we can hang out till then. I'll call the pilot and get him to pick us up from the roof.'

'The roof!' said Alfredo.

'Yes, when I checked out this place I noticed there's a flat area, large enough for a chopper to land. It worried me at the time, could have been a security risk, but now it's gonna save us. We'll pick up Davey and Keanan on the way up there. Let's go before the others find out what's happened.'

CHAPTER 32

FIFTEEN DAYS after Barnabus died, one hundred and seventeen cardinals formed a conclave in the Vatican to elect the new Pope. Michael Heaney sat glued to the TV in his Little Rock offices. He had little time for the tradition of the whole occasion.

'Black smoke, white smoke, who gives a fuck? Just get on and announce it why don't you. Don't let me down, Bilo boy. I have a lot riding on you.'

As he spoke, the TV cameras focused on a plume of white smoke rising from the Vatican.

Heaney's mouth went dry. He felt his pulse quicken. Crowds and the world's media filled St Peter's Square. Everyone focused on the balcony. For Heaney, the wait felt like an eternity. Eventually the spokesman appeared dressed in the red and white robes of a Cardinal. Quickly the din quietened. A cheer went up from the crowd as he spoke. The only English words Heaney could make out were brothers and sisters. Then he heard the name Cardinal Biloweiki.

'That'll do me,' said Heaney, as he reached for the remote to switch off the TV.

* * *

Rodeo sat in his cell strumming his guitar. The new song he worked on wouldn't come together. *Maybe the lyrics are wrong*, he thought. However, deep down he knew he had other things on his mind.

He turned his head when he heard keys turning in the cell door.

'Come with me, you have a visitor' said the guard in a heavy French accent.

He led Rodeo through the corridor into another room. Philippe Revel stood to greet him.

'Rodeo, please excuse me, I won't shake your hand as any body contact is strictly forbidden.'

He sat down again. Rodeo sat the other side of the plain wooden table. The guard sat on a chair by the door.

'Rodeo, my name is Philippe Revel and, providing you agree, I'm to be your defense lawyer. Your friend and head of security, Mr Lopez, retained my services. So Rodeo, tell me, who are you?'

'Wouldn't you rather know if I'm innocent or guilty? In the movies isn't that what they always ask?'

'No, the court will decide that. I want to know everything about you. I want everything, warts and all. I do not want any surprises sprung on me by the prosecutor in court. There can be no skeletons left in the closet. Do you understand?'

'It's your call,' said Rodeo.

'It may be my call, but it's your life on the line.'

'Philippe – may I call you Philippe?' He nodded. 'There's one certainty in this life, and that is that we all die one day. But I kind of like life and if I were to be executed for the rape and murder of a child, my life would have served no purpose. No one would play my music or listen to things I've said about love and how love is all there really is. I just feel there'd be a lot less love in the world. So where do you want me to start?'

Rodeo spoke about his childhood, how he went to jail because of the Reverend Claymore and how, because of love, he's now one of his best friends. Then he moved on to his early years as a rock musician and his rise to stardom. Philippe listened intently, occasionally taking notes, sometimes nodding his approval or understanding, sometimes smiling and occasionally looking a little shocked but doing his best to hide it.

'So Rodeo, tell me a little more about Heaven's Door.'

Rodeo smiled. 'What do you want to know?'

'Rodeo, please don't play with me. You know what I'm alluding to.'

Rodeo looked a little taken back. Philippe softened his tone a little. 'You must understand the whole case could be won or lost on this.'

'You want to know did I have sex with underage kids at Heaven's Door?' Philippe nodded. 'The truthful answer is no. I know I have a reputation, you know, groupies, but that's all for show. Who would take me seriously as a rock star if I didn't? Not that it's wrong, you understand. It's just that I don't need physical love. The first girl I slept with for many years is Kamna. She's different. I think she's maybe a soul mate.'

'Go on,' said Philippe quietly.

'Mathew was supposed to check the age of anyone attending a party at Heaven's Door and get some ID. We have paper records going back to the very first party, copies of driving licenses and ID cards. It's possible some were faked, doctored or something, but we never knowingly let anyone attend who was under eighteen.'

'Where were the records kept?' asked Philippe.

'In an office at Heaven's Door.'

'Rodeo, it is unlikely they are still there.' Rodeo looked puzzled. 'I am sorry to tell you this, but last night fire destroyed Heaven's Door Ranch. Your staff there, who are all safe by the way, claim a right wing Christian evangelical group did it. They invited people to go along and put Rodeo memorabilia and music albums on the flames to stoke up the fire. I'm so sorry.'

Rodeo put his head in his hands.

'Look… Rodeo…' Philippe could see the pain in his face. 'I think, as you say in English, we'll call it a day. I'll be back tomorrow. Au revoir.'

CHAPTER 33

As Château de Montvillargenne disappeared beyond the horizon, Mathew relaxed a little.

'So where to now?' Mathew asked Alfredo, who sat next to him.

'Now we go and save Laura and Edith. I've given the pilot the coordinates, I just hope they're there.'

'Are they in trouble?' asked Douglas, overhearing.

'No, luckily we got to them first, but we need to move them quickly.'

'Thank God,' said Douglas.

'What would you like me to do with this?' He took a package from inside his shirt.

'Is that what I think it is?' said Mathew.

'Yes, it's the original package from Barnabus,' replied Douglas.

'So what did they burn then?' said Alfredo.

'When you left the room to find out what was going on, I hid the original and just left my translation scribble on the table with an old envelope. I scrapped some wax from a candle I found in the room, stamped it with my ring, made it look like a realistic seal and pressed it onto the envelop.'

'You son of a gun,' said Mathew.

'It won't take them long to find out,' said Alfredo. 'They'll send the ashes to a laboratory for tests. We have to assume they know we still have the package.'

* * *

Cardinal Lejon, Edith and Laura made their way through a narrow, damp tunnel barely high enough to stand upright in. Cardinal Lejon's small flashlight provided the only light.

'The Huguenots used to use this tunnel in the religious wars of the sixteenth century and then again in the seventeenth century. More recently the French Resistance used it in World War Two. It has saved many lives. It is thirteen hundred metres long.'

The tunnel ended in a densely overgrown copse which, to Edith, seemed almost as dark as the tunnel.

'Keep still and be silent,' said Cardinal Lejon. 'This is where we are being met, but I have no idea how long we will have to wait.'

An hour later they all heard the sound of a helicopter.

'They are using a helicopter to try and find us. Try and cover yourselves with some branches,' said Cardinal Lejon. Laura peeked at the helicopter through gaps in the leaves.

'It's Rodeo's, I know it is. I recognise it.'

'Are you certain?' said Cardinal Lejon. They watched it circle, searching for somewhere to land.

Laura spoke. 'Come on, let's make a dash for it.'

'I hope you're right,' said Cardinal Lejon.

They wasted no time in getting them on board before taking off again.

'Where to now?' said Mathew. 'We're running short of places to go.'

The Abbaye Notre-Dame de Senanque stood in isolated splendour in a valley filled with chestnut trees. Lavender fields surrounded the Abbey.

'The Cistercian Monks work in these fields,' said Cardinal Lejon. 'The lavender helps the bees produce splendid honey, which the monks sell to provide for the few necessities they need. Otherwise they are self-sufficient. When they're not working they are either singing in a choir or praying, or of course sleeping. The bees, on the other hand, just work and sleep.'

Cardinal Lejon had a kind of freshness about him. Mathew liked him. But what made him believe Rodeo was the reincarnation of Christ? That he, Laura, Douglas, Alfredo, Davey, Keanan and Edith were all his disciples?

Douglas looked like a cat with two tails. 'Eureka!' he shouted, as he entered the refectory. Since they had arrived at the Abbey, twenty-four hours earlier, he'd shut himself away, even from Laura, to work on the translation.

'Let's all go sit in the lavender fields and take in that gorgeous scent, while I read what Barnabus wants us to communicate to the world.'

Gregorian chants could be heard coming from the Abbey. Everyone sat except Douglas, who remained standing.

'I have a letter written by Barnabus to the Catholic Church. A letter that would do justice to Saint Paul himself. He begins as follows. On Earth as it is in Heaven, this is our destiny. In Heaven there is only love. Love is all there is. There is no Hell or Purgatory. Hell and Purgatory only exist in the imagination of humans and are used by some as a means of power and control. The reality is, there is only love. Jesus Christ told us to love thy neighbour as thyself. But how can we do that if we ourselves are weighed down by guilt and by sin? So what happens is we then judge our neighbours as we judge ourselves. We make moral judgements based on guilt and sin rather than love. So I tell you, love yourself first. If you do not love yourself how can you love others? Are you able to look in the mirror and honestly say I'm proud of my actions because they are born out of love? Or do you look in the mirror and feel ashamed because your actions are born from a desire for power or possessions? Do I treat people how I would like to be treated? Look at what you do. Is it with love or is it without love? If everything we did was with love then we are truly creating Heaven on Earth. I tell you God demands nothing from us and he gives us only love.

'Christ was crucified because there was not enough love in the world. By dying on the cross he showed us the ultimate example of love. For over two thousand years we have waited for the second coming of Christ. But we have learned nothing. Yes, we pray to him and sing his praises, though in reality there is no more love now than over two thousand years ago. Now that he is once again here on Earth we are intent on repeating our mistake.

'Yes, he is here on Earth. Does that shock you? Did you expect to hear fanfares of trumpets? My brothers and sisters, listen and you will hear. Listen to his music and all you will hear is love. Listen to his words and all you will hear is God, but of course they are one of the same.

'This man I speak of, if he is crucified, humankind will endure another two thousand years of a world without enough love. A world with endless wars. A world where people are slaves to religious or political dogma. A world with misery and hunger. A world in which people are not allowed to think for themselves. A world where love is forced to take a back seat.

'The man I speak of is the American musician Rodeo. He is in prison awaiting trial for a crime he did not commit. Once again religious zealots and corrupt politicians are making false allegations against a man who has bought only love into the world. Why are they doing this? I believe it is out of a misguided sense of loyalty to God. But all God needs is love. The religious zealots also want to destroy Islam, but I say to you the only way forward is love. Show Islam what love can achieve. Invite them to be a part of a new world of love. But I also say to you do not give up love for a world of tyranny, where a person is forced to worship a God they do not recognise, and where people are told how to behave morally with the threat of barbaric punishments if they break these false rules. For these rules do not come from God, they come from men who command power by saying they know what God demands or wants. If they don't know love, they don't know God. If these men persist in their doctrine then you must resist. Resistance under these circumstances is an act of love for yourself and humankind. I know this is a paradox, but giving in and surrendering or allowing something to happen is not an act of love, but neither is wholesale annihilation. If these corrupt politicians and religious zealots have their way, all they will succeed in doing is delaying the time when life on Earth is as it is in Heaven for all people.

'As the head of the Roman Catholic Church I urge all Catholics to adopt Rodeo's philosophy of love and seek spiritual enrichment through love. Do not worship God, instead love God, because if you truly love God you will love yourself and all humanity, because we are all one.'

Everyone sat in stoned silence. The Gregorian chants continued in the background helping to create a surreal spiritual dimension. Douglas sat down on the dusty ground next to Laura.

'The picture deciphered by Mathew tells us about Armageddon.'

'This is really heavy shit,' replied Matthew after a while. 'Hell, what do we do? I'm lost.'

Laura looked around at everyone before interjecting. 'Rodeo would ask the question, what would love do now?'

'I know,' said Davey.

'Go on,' said Mathew, trying to encourage him.

'Well, Kalma-diva must not be crucified, so we must rescue him. Then we go to India where I have many friends who will look after all of us.'

'Yeah right,' said Keanan. 'They're just going to let us walk in and walk out with him out just like that?'

'We'll think of something between us,' said Alfredo.

Mathew stood. 'Right now we all need to be on our guard and keep our wits about us. Cardinal Lejon has told me his men will do what they can to protect us, but that doesn't mean we can rest easy. Just be careful everyone.' Cardinal Lejon nodded in agreement.

CHAPTER 34

MICHAEL HEANEY stood to huge applause.

'Mr Chairman, Mr Vice President to be, this convention and citizens of our great nation. I stand before you and before God to accept your nomination for the presidency of the United States, thank you. I would also like to express the gratitude of this convention to the good Christian people of Kansas and the city of Topeka for their warm hospitality.

'Our party deserves to be proud of itself. We are united in our values of freedom, family, work and peace. We have another value, in God we trust…a Christian God. When I hear folk dismissing Christianity as irrelevant I feel sad and uncomfortable because our country was forged and moulded by people who held deep Christian beliefs. The puritans who sailed on the Mayflower, African slaves who came to know Christ through all their sufferings and hardships, refugees from Europe who came here because they wanted the freedom to worship God in their own way. They all embraced our laws, our politics. They didn't want to change anything. We owe everything we have to our Christian heritage. I promise, I will maintain our heritage. I will do whatever it takes to ensure our freedom and the freedom of Christians around the world to follow their Christian faith.'

Mathew picked up the TV remote control and pointed it at the TV.

'I tell you, if that man becomes president we are going to have a war on our hands.'

'This is why it is imperative Rodeo lives,' said Cardinal Lejon. 'He is the world's only hope.'

'But did you hear that applause when he stood to speak?' said

Douglas. 'Surely the American people have more sense than to vote for him as president?'

'At the moment yes, you're right, but if there's another 9/11 he'll win by a landslide,' said Alfredo. 'And you know what, I can almost guarantee it's gonna happen.'

*   *   *

Rodeo sat across the table to Philippe. The guard sat in his usual chair.

'I have some news. A date for the trial has been set. The first day of October.'

'Next month,' said Rodeo, a little surprised it was so soon. Philippe read his thoughts.

'Yes, it is soon. We have only forty days. The prosecution must feel confident of their case.'

'Does it give you enough time?' asked Rodeo.

'I didn't object, I wanted them to know we are also confident.'

'Are we?'

'If you want the honest answer, no.'

Rodeo smiled. 'You know Philippe, I could be your first ever failure.'

'Maybe not. We have a new star witness. Tell me about the girl you know called Kamna.' Rodeo sat back in his chair and threw his head back.

'You know, she's something else, but I don't understand. I made love to her. What the fuck's she gonna say in court that's gonna help me?'

'She's going to say that after you made love she left and went to a hospital where a doctor recovered your sperm. The doctor then tried to kill her. She managed to escape by killing the doctor. That is documented, or rather that a doctor was killed on the same day and at the same clinic.'

Rodeo sat up. Philippe continued.

'She also says a woman put her up to it, the same woman who attacked her after she arrived in Paris. I'm sorry, you didn't know about that. I will also warn you, when you see Kamna in court, she will not be the girl you knew. Her face…' Philippe stopped, not knowing what to say.

Rodeo closed his eyes.

'She believes the woman is an associate of the American Senator, Michael Heaney. Kamna worked in Little Rock at a software company owned by an Indian guy.'

'Now there's a coincidence,' said Rodeo, rocking back in his chair. 'Michael Heaney comes from Little Rock. The same Michael Heaney who zapped Douglas and raped his fiancé. Of course we have no proof, but that's the kind of man he is. I'm not judging him by the way, he just hasn't found love. Maybe Mathew wasn't so crazy after all. You know, he believed Heaney wanted me alive and well so he could blame all America's problems on a moral decline caused by me. So he wanted me accused of a heinous crime, and what could be worse than the rape and murder of a child? Anyone who supports me or fails to speak out against me is automatically guilty by association. Which leaves the way open for him to win the Republican Presidential Nomination and then the Presidency.'

'Voila,' said Philippe, 'you have solved the crime. Now all we have to do is convince three judges.'

'Where's Kamna now?' asked Rodeo.

'She is staying at the Indian Consulate in Paris. They are protecting her.'

'Yeah, but is she safe?'

'As safe as she can be under the circumstances.'

* * *

At the Abbaye Notre-Dame de Senanque, the monks silently filed into the chapel for the dawn mass. The sun had yet to rise across the valley. Alfredo couldn't sleep. He'd been awake most of the night. Something wasn't right. He couldn't put his finger on it exactly. It felt like they were being watched. He looked around the dormitory. All the shutters were closed. The only light came from a moonbeam shining through a skylight.

'Everyone.' Alfredo spoke in a low, calm authoritative voice. 'Everyone wake up. We have to leave, now. Come on.'

'Mr Alfredo, what is wrong?' asked Davey, still half asleep

'Come on, we have to leave quickly.'

'Where we going at this God damn hour?' said Keanan, yawning.

'Just get dressed, quick as you can.'

The chopper pilot looked at Mathew. 'I'll go get her up and meet you shortly.'

Alfredo allowed everyone two minutes.

'Are you all ready?' He didn't wait for an answer. 'Bring a coat or sweater or something, it's cold out, and follow me.'

He led them through a door to the library then through another door into the grounds at the rear of the Abbey. They could hear the monks singing.

'Where's Cardinal Lejon?' asked Laura.

'He must have joined his brothers for dawn mass,' said Alfredo. Just as he spoke, a massive explosion destroyed the dormitory they'd just left. Douglas felt the ground shake under his feet.

'Run to the trees,' shouted Mathew. He pointed to the edge of the lavender field over two hundred metres away. They all ran except Davey, who just stood and gawped at the flames leaping from the Abbey roofs. Laura grasped his hand and pulled him towards the trees. Edith tripped and clutched her knee. Mathew lifted her up and carried her over his shoulder. Four more explosions rocked the Abbey. The whole building became one giant bonfire.

'Boss, I can hear the chopper,' said Davey excitedly, as they stood amongst the trees. They all looked to where the sound came from and saw it rise from the ground. It reached a height of around two hundred feet then exploded. The ensuing fire ball appeared to consume itself before hitting the ground.

'We can't stay here,' said Alfredo, turning away from the wreckage of the chopper. 'We have to keep moving. I'm praying they think we perished in the Abbey, but it won't take them long to realise we are still very much alive.'

'Can you walk?' said Mathew to Edith.

'I think so, but it is very painful,' she said tearfully.

'Here, put your arm round my shoulder,' said Keanan.

One thing puzzled Mathew. How did Alfredo know something was wrong? Was it sixth sense or did he know something the rest of them didn't?

'We'll head towards the main road. Maybe we can catch a bus that's heading to one of the local markets,' said Alfredo.

'I think the road's over the other side of that hill,' said Douglas pointing. 'It's at least five miles away. I remember thinking how secluded this place looked when we flew in.'

'Okay, we keep moving, but we take it steady,' said Mathew. Keanan sidled up to Mathew and whispered.

'There's something moving through the trees. Just down there to our right, on the edge of the field. Look.' Mathew looked. 'There, did you see?' said Keanan.

Mathew nodded. 'You wait here.'

He moved surprisingly nimbly for a large man, down a steep bank through undergrowth and trees. As he neared the spot Keanan had pointed to, he froze.

'Alfredo, Douglas, here. Come here and bring a knife. Keep the others back.' After scrambling down to where Mathew stood, they looked in horror at Cardinal Lejon's naked body hanging from a bow. His hands were bound behind his back with plastic ties. Bruises, blood and what looked like burns covered every part of his body. Then Mathew saw he had no eyes.

They cut him down and laid him on a small grassy patch. Douglas placed his rain coat over the body to cover it as best he could and said a short silent prayer.

'What's fucking going on?' said Mathew accusingly to Alfredo. 'How did you know something was going to happen minutes before it did? What kind of butcher did this to a human being? I want some answers and I want them now.'

Mathew scowled. He looked as if he would break into an uncontrollable rage at any second.

'Can't you see?' said Alfredo. 'Look at him. Look! He's a victim of the inquisition.'

'What fucking God damn inquisition?' shouted Mathew, already at boiling point.

'The inquisition that killed my three colleagues, the inquisition that killed Barnabus and now wants the documents destroyed. The inquisition that wants Rodeo dead because of what's written in the hidden Testaments. Do I need to spell it out any more?'

CHAPTER 35

PHILIPPE REVEL paced the floor of the small, musty-smelling interview room.

'There's still no sign of Mathew and the rest of your entourage. Why did they leave Château De Montvillargenne in such a hurry? Why has no one seen them since? Your trial begins tomorrow and three of our key witnesses are missing.

'Can't you ask for a postponement or something?' asked Rodeo.

'I have already and the Judge refused.'

'So who are their witnesses?'

'A forensic DNA expert, the doctor who pronounced Carlotta dead, Chief Inspector Partis, Sister Louisa the convent's Mother Superior and Sister Teresa who found Carlotta dead. Plus anyone else they wish to call, because I have no doubt the Judge will agree.' Philippe banged on the table in frustration.

'So what's the defense strategy going to be?' said Rodeo.

'Good question. If I was in America I would listen to the prosecution case very carefully and identify any weaknesses. Then bit by bit challenge their assertions, enough to sow the seeds of doubt and then, only then, introduce our star witness, Kamna.'

'Sounds good to me,' said Rodeo.

'But this is not America, this is France. First of all you will be questioned by the Judge. How you respond will determine in the jurors' minds whether you are guilty or innocent. You see, in the assizes court there is one Judge and two magistrates. They, along with nine jurors, form a tribunal and it is the tribunal who will decide on the verdict and sentence.'

'Okay.'

'By the way, you'll wear headphones so you can hear everything in English.'

* * *

The court room appeared smaller than Rodeo envisaged. Wooden benches, tricolours and bright blue robes of the court staff made it look like a scene from a movie about the French Revolution. He tried to make out who the various people were.

'Here, put these on,' said Philippe, passing him the headphones.

'The people will rise,' were the first words Rodeo heard.

The Judge followed by the two magistrates and nine jurors entered and took their places on the benches. Rodeo smiled. The voice in his headphones belonged to what sounded like a very sexy French lady with a wonderful accent. *Maybe this won't be so bad after all!* He looked around to see if he could see her.

Philippe nudged him. 'The usher will lead you to the dock while the Judge is speaking.'

The sexy voice continued. 'The people maybe seated.'

The usher walked across the floor to Rodeo and beckoned him to follow him as the voice in the headphones continued.

'This tribunal is set to examine the charge that Rodeo, who is charged under his real name Rodeo Rickets, murdered and raped Carlotta Benando. The accused will face the bench.'

Rodeo stood on his own facing the Judge and the magistrates. He could see Philippe to his left. He nodded, to try and put Rodeo at ease. Rodeo looked directly ahead to the bench. The Judge was a man, but the two magistrates were women. *Well, I'll be damned*, thought Rodeo. Not that it made any difference, but somehow he felt more at ease.

'Rodeo Rickets,' spoke his interpreter. 'Through your lawyer you have pleaded not guilty. I'm going to ask you some questions which you are required to answer.'

Shit! The voice in his headphones was giving him a hard on. She sounded so seductively gorgeous.

The questioning continued for two hours before the Judge called a two hour recess for lunch.

'You did well,' said Philippe, walking over to him. 'I watched the jury. They were all listening, which is always a good sign and the Judge, he only tried to identify the facts of the case.'

After the recess the Judge continued with the questioning.

'Mr Rickets, how long had you known Carlotta?'

'Well, her father, a friend of mine, asked if we could take care of her as he had to go away on business. Because her mother, his wife, had died and he had no one else to look after her.'

'I see. Why did it not occur to you to seek professional help from welfare services who could possibly have arranged foster care?'

'Well Sir, Carlotta's daddy was in some kind of trouble and he believed the people who were after him could have tried to get to him through her, so it was a secret arrangement. No one was to know, apart from the people around me, my friends and staff, that she was with us.' Philippe cringed.

'Your friends and staff. Are they available to be questioned?'

'No, they've disappeared. I don't know where or why.'

'I see, how very convenient,' spoke the Judge. 'What trouble was Carlotta's father in exactly and how did you come to know him?'

Philippe smiled as Rodeo answered.

'One day my head of security found him bleeding on the sidewalk. We took him to hospital and I paid for his treatment. We didn't even know he had a daughter until he phoned one evening before a concert, said he was in some kind of trouble and would we take care of Carlotta till things had settled down.'

'Mr Rickets, I have to ask you. Did you kill her so her father would not find out you were sexually assaulting her while he was away?'

'No Sir, I loved her, same way I love everyone. She was like my own daughter.'

'I have in front of me press cuttings from various publications in the United States which suggest you are a paedophile. Many paedophiles are fathers who think nothing of raping their own daughters, so why would thinking of Carlotta as your daughter stop you?'

Philippe wanted to shout 'objection', but this inquisition was only between the Judge and the defendant.

'They're just rumours put about by people who don't like what I have to say.'

'And what do you have to say? Particularly about pedophilia? Shall I remind you? I will quote you. I believe that nothing we do is right or wrong, only with love or without love. I will not condemn because God will not condemn. Did you say this?'

'Yes I did, but I also said anyone who indulges in personal satisfaction with children is without love, for themselves and the child and because of that, society needs to show love to the child by stopping the person. Then we should help the person by helping them find love in their lives rather than physical satisfaction.'

'The night of the rape and murder, you said to the police you were tired after the concert. Yet you wanted to drive yourself back to the hotel.'

'Yes, that's correct.'

'Why did you drive yourself?'

'I wanted time on my own.'

'What for? To go to the convent of the Sisters of Charity in Saint-Omer?'

'No, I just drove back to the Chateau.'

'But the staff on duty say you didn't arrive back until five o'clock in the morning. So what were you doing and where did you go?'

'I don't remember. I think maybe I pulled over somewhere and did some meditation. When I'm meditating time doesn't come into it.'

'The tribunal will recess for today.'

'The people will rise.'

Philippe walked across to Rodeo.

'How did I do?' said Rodeo.

'Okay. But I think, as you would say, we have an uphill battle on our hands.'

On day two, the first of the prosecution witnesses gave their evidence. Rodeo listened intently through his headphones as the forensic DNA expert answered the Judge's questions.

'Tell me, where was the DNA recovered from?'

'From sperms found in the vagina of the deceased.'

'The DNA match with the accused, what are the chances of an error or of someone else having the same match?'

'The chances are zero. The reliability of tests today are absolute.'

Philippe stood and addressed the Judge. 'I have some questions I would like to ask the witness.'

'As you wish.'

'Sir, apart from the sperm, what other DNA samples did you test?'

'None.'

'You mean you were not given any to test?'

'No, I collected the samples myself. There was nothing else to test, only the sperm'

'Don't you find that a little surprising? Wouldn't there have been hairs or skin or something?'

'Not necessarily.'

'Is that yes or no?' Philippe's voice became sharp and terse.

The Judge intervened. 'Mr Revel, please allow the witness to explain.'

'Okay, your explanation, please,' said Philippe.

'Other DNA being available depends on, for example, if the attacker wore gloves, had they shaved their body beforehand, were they wearing a hairnet?'

'A hairnet? How many times in an attack of this nature, where the victim has been raped and murdered, have you failed to find sources of DNA other than sperm?'

'None, however please believe me it is possible.'

'And so is a meteorite falling on my head. I have no further questions for this witness.'

'Fifteen love,' said Rodeo to himself.

The next witness, Doctor Levine, looked across the courtroom to Rodeo. Rodeo never flinched or looked away as the doctor's eyes bored into him.

'Doctor Levine,' the Judge began. 'Am I correct in saying you pronounced the victim dead at the scene and you also carried out the autopsy?'

'Yes, that is correct.'

'Please tell the tribunal, how, in your opinion, the victim died.'

'Suffocation, probably with a pillow.'

'Were there any other injuries?'

'Yes, her wrists were raw and bleeding from being tied together with plastic ties and she had bruises on her upper and lower abdomen that are consistent with a rape of this type. There were also marks around her mouth and the back of the head that I believe were caused by a very tight gag.'

'At what time would you say death occurred?'

'Two o'clock in the morning, give or take five minutes either way.' 'Thank you Doctor, I have no more questions. Mr Revel, do you have any questions for this witness?'

'Yes I have. Doctor, what were the injuries to her genital regions?'

'They were consistent with being raped.'

'What does that mean exactly?'

'Well, her hymen was broken at the time of the assault.'

'And what other injuries?'

'Sir, I must object to this questioning.' The Doctor looked flustered and sweated profusely. The Judge intervened.

'Doctor, please answer the question, however insensitive it appears to be.' The Judge glared at Philippe.

'There were none, but I could tell intercourse had taken place.'

'Doctor, please correct me if I'm wrong, but is it not consistent with being raped that there would be signs of bruising around the genital regions, especially in such a young girl?'

'Yes, you are right.'

'Would it be possible to break the hymen and not cause any bruising?'

'I really cannot say.'

'Okay, let me refresh your memory. I speak of a case that came to trial three years ago when you were working for the defense. You said and I quote, it is not possible to rape a girl this age and break the hymen without causing even slight bruising. So I ask you again, would it be possible to break the hymen and not cause any bruising?'

'No, it is not possible.'

'Thank you Doctor, I have no further questions. However, I would like to remind the tribunal that if, as suggested, Rodeo killed her so her father wouldn't find out he had been sexually assaulting her while he cared for her, doesn't it seem strange her hymen remained intact until the night of the murder?'

Thirty love, thought Rodeo.

On day four, Rodeo felt a little more relaxed in the austere surroundings of the court room. Philippe sat next to him and spoke quietly.

'The prosecution have asked if a witness, who's not listed because he came forward at a late stage, can give evidence. I have seen his statement. I argued against him giving evidence but the Judge sided with the prosecution. I need to play for time, what you would call delaying tactics while my people do a little digging into this witness' background.'

'The people will rise.'

Rodeo stood with the rest of the court while the tribunal took their seats. After everyone else sat down, one witness stood facing the tribunal. He appeared miserable, yet at the same time arrogant. The Judge spoke.

'Please tell the tribunal your name and occupation.'

'My name is Monsieur Pascal Leon and I am an undertaker.' Rodeo smiled to himself. The sexy voice in his headphones mimicked what the witness must have sounded like. If Rodeo didn't know better, he would have described him as nasty or wholly disagreeable. In reality, Rodeo knew this man had never experienced what it was like to give or receive love.

The Judge continued. 'Monsieur Leon, what were you doing on the night Carlotta Benando was murdered?'

'I live on my own. At ten o'clock I went to bed as I normally do. I read for a while before falling asleep. At exactly one o'clock in the morning I was woken by my phone ringing. I know it was one o'clock because I looked at my radio alarm. It was Doctor Lemare. One of his patients had died and my services were required.'

'So Monsieur Leon, what did you do?'

'I dressed quickly and drove in the hearse to the address in St Etoise. When I turned out of my drive I saw a car, a large car, parked at the side of the lane. You must realise this is very unusual because I live in a very rural location, there are no other houses. So I drove very slowly. I'm ashamed to say I thought it might be lovers, but there was only one person in the car.'

'Monsieur Leon,' said the Judge, 'please tell the tribunal who you saw in the car.'

The witness looked across the court to Rodeo. 'The defendant, Rodeo.'

'How can you be sure?'

'Because he is well known, easily recognisable. I have seen him on television many times. I know I'm not mistaken.'

'How far from the convent at St Omer do you live?'

'Three kilometers.'

'Thank you Monsieur Leon, I have no further questions for you.

The Judge spoke again. 'I have evidence from the police. Tyre tracks which match the tyres of the car used by Mr Rickets on the night of the murder were found exactly where Monsieur Leon claims to have seen Mr Rickets in a car.'

Philippe Revel stood to speak. 'Sir, I need to spend some time with my client before I question this witness.'

'Very well, you have two hours. The tribunal is adjourned till two o'clock.'

Philippe looked angry. 'Why did you not tell me you were only three kilometers from the Convent?'

'Because I wasn't. After the gig I went south, don't ask me where exactly. I only know it was south, not north.'

'How can you be so sure?'

'The car's sat nav showed me going south.'

'You're absolutely sure?'

'Absolutely, and the car I drove was brand new, with no wear on the tyres. It had only around two hundred kilometres on the clock, so those tracks they found prove nothing.'

'Okay, so our undertaker's lying. Now all we have to do is discredit him, sow some seeds of doubt on his testimony. You stay here while I speak to my people.'

'Well, I hadn't planned on going anywhere.' Philippe smiled and touched Rodeo on the shoulder. As he walked towards the door he stopped and turned round.

'What are you prepared to do to help your case?'

'I'm all yours,' said Rodeo.

Two hours later the tribunal reconvened.

'Monsieur Leon,' said Philippe. Rodeo felt anyone questioned in court by Philippe would almost certainly be reduced to the status of a quivering jelly. Philippe's huge personality, coupled with his sheer presence, appeared to terrify all who stood before him. 'You say you saw Rodeo in a car, parked in a lane near where you live?'

'Yes I did.'

'Tell me, what did he look like?'

'Like he does now, no difference.' Monsieur Leon looked across to Rodeo.

'Monsieur Leon, are you sure about that?'

'Yes, absolutely,' he replied in a voice tinged with pride.

Philippe gave a wry smile before continuing.

'Everyone knows what Rodeo looks like, but his dreadlocks are actually hair extensions, added by a hairdresser before he goes on stage. At the end of each performance a hairdresser removes them.

The reason he is wearing them now is because he was arrested on stage and the hairdresser didn't have an opportunity to remove them. But they were removed by the hairdresser after the concert on the night of the murder. If necessary, the hairdresser will testify to that effect.'

'That will not be necessary,' replied the Judge. 'Monsieur Leon's testimony will be struck from the record and disregarded by the tribunal. The tribunal will recess and reconvene tomorrow at nine thirty. The people will rise.'

'Forty love,' said Rodeo under his breath.

CHAPTER 36

O N THE long walk back to the road they all agreed they'd be safer in the centre of Paris, somewhere like the Ritz Hotel. Maybe we've just had enough of roughing it, thought Mathew, but at least security would be manageable and Paris is where they needed to be to help Rodeo. Not holed up in some God forsaken monastery in the middle of nowhere. Surely no one would risk attacking them at the Ritz?

The packed bus made its way along the picturesque country road. Davey and Keanan stood at the front. A man wearing a traditional beret gave up his seat for Laura.

Mathew recoiled in horror as he saw at a photo of Edith on the front page of a passenger's newspaper. He hadn't thought of that. Of course, her parents would have reported her as missing. Mathew looked along the bus to where she sat. She had her jacket collar up which did a pretty good job of hiding her face. In the photo she had her hair tied back, but on the bus it flowed and helped hide her face. She could be any teenager.

Another bus and two trains later, they walked into the lobby of the Ritz. Hotel security immediately pounced on the bedraggled-looking group. One of them spoke.

'Can we help you people?' His tone sounded aggressive and condescending.

'I would like to see the manager please,' replied Mathew.

'You tell me what you want first and then I'll see if the manager's available.'

'If you value your job you'll go get him right now.' Mathew didn't take his eyes off him. The security man reluctantly caved in. 'I'll call the manager for you Sir.'

'Thank you,' said Mathew, with a touch of sarcasm.

'How may I help you Sir?' said the manager with genuine politeness.

'We'd like to stay here for as long as necessary. We'll require three suites with two bedrooms and one with one bedroom.'

'How long for Sir?'

'Till whenever,' said Mathew nonchalantly.

'I'll check what we have available Sir. May I have your credit card please? The concierge will take your luggage.'

'We're traveling light,' said Mathew, a trifle embarrassed as he took a card from his wallet.

A few minutes later the manager reappeared.

'Thank you Mr Lopez. We have allocated you beautiful deluxe suites, all on the same floor. I will personally show you to your suites. If there is anything you or your party need during your stay, please let me know.'

'There is one thing,' said Mathew. 'I like your security. They're on top of things and security's important to me. I need to speak to the guy who stopped us when we came in.'

'Certainly Sir.'

'How come he's being so nice to us?' asked Douglas.

'Because we were originally going to use this hotel and Old Iron Knickers sent the manager complimentary front row seats for him and his friends.'

'I see,' said Douglas, still wondering how the manager knew they were connected with Rodeo.

*   *   *

Kamna lay in the bath, looking up at the painted ceiling. How did someone paint that upside down in all that intricate detail? How come I'm looking at fucking ceilings?

To her right a mirror made up of hundreds of small decorated tiles put together like a glass mosaic reflected her image. Analysing herself, she admitted she'd rather look at paint dry than a mirror. She looked at her body, soaking in the hot scented water. Everything perfect, her breasts, waist, hips, legs… She wondered what Rodeo would think of her now? Would he be able to look at her and still think her beautiful? Would she still be able to entrance him? The thought that he would no longer be turned on by her frightened her more than anything. Why did she care what Rodeo thought?

'Who the fuck is Rodeo to me anyway?' she said out loud.

Just thinking about him made her moist. Laying back in the water, she imagined Rodeo's tongue working its magic as she teased a nipple. Her other hand reached down between her legs. She moaned as her long fingers delicately caressed the puffy outer lips of her smooth vagina. Nectar like love juices flowed as she imagined Rodeo sucking on and licking her ultra sensitive clitoris. The heavenly sensations built and ebbed until an intense double orgasm overtook her and somewhere, in time and space, her soul became one with Rodeo. Gradually the cosmic sensations subsided.

'See what you do to me, you fucking horny bastard?' Slowly she opened her eyes and found herself involuntarily looking at the reflective glass mosaic. Staring at herself she willed it to shatter into a million pieces.

* * *

In the courtroom on day five, Rodeo listened to Sister Louisa give evidence. His mind drifted. He imagined what she looked like naked. In her fifties, a slightly built woman but with generous breasts, which her nun's robes had difficulty concealing.

A nudge in the ribs from Philippe bought Rodeo back to reality.

'I trust her,' said Philippe. 'I can't say why, but I know I'm right.'

Rodeo put her breasts to the back of his mind and listened to the proceedings.

'Sister Louisa, who had access to the security code for the front door?'

'Only myself and the other sisters.'

'You're sure about that?'

'Yes, it is changed every month and everyone is under strict instructions not to divulge it.'

'When was it last changed?'

'The day before little Carl… I remember because we had a visitor, Sister Maria, from England. She passed through on her way to Lourdes. She only stayed the one night.'

'Was she given the code?'

'No, she had no need. She departed early in the morning on the day Carlotta was attacked.'

'Thank you Sister, I have no further questions. Mr Revel,' continued the Judge, turning to Philippe, 'do you have any questions for this witness?'

'Yes I do. Sister Louisa, this Sister Maria, what do you know about her?'

'Nothing really.'

'Yet you allowed her to stay without knowing who she was. What did she do while she stayed at the convent?'

'I don't know.'

'Excuse me, I know,' said a voice from the back of the court. The voice belonged to a young nun who sat on the witness benches. Philippe turned to look at her. Before he could speak the Judge interrupted.

'Thank you sister, we will come to your evidence on another day.'

'I have no further questions for this witness,' said Philippe.

'Very well,' responded the Judge. 'The tribunal will adjourn till Monday at nine thirty. The people will stand.'

*   *   *

Kamna looked longingly out of the fourth floor, down to the shops below. Rue De Paradis bustled with activity. The crystals didn't much interest her, but the furs and leather…oh to try on some of those.

'The streets are busy. Maybe no one will notice me, if I'm discreet,' she said to herself. Three weeks trapped in the embassy had left her feeling somewhat depressed.

'But,' she argued with herself, 'a little shopping therapy will make me feel better. Okay, I know I'll be taking a risk, but I can look after myself. Maybe going shopping will help put it to the back of my mind. Anyway, once I go back to India, plastic surgeons there can work miracles. However, I do need a new outfit for my court appearance.'

The last statement clinched it. Grabbing her handbag she made a beeline to the lift. No one stopped or spoke to her as she left the embassy through the large solid oak doors. She looked around then stepped out onto the busy pavement. No one seemed the slightest interested in her. *Good. Now to the shops.*

*   *   *

Davey wanted to see his sister more than anything else in the world. Mathew told him she was safe, probably at the Indian Embassy. He knew he shouldn't have sneaked out, but surely no one would miss him. After all, he would only be gone a couple of hours.

Standing on the pavement opposite the Embassy, he tried to pluck up the courage to go in. *What if they arrest me*, he thought, *and make me go home?* Then the impossible happened. The large solid oak doors opened and Kamna walked out onto the pavement. Davey stared, open mouthed. A scarf covered part of her face but he'd know his sister anywhere. His heart beat faster with excitement and love.

Despite his excitement, something told him this was not the time or place for a reunion. There were too many people around. He followed her towards a parade of shops. She didn't even bother to look in the window. She went straight into the first shop. Davey went to follow but stopped suddenly. Some of the female mannequins were dressed in tight leather skirts and tops. Others wore leather bras and thongs. One mannequin with large breasts even sported a furry basque.

'Okay,' said Davey to himself. He'd wait until she came out. Twenty minutes passed, then thirty.

'What is she doing in there?' After forty minutes she came out holding a couple of bags. Davey breathed a sigh of relief.

He followed her to another shop. This time there were male and female mannequins dressed in what Davey thought to be more normal attire – leather coats, dresses and jackets. He waited for five minutes before following her into the shop.

Davey looked around. The staff all appeared to be Indian.

'Cool,' he said to himself. One of them spoke to Davey in Hindi.

'What do you want here?' Davey responded quickly.

'I'm with my elder sister, but I have lost her.'

'Oh, she is over there trying on a dress,' the man said, pointing.

'Thank you,' said Davey. He walked across to where the sales assistant had pointed. There were ladies and gents changing rooms. No one was looking. He sneaked into the ladies changing area.

Hearing voices from one of the changing booths, he stopped to listen.

'You thought we wouldn't be watching for you? You fucking stupid cow. Now you come with me and remember, I won't hesitate to kill you.'

Davey felt in his pocket for the taser Mathew had given him for self-defence. Hiding behind a curtain, he waited for Kamna and her captor to appear. The look on the man's face as the paralysing voltage surged through his body would have been worth millions of Rupees. *If only I could have photographed it!* thought Davey.

Kamna didn't have a clue what was happening until she saw Davey, beaming.

'Davey, what are you doing here?' she said in amazement. Davey belied his fifteen years. Suddenly he'd grown up.

'I'll tell you later, but for now come with me before he recovers,' he said in a mature, commanding tone.

They left the shop. Kamna's assailant lay on the floor of the changing room, still disorientated and in agonising pain.

Davey hailed a cab. 'The Ritz Hotel please.'

'My, you have come up in the world,' said Kamna as she pulled him close to her.

Davey beamed when Kamna related to everyone of how Davey, single handedly, had rescued her. Laura decreed that they should have a party in celebration of Davey's heroics and Kamna's safety.

Everyone joined in the fun. Keanan even plucked up the courage to ask Kamna to dance. Mathew looked on contentedly. Privately he'd spoken to Davey about the necessity to tell him or someone where he was going. Davey nodded in acknowledgement and apologised.

Laura and Douglas smooched to one of Rodeo's slower numbers.

'What's going to happen to us?' asked Laura, as she rested her head on Douglas' shoulder.

'Do you want to know the truth?' replied Douglas, holding her tighter.

'Not really. Once I thought I knew what life was about. Now I'm not sure any more. Okay, I know it's about love and how that's all there is, but where do I fit in? I'm caught up in all this. If it hadn't been for Laladee I'd never have met Rodeo or you. Are our lives planned, are our destinies set in stone?' Douglas kissed her ear.

'Maybe our lives are planned,' he said. 'Maybe the people we'll meet or the places we'll go are written in the stars or some great book. But the essence of life isn't planned. That depends on how much love is in our lives. When you think about it, when we go to Heaven we can't take our houses or possessions, but we can take our experiences and memories. The lucky ones are those who have lots of happy memories of love in their lives that they can take with them. Without love an...' Laura stopped him with a sloppy kiss on the lips.

CHAPTER 37

WHEN POPE Innocent XIV returned to his native United States, huge crowds turned out, all eager to catch a glimpse of the first American Pope. The crowds were by no means all Catholic, a fact that pleased Michael Heaney immensely.

Towards the end of his visit, Pope Innocent and Michael Heaney held a private meeting under the guise of the COACC at Heaney's Little Rock HQ.

'So Bilo, you old fox, you finally got your wish.'

'Yes, the Catholic Church needs a strong leader and at last the cardinals recognised that fact. I'll be like Saint Peter, a rock. I intend to lay the foundations for a Church that demands obedience to God and his laws and…'

'Great,' said Heaney interrupting. 'If I drank, which I don't, I'd drink to that. You know my presidential opponent? His Achilles Heel is his previous support for Rodeo. So when Rodeo is found guilty, dear old Whitehouse here I come.' His eyes misted over as he contemplated the thought.

Pope Innocent removed his gold-rimmed spectacles as he spoke. 'And if he's not found guilty?' He stared at Heaney who smiled, slightly nervously, before speaking.

'Don't worry, everything's taken care of. He's history.'

'I hope you're right,' said Pope Innocent, 'because without you in the Whitehouse our plans and my Papacy…'

'Stop worrying,' said Heaney. 'Believe me, you're speaking to the next US President. However, I do have one pretty little problem, an Indian slut called Kamna. She worked in Little Rock.' Pope Innocent raised his eyebrows. 'Don't worry, we covered our tracks,' continued Heaney 'But she's going to give evidence for

Rodeo's defense, and that might make it more difficult to convict him.'

'So what do you want from me?'

'She's holed up at the Paris Ritz with all of Rodeo's cronies.'

'Interesting,' said Pope Innocent. 'Before Barnabus died, he sent some documents to Douglas Claymore. Those documents could jeopardise everything we're working for. My people have already failed three times in their efforts to either destroy or retrieve them. I feel we have a mutual problem.'

'So what do we do?' said Heaney.

'We wait. Let this Indian slut give her evidence. In the meantime, you dig up some dirt on her background and her evidence will be discredited.'

'And what about your documents?'

'When Rodeo is found guilty and I release evidence which shows Barnabus undermining Christianity and the Catholic Church, they will become irrelevant. They will be nothing more than the last ramblings of a senile old fool.'

*   *   *

On day six of the trial, Philippe addressed a young nun, Sister Helene.

'Sister Helene, please tell the tribunal what you and Sister Maria from England did when she stayed at your convent.

'We communicated in English, even though she had a strong accent, maybe Spanish or Portuguese. You see, I wanted to practice my English. In the morning we went to the town with some books from our library for some of our elderly to borrow. On the way back we stopped off at the convent orchard to pick some apples.'

'And when you went back into the convent, what did you do?'

'I went to the kitchen with the apples.'

'No before that, how did you open the door to enter the convent?'

'I entered the five digit code.'

'Did Sister Maria see you enter the code?'

'I suppose she could have seen me...'

'Thank you sister Helene. I have checked with the authorities in England, they have no knowledge of a nun called Maria who has traveled to Lourdes recently. I have no further questions.'

One game to love, thought Rodeo.

The prosecutor stood. 'I'd like to bring Inspector Partis to the witness bench.'

The Inspector stood straight, almost to attention. 'Inspector, please tell the tribunal about some further evidence you discovered.'

The Inspector stammered before answering. 'Some keys on the door security key pad had UV paint on them, others just a very faint trace. The numbers with the faint trace were the five numbers that formed the code to gain entry. As soon as those keys were used the UV paint rubbed off. All someone needed to do was to shine a UV torch onto the keys and instantly they could see which five formed the code.'

'But that in itself would not tell the person what order the numbers were in?'

'You're right. However, the number is changed every month and not written down. To make it easy to remember, the numbers chosen are usually in either ascending or descending order.'

'What was the number on the night of the murder?' asked the prosecutor.

'Eight, six, four, two, zero,' replied Inspector Partis.

Philippe stood. 'Monsieur I must protest. It is not a scientific fact that numbers are chosen in ascending or descending order.'

The Judge spoke in a no-nonsense tone of voice. 'Monsieur Revel, may I remind you the tribunal will decide what is and what is not conclusive evidence.'

The prosecutor continued. 'What other evidence have you found Inspector?'

Before answering, the Inspector glanced across to Rodeo. 'Traces of UV paint which matched the paint on the keypad were found in the car used by Mr Rickets.'

Rodeo leaned across to Philippe.

'He's lying. That look he just gave me was an involuntary plea for forgiveness.'

The Judge spoke. 'Mr Revel, do you have any questions for this witness?'

'Not at this stage,' said Philippe, deep in thought.

'In that case, the tribunal will adjourn until nine thirty tomorrow. The people will rise.'

*   *   *

Mathew lay back in a tub of warm soapy water and closed his eyes. He had a busy day ahead of him. The phone rang.

'Shit, who wants me now?' Naked and dripping wet, he walked through to his bedroom to answer the phone.

'Hello.'

'Mr Lopez, this is reception. There is an American lady here who wants to see you. She says, tell him it's O, I, K.'

'I don't know anyone called O…shit! It's Old Iron Knickers. Send her up.' He put the phone down. 'I better put some clothes on.'

Mathew opened the suite door in anticipation. The lift doors opened and Mable stepped out.

'You're up then, thought you'd still be in bed.' *She's in top form,* thought Mathew.

'Mable, lovely to see you.'

'Yeah right. I brought all the records for the trial.' Mathew looked at her blankly. 'Records of people attending your parties, you know, their ID with their ages.'

'Right,' said Mathew.

'Lucky someone thought to make back-ups,' said Mable. 'How does someone get some breakfast around here?'

'Now that I *can* help you with. Come with me, Mable.'

*   *   *

Rodeo couldn't believe it. Of all the people, Old Iron Knickers, who'd never, ever, traveled abroad before and Mathew, Douglas,

Laura and…Kamna. Her hair and large sunglasses covered most of her face. She still looked beautiful, her figure, her poise.

'Philippe, did you know?' said Rodeo.

'I only found out this morning. Your business manager Mable, she has back-ups of your party records. Today's a big day for us. It could be make or break.'

'The people will rise.'

The tribunal took their seats. The Judge spoke.

'The defence calls Mable Hillthorpe to give evidence.' Mable moved to the witness bench and put on the headphones.

'Mable, please tell the court your name and your relationship with Rodeo,' began Philippe.

'My name is Mable Hillthorpe and I'm Rodeo's Business Manager.'

'Mable, how long have you known Rodeo?'

'I've known him since he were knee high to a grasshopper. You see, I knew his mother and I'll tell you there's not a finer, kinder human being on the planet than Rodeo.'

'Thank you Mable. What exactly does the role of Business Manager entail?'

'I book the venues, negotiate TV and radio rights, and deal with anything financial.'

'You have brought with you some evidence which has been submitted to the court for scrutiny.'

'Yes. I have with me the records of everyone who's ever attended one of Rodeo's parties. I know you thought they were destroyed by the fire that destroyed Heaven's Door, which is Rodeo's ranch. But I know what his head of security is like.' She looked across and glared at Mathew. He glared back. 'So I took it on myself to make back-up records. There's over three thousand names and addresses with their ages all confirmed with official ID. Everyone is over eighteen. You can contact anyone of them and they'll confirm the details.'

'Thank you Mable. I have no further questions for this witness.'

The prosecutor stood.

'I have some questions for this witness. Madame, I do not dispute your records. However, what was to stop underage girls or boys being smuggled into the parties with the collusion of security without any records being kept?'

'He wouldn't do that. He's never broken any law in his life.'

'What was your relationship to the accused's mother?'

'I'm his aunt.'

'Please be more…specific.'

'I was her pimp's sister.'

'Thank you, I have no further questions for this witness.'

Rodeo dropped his head. Painful, distant memories returned in the form of vague pictures of people fighting and cursing. Seeing images of his mother unleashed a tremendous love that until now he'd kept pushing away.

Philippe stood. 'The defence would like to call Mathew Lopez.'

Mathew moved his large frame to the witness bench.

'Please state your name and your relationship with Rodeo.'

Mathew cleared his throat. 'My name is Mathew Lopez and I'm in charge of his security. He's also my best friend.'

'Mr Lopez,' Philippe continued, 'how long have you known Mr Rickets?'

Mathew answered loud and proud. 'Since we were in jail together. He saved my life and I've been proud to be by his side since.'

'How did he save your life?'

'I was bad, real bad, because I'd never known anything else. He weren't scared of me like everyone else. Instead, he respected me. He talked with me about love, about God within us. He began to write and sing songs and I kind of kept an eye out for him. Other prisoners, instead of trying to pick fights with me, they began to respect me. The whole wing sort of settled down. You want to know what Rodeo said? I'll tell you. If some hell hole like this can become a better place because there's a little more love around, there's hope for the whole world.'

'Did you ever smuggle or allow underage girls or boys into parties at Rodeo's Heaven's Door ranch?'

'No Sir'

'Were you ever aware of underage girls being present at the parties?'

'No Sir, never.'

'Thank you, I have no further questions, Mr Lopez.'

The prosecutor stood and looked disdainfully at Mathew.

'I have some questions.' The Judge nodded.

'Mr Lopez, what was your crime? Why were you in jail?'

'I had raped a woman at knifepoint.'

'And you expect the court to believe your testimony? I have no further questions for this witness.'

The Judge spoke. 'The tribunal will adjourn for two hours.'

Two guards escorted Rodeo back to the court cells. Philippe spoke to Mathew.

'You did well. I saw the Judge listening to you. His expressions were very positive.'

'Don't bullshit me, you heard the prosecutor. Who's gonna believe the testimony of a rapist? And poor Mable, so what if her brother was a fucking pimp? Does it make her a bad person?'

'The people will rise.'

The tribunal entered and sat on their raised benches, then everyone else sat. Philippe remained standing.

'The defense calls Kamna Dhillon.'

Kamna walked gracefully to the witness bench. The Judge spoke.

'Miss Dhillon, please remove your sunglasses so the tribunal can clearly see you.'

Rodeo felt her pain as she removed her large glasses and looked directly at the Judge.

Philippe spoke. 'Please state your name and your relationship with Rodeo.'

'My name is Kamna Dhillon. I met Rodeo after a concert in my home city of Hyderabad and we made love at his hotel.'

'How did he meet you?'

'It is his custom to invite an audience member onto the stage during the show and he chose me.'

'But you had planned to meet and seduce him, had you not?'

'Yes, that is correct.'

'Why was that?'

'I had been paid one hundred thousand dollars to sleep with him and collect his sperm.'

'Who paid you to do this?'

'Who paid the money? I don't know, but I was approached by a woman. I thought at the time, why not? If she wanted Rodeo as a donor for her baby that's her business. It was easy money and I quite fancied him anyway.'

'So after you slept with him, what happened?'

'I left him asleep and met a man in the grounds who took me to a clinic to collect the sperm. After he retrieved the sperm, the doctor tried to kill me by injecting me with something nasty in a hypodermic syringe. I managed to stick it in him instead and escaped.'

'Who was the woman who approached you?'

Kamna almost screamed out her answer. 'The same woman who did this to me.' She motioned towards her face.

'And where did she approach you?'

'While I worked in Little Rock, USA.'

'And then, when you decided to come to France from India to give evidence on behalf of Mr Rickets, you were attacked in a Paris café by this woman.'

'Yes that is right.'

Philippe addressed the whole court. 'Whoever did this wanted to stop you giving evidence.' He pulled her hair off her face. The whole court groaned in sympathy. 'They killed little Carlotta and framed Rodeo for the crime.'

The Judge spoke sternly. 'Monsieur Revel, must I remind you again that is up to the tribunal to decide. You must only present the facts.'

Kamna looked across the court to Rodeo. He mouthed to her the words, 'I love you.'

A tear ran down her cheek. She looked into his eyes and realised he meant it.

'I have no further questions at this stage,' said Philippe.

The prosecutor stood.

'I have some questions for the witness.' He looked at his notes then at her.

'Mademoiselle Dhillon, have you ever slept with men for money? Before you answer, consider carefully.'

Kamna looked scared. Her eyes betrayed fear. She looked across to Rodeo. Rodeo nodded and winked at her, then smiled. Of course, she thought, he wouldn't judge her whatever she had done.

'Yes,' she replied, barely audible.

The prosecutor addressed the tribunal. 'I have given to the tribunal video footage that is available on the internet. It shows Mademoiselle Dhillon having sex with westerners from a young age. Also, in the last forty-eight hours, the man you worked for in Little Rock, USA has been arrested for living off immoral earnings.'

He redirected his attention to Kamna. 'Mademoiselle Dhillon, you are no more than a common prostitute, a gold digger seeking publicity. Your story is worthless. I have no further questions.'

The judge spoke. 'The tribunal will adjourn until nine thirty tomorrow. The people will rise.'

CHAPTER 38

MICHAEL HEANEY smiled at the camera, showing off his perfect white teeth. Preston Quick shook his hand and they sat down.

'Senator Heaney, thank you for agreeing to take part in my show. How's the campaign going?'

'Great, just great. My campaign team are doing a magnificent job and the polls currently reflect that.'

'The fact that you're level at this stage, no one can call which way it's going to go. How much is that down to your promise to put Americans and God at the forefront of everything you do?'

'As I said before, this great country of ours only became great because of its people and their belief in God. The people connect with me because they know I have their interests and the interests of America close to my heart.'

'When exactly did you decide to give up the church to pursue a career in politics?'

'While at evangelical college I felt a great sadness at the direction our country was headed. I prayed and prayed for guidance for what I should do. I believe God told me I could reach a wider audience from a political pulpit than I could from a Baptist Church pulpit.'

'When you say God told you, do you mean he actually spoke to you?'

'No, not at all. It was a feeling I had inside that became stronger the more I prayed.'

'Now your opponents accuse you of being politically far to the right of centre on issues like abortion.'

'If wanting to protect unborn babies that have been created in God's image is being politically far to the right, then I'm guilty.'

'The rock star Rodeo is currently on trial in France for the rape and murder of a ten-year-old girl. Now you have always been outspoken against him. Is that helping your campaign?'

'I believe it is. When Rodeo is found guilty and executed for his heinous crime, I suspect many Americans who may have supported him will return to traditional Christian values. My opponents on the other hand, although never giving him wholesale support, never spoke out in public against him.'

'And you believe that could swing the vote?'

'Yes, I believe it will.'

* * *

Douglas pressed the off switch on the remote control.

'If Rodeo's found guilty that man will become president,' said Douglas. 'He'll make George W Bush look like Mother fucking Teresa.'

Philippe, who'd been invited back to the Ritz, spoke.

'Tomorrow is a big day in court. The prosecutor will begin his summing up…'

'Monsieur Revel,' said Edith, interrupting him in mid sentence. 'I would like to give evidence. I spoke to Father Jacques on the telephone. He reassured my parents I'm safe and they are no longer searching for me. Please, it's because of me that Rodeo faces the death penalty. Instead of being the face and voice for revenge, I would like to speak out for love. Please, monsieur.' She looked at Philippe with wide, angelic eyes.

'Okay, you win. I will approach the Judge before our Monsieur the Prosecutor begins his character assassination of all my witnesses. That is, apart from you, of course.' Edith threw her arms round him.

'I won't let you down,' she said, while giving him a big kiss on the cheek.

* * *

On day eight of the trial, Edith stood on the witness bench facing the tribunal.

'Please tell the tribunal your name and your relationship with Rodeo,' said Philippe gently.

'My name is Edith Llitjos and my relationship with Rodeo is…well, I have seen him at a concert, I pleaded for him at a private audience with Pope Barnabus…and his friends all looked after me really well after Laura and I were almost kidnapped and…' The prosecutor jumped to his feet. Edith stopped, not sure whether to carry on. The Judge intervened before the prosecutor could speak.

'Carry on my dear.' He looked disdainfully at the prosecutor through the thick bifocals perched on the end of his nose.

'And we were all nearly blown up by people who want us all dead,' continued Edith.

'What has this got to do with the case we are trying?' said the Prosecutor angrily.

'That is for the tribunal to decide,' replied the Judge. 'Monsieur Revel, please continue.'

'Edith, please tell the tribunal exactly what happened when you saw Rodeo at his concert in Paris.'

'I adored the atmosphere, the music and Rodeo's voice and the spirituality of the occasion. I remember him saying all we need to do is choose love, every time, and you know we have that choice. It's up to us. It's always our choice, our responsibility. It makes no difference what someone else has done to us or what we've been through or what we want from a situation. If you choose love, you and the whole world will always be a winner, they'll be no losers and we'll be creating a better place. I will never forget those words. I want the tribunal to know.' She stopped and looked at Rodeo, using the pause to good effect. Everyone strained to hear what she was about to say. Her voice, strong and assertive, demanded to be heard.

'When I looked into the eyes of the man who killed my friend and raped me, I saw nothing. But when I look into Rodeo's eyes, all I see is love. I know he did not rape and kill Carlotta.'

'Thank you Edith,' said Philippe. 'I have no more questions.'

The Judge spoke. 'The tribunal will adjourn for two hours. The people will rise.'

*   *   *

Keanan and Alfredo sat opposite each other in a small bar on Rue Auber.

'I'll get these,' said Keanan.

'I'll just have an orange juice this time,' said Alfredo. 'I need to keep my wits about me, an' you better do the same.'

'No, I'm gonna have another beer.' Alfredo looked at him disapprovingly.

'Don't worry, I'll be fine,' said Keanan.

As he walked across to the bar, Alfredo cautiously looked around. *You can never be too careful.*

Keanan put the drinks on the table and sat down. He looked at Alfredo thoughtfully before speaking while Alfredo took a sip of his orange.

'Do you think they'll find Rodeo guilty an' execute him?' asked Keanan while pouring the ice cold beer into his glass.

'I'd say it's fifty-fifty. If they do, an' Heaney's elected president, you better be ready for Armageddon.'

'I'm done with sitting round doing nothing. We have to do something,' said Keanan, staring into his beer.

'You tell me what and I'll help you.'

'Heaney was after you, he wanted to use Carlotta to get to you.' His voice slightly slurred.

'I know,' said Alfredo, 'you told me before. But what I don't understand is why is Heaney after me? It doesn't add up, unless him and Innocent Biloweiki teamed up. When you think about it, it makes sense. One of my colleagues found out about the inquisition. Now, apart from me they're all dead. I'm the only one alive, so I'm a threat to Innocent who I believe is the person leading the inquisition. The people I tagged along with, who busted into Château De Montvillargenne, were all part of the inquisition.'

'Were they really gendarmes?'

'No, no, I'd describe them as more like Nazi Brown Shirts, Biloweiki's private army. After I died I infiltrated them, if you catch my drift. Innocent Biloweiki fears what's written in the hidden testaments. Him and Heaney want the same thing but for different reasons. They both need to get rid of Rodeo. The question is, how do we stop them?'

'What if I could get a virtual camera into his offices at Little Rock? Maybe we could find something that would nail him and Pope Innocent.'

'You've already checked out his computers, he's clean as a whistle.'

'No, there has to be something…look we got to do this.'

'You're right kid,' said Alfredo. 'It's no good just sitting here getting drunk. You go get your virtual camera working. I'm going to the Vatican. The one thing Innocent wants are the original documents from Barnabus. Maybe I can tempt him, you know, like the spider to the fly.'

'You're on!' said Keanan, gulping down his last drop of beer.

*   *   *

Two hours later the prosecutor addressed the tribunal.

'Ladies and gentlemen of the tribunal. Fact one, a little ten-year-old girl was cruelly raped and murdered. Fact two, the sperm of Rodeo was found in her vagina. Fact three, Rodeo was being investigated as a paedophile. Fact four, he has no alibi. Fact five, traces of UV paint were found in his car and UV paint was found on the security buttons on the front door.'

For the next three hours he meticulously summed up all the prosecution evidence. The tribunal sat silently, listening and concentrating. There were no interruptions from the Judge.

Rodeo kept looking over to Kamna, trying to catch her eye. Every now and then their eyes met. He even managed to surreptitiously blow her a kiss.

Philippe looked at his watch. In five minutes it will be time for the tribunal to adjourn. The prosecutor timed his summing up to perfection. With one minute to go, he gave his final plea.

'The man on trial hides behind a façade of deception. He pretends to talk of love for humanity and the whole world, whereas in reality he is a vicious rapist, killer and paedophile. He shows no remorse for his crimes. I ask the tribunal to find him guilty and to impose the maximum sentence…death!'

Mathew sat with his head in his hands. Philippe knew he would have his work cut out if he was to persuade the tribunal to find otherwise.

The Judge spoke. 'The tribunal will adjourn till nine thirty tomorrow. The people will rise.'

As the guards led Rodeo back to his cell, Kamna mouthed 'I love you too.' She hoped he'd seen her, but wasn't sure.

That evening in his suite at the Ritz, Mathew sat on the Louis IV chaise lounges with Alfredo and Keanan. Mathew ordered some coffee.

'Mathew, my friend,' said Alfredo. 'Keanan and I feel we should try and somehow stop Michael Heaney.' He then told him of their suspicions, that Heaney and Biloweiki Innocent were somehow in it together. Mathew nodded.

'So what do you want to do?' said Mathew.

'Alfredo's going to the Vatican and Douglas and Laura are going to Little Rock.'

'And what do you intend to do when you get there?'

'Kick ass!' said Keanan.

'I intend to lure Pope Innocent into a trap, using the documents from Barnabus as the bait.'

'Well, things aren't going too good in court. That may be our only hope,' sighed Mathew resignedly.

The next morning, Philippe appeared in a pensive mood when Mathew spoke to him.

'Why are you so wound up? You never lost a case yet and you're not gonna start now.'

Philippe put his hand on Mathew's shoulder. 'I hope you're right.'

Everyone took their positions on the benches.

'The people will rise.' The tribunal entered and sat down.

The Judge spoke. 'Mr Revel, please begin your summing up.

Philippe addressed the tribunal. His voice, confident and commanding, ensured everyone's attention. For three hours Philippe tore into the prosecution's case. Bit by bit he attempted to cast doubt.

'Of course traces of UV paint were found in his car. UV paint is used on stage. Traces are bound to end up on his clothes and in his car. There's bound to be some contamination. UV paint is available anywhere, anyone could have used it.

'There is no evidence of Rodeo ever having underage sex. No one has ever come forward and made a claim. There has only ever been innuendo by people who disagree with his views on life. Rodeo, on the other hand, has provided detailed evidence of age checks which were carried out on everyone before they were allowed to attend one of his parties at his ranch. Who else in this court does that before they hold a party?

'The prosecution failed to give an explanation as to why there were no marks or bruising which are always a hallmark of this kind of attack. In fact, the prosecution has no evidence that Rodeo Rickets raped and murdered Carlotta.' His voice raised to a crescendo. 'Their whole case is circumstantial and based on flawed arguments.'

Philippe sat down, exhausted. Sweat ran down his forehead.

'The tribunal will leave the court to deliberate on the verdict,' announced the Judge.' We will notify you when we have reached our verdict. The people will stand.'

Rodeo leant across to Philippe.

'I want you to know, whatever the verdict, you've done a great job.'

'I hope so, I hope so.'

'Mr Revel,' said Mathew. 'How long are they gonna take?'

'I don't know. It could be hours or even days. We just have to wait.'

CHAPTER 39

AT THE RITZ, Mathew paced up and down as he spoke. 'They've been deliberating now all yesterday afternoon an' all day today. How fucking long do they need?'

The phone rang. It was Philippe.

'Mathew, the tribunal has reached a verdict. The court will reconvene in one hour. I'll see you there.'

Crowds of people gathered outside the court. A few had placards supporting Rodeo, but most were chanting for his execution. TV cameras and news teams interviewed people in the crowd. The police kept a clear pathway for people to enter the court.

Only Mathew and Kamna went to the court. Everyone else decided to stay behind and watch the TV. Besides, the chances of them all being allowed in was small.

Philippe met Mathew and Kamna in the corridor outside the courtroom.

'How's it looking?' said Mathew.

'I honestly don't know,' replied Philippe. 'Very often, if it is a quick deliberation, it is favorable for the defendant. However, if it is long there are obviously some disagreements. But in this case, a day and a half of deliberation, I can't predict.'

Mathew, Kamna and Philippe took their seats. The guards escorted Rodeo into the court. Instead of leading him next to Philippe, they sat him on a small bench directly in front of the Judge and the two magistrates. He put on his headphones. In the last two days the girl with the sexy, kind voice had been replaced by a man with a bored, sneering voice. He wondered which one it would be today.

'The people will rise.' Shit! It was the latter.

The tribunal entered and took their seats. Philippe closely watched them to see if he could gain any clues. None of them were giving anything away. They all appeared totally neutral.

'The defendant will stand,' ordered the Judge.

Rodeo stood. He looked around to try and catch a glimpse of Mathew and Kamna. The Judge reprimanded him.

'You will face the tribunal.' Rodeo turned his head slowly back toward the tribunal.

'Mr Rodeo Rickets, after careful consideration of the facts, the evidence given and the court protocols which were followed, the tribunal has reached a verdict and the verdict is unanimous.'

Rumbles went around the court room like a Mexican wave at a soccer match. Mathew held Philippe's arm.

'The court will remain silent,' said the Judge.

Rodeo desperately wanted to hug Mathew and all his friends. God knows what they are going through at the moment.

'Rodeo Rickets…'

For Mathew, time seemed to stand still. His whole life with Rodeo seemed to pass in front of his eyes in the split second before the Judge made his announcement.

'The verdict is guilty of the rape and murder of Carlotta Benando.'

The court room erupted.

'The court will remain silent while sentence is passed.'

He banged the gravel. Rodeo turned round to look at Mathew and Kamna. Tears ran down both their faces. Tears that were born out of love. The hubbub subsided.

'You will be executed by lethal injection at La Santé prison twenty-eight days from today.' The court remained silent. 'There will be an automatic appeal in two weeks. Take the guilty to the cells.'

The whole court watched as the guards unnecessarily manhandled Rodeo from the court room.

'The people will rise.'

Philippe stayed sitting down, shaking his head.

'Something is wrong. How could it possibly be unanimous?'

Mathew sat down again next to him and held his hands.

'For what its worth, I know you did your best, no one could have done any more. That Judge has been a shit from the start.'

'He's always been a shit. Right from the day my mother first met him. Why she married him I don't know.'

'He's your father?' exclaimed Mathew in disbelief.

'My step father.'

'Does that mean you could…you know, speak with him before the appeal and…'

'Non, the appeal is heard by a different tribunal. You must understand. In France the appeal is often seen as no more than a formality. Unless there is new evidence they tend to just rubber stamp the verdict.'

*   *   *

Mathew switched on the TV to listen to the news.

'Voting takes place next week in what we thought would be a close run race. But since rock star Rodeo was found guilty of the rape and murder of a young girl and sentenced to die by lethal injection next month, all the polls show Senator Heaney has a ten point lead and could win an historical landslide victory.'

'Not if I have my way,' said Mathew as he pressed the off button.

CHAPTER 40

'ITALIAN DRIVERS are crazy,' said Alfredo to himself as he battled with the Roman traffic. After three near misses and several altercations, he arrived safely at the parcheggi di scambio.

The subway ride to Lepanto metro station passed uneventfully, apart from being accosted by three gypsy children. The eldest bore an uncanny resemblance to Carlotta. Fishing in his inside pocket, he brought out three expensive pens and gave them one each.

'Here, a present,' he said in Italian. 'Go to school and learn to become great writers.' The children laughed and ran off down the carriage and through the connecting door.

He walked the two hundred metres to Hotel Farnese and checked in. The desk clerk, seeing the elderly frail gentleman, offered the service of the hotel porter to carry his small case to his room, an offer Alfredo gratefully accepted. After all, keeping up the pretence is all part of the disguise.

After double locking the door, he opened his case on the bed and felt for his revolver, sandwiched between his clothes and a wet suit. He placed it under his pillow and lay on the bed. Tonight he would be busy. Might as well rest now.

At seven o'clock he soaked in the tub, overflowing with scented bubbles. *How come I always overdo the bubbles?* he thought to himself.

The grey colouring he sprayed on his hair and moustache gave him a rather distinguished look, he felt. He put on the wet suit then his smart old man clothes over the top. Bifocals, coupled with padding that created a slight but distinguishable hump on his back and a walking stick, completed his disguise.

'I won't be in for dinner,' he said as he walked past the front desk. 'In fact, I might not even be back till breakfast,' he said, winking. The desk clerk looked up and gave a knowing smile.

The sun had nearly disappeared from the sky as Alfredo approached the Ponte Umberto. He walked across the bridge over the River Tiber and looked in awe at St Peter's Basilica with the magnificent Michelangelo's Dome. At the far side of the bridge, he climbed down some steps to a path with grassy banks that ran along the side of the river.

There appeared to be no one around. The sun had now set completely. The moonlight glistened on the water. Standing under the bridge, he removed and carefully folded all his clothes and walking stick, then placed them in a watertight bag attached to a piece of monofilament fishing line. He tied the end of the line to a small metal rod protruding from the bank. Gently he let the bag disappear into the murky water.

Creating no splash, he silently slipped into the water. For reassurance he found himself feeling for his revolver strapped to his inner thigh in a waterproof holster. His only light came from a small hand-held, wind-up torch.

Taking a deep breath, he dived below the surface. Straight away he saw it, a tunnel in the side of the river bank. Only eighty centimeters in diameter, it looked like a drain pipe if the water was very low. His lungs strained as he swam the six metres through the tunnel. He broke the surface, gasping for air.

The small chamber looked exactly as he remembered it. He pulled himself out of the water onto a narrow ledge. While he rested, he shone the torch onto the brickwork. *That's the one.*

The brick looked exactly the same as all the others in the chamber but, as he pulled, it came away. Inside were some papers – maps of the subterranean passages beneath the Vatican City.

'They're still here, thank God.'

He put them into a pocket in the front of his wetsuit. A rat scurried past him. The torchlight grew stronger as he gave it a few more winds.

Because of their Papal bodyguard role, Alfredo and his

murdered compatriots were the only people who knew the geography of the passages. Others knew they existed but were not privy to where the entrances or exits were. Even the famous Swiss Guards had no idea. The maps in Alfredo's pockets were drawn in such a way that they would be of no use to someone who did not already have a good knowledge of the geography.

He shone the torch along the passageway to his right. The passage to his left led to a nightmarish maze of tunnels that, rumour had it, contained the skeletons of people who lost their way for ever, many centuries ago.

* * *

Pope Innocent sat reading in a comfortable reclining chair with built-in foot stool. Light came from an old-fashioned standard lamp behind him. The library contained over fifty thousand books, some of which were very ancient. Alfredo watched him intently from the shadows, careful not to make a sound or disrupt the light patterns in the room. At exactly eleven o'clock, Pope Innocent retired to his chamber on the top floor of the Vatican Palace.

Alfredo placed a note inside the book at the page where Pope Innocent left the bookmark. Rubber gloves meant there would be no tell tale finger prints. *Oh to be a fly on wall when Innocent Biloweiki opens his book*, thought Alfredo.

The same desk clerk sat at the reception desk as Alfredo returned, just after one o'clock in the morning. He smiled.

'No luck then Sir?' he enquired.

'No, all too ugly,' said Alfredo, pulling a disgusted face to add a little credence to his story.

* * *

Douglas and Laura listened intently as Keanan explained how his system worked. His technical wizardry fascinated them.

'So what you're saying,' said Douglas, 'is that you've developed software which rides piggyback on the GPs system?'

'Exactly,' said Keanan.

'But how do we use it to our advantage?' asked Laura.

'Well, that's the clever bit. Originally I could access any computer, whether standalone, networked, on or offline, and using a really neat programme I developed I could observe the person using the computer and the area around the computer. I effectively turned the computer into a remote controlled camera. I could also place things like images onto the screen, as well as read and alter files. That's how Heaney tapped into Carlotta's laptop, hoping to get to her dad through her.'

'Can Heaney still use it?'

'Unfortunately, yes. However, I've built a jammer which protects any computer within a radius of about a hundred metres, so we're safe. But listen to this. I have a new system. While my compatriots watched The Simpsons, I studied nanotechnology. In a couple of days when my virtual parasites have hatched, I'll be able use the GPS signal as a remote camera without having a laptop at the other end. I'll be able to film anyone, anywhere, at any time, providing they're infected with the parasites.'

'Sure your name's not Einstein?' mocked Laura.

'Einstein? Who's he?' said Keanan, puzzled.

'Never mind Einstein,' said Douglas. 'If that got into the wrong hands, God help us. But how can we use this technology to expose Heaney and save Rodeo?'

'We need someone to plant a female virtual parasite on Heaney,' said Keanan.

'A female virtual parasite? You're kidding me?' Douglas looked incredulously at Keanan.

'No, its logical. The parasites I'm waiting on to hatch are all female. The males, which don't need to hatch, attach themselves to the GPS signal and hunt for females of their own species. If Heaney has female parasites attached to him, the males will find them and then we have live movies in glorious Technicolor wherever he is.'

'So,' said Laura, 'all we need now is a volunteer to go and attach some virtual female parasites to him. Any volunteers?'

Douglas and Keanan looked at each other.

'Looks like it'll have to be me then,' she said.

'Now wait,' said Douglas.

'No, you wait,' said Laura. 'Just listen to what I have to say.'

Douglas went to speak, but Laura put her fingers over his lips. 'He's never met me. Okay, he probably knows I'm tagging along with Rodeo. But he knows zilch about me. I'll play to his ego, you know, make him think I've changed sides because I like winners and powerful men.'

'I don't like it,' said Douglas. 'You don't know what he's like. It's too dangerous.'

'Do you have a better idea?' answered Laura. 'I promise I won't do anything stupid. Look, the election is only three weeks away. He's not going to want to draw attention to himself. Besides, as soon as I've attached the female parasites I can make good my getaway. Keanan, these virtual parasites, what do they look like and how are they attached?'

'Until they hatch I don't know.'

'Can you see them? Do they move?'

'Probably.'

'What if they drop off the skin?'

'They won't if they're internal,' said Keanan.

'You mean he swallows them in a drink?' said Douglas.

'No, they can't survive in liquid.'

'So how do we get them into him internally then?' said Laura. 'Inject them, or in food?'

'I haven't figured that out yet, but they'll be too large to inject. Maybe we have to shove 'em up his ass.' Keanan saw the look on Douglas' face. 'Look, I don't know. We have to wait till they're hatched.'

That night Douglas held Laura in his arms.

'For once in my life I've found love with you and Rodeo an' everyone…now my love's going to be tested to the limit…' Douglas paused. 'The girl I love has to probably go and sleep with the man who raped my fiancé in order to save a man I love who will save the world.' Laura felt his tears on her shoulder as she pulled him to her.

*   *   *

The following evening, Pope Innocent sat in his reclining chair and picked up his book from the small table beside him. He opened the page at the bookmark. Alfredo's note fell out. Slowly he picked it up and unfolded it, wondering where it had come from.

He read the note out loud. His face turned a bright shade of Papal scarlet.

'Innocent XIV, Permaneo Pope.' He digested the words. 'The last Pope!'

Alfredo sat in the hotel bar contemplating the look on Pope Innocent's face. What the note lacked in words was more than made up for by intrigue. He could just imagine the torment going through his mind. Who put this in my book? Someone's playing games with me. Who has access to the library? His staff would be going through hell but, more importantly, so would he.

Alfredo sipped a little of his Napoleon brandy.

'Carlotta, my little angel. I let you down, but I'm going to make it up to you, I promise.' He raised his glass. 'To Carlotta,' then took another sip.

Three nights later, Alfredo returned to the Vatican City through the underground tunnels. While Pope Innocent read in the library, he left an envelope on his bed in his personal chambers.

Pope Innocent picked it up and opened it. Inside were three photos, all newspaper cuttings and a note. The photos were of Carlotta, Michael Heaney and Barnabus. He read the note out loud. 'Nos teneo,' then translated it in his mind. 'We know.'

Pope Innocent, not wanting to draw attention to himself, lit a candle and burnt the photos and both notes.

'I'll deal with this my way,' he said to himself. 'Knowing is one thing, proving it is another.'

The next evening, Alfredo took a call on his hotel room phone.

'Alfredo, its Mathew. Keanan's waiting for his little friends to hatch. He's not sure exactly when that's likely to be, so we could be cutting things a little fine.'

'Okay,' said Alfredo, 'I'll hold on till I hear from you. You'll be pleased to know the messages have been passed.' Alfredo hung up.

CHAPTER 41

RODEO SAT facing Mathew across a small table. His hands were cuffed together and his feet manacled.

'Don't think I'll be going anywhere for a while,' joked Rodeo. 'I guess I'll just have to settle for some quiet nights in.'

'We're all missing you boss,' said Mathew. 'We're planning the biggest party ever for when you're free.' Rodeo smiled to himself at Mathew's attempt to boost his morale.

'Mathew, if that day ever comes, I'd like that very much.'

'Your appeal's tomorrow. How's things going with Philippe?'

'Not so good. We have no new evidence and he can't even appeal against the sentence because, under French law, death is mandatory in these cases.'

'Hey, maybe Pope Innocent will appeal for clemency on your behalf?' joked Mathew, trying to hide the tears which weren't far from the surface. 'Boss, there's someone else here who wants to see you. I'll go so they can come in. I'll see you soon boss.'

As Mathew walked away towards the door the dam burst.

Five minutes later the door opened. A guard led Kamna to the table. She wore a traditional sari, which highlighted more curves than it hid.

She sat down opposite Rodeo. Putting her fingers to her lips she stopped him speaking. Instead, she put her hand on his face and explored it with the tips of her fingers. The guard looked across. She shouldn't be touching him but he decided to turn the other way.

The touch reinvigorated his senses and feelings. Her fingers strayed toward his lips. He opened his mouth a fraction and felt her finger force its way in. His tongue toyed with her finger. Fifteen minutes passed without a word passing between them. Then the guard spoke.

'La visite est finie.'

Rodeo watched her as she slowly made her way to the door. He'd never ever known a woman quite like her. If only he had more time. She turned and smiled as she walked through the door. Rodeo noticed a single tear on her cheek.

A newly convened tribunal heard the appeal without Rodeo being present.

'The appeal hearing lasted only four hours and then it only took another two hours for the tribunal to decide to uphold the original verdict and sentence.'

Philippe's anger and desperation showed on his face. Rodeo felt Philippe had aged ten years since that first day in court.

'If you are executed I've decided to end my career in France and fight against injustice, wherever it occurs in the world,' said Philippe in a voice stilled in passion. 'Even if I only make a very small difference, it will be better than nothing.'

In La Santé prison, arrangements for Rodeo's execution were in full swing. Rodeo welcomed his transfer to a new holding cell because it contained a few more comforts. It had a shower, the bed had a sprung mattress, he even had a TV with satellite channels.

'Home from home,' said Rodeo, as he lay on his new bed.

He had to fill out a form stating what he would like for his last meal and who he would like his last visitors to be. Only three were allowed.

He chose anchovy pizza. *I know it won't be up to Mathew's standard*, he thought, as he wrote it on the form. For his three visitors he wrote Mathew Lopez, Douglas Claymore and Kamna Dhillon.

CHAPTER 42

KEANAN WATCHED the virtual eggs through a strong magnifying glass. Each one had started off invisible to the naked eye, but now he could clearly see them. Two hundred female eggs, each about the size of a pinhead.

'Another couple of hours and they'll hatch.'

Davey looked at them in awe.

'These little things are going to save Rodeo?'

'That's the plan,' said Keanan.

'You are so clever. I wish I could be clever like you.' Keanan swelled inside, but his natural modesty took over.

'I'm not really clever. I just have natural curiosity.'

'But it is a clever curiosity,' said Davey.

The eggs sat in a tray that looked like a laptop which had been reversed, with the screen flat and the keyboard vertical.

'How will you move them?' asked Davey.

'Well at the moment all you can see are two-dimensional images. When they hatch the two-dimensional image, which is really coding, combines with bacteria on the screen and forms real live critters which are programmed by the code.'

'How come they take so long to hatch?'

'I'm limited by the power of my computer – the more powerful the computer the quicker the process. It's a bit like uploading a large file. The part I like is the fact that they're programmed to reproduce themselves, you know like a computer virus when they're fertilised by the males.'

'Wow,' said Davey. 'Can I watch them hatch?'

'Sure,' replied Keanan, 'and you can help me test them out. That is, providing you don't mind little critters on you.'

'No, I don't mind,' said Davey, pulling a face which communicated the opposite. Keanan smiled.

'They won't harm you, I promise.'

They both watched the tray expectantly. The eggs slowly changed from a dark grey colour to a light, almost pinkish red.

Slowly the eggs started to move. At first the movements were barely noticeable. Then they rolled around the tray, almost like marbles.

'Don't worry, when they hatch they won't move much.'

As Keanan and Davey watched, one by one the eggs split open and on the screen were real three-dimensional worm-like creatures. Each one measured around two millimetres in length.

'They're green,' said Davey excitedly.

'I've programmed them to change to the colour of their environment when they've been fertilised so they'll be virtually invisible.'

Keanan carefully picked up one of them with a pair of tweezers.

'Hold out you hand, palm down,' said Keanan. Davey did as he was told, then Keanan very carefully put the parasite on the back of Davey's hand.

'Right, now hold it there.'

Keanan typed a code into another laptop. Davy watched the green thing on his hand. It didn't move.

'I think it's dead.'

'No, hopefully it's being fertilized.'

'It's gone,' said Davy incredulously.

'No it's still there, only it's changed colour.'

* * *

Mathew sat in his hotel suite watching news of the American election. Heaney's lead appeared unassailable.

'You haven't won yet,' said Mathew. 'It's not over until the fat lady sings, or at least until Rodeo doesn't sing anymore.'

Suddenly, instead of watching pundits talk about Heaney, the picture showed Keanan and Davey. Clear as a bell with full sound.

'Mathew, I hope you're watching this,' said Keanan.

'And I have a creature on my hand that you can't see,' said Davey.

Mathew stood up and walked down the corridor towards the suite shared by Keanan and Davey. He knocked on the door.

'Hey, what's going on in there?'

'Come on in.'

Mathew entered. 'What are you two guys playing at?'

'Mathew, it works! They've hatched and it works.' Keanan explained what had happened.

'Well I'll be damned,' said Mathew. 'Now maybe we can kick some ass, in a non violent way of course. Those pictures on my TV, how did you override what I'm watching?'

'It's like I attached our pictures to the satellite signal. You know how on a computer you can send to back? Well I just send the TV picture to the back so only our picture can be seen.'

'So let me get this right, you can put live film on any TV in the world?'

'Yes, but don't worry, just now I only interrupted your TV. No one else saw it.'

'Could you broadcast two live streams at the same time? I mean, have a double picture on the TV screens, half an' half?'

'Sure, no problem,' said Keanan.

'Guys, I feel I have the beginnings of a plan.'

CHAPTER 43

FOR MARIA VON HIND, being on the payroll of the next president of the United States and then being asked to assist Pope Innocent with his security was her idea of Heaven. Two of the most powerful men in the world needed her. The headscarf she wore to hide her severed ear only served as a temporary measure until she had the time for a plastic surgeon to rebuild it.

When she visited Pope Innocent, the nun's habit served her equally as well.

'Sister Maria,' said Pope Innocent. 'I appreciate you coming here to help. Your reputation precedes you. I understand you are extremely well qualified to handle the situation.'

'Most Holy Father, thank you for your praise. Coming from you it is most welcome.'

Pope Innocent continued. 'A rodent has twice entered and left nasty messages in my personal apartment and my library. I want it caught and destroyed. Do whatever you need to. Feel free to lay traps, for example.'

'I will start work right away.'

'By the way,' said Pope Innocent. 'I believe this rodent is of the same breed that has caused problems in France and is now nesting in Paris.'

'I understand,' she said with a glimmer of a smile on her face.

* * *

Alfredo walked past the hotel reception.

Signore, a small package has arrived for you.'

'Thank you,' said Alfredo, as the desk clerk handed it to him.

In his suite, Alfredo carefully opened the jiffy bag, not quite knowing what to expect. He took out a handwritten piece of paper and two small flat tins of…hand lotion?

He read the handwritten note.

'In the tins is gelatine which contains the necessary "proteins". Apply liberally in either the mouth, vagina or anus. This ensures the proteins, which are completely harmless, cannot be wiped off and gives them a chance to replicate. If unable to apply in those regions, anywhere on exposed skin will do or on any object, but the proteins will not be effective for so long because it is unlikely they would have the time to replicate. Good luck, Keanan.

PS I suggest you apply some to yourself. Don't worry, they are completely harmless. Davey and I will be watching our TV channels continuously, ready to broadcast any progress.'

Alfredo cautiously opened one of the tins. Inside the jelly were what looked like tiny lengths of green cotton.

'Tonight, my friends, you will begin your work. Good luck and good filming.' He carefully replaced the lid, then tore up the handwritten note into bite size pieces and proceeded to eat them.

* * *

Even as a child, Maria Von Hind enjoyed killing. Her favourites were rats. Before school she'd set traps down by the river and as soon as school finished she went to see how many she'd caught. She gained many hours of pleasure by inventing different ways of killing them and listening to their squeals of terror as she held them down and dissected them.

From what Pope Innocent told her, the intruder came from outside the Vatican City. Maybe one of those holed up in Paris where their beloved Rodeo would soon be executed. But who would have the skill and knowledge to gain entry, bypass security and…? Only one man, but he was dead…or was he? At the time she thought his death suspect, so public and so soon after his daughter.

She tagged on to one of the tours in St Peter's Square.

'Excuse me,' she asked the guide. 'Are there tunnels and things under here?'

'Yes there are hundreds, many of them over two thousand years old, some predating Christianity. A few lead to burial chambers, others were built to allow escape or even to secretly bring in women. Rumour has it boats would come along the river to where Pope Gregory, who promoted celibacy, built a secret entrance for his women.'

'Thank you.' She slipped away from the party. *Well, I have to start somewhere*, she thought.

Why build a tunnel any longer than it need be? She studied a map. The river is nearest the Vatican City at the Ponte Umberto.

'I think a little stakeout is in order,' she said to herself.

* * *

Douglas and Laura watched the CBS reporter on the TV in the airport lounge.

'The Michael Heaney presidential Bandwagon rolls around the United States, state to state and city to city, building up an unstoppable momentum as it goes.'

One of his supporters in the crowd passed him a young child to hold before the camera panned on to him.

'Senator Heaney, the day after tomorrow you're campaigning in Oregon. How's your vote holding up there?'

'Yup, I'm on my way to Portland and Salem to thank the people of Oregon for their support and to try and whip up a little more from those who are as yet undecided. As you know, Oregon could go either way. But I'm praying for the people of Oregon's support.'

Michael Heaney had a disdainful look on his face as he turned away from the camera and handed the child back, before strolling into a restaurant adorned with posters and banners.

'Well, at least we know where he's gonna be,' said Laura, stoically. 'How am I going to get to see him?'

'He doesn't know you,' said Douglas. 'But he probably knows of you and he probably knows we're an item. So how about we go together? I give him some cock and bull story about being deceived by Rodeo and wanting to help him in his campaign. I apologise for trying to attack him last time I saw him and accept his plea for forgiveness for not having the strength to resist my fiancé when she came on to him.'

'Do you think you can do that? Can you carry it off convincingly?'

'Look, I just want to see this…monster receive his just desserts and anything I can do…I know what makes him tick. He won't be able to resist coming on to you. He'll see it as a challenge to put one over on me again. It's a power thing.'

'Will you be able to handle it when he does come on to me and I respond?' Douglas didn't answer. Instead, he stood up and grabbed his jacket.

'Come on, let's eat.'

* * *

Maria Von Hind felt like a prostitute as she lingered around near the bridge. *You never know, if someone approaches me I might take them up,* she thought. *I haven't had a fuck in weeks.*

As the evening drew on there were fewer people around. The sun had nearly set. An elderly gentleman walked slowly across the bridge. For some reason she slid deeper into the shadows.

She watched the elderly gentleman sit down by the side of the bridge and put some lip balm on his lips. A car crossed over the bridge and a teenage girl and boy jumped out and walked hand in hand by the river towards the stone steps.

That would be good cover, she thought. They stood at the top of the steps, kissing and fondling each other. Maria watched jealously. Eventually they broke their embrace. The girl walked back across the bridge. She watched the young man take out a cigarette and light it before he walked off in the opposite direction.

Her attention turned back to the old man. Where'd he gone? He'd vanished, simply disappeared. She walked down the stone steps towards the grassy bank. Taking out a small battery torch, she searched along the bank. The light shone on a metal rod sticking out of the bank under the bridge. Something caught the torch light. She looked closer. Just a piece of fishing line. Then she turned back. *Why's it tight?* She pulled the line.

'Something's attached to it,' she said to herself as she pulled it up.

Shinning the torch into the bag she searched through it, being careful not to disturb the contents too much. A folded walking stick, pants, shirt, socks, shoes…a small tin. She opened the tin and dipped her finger into the jelly then put a little on her tongue to taste it.

'No taste. It must be his lip balm,' she said as she replaced the lid.

* * *

Keanan and Davey carefully watched their screens. Whoops of joy went up when pictures from Alfredo came up. Mathew heard them and went through to find out what was going on.

'I take it by that noise that we have some pictures come through?'

'Mathew, look at the screen,' said Keanan. 'Look!' Mathew looked.

'I don't understand,' said Mathew. If the creatures on Alfredo are filming the pictures, how come we can also see Alfredo?'

'You have to remember these pictures are digital representations of what the critters are picking up. They pick up everything around them, including their host.'

'I see,' said Mathew, who was really none the wiser.

He sat down with Davey and Keanan to watch. When Alfredo entered the water the picture quality dropped to almost nothing. A couple of minutes later Keanan's attention was caught by something else on his computer screen.

'There's another transmission, but it can't be happening yet. It's impossible. Douglas and Laura aren't ready. Alfredo couldn't have got to Pope Innocent's apartment yet.'

Then the picture came onto the screen.

'Keanan, you look like you've seen a ghost or something,' said Mathew, as he looked at the woman in a headscarf lowering a bag back into the water.

'No, a ghost I can handle, but she's worse than evil. It's Maria Von Hind. She's the one that killed Harry and tried to kill me and Kamna.'

Davey screamed at the woman in the picture. 'I hate you! I hate you!'

'Are you sure it's her?' said Mathew.

'One hundred percent,' answered Keanan.

'We have to warn Alfredo.'

'How?' said Keanan. 'He doesn't even carry a cell phone. All we can do is sit and watch.'

They watched the two pictures on the screen. Maria Von Hind took up a position on the bridge close to the top of the stone steps and lit a cigarette.

Once Alfredo climbed out of the water, the picture quality improved.

'I thought you said those critters couldn't survive in liquid?' said Mathew.

'They can't,' said Keanan. 'But in his mouth they'll stay safe, even if he has a drink. They'll probably have buried themselves under his skin.' Mathew pulled a face.

Alfredo made his way through the tunnels till he came to a fork. He stopped to check his map.

'There should be a fish sign directly ahead of me.' He shone his torch around. There it is, on the ceiling, a fish pointing to the left. Alfredo took the right fork. The left led to the never-ending maze.

'That man's something else,' said Mathew while watching intently.

The passage wound sharply to the right. Alfredo bent down. The passage appeared to be shrinking. All of a sudden it broke out into a chamber.

'Hey,' said Alfredo aloud, 'if you guys are able to see me, this is where I'm about to enter the Pope's private chapel. With a little luck he'll be at home.'

His voice came through loud and clear.

'You are amazing Keanan, you know that? Amazing,' said Mathew.

They watched Alfredo push against what looked like a solid wall. It began to move.

'I hope you're ready to broadcast to the world if it's what we want them to see and hear,' Mathew said to Keanan.

'Sure, there's a thirty second delay so we can decide whether or not to broadcast.'

'Good.'

The wall moved as Alfredo pushed until there was enough space for him to squeeze through. He entered an ornate chapel. Initially it appeared to be just large enough for the High Alter, which stretched across to the far end of the chapel. On closer inspection, the chapel had four large coves that almost doubled the available space. Seven large candles lit the alter area.

Alfredo took an envelope out of a pocket in his wet suit and placed it on the far end of the alter before crouching down and waiting. Ten minutes passed before Pope Innocent entered alone. He knelt in front of the alter, put his hands together and silently prayed.

For Mathew, Keanan and Davey, it was like watching a real-life movie, but far more tense.

'How's he going to get the critters into the Pope?' said Mathew.

'He will think of a way,' said Davey.

Pope Innocent prayed for ten minutes and proceeded to read from a Bible that lay on the alter with its pages open. He read quietly to himself. Then he stopped and did a double take.

'Look, he's seen the envelope,' said Keanan.

Taking four paces to his left he gingerly picked it up and tucked it inside his robe, all the time looking around in case someone happened to be watching.

'Yeah, you're fucking right we're watching,' said Mathew, almost triumphantly.

Pope Innocent left the chapel.

Alfredo made his way back to the wall and squeezed through the gap, pushing it shut behind him.

'If you guys are watching, which I hope you are, I'm coming back tomorrow night to confront him after he's read a copy of the letter from Barnabus. Be ready to broadcast to the world.'

He retraced his steps. The six metre swim through the tunnel became easier each time as his lungs became accustomed to it.

They watched Alfredo climb out the water onto the path under the bridge. From the other picture it became obvious Maria Von Hind had spotted him. She kept her distance while Alfredo retrieved his clothes and changed. He looked around. Everywhere appeared deserted.

For once in her life Maria Von Hind did not act on impulse. She would kill him, yes, but she would decide when and where. Instead, she decided to follow him back to his hotel.

'What's she doing?' said Keanan.

'Quickly, find me the phone number of his hotel, the Farnese I think it is,' said Mathew.

Keanan typed Hotel Farnese Rome into Google.

'Now translate this into Italian – There is a bomb primed to go off in Hotel Farnese in ten minutes. Take this warning seriously or many people will die.'

Keanan typed it into a translation programme.

'Here, it's on the screen.'

Mathew read it.

'Ci è una bomba innescata per andare fuori in hotel Farnese in dieci minuti. Prenda seriamente questo avvertimento o molta gente morirà.

'Okay, dial the number.'

Keanan dialed. The phone rang three times before a female voice answered.

'Hotel Farnese, buona sera.'

Mathew put on his most menacing voice and read from the screen. As soon as he finished he put the phone down.

'Now, let's watch what happens.'

As Alfredo approached the hotel he realised straight away something was wrong. People were being moved away from the building by police who were everywhere. Sirens sounded. There were even fire trucks. Instinctively he looked around. Maria Von Hind slid into the shadows.

'Guys, if you're watching and this is something you've done to warn me, I owe you. I'll call from a public phone at the metro station.'

They watched him walk the two hundred metres or so and pick up a phone in the metro entrance. Mathew hardly let the phone ring before picking it up.

'Alfredo, we needed to warn you. We have Maria Von Hind on camera. She must have waited down by the river and pulled your clothes bag out. She probably searched through it and tried some of the jelly on her tongue, 'cause now we have pictures. She put your bag back, waited for you to come out the water an' followed you back to your hotel.'

'Where is she now?' said Alfredo.

Mathew looked at the picture.

'I don't recognise it.

Keenan chipped in.

'The GPS shows she's four hundred metres from you and still moving away.'

'Okay, I'll stay somewhere else tonight. Tomorrow I'll be waiting for her.'

He walked out of the metro.

'I think I'll take a stroll and see what the night throws up,' he casually said to himself.

He'd only walked a hundred yards when a very pretty black girl approached him.

'Signore, American?'

'Yeah,' he stopped. She looked about eighteen, had a stunning figure, flawless complexion and gorgeous lips.

'One hundred fifty euros for a half hour.'

'How much for the whole night?'

'For you, five hundred euros.'

When Alfredo stripped off in her apartment she couldn't believe he wasn't old, and the wet suit?

'I only charged five hundred euros because I thought you were old man who would only come once. Now I see you are also a rubber fetish.'

'Don't worry, you look after me an' I'll give you a large bonus. How about an extra hundred euros for every time I come?'

'Okay, you are going to come many times!'

'Oh, an' boys if you're still watching, you can turn the pictures off.'

'Who are you talking to?' she asked.

'Oh no one, just some friends who sometimes haunt me.'

She moved towards him and explored his rubber suited body with her hands and mouth. She felt the revolver in the waterproof holster but knew better than to comment.

In the morning Alfredo sat up.

'That will be an extra six hundred euros,' she said as she plugged in the kettle.

'Six hundred? You're kidding!' said Alfredo, with a smile on his face.

CHAPTER 44

'THIS MUST be the place,' said Laura. 'Look at all the security.'
'Pretty impressive for an art museum,' replied Douglas, looking up at what he thought looked more like a temple than a museum.

'Let's have a wander round and try to work out how we get an invite inside.'

Crowds had gathered along a route flanked by tree-lined parks on either side.

'Might as well join them,' said Douglas, 'and watch Senator Heaney parade into town.'

Half an hour later, three police motor cycles headed the procession followed by a college band, complete with cheerleaders, then a four-car motorcade. People in the crowd held up placards, saying 'Put Jesus first, vote for Heaney', 'Vote Heaney for President and Return to Christian Values', 'Stop Immorality, vote Heaney'.

In the front car, an open-top limo, some of Heaney's security team stood looking around, watching for any signs of danger.

'Hey, I recognise those guys,' said Laura. 'After I first went to Heaven's Door after a concert, they visited me, asked me to go back and inform on what went on there. Told me they were FBI agents investigating claims Rodeo had sex with underage girls and boys.'

Douglas thought back to when the FBI had visited him.

'You know, I also had a visit and now you come to mention it, I think those were the guys.'

He felt in his pocket for his wallet.

'Somewhere in here I have a card with a phone number…here it is.' He proudly held up the business card which had seen better days.

'Okay, we give it a couple of hours then we call,' said Laura.

*   *   *

'Hey Keanan,' said Mathew. 'Do you have any more of those critters in jelly?'

'Sure, second batch hatched a couple of hours ago.'

'Put some in a paracetamol capsule for me. I have an idea.'

Two hours later, Mathew passed through security at La Santé prison with the paracetamol capsule carefully hidden under his top lip.

Rodeo sounded down, his eyes looked tired.

'Matty, all my estate goes to you. Whatever you want to do with it, you decide.'

'You ain't gone yet boss. Things are happening that you an' sometimes me have no idea about. Talking about things happening, Douglas won't be able to see you. You see, he's one of the things that's happening, if you catch my drift, but Mable desperately wants to be with you before…'

'Okay, I'll ask to change my list and Matty, will you cook me one of your special anchovy pizzas?'

'Sure boss, anything. But we still have a couple of days.' Mathew's voice dropped. Boss, I'm gonna put a capsule in your mouth,' he whispered. 'When I do just crunch it open. Don't worry, it's nothing nasty.' Rodeo nodded.

Mathew took the capsule from his mouth and, making sure that he was not being watched by the security guard, placed it in Rodeo's. Straight away Rodeo crunched down on it, releasing the gel-encrusted critters.

*   *   *

Douglas dialled the number on Laura's cell phone.

'Security agent Booth speaking, how may I help you?'

'This is Douglas Claymore. Tell your boss, Mr Heaney, that Laura Sable and I would like to meet with him. You can call me back on this number.' Douglas pressed the end button without waiting for an answer.

Three hours later, while Laura and Douglas were enjoying a coffee in a student café on the college campus next to the museum, the phone rang. Douglas answered it.

'Douglas Claymore.'

'Hi Mr Claymore, this is security agent Booth. Mr Heaney will be delighted to see both you and Miss Sable. He asked me to remind you to bring some original documents that he's interested in. Come to the reception desk at the Grand Phoenix Hotel in Salem at five o'clock tomorrow.' The phone cut off.

'What did he say?' asked Laura.

Douglas repeated the instructions. He looked at her with a worried face.

'That doesn't give us much time. That's only…with the time difference about…nine hours before the execution. One more thing. He wants the original documents from Barnabus.'

'Shit,' said Laura.

*   *   *

'Hi guys,' said Alfredo, waving. 'I need to know where Maria is. I'll call you in ten minutes.'

Keanan had been watching her like a hawk for the past two hours. Even he had to admire her body as she showered.

'Davey, I'll take the call. You watch Maria for me.'

'Where is she?' asked Alfredo.

'Davey, update.'

'She is walking over the bridge.'

'Describe what she's wearing?' said Alfredo.

'Davey, what's she wearing?'

'She is wearing a long-sleeved jacket, baggy trousers and a wet suit under her clothes. I saw her put it on after she showered.'

'Well observed, Davey.'

Davey felt a sense of pride that he'd been able to provide some valuable information.

'Alfredo, she's wearing a wet suit under her clothes, Davey confirmed it.'

Alfredo smiled. 'He's too young, he shouldn't be watching such things.'

'I'll catch you later, out.'

If she's wearing a wet suit then she intends to follow me, thought Alfredo. *It's nice being one step ahead of the game.*

Alfredo went through the same process, carefully folding his clothes, tying the fishing line to the protruding metal rod. He did everything the same so that nothing would arouse her suspicion.

As he made his way through the tunnels he wondered how far behind him she was. Every now and then he'd stop and listen. He couldn't hear anything apart from the occasional rat scampering around. With a little luck she'd become lost and stumbled into the never-ending maze.

Alfredo arrived at a large wooden door secured by one bolt. He slid open the bolt and pulled open the door, then walked through and closed it by sliding the bolt on the other side.

'There, that does it. Now Biloweiki Innocent, it's just you and I.'

He climbed up a wooden staircase. At the top he lifted a hatch covered by an ornately decorated wooden panel. Pulling himself up, he climbed through and walked along the narrow passage till he came to a door.

Keanan and Davey watched the two screens. Maria moved surprisingly quickly through the tunnels, every now and then stopping as if listening for clues as to which tunnel Alfredo had taken. She arrived at the wooden door only ninety seconds after Alfredo bolted it from the other side.

'How can we see so clearly when it is so dark in there?' asked Davey.

'That's because the critters are programmed to input the necessary light into the images they beam back.'

'Wow.'

Alfredo opened the door that led into Pope Innocent's private offices. From the other side the door formed part of the ornate paneling that covered all the walls in the office.

All the electric lights were off. There were no candles. The offices appeared empty. Alfredo walked across to a large desk and shone his torch. He hoped to find evidence of the inquisition that he believed Cardinal Biloweiki had ordered when he first became Secretary of the Congregation for the Doctrine of the Faith. It was like looking for a needle in a fucking haystack.

He tried to open all the desk drawers – only one wouldn't open. Then he tried the drawers of the two filing cabinets. They all opened.

Keanan and Davey watched Maria retrace her steps.

'What is she doing?' asked Davey.

'I don't know,' replied Keanan.

They watched her move through the tunnels. When she arrived at the fork with the fish she removed the rucksack she was carrying on her back.

'What the fuck?' said Keanan, as she took out what looked like a grenade. They watched her attach a long cord to the pin. 'I don't like the look of this.'

On the other screen they watched Alfredo take his revolver from the holster and fit a silencer. He fired a single shot at the one lock on the drawer which wouldn't open. The lock shattered. He opened the drawer and removed some ancient-looking manuscripts and papers.

'Boys, I hope you're watching, 'cause I want you to focus in on these papers. Don't broadcast them live, just record the details.'

He spread them out on the desk top. Keanan zoomed in on each in turn. Alfredo didn't bother to put them back. He left the private office and made his way down a corridor to the library.

'I hope you're still recording, me boys.'

Alfredo silently opened the library door. He avoided altering any shadows as he made his way towards the far end where Pope Innocent sat reading. The light from the candles produced an eerie glow around him.

He felt for the capsule in a pouch in his wet suit.

'Oh my God,' said Keanan as he looked at the pictures on screen. The critters had picked out three figures dressed in black who were totally invisible to Alfredo. They all had guns and all wore night goggles.

Keanan and Davey watched the nightmare scenario unfolding in front of their eyes.

Alfredo took his revolver from the holster around his waist and released the safety catch. In one movement he rolled across the floor to where Pope Innocent sat reading. Three shots rang out from the figures dressed in black. They all missed.

'So you brought in help, did you?' said Alfredo, crouching behind Innocent's chair. 'I had a hunch you would, you fucking coward! I bet you're not even Innocent. No pun intended. Here goes.'

He fired three shots while rolling across the floor to the movable wall. Only one shot came back at him, just nicking his shoulder.

'Well, two out of three ain't bad,' he said to himself, as he pushed the wall and slid through the gap. 'Now where are you likely to be? I think I'll try…your private chapel.' The empty chapel was in darkness.

'Fucking shit!' said Alfredo in frustration. 'We're running out of time.' Then he had an idea. He walked across to the confessional and took out one of his tins. He spread the gel around, on the kneeler, everywhere.

'That should do, boys.'

All Keanan and Davey could do as Alfredo made his way back through the tunnels was watch. They could see Maria waiting, the cord, the grenade. Davey couldn't bare to look as Alfredo approached the cord with his revolver drawn, ready to take on Maria.

The explosion wasn't as big as Keanan expected, but Alfredo lay motionless. Then something happened that would change Keanan and Davey's lives forever.

'Would you look at this,' said Keanan in disbelief.

Davey uncovered his eyes. They both watched as Carlotta kissed her daddy. Then, with his physical body still on the floor of the tunnel, he (or his spirit, as Keanan would later describe it) stood up and hugged Carlotta. Then they faded away through the tunnel wall. Keanan and Davey just looked at one another.

'Did you see what I saw?' said Keanan. Davey just nodded in agreement.

'The little critters must have been able to pick up what our human eyes can't see,' said Keanan.

*   *   *

Blood wept from a wound on Maria's leg.

'A piece of rock must have hit her,' said Davey.

She made her way through the tunnel. Gradually her torch began to fade. When she came to the chamber with the water and the pipe leading to the river bank she just kept on going.

'She's missed it,' said Keanan.

The two boys watched her enter the never-ending maze. Maria panicked. After walking a hundred metres or so, she knew she'd gone too far. All she could see was blackness and all she could hear were rats. Turning back to retrace her steps, she inadvertently took a wrong fork. She knew she was lost but had no other option than to keep on moving.

Suddenly the floor gave way. She dropped three metres into a small chamber. Her leg hurt, she couldn't bend it. Pulling herself around, dragging her damaged leg, she felt the walls, trying to find an exit. Suddenly she screamed as a rat bit into the weeping wound on her leg. Then another and another.

Davey wanted to be sick, but Keanan watched as maybe a hundred rats ate her alive. It took five minutes for her screams to stop and the picture to go dead. One thing Keanan learned as he ran to the bathroom: revenge wasn't sweet.

CHAPTER 45

DOUGLAS AND Laura approached the main doors of the Grand Phoenix Hotel. A young woman stopped them.

'Excuse me, may I see your security passes please' she said with a smile and a friendly voice.

'We have an appointment with Senator Heaney.'

'May I have your names please?'

'My name's Miss Sable.'

'And I'm Mr Claymore.'

'Wait here please.'

She disappeared for a couple of minutes. When she returned a slightly older woman accompanied her.

'Come with us please,' said the older woman.

The two women accompanied them through the hotel reception to the Bar area.

'Take a seat,' said the older woman. 'Mr Heaney knows you're here. He's keen to see you, but he is busy. He'll catch up with you as soon as possible. In the meantime, Caitlyn here,' she pointed to the young woman, 'will look after you. If you want anything, just ask.' She turned and left.

'Can I get you anything?' asked Caitlyn.

'I think I'll have a glass of medium white wine,' said Laura.

'And I'll have a dry red. I don't normally drink but I'll make an exception today, seeing as we are going to meet the future president of the United States of America. Might as well drink to his health.'

'May I use the washroom?' said Laura.

'Sure, it's just over the other side of the bar area, through those double doors.'

Douglas sat pondering. How could they guarantee Heaney would do or say something out of place that could be broadcast, which in turn would lose him the election and hopefully free Rodeo? The bottom line is they couldn't. If he has any sense he'll stay squeaky clean. He already has a phobia against wires and cameras. No, he'll stick to public places. Maybe Laura could…his mind didn't want to go there. He looked at his watch.

The execution loomed nearer. Only eight and a half hours.

*　*　*

'You boys better get some sleep,' said Mathew. 'I'll keep an eye on what's going on. Any problems, I'll call you.'

Mathew watched the screens. When Keanan and Davey told him what had happened to Alfredo and Maria Von Hind he had mixed emotions. He wondered what Rodeo would have said. He looked at the computer screen and saw an icon named Rodeo. He used the mouse to position the cursor, then left clicked.

'Well I'll be damned.' Rodeo appeared on the screen, sitting in his cell writing.

'What are you writing boss?'

How do I zoom this in? He turned the wheel in the middle of the mouse and saw more of the cell around Rodeo. Turning the wheel the other way the picture zoomed in on Rodeo. It zoomed in further still until he could see the words he'd written.

'I hope you don't mind me looking, boss.'

Mathew read out loud what he saw.

'Dear Matty, when you read this I'll be in Heaven. I guess the new songs I had planned to write won't now happen, which is a shame because I thought I could somehow heal the world with my music and my love for people. If I'd had more time I would have liked Kamna to be my long term partner and maybe even have children with her. One day, when the time is right and she's stopped grieving, maybe you can share that with her, and show her this letter.

We've had good times together – remember them, remember all the things we spoke about over endless coffees into the early hours. Carry on for me. Tell everyone how much I love them, Douglas, Laura, Alfredo…' A tear ran down Mathew's cheek. He carried on reading.

'Davey, Keanan, Edith, Mable, Philippe and all the band an' crew. You know, you can all still make a difference. Just because I'm not around anymore doesn't mean our quest for more love in the world has to stop. One day Mathew, you will write a book and that book will rekindle what we started.

Your loving pal, Rodeo.'

* * *

In the washroom cubicle, Laura slipped off her panties and put them in her handbag. Then she put on some bright red lipstick. What am I doing? she asked herself. He's not going to look at me, he's not going to risk anything when he's so close to his goal. No, Douglas and I have to be cleverer than that. Besides, I love you, Douglas.

She walked back to where Douglas sat and sat down next to him.

'Change of plan. I can't go through with it. I love you too much.' She bent over and kissed him on the lips.

'But…' said Douglas.

'No buts, besides he's not going to fall for it. He won't take the risk of me shouting rape or something. We have to be cleverer.'

'What do you suggest then?'

'I don't know. Let's just wait and see what comes along.'

Caitlyn brought over the drinks on a tray.

'Anything else you'd like, just ask. I'm only over by the double doors.' She smiled and left. Douglas watched her walk away.

'If Heaney's not making out with *her* I'm a Dutch uncle,' said Douglas.

'Oh, you noticed her then,' teased Laura.

'How we going to get the gel onto Heaney?' said Douglas, quickly changing the subject. 'We have to think. We don't have much time.'

'We could put some on our palms so when we shake hands…'

'No it won't work, as soon as he washes his hands…'

Just then, Heaney walked through the double doors flanked by two burley security guys. He walked straight across to Laura and Douglas.

'Good of you to drop by,' he said as he shook their hands. 'I believe you two have become a little disillusioned by Rodeo... and have left a sinking ship, so to speak.'

'Sort of...' said Douglas. 'Michael...first of all, I want to apologise for my behaviour the last time we met...'

'Douglas, that's all in the...'

'No I shouldn't have tried to attack you.'

'Look,' said Heaney with a sickly smile. 'To show there's no hard feelings, when I'm elected President how would you like to be my spiritual advisor?' All the while he was looking at Laura and mentally undressing her.

'Well, I...'

'I know, you feel...embarrassed because you have some documents sent to you by Pope Barnabus. Well, don't be. Pope Innocent explained to me...yes, Pope Innocent and I know each other. When he was just plain old Cardinal Biloweiki we used to meet as part of the COACC. Anyway, he told me Pope Barnabus was becoming deluded, you know, out of touch with reality. Pope Innocent feels those documents belong to the Catholic Church.'

'Well, yes,' said Douglas, 'I can understand that.'

'Good,' said Heaney. 'Laura, with Douglas working for me, I'm sure we'll see a lot more of each other.'

'Maybe,' said Laura, fiddling with her hair and running her tongue across her lips.

'Here are those documents,' said Douglas.

'Thank you Douglas.'

'I just have to go to the wash room again,' said Laura. She turned and left.

'Well, keep in touch. Call me when the election's over and we'll discuss your role.' Heaney shook hands, turned and left with his two minders.

'Wait outside,' said Heaney to his minders as he entered the washroom.

Laura stood facing the mirror. She saw Heaney walk in and stand behind her. She turned to face him while her fingers toyed with the top button of her shirt.

'Douglas is a lucky man.'

She opened her mouth as he kissed her and forced his tongue inside, exploring every corner. Some of the critters readily transferred to their new host. He broke the kiss.

'I'll catch you again when he's working for me.' She turned to face the mirror and watched him leave.

Douglas breathed a sigh of relief when the double doors opened and she walked back through.

'Mission accomplished,' she said. 'Now what?'

'Now we get as far away from here as possible. When he finds out those documents are fake…'

'And I don't want to be around when he suddenly finds himself on TV.'

*   *   *

Three hours before the scheduled execution, Mathew arrived at La Santé prison with Kamna, Mable and Philippe.

Philippe went through to see him. He put his arms around Rodeo and hugged him. The guard turned a blind eye. After all, the prisoner wore handcuffs and manacles. What harm could be done?

'We haven't given up,' said Philippe. 'I'm still hopeful of a last minute stay.'

'Philippe, I appreciate all you're doing, but I want you to know if you're not successful, I'm ready. I know what awaits me when I pass over. I'm just sad to leave everyone.'

'I understand. You are a brave man Rodeo. I must go, there are others who want to see you.'

Mable came in with Mathew. Rodeo kissed Mable on the cheek.

'You know what, despite the predicament you find yourself in, your mother would have been proud of you and what you have achieved.'

'Thanks Mable, that means a lot.' He paused. 'Mable, I want you to do one thing for me.'

'Sure.'

'Look after Mathew here.' Rodeo winked at him and Mathew looked to the heavens.

'Boss, I don't need looking after.'

'You heard him,' said Mable. 'I intend to make sure I uphold his wishes.' Mable hugged Rodeo.

'I love you boss,' said Mathew, hugging him. 'If I could change places I would.' .

'And I love you too Mathew.'

Two minutes after they left, Kamna walked into the room. Rodeo could see she'd been crying.

'This is all my fault. If only I hadn't been so greedy…'

'No Kamna, it's not your fault. Never believe that, 'cause I don't. What I said in court is true. I love you… You are a special person. The love inside your soul is powerful and will one day help to change the world for the better. Believe me. In fact, all the love songs I have ever sung, if I could sing them now, they would all be dedicated to you.'

She placed her arms around him and cried.

Keanan and Davey watched and listened on screen.

'He sure loves your sister.'

'And she loves him too.'

An hour before his execution, a priest entered the cell. Rodeo assumed it was to give the last rites.

'Father I know you mean well, but I…'

'It's your choice, but I am Father Jacques, Edith's Parish Priest. She has told me all about you. She told me about the letter she received from Our Most Holy Father Pope Barnabus to deliver to Douglas. She also told me broadly what it said.'

'Edith is a very special person,' said Rodeo.

'Yes she is, and I know you are special to her. I want to promise you I will do everything possible to clear your name and encourage people to live with more love as both you and Jesus Christ espoused. I will carry on doing that from within the Catholic Church, because I feel I will have more impact.'

'Do you know Father, I think you'll have more impact than you can ever imagine, especially when you're occupying the Holy See in Rome.'

'You joke of course. But if I can make a difference in my own parish…well, I will be happy. May God bless you and be with you. Amen.'

* * *

The small motel room looked clean. The sheets on the bed were freshly laundered and the satellite TV worked.

'We'll take it,' said Douglas to the elderly Spanish lady.

'Eighty dollars please and you check out by ten in the morning.' Douglas counted out the cash. She left, closing the door behind her.

Laura turned on the TV and set the channel to CBS news. They both sat on the edge of the bed, watching, waiting and hoping.

CHAPTER 46

'RIGHT GUYS,' said Mathew. 'We need to be ready. As soon as they come into Rodeo's cell I want the pictures beamed live to the world.'

'I have Heaney on screen as well,' said Keanan.

'Good, but I don't expect too much to happen from that end yet, but you never know. Just keep a watchful eye on things, an' Davey, you keep an eye on not so Innocent's confessional. Any movement there, just shout.

'They're coming!' shouted Keanan. 'We're going live.'

Televisions throughout the world lost their pictures, replaced by the grim sight of Rodeo being led to the execution chamber. Every channel in every country. The whole world watched.

At the Vatican, Pope Innocent looked at his watch.

'Soon the world will return to normal and the Roman Catholic Church will lead Christians the world over to salvation through their faith in Jesus Christ. With a little help from soon to be President Heaney, Islam will be confined to the history books. Barnabus, you were so wrong. Why didn't you join us when you had the chance?'

'Mathew, Heaney's watching our pictures on the TV,' said Keanan excitedly.

'Ok, keep monitoring.'

'The phone's ringing in the execution chamber. Listen.'

'C'est impossible. Personne n'a un appareil-photo ici…À la télévision? Tous les canaux? Impossible…Nous ne sommes pas les exécuteurs publics que nous devrons nous arrêter…Peut-être quelqu'un a planté un appareil-photo sur le prisonnier. Nous l'enlèverons et le rechercherons.'

'What's he saying?' said Mathew.

'I don't know, but they're opening the chamber door.'

'Good, keep the live pictures coming.'

The guards walked Rodeo through to a side room.

Roughly unzipping him, they removed the blue sleeveless overall leaving him totally naked. After an intimate body search they replaced the overall with what looked like a surgeon's gown. Again the guards took him into the execution chamber and again the phone rang.

'I don't know what they're saying, but they're taking him out again,' said Mathew.' They watched him being taken back to his cell.

'Ok, keep the live transmission going, but in one of those small boxes on the screen. Let's hear what CBC news has to say, an' keep an eye on Heaney.'

'In the last half an hour TV viewers around the world have been watching the attempted execution of the rock superstar Rodeo at La Santé prison in Paris. Rodeo was convicted and sentenced to death in France for the rape and murder of ten-year-old Carlotta Benando, a charge he has always denied. Governments around the world are demanding an explanation from the French Government, which at the moment it seems they are either unwilling or unable to give. They have said that the execution has been suspended pending an investigation. We're going to go live to our French correspondent Charles Courtois, who is outside La Santé prison. Charles, what's the situation there?'

'At the moment it's pretty quiet, although there's a steady stream of people turning up. Some are saying it's a miracle, that God has intervened.'

'Do you hear that?' said Mathew. 'A miracle.'

'Others appear to be anti-capital punishment,' continued the reporter. 'The trial was widely reported on in the French press and on TV in France and many are saying they felt uncomfortable with the verdict. Some are even demanding a retrial.'

'Keep an eye on Heaney,' said Mathew. 'He's not going to like this. Davey, bring up Douglas and Laura on your monitor. I want to see if they're okay.'

'We got him! We got him!' shouted Keanan. 'Going live with a thirty second delay.'

The TV showed senator Heaney sitting in a room at the Grand Phoenix Hotel, watching a TV.

'I didn't go to all the trouble of framing him for you to fuck up the execution and then have a retrial,' Heaney shouted. 'What the fuck are you fucking frogs playing at?'

His face turned white as he saw himself on TV saying those words. He stormed out of the room, totally unaware he was still being broadcast live.

'Who's put a fucking camera in my room? Those fuckers that were here today, Laura Sable and Douglas Claymore. I want them dead, do you hear me? Fucking dead. Did you did put a tail on them like I said?'

'Yeah sure,' one of the security team answered.

'Right, get it done. Now.'

'Senator Heaney, you're still on live TV. The camera isn't just in your room, you're still fucking live, on every fucking channel. Where the fuck's the camera then and how come its live on TV?'

* * *

Douglas and Laura watched the unfolding events in their motel room.

'What do we do?' said Laura 'They know where we are.'

'As I see it, we have two choices. We can either run, we might escape but I suspect not, or we stay here, together. Barnabus said there's not enough love in the world, well let's show there is more love than two thousand years ago.'

Laura pulled him towards her, her mouth covering his.

Mathew shouted at Davey. 'Turn the picture off! turn it off!'

When the motel room door burst open they carried on kissing, ignoring the three men.

They fired six shots at close range. One of the men then made a call on his cell phone.

'Tell Heaney it's done.'

Five minutes later, Senator Heaney walked into the washroom and went into a cubicle. He took a gun out of his pocket and pondered for about ten seconds. Placing the barrel in his mouth he pulled the trigger.

Thanks to the thirty second delay, Keanan was able to stop it being broadcast.

Kamna and Mable came into the room.

'Come here you guys,' said Mable. 'You need some hugs and TLC.'

Mathew sat down with his head in his hands, sobbing. Mable put her arm around his broad shoulders.

'You have a good cry,' said Mable. 'Do you good.'

'I'm so proud of you, my brother,' said Kamna. Davey beamed as she squeezed him.

'And Keanan, you need a cuddle too. Come here please.'

Davey pulled away. 'I have to watch the confessional.'

'Davey, it's over,' said Kamna.

'No it's not! Not yet!' shouted Davey. He sat down, looking at the screen. 'Keanan, look, there's another picture!' Keanan walked across and opened it up.

'It's Pope Innocent.'

'What's he doing?' said Davey

'He reading something. A document'

'Zoom in.'

'If we're watching him it must be the one Alfredo left on the alter. He put critters on it.'

'Keanan,' said Mathew, 'let's broadcast live and show the world Douglas' translation. Let the world hear Barnabus through the mouth of the man who killed him.'

EPILOGUE
THREE YEARS LATER

THE LARGE black four by four sped along the dusty road towards Hebbagodi with its headlamps on full beam, lighting up the night sky.

'Hurry or we'll be late,' said Keanan to Davey.

'I'm driving as fast as I can.'

'Are you sure? A camel could go faster. Look, there's one overtaking us now.' Davey looked to where Keanan pointed.

'Caught you.' Davey smiled.

Since the events in Paris, Keanan had patented his critters and licensed it to NASA, who he now worked for. Davey had just accepted a place at Hyderabad University to study medicine.

Davey looked at the sat nav. Only twenty-five kilometres to go. We'll make it easily…if I put my foot down. The four by four accelerated, the force pushing Keanan back into his seat.

'Slow down,' said Keanan, 'you'll kill us both.' Davey looked at Keanan and they both laughed.

The concert at Hebbagodi took a year to plan. Mathew worked with his wife, Mable, to plan what the world's media described as the biggest party ever.

Mathew and Mable had married a year ago today in a double ceremony with Rodeo and Kamna. Father Jacques presided over the ceremony. Edith performed the bridesmaid duties. Philippe, Keanan and Davey were all best men. The ceremony, just a declaration of love, took place in Hebbagodi. All the villagers were guests.

Pope Innocent couldn't resist calls for an autopsy to be carried out on Pope Barnabus. The cause of death was recorded as heart failure caused by chronic cyanide poisoning. Innocent stepped down and was rumoured to have confessed all to a Vatican court. It is not known were he is or what became of him.

'Look,' said Keanan. 'The lights.' In the distance laser beams, all colours of the rainbow, lit up the night sky.

The four by four pulled up at the specially built arena. Keanan and Davey rushed through to the backstage area.

'Davey, Keanan,' said Kamna, hugging them both 'I was worried you weren't going to make it. Quickly, come and take your seats. It will start in five minutes.' They sat with Mathew, Mable and Edith.

'Kalma-diva...Kalma-diva...' the crowd chanted.

Davey and Keanan joined in. Outside the arena, those who couldn't get in watched for free on giant cinema screens erected around the village.

The band played. A huge cheer went up. Rodeo's backing singers joined in with the band.

Philippe came onto the stage.

'Please give a huge cheer for Rodeo.'

The crowds inside and outside the arena went crazy.

'Kalma-diva... Kalma-diva... Kalma-diva... Kalma-diva...'

Rodeo entered to thunderous applause. He went straight into a song. At the end of the song, Rodeo addressed the audience.

'As you know, tonight is special. It's a celebration of all that's good about humankind. It's a celebration of Love. Three years ago some friends of mine gave their lives so that we could move our world forward to an era of peace, happiness, love and creation. I'd like to honour their lives by applauding them. Their names are... Carlotta Benando, Alfredo Benando, Harry Day, Pope Barnabus the First, Douglas Claymore, Laura Sable and their baby. Laura and Douglas didn't know she was expecting, but they'll be with their baby in heaven sharing this moment with us. I'd also like to honour Davey Dhillon, Keanan Horris, Edith Llitjos, Mable Lopez and my wife Kamna. All of you, come on up on stage.'

Massive applause accompanied their walk onto the stage.

'I also have two very, very special announcements that I'm mighty proud to make. Mathew Lopez, I know you're shy Matty, but come on up and join us. Everyone, I've just been informed today that Mathew Lopez has been awarded the Presidential Medal Of Freedom, with Distinction, the American Nation's highest civilian award.' Mathew and Rodeo hugged. 'Also today comes the news that Douglas Claymore, Laura Sable and Pope Barnabus have been jointly posthumously awarded the Nobel Peace Prize.'

The applause continued for ten minutes before Rodeo interrupted.

'Okay, now let's show the world how to party, how to rock and, more importantly, how to love.'

THE END